HEROES & VILLAINS

FICTION WRITERS GROUP

To all of our heroes.

A collection of short stories from the Writers' Anarchy series.
a FICTION WRITERS GROUP anthology

Published 2014
by Fiction Writers Group
First Edition.

Copyright © 2014 by Fiction Writers Group
Cover Design and Layout by Alex Hurst

ISBN-13: 978-0692230480

ALSO BY FICTION WRITERS GROUP

WRITERS' ANARCHY I
WRITERS' ANARCHY II: THE END OF THE WORLD AS WE WROTE IT
FLASH IT!
ANYTHING GOES

Table of CONTENTS

A Matter of Extraction

LYNN MOHNEY

THE DENTIST

BLACK ROTTEN HOLES of decomposed tooth enamel. The yellow ochre crust of gingivitis as it spreads along the edge of bloody sore gums. Putrid breath as it wafts through the air. Teeth so affected by disease, the surrounding bone is deteriorating, leaving nothing to hold those suckers in.

That's what I, Dr. Ginger V. DeKay, am talking about.

People who don't floss. Really. What is so hard to understand about using a little mouth wash and brushing after each and every meal? I don't mean to be a heel, but it would make my life a lot easier. All I ever wanted was a world with perfect, straight teeth. I've tried to schedule people in for appointments, but for some reason they don't appreciate my skills. Perhaps this is because they rarely leave my care alive. I've tried to keep a dental hygienist on staff, but every one of them quits on me after a mere two days. They don't like my practices, they say. Ha! They just don't want me to see the subtle traces of plaque they have left behind in their mouths. I've taken care of each and every one of them.

My theory is simple. If you show me you don't have the maturity to handle the important responsibility of the proper care of teeth and gums, you don't deserve the privilege of ownership of these pearly white gems. I rip them out, one by one, and set them free from a torturous lifestyle of abuse. I maintain them in a special case—a home for underprivileged teeth, you might say. I don't use Novocain on my patients. If you have neglected your teeth, you get what you deserve.

I mean to free each and every tooth from their life of slavery and mistreatment, one poor defenseless incisor at a time. No one can stop me. Don't bother trying to avoid my office. I make house calls. I will find you and your little rotten teeth too.

I HAD JUST RETURNED to my office after an exciting appointment. I was still glowing from the memory of the pleasure of taking care of a vile putrid mouth. Lara Larsson had required skills only an expert such as myself could have provided. We met in the grocery store, in the candy aisle. I find some of my best patients there, and Ms. Larsson was no exception. She was missing two top right bicuspids and a bottom incisor. My special vision could see a cavity was already forming in her left canine, and if not treated soon, the tooth would fall out. Irreprehensible!

How can I tell someone has a cavity from half way down a grocery aisle, you ask? Don't I need an x-ray machine to be able to see the decay in Lara Larsson's mouth? An ordinary dentist certainly would, but I am no ordinary dentist. I have been able to see each and every person's mouth with intimate detail, since birth.

The deterioration of Ms. Larsson's teeth made my blood boil with surmounting anger. I felt nauseated, as I imagined her eating chocolates and other sugary sweets, abusing those poor remaining teeth. Sugar would stick to the enamel and turn into acid, eating away at the precious enamel. Ms. Larsson wouldn't take the time and care to brush her remaining teeth, and they too would rot and suffer an anguishing death. I could hear each molar in her mouth screaming in agony as she tortured them repeatedly.

Ms. Larsson waddled towards me, meaty fists clenching bags of chocolates and gumdrops. Her smile was huge, showing her remaining teeth. Had she no shame? I gritted my own teeth in horror.

"Girl's gotta have her chocolate, y'know?" Ms. Larsson held up a candy bar.

I wasn't certain, but I think I was supposed to laugh. I forced a smile. Her expression changed to a grimace as she raised an eyebrow and snarled her lip, brushing past me. I could hear her teeth rattling, begging to be rescued. I decided she had to be my next patient.

Following Ms. Larsson to her home proved to not be as simple as it sounded. She liked to drive fast, and wove in and out of oncoming traffic; nonetheless I managed to keep up and parked my Mercedes a few houses away from a beat up ranch. I kept a slower pace; allowing Ms. Larsson time to hobble up her walkway, so as to not let on she was being followed. I checked her mail and learned her name. I liked having the name of my patients so I could bill them later should they live.

I considered knocking, but decided I preferred to let myself in quietly. Sometimes patients reacted adversely to the idea of an unplanned house call from the dentist and refused to let me in. It could turn into a rather ugly scene, one I liked to avoid. No need getting the neighbors involved. I could only do so many house calls in one day.

The screen door creaked, and hit my black bag of tools as I entered, but Ms. Larsson didn't seem to notice. I crept along the beaten, stained carpet, climbing over full trash bags and cat excrement to what I believed to be the kitchen. My nose stung from the pungent smell of urine. I was doing those poor teeth a favor, taking them out of this place. Ms. Larsson's back was to me, humming, as she blew dust out of a bowl and poured her candy into it. The corners of my mouth turned down and I fought the urge to gag. I slid my hand into my bag and pulled out a silk scarf.

I am a tall woman, in good physical health. I stood a few inches over my victim, and made easy work of gagging her, and tying her hands behind her back. Her eyes bulged from her head, recognition apparent. Ms. Larsson struggled to get away from me as I pushed her to the chair in her living room. Not as convenient as a dentist chair, but it would have to do.

I like to work in silence. I feel my victims understand their crimes well enough without me blathering on about it. I tied her to the wooden chair so she could not move while I performed my art. I made eye contact with Ms. Larsson as I removed the gag. She tried to scream, but her voice had escaped her. It was another talent of mine, but it only worked if I could see the pupils of my patient. I have special custom made clamps I stuffed into her mouth, pushing up on the palate and down on the tongue, so she couldn't clench her teeth or try to bite me. One by one, I ripped each tooth out of her mouth with my forceps. I didn't hesitate to slice the gum or cut away part of her jawbone to remove full teeth. Only the safety of the tooth mattered. I relished in Ms. Larsson's attempts at garbled screams. After I had removed a mere six teeth, Ms. Larrson lost all consciousness. I may have accidentally slit her throat when I was finished. Each tooth was placed in its own special black silk drawstring bag, where it could be comfortable until I was able to place it properly amongst my other teeth. I left Ms. Larsson to bleed. I no longer cared about her fate. If she bled to death, I didn't believe the world would miss her.

It had been exhausting but exhilarating work, and I was experiencing quite the adrenaline high upon returning to my office. I was surprised to find a small blonde woman in my waiting room. I had not scheduled any appointments, and I almost never had walk-ins. I looked down my aquiline nose at the tiny woman. She adjusted black wire framed glasses, and offered me her hand.

"Hello, Dr. DeKay?" I allowed myself to look into her mouth as she spoke. Every tooth in her mouth was neatly placed: straight and erect. I didn't see the slightest trace of plaque, and this woman had never had a cavity in her life. Either she had the best orthodontist, or she had the best orthodontia I had ever seen. She was in no need of a dentist. This made me suspicious.

"Yes."

"Um. I'm Candi Kayne. I noticed you were hiring dental hygienists, and, um, I'd be interested in applying for the job."

I took her offered hand. "My what beautiful teeth you have."

"Thank you. I brush and floss every chance I get." Candi blushed.

"I have very low tolerance for people who don't take care of their teeth properly."

"Oh me too. Really there is no worse crime, is there?"

"I don't believe so."

"Sometimes I wonder if people even deserve to have teeth."

This was turning into the perfect day. Regardless, hired help rarely lasted. "You're hired. I work a lot of evening hours. Will that be an issue?"

Candi's brow wrinkled and she hesitated. "Don't you need to see my resume? I can show you my credentials."

"Your teeth are enough to convince me, darling. So, evenings?"

"Evenings."

THE PATIENT

HARLAND TOSIS, or Hal as everyone knew him, had been turned down by three different women in one night. It was an all time record, and he was feeling rather dejected. He wasn't trying to get laid or anything. Hal didn't even expect to get a date. He wasn't the type of guy who managed to pick up women in bars. He was a brilliant salesman, specializing in bio-electronic turbo toothbrushes.

Hal had been laid off three times during his career as a software engineer, before he decided he just didn't have the talent to succeed in that field. With no other training to speak of, he had wallowed in self-pity for a few months as the bills began to creep up. Then, after a harrowing trip to the dentist, he had come up with his idea for a specialized toothbrush that would eliminate the need to ever go to the dentist for a regular cleaning again. After several trials, he managed to create a toothbrush that flossed, irrigated, scaled, and polished regularly.

Only, dentists refused to sell Hal's devices in their offices as they worked too well, and decreased patients. Hal had to be more creative in how he found potential customers. He had some success in door-to-door sales, and a few stores were willing to carry his product. Hal was hoping to get the sponsoring he needed for a real infomercial. Then he was certain his business would really take off.

One might not think people would buy toothbrushes from some random man in a bar; however, Hal had made a booming success of it. Hal had a boy-like charm, which made people willing to talk to him. People didn't expect to meet up with someone trying to sell them anything other than booze or sex in a bar, so they were more inclined to hear him out, if only for the novelty of the matter. After a few drinks, people were also a lot looser with how they spent their hard-earned cash. Hal felt no guilt taking advantage of the situation, as he was confident in the quality of his product. Even if they had buyer's regret in the morning, they now were the proud owner of a fine new toothbrush.

However, Hal could not score tonight. The first woman had told him to bug off. The next had thrown a drink at him, and accused him of hitting on her. The third refused to even acknowledge his existence.

Hal knew some nights were like this. He decided it was time to pack it in and head home to where the most beautiful woman in the world waited for him. All right, maybe Candi Kayne was rather plain, but she loved him, and that made her amazing. She wouldn't care that he'd had a bad night. She would kiss his wounds and all would be right in the world. He knew she was proud of the work he did.

He finished packing up his supplies, took a swig of his beer, and rose to leave, when his cell phone buzzed. He would have ignored it, but it was Candi. Hal loved the sound of her melodic voice.

"Hal?"

"Yes, sweety."

"How's work going?"

"Meh. Could be better. I was just packing up to leave, and come over for a little visit. Is that cool?"

"Well. No. I wanted to see you, but I can't. Work called. You know how it is."

No. Hal didn't understand how it was. How could a dental hygienist work such strange hours all the time? It was nine o'clock at night. Hal didn't get it, but he loved Candi too much to start an argument, even if it was the third time this week. He would have been suspicious of an affair, except Candi was just not the type of girl who would do that.

"Bummer. You know, that McKay really ought to keep more normal hours, don't you think? I know it's a brand new job and all, but maybe you should find a job with a different dentist."

"It's Dr. DeKay. I don't think so. This is the right place for me." Candi's voice sounded funny.

"What time do you think you'll get out? Maybe I can come over after?"

Candi stifled a yawn. "How about tomorrow night? I'll even cook dinner, ok?"

"Ok, I guess. I look forward to it."

Hal disconnected from the call and sat back down, hailing a waitress over. If he was eating alone, he might as well just order a burger right here. Elbow on the table, cheek resting on his fist, he watched the ball game on the wide screen television. He wasn't certain who was playing, but apparently his team was winning, given the roars of the rest of the crowd. Fists were shaking at the screen as the game flipped off and a newscaster appeared. Hal sat straighter, eyes alert.

"We interrupt this broadcast to provide you with updated information about The Extreme Exodontist." Hal couldn't hear Abby Abbson over the other patrons, but dialog ran across the bottom of the set at a speed the man could follow well enough. "The police believe the Extreme Exodontist is female, approximately five foot-eight, but this has not been confirmed to date. They are urging everyone to be cautious and keep all doors and windows locked. The Extreme Exodontist is considered to be armed and dangerous. She breaks into homes while people sleep, forcefully removing the teeth of her victims and leaving them for dead. Again, she's considered to be armed and dangerous. Please exhibit caution as she has already taken the lives of at least ten people, maybe more."

Hal thought of Candi alone working at night. He hoped this Dr. DeKay had taken security measures. *What was the world coming to?* Dentists stealing teeth was a new one. He shook his head.

WHEN THE BURGER ARRIVED, the bun was limp, the meat overcooked, and the fries were soggy, but at least Hal didn't have to cook it himself. Hal was not known for his cooking ability. Opening his mouth wide to take in the dry bun, Hal didn't expect to find something rock hard in the middle of the ground meat. He let out a sharp scream as he felt the searing pain of a cracked tooth. Spitting out chunks of hamburger, Hal found the culprit.

"How the hell did they get a rock in my hamburger?" It was near impossible to understand Hal, as he held onto his cheek and spit out a glob of blood. Within moments, the manager was at his side making a big fuss over keeping the incident quiet, and offering his meal for free. Aghast, Hal picked up his belongings, figuring he was in need of a dentist. Fortunately, he knew of one open this late. Dr. DeKay probably didn't take walk-ins normally, but perhaps she would make an exception for her hygienist's boyfriend.

THE DENTIST

I WAS AMAZED. It had been a month and Candi Kayne had been the perfect hygienist. Granted, I hadn't shared with her the depths of my practice techniques, but I sensed she would understand. I had observed her days before with a patient who had a disgusting case of halitosis and bleeding gums. Candi's pallor was green, her face scrunched up as though she had been sucking on lemons. You can't fake a response as strongly as she was exhibiting. The patient let Candi know she was being rough on him, and he was experiencing pain. Candi responded by tipping his head further back, forcing his mouth to open wider as she scraped the back wisdom teeth.

Candi would be pleased; I'm sure, of how I resolved her case following her appointment. I allowed Candi to leave before the end of her shift. I followed the patient to his home, and dispatched the gentleman of his teeth, removing his tongue for good measure. I have no use of the tongue, but it is the fastest way to cure someone of intolerable breath. Candi had been such a good employee; I was considering allowing her to come with me in my next house call. I believed, with Candi by my side, we would be a formidable team.

There was one more patient for the evening, and then Candi and I were going to discuss her progress as an employee. I was planning to offer her a raise, and let her in as part of the team. I liked to work alone, but there was something special about this girl. I felt a kinship with her I had never experienced before.

Candi was on her cell phone at the front desk, when I left the exam room. Her mouth turned at the corners as she spoke softly. I hadn't been too keen about other employees using cell phones, but Candi had been such an exemplary employee, I chose to overlook the transgression. She disconnected the call and forced a smile in my direction.

"Is everything all right, Candi?"

"I'm sorry, I was on my phone. I won't let it happen again. I needed to let my boyfriend know I'd be late for dinner. I think he's having trouble understanding why we work so many evenings."

"I'm sure it can be frustrating. I've always been more comfortable working in the evenings, and it is terribly convenient for working people."

"Oh, I totally get it. Hal gets it too. He's just disappointed because he was looking forward to it."

"Hal. What a nice name. What does he do?" I didn't really care, as long as he paid proper attention to his teeth; however, it was a good idea to keep a good employee happy.

Candi's face brightened at the opportunity to discuss her boyfriend. "He sells toothbrushes. Really awesome toothbrushes. He calls them bio-electronic turbo toothbrushes; he's such a dweeb. The toothbrush is cool though. It flosses, irrigates, scales, polishes, and probably would do the dishes too, if you asked."

"Why would anyone go to the dentist if they had a toothbrush like that?" I wasn't sure if I liked this Hal.

"That's his biggest problem. No dentist wants to sell the product." Candi moved to the computer, banged the monitor a few times, and punched a few keys. "Looks like our last patient is Alice Anderson. How is she as a patient?"

"Oh, lovely woman. Barely needs cleanings. Near perfect teeth. Won't be bad, and then I'd like to discuss your career here, Candi."

Candi's eyes widened. "I hope I'm doing all right. I can try to do better."

I waved my hand at the younger woman to hush her. "Candi, you are the best hygienist I've ever had."

Ms. Anderson didn't fail me with her excellent teeth. I'm really a sweet person if your mouth is in tip-top shape. Ms. Anderson can attest, as she is one of my few regular customers. Candi barely had to clean the teeth before I performed an oral exam. Ms. Anderson's teeth assured me they were comfortable where they were, and once again I determined there was no reason to forcefully remove them from their loving home. The appointment was short enough; I believed Candi might even be able to get home to her dinner after all.

I directed Candi to my office. It was nothing flashy, but I had a newer mahogany desk, and two comfortable chairs. The wall displayed my numerous degrees and proof of my credentials to provide general dentistry to the public. I motioned for her to be seated in the chair up front, while I sat behind my desk, resting long shapely legs and cherry red pumps on the desktop.

Candi chuckled as she wrung her hands. "Wow, I've never gotten to sit in here. Not even when you interviewed me."

"I could tell I had a qualified candidate, and I was right. Candi, I am very pleased with your performance. I think you are going to go far with me by your side. I can tell you share my, how should I say it? My distaste for people who don't know how to care for their teeth. I hope I haven't misinterpreted your response."

Candi wrinkled her nose. "I can't believe the disregard people have for their teeth. I mean really. How hard is it to use a toothbrush. I wish some of them would buy a brush from Hal. I mean, I never suggest that. I know enough not to try to send your customers away."

I brought my hands together in front of me. "I believe some people shouldn't even have the right to teeth. If you abuse your child, family services comes and takes them away from you. Why not teeth?"

Candi's eyes widened and she wrinkled her forehead as she leaned forward. "What do you mean?"

The buzzer at the front door of the practice waiting room started going off. Someone was here. We had no more scheduled patients, dammit! Whoever it was, they were going to feel my wrath. A stunned Candi and I bolted to the front of the office to see who was there at this late hour. A short man with scruffy black hair and wire rimmed spectacles stood at my entrance holding his cheek. I could see with my special vision, he had cracked his tooth. I could hear it screaming for help. I wanted to cover my ears to block out the high whine of the poor little creature. It was no use. I couldn't save the tooth, and it would die. This man had committed murder, and he would have to pay the price.

"Hal, what are you doing here?" Candi's pallor was whiter than usual.

THE TOOTH FAIRY

L IFE WAS GETTING more and more complicated day by day. I feared I would fail my special mission. Flossy Sugarfield herself, High Tooth Fairy, had asked for me, and no one else to deal with a little transgression. It might not have been so difficult had I not kept all of my normal duties as well. The responsibility of gathering lost teeth for two hundred children a night could be quite exhausting, and it was considered a full time job for most of us. I was expected to maintain the normal duties of a tooth fairy, but I was also a special agent. I took care of special situations.

Ginger V. DeKay was definitely one such problem. She had been a nice kid, but something went terribly wrong. She had been playing capture the tooth, not dissimilar to capture the flag, like some humans play. Ginger was knocked on the side of the head, and was never the same. She forgot all of her tooth fairy training, and started behaving like a human mortal. The general consensus had been to just let her be as there was no way to regain her memories. No one had considered she hadn't lost her tooth fairy abilities when she started dental school. The rumors of a serial dentist in the human world didn't start until much later, and it was not immediately connected to a fairy. Flossy brought me into her confidence, noting she believed the voices of teeth were still speaking to Ginger. Flossy was concerned the voices could be causing madness. She had heard the reports of strange occurrences where adult humans were having their teeth stolen and left for dead. Flossy was suspicious a fairy was involved, though why she didn't share. She strongly believed Ginger was involved. If she was, Ginger was breaking fairy code and would need to be stopped, but first I had to confirm she really was the culprit.

I could have complained about my insane schedule. Like most fairies, Ginger was programmed to work nights, which meant I had to gather all of my teeth and keep an eye on her at the same time. It was no use to mention the inconvenience. Flossy would have just pointed out it was probably unwise of me to have a human mortal boyfriend. I liked Hal though. He was a good guy, and dedicated to proper oral hygiene. I couldn't see how his presence in my life would have a negative impact on my job. That is, until Hal walked into Ginger's dental practice right as I was getting a confession out of her.

IT WAS EASIER THAN I EXPECTED to convince Ginger she should hire me. I hadn't expected her to trust me. If she believed herself to be a mortal human, Ginger should have been a bit paranoid regarding why teeth were speaking to her. I had considered the possibility she could sense she and I had more in common than she normally experienced with other people. True she was not aware either of us were tooth fairies, but she was still one of us.

Ginger was very careful not to allow me to witness her with patients, making it difficult to prove she was, without a doubt, guilty, as Flossy had suggested. Nonetheless, I had confirmed several of my patients had their teeth stolen and had died soon after seeing me. I was going to need to tread carefully, to make certain somehow I didn't end up a suspect with the police.

Ginger sat in her chair across from me, red pumps on top of the desk. Wild fiery hair framed her white porcelain face and green eyes which shown with a madness I cannot describe. Her voice was cool as she started explaining to me her belief teeth were like abused children who needed to be rescued. My heart beat faster in excitement. She was going to explain everything to me right here. I reminded myself to play it cool. I was little quiet Candi, who agreed people took awful care of their teeth. I would be shocked to learn my boss was stealing teeth when I was not looking. I had not expected her to come to me with the information I sought. I had firmly believed I would have to take her by force. Perhaps I could convince her to come with me at her own free will?

I was lost in those thoughts when I heard the front buzzer ring. My stomach dropped to the floor when I saw Hal standing there, clutching his cheek. Of all the choices, why couldn't he have chosen an emergency room?

THE VICTIM

D
R. DeKay's office was set in a small cape just outside the commercial district of Cavity Falls. Hal noticed Candi's small compact car parked out back in the driveway, as he headed up the walkway. The lawn had been mowed, but there were no flowers or bushes to be seen. A small non-descript sign stood in the front lawn marking the location as Dr. DeKay's practice, otherwise there was little to make the place stand out.

Hal jumped a little when he heard a buzzing sound as he entered the office, but he easily determined its purpose. His mouth jogged, causing a new wave of pain. It had worsened since entering the office, but he figured it was mostly due to anticipation. He had never been a fan of dentists. Despite his business, Hal had always had terrible teeth, and figured he was facing dentures in old age. He had a number of fillings and it was probable he needed another.

Hal expected Candi to be surprised to see him; he had not expected her to turn green. Her eyes were wide, mouth in a wide "O", legs standing apart. She brushed her short blonde pixie hair out of her face and forced a weak smile.

"Hal! What are you doing here?"

Another woman entered the room. Candi was an attractive woman, but she faded into the background with Dr. DeKay standing behind her. Hal found himself immediately drawn to the dentist's full lips in a half smirk, which did not reach the empty emerald eyes. Luxuriant fiery curls fell about her shoulders, drawing his eyes down to a perfect body and legs. Lots and lots of legs. Hal found himself wishing he could work a late night or two himself with Dr. DeKay. He shook himself and reminded himself he was in love with Candi.

"He broke his tooth, the poor dear. Is this your sweetheart?" Dr. Dekay put a long manicured hand on Hal's shoulder. He felt the warmth tingle through his body. Only one other woman had made him feel a similar tingle—Candi. He liked it, and wanted her hand to remain there. *How did she know my tooth was broken?*

"Yes." Candi hesitated before she answered. *What was her problem anyway? Was she embarrassed?* Hal wasn't perfect, but he wasn't bad looking. "Hal, maybe you should go to the emergency room. Dr. DeKay and I were just closing up the office."

She wasn't embarrassed. She was jealous, Hal thought. *Candi doesn't want Dr. DeKay's warm sensual hands to touch me.* The idea made him smile.

"Nonsense. He's family. Come on into the treatment room, Hal dear. I'd like to show Candi a few new techniques." Dr. DeKay gestured towards the door and headed there.

Candi shook her head and mouthed no. Hal shrugged. She pointed towards the exit to the street, her face almost angry now. Hal shook his head. He saw no reason why he should go to the emergency room when the lovely Dr. DeKay was more than happy to treat him. Candi pulled at his elbow, as he turned to follow the doctor.

The exam room was typical for a dentist, but something didn't feel right. Hal wished now he had listened to Candi and left. She hadn't been a jealous girlfriend. Bad things happened in this room. He turned to look Dr. DeKay in the eye, and he didn't like what he saw there. With more strength than he had expected, she pushed him into the exam chair and straddled him. A moment ago, Hal would have loved to find himself in this position, but he was no longer certain. His mind flashed to the television screen at the bar earlier. Recognition hit hard.

"You're the Extreme Exodontist."

Dr. DeKay nodded slowly, pleased with herself. Hal felt his bowels turn to water. He feared he would urinate his pants. *Why didn't I believe Candi?* Candi. What did she have to do with all of this? She must know something, but Hal refused to believe she could be helping this demon.

"Candi, I want you to observe appropriate treatment for a loser like Hal here, who doesn't take proper care of his teeth. He should be ashamed of himself, really. Sells special toothbrushes but he damages his own teeth. I thought better of you, too, Candi. I thought you understood, but to think you actually kiss this vile mouth." Dr. DeKay shook her head, disgusted. "I am going to remove all of your teeth, Hal. One by one, I am going to save them from you. I'm not going to use Novocain. I want you to feel the pain. Then I'm going to kill you in front of your pathetic girlfriend. Look at her. She's so shell-shocked; she can't help you. Poor, poor Hal."

Candi stood, eyes closed, mouth agape, legs akimbo, entranced by the scene before her. At least before Hal died, he knew Candi wasn't a part of this nightmare. It was a small comfort. Hal noticed odd changes in his girlfriend. She had never been tall, but he was certain she was shrinking. Her skin was taking an iridescent purple glow, and was she growing wings? She reached out and punched Hal, causing his world to go black.

THE DENTIST

FROM THE MOMENT that man entered my office, his teeth were screeching at me, begging me to rescue them. Hal didn't neglect his teeth like most of the people I contended with. He was physically beating them with his damned fandangled toothbrush. I would leave every last neglected tooth with their horrid owners in exchange to be able to save Hal's teeth, and any other teeth being abused by his foolish invention. No wonder no dentist would promote the evil device.

I fought to keep calm and not allow Hal to see the pain I experienced. The piercing whine of those enameled beauties made my ears feel as though they would bleed. I couldn't rescue them fast enough so they could stop screaming at me. I paced myself. I wanted Candi to understand what sort of monster she had been dating.

Mounted on top of Hal, I began fishing for my mouth clamps. I wasn't surprised to see Candi's fist. If she was truly in love with this detestable man, she might try to protect him. I had not expected her to punch Hal.

"Good girl, Candi. Now we can get to work."

"Not so fast." Candi's voice was shrill and higher pitched than normal. "I just don't want him to get hurt, so he's best unconscious."

Fair enough.

I moved my head so more of Candi's body should have been in my vision, but I couldn't see her. I whipped around to look all around me, but I couldn't find her anywhere. She couldn't have left the room without my hearing the door open and close. I waved a mosquito out of my face as I continued my fruitless search.

"I'm right here, Ginger."

I was already angry. Now I was pissed. It wouldn't have been as bad if the damned mosquito hadn't landed in my hair. I swatted at it, causing it to fly away and land directly on my nose, staring into my eyes. It wasn't a mosquito. It was a tiny person with purple iridescent skin, delicate butterfly wings and the face of my hygienist. I wanted to smack her with the palm of my hand, but I was too startled to react before she flew again out of reach.

"I'm too fast for you. Don't bother."

Regaining my composure, I shrugged and returned to fishing for my mouth clamps. "I don't think you can really stop me at that size, sweetheart."

"You'd be surprised by how much more we can do at this size, Ginger. Why don't you shrink yourself down and you'll see. You can't hear the teeth at my size."

I snickered. I couldn't shrink myself—of course I had never seen anyone else manage such a transformation, either.

"You can do it, Ginger. You just forgot how."

It was time to accept I might really be losing my mind. I had accepted I could see teeth with x-ray clarity. I was tired of hearing teeth speak to me, but I had found a way to stop it. Little talking fairies were more than I could believe.

"I'm real, Ginger. I'm a tooth fairy, just like you. I hear the teeth. I know how to block out the sounds, but they are there. I know why you steal them. I know you can see them with your bare eyes, while other dentists need special machines. Let me help you."

"This is ridiculous." I opened the unconscious man's mouth to place the clamps. A blinding flash of light and cutting pain in my fingers forced me to hesitate.

"Humor me. Try it. Close your eyes and picture yourself small. If you are crazy, it won't change anything. If I'm right, I'll make the teeth stop."

I held my hand, examining it for damage, but found none. I closed my eyes. I'd make a hot little fairy. I wanted dragonfly wings, and none of that purple skin garbage. I wanted soft pink skin, and no one was taking my hair from me. I felt a gentle warm tingling in my limbs, like a soft caress of a man's strong but capable hands. I imagined myself wearing a floral print flowing dress just covering the essentials. A gentle breeze wisped through my hair and wrapped around my torso. I felt my body lift off Hal. I was floating. It was the most beautiful feeling I had ever experienced. The teeth stopped screaming.

"Ginger. You're flying."

I opened my eyes and smiled; a refreshed feeling washed over me. I had never felt so free. The ground was gone, and I lifted in the air. Candi was right; she had helped me. Most importantly, the teeth were silent. I wondered, how many more ways were there I could save those teeth now? If transformation between human and fairy was this easy, I could perform searches with my human ears, shrink down and fly into the patients' homes completely undetected. I would have no need for apparatuses to tie people up, which had always been sloppy and risky.

Candi's face was stone cold. She threw something at my face, and everything else went dark as I fell the long distance to the ground.

THE TOOTH FAIRY

HATED DOING IT. As soon as Ginger managed to pull herself back into her fairy form, I could see her madness would come to an end. She didn't remember. She might never remember, but she had been

released. My duty was to bring Ginger back to Flossy unharmed. I couldn't do it in a more human form. The fairy dust I threw at her would cause her to sleep until I returned her to our home. I just wished Flossy would order problems such as this to be rectified before it was a full disaster, but that was my personal opinion. There was no room for personal opinions in my world.

I looked to Hal, still passed out. He had missed the majority, but he had seen me in my fairy form. He probably would think it a dream, or no one would believe him. I decided it was best to let him forget me completely. It wouldn't hurt if he forgot how to build those damned toothbrushes either. I sprinkled fairy dust on his tongue, whispered in his ear, picked up Ginger's limp body, and flew away into the night.

AFTER FIFTEEN years in the rat race, Lynn Mohney left a career to pursue her lifelong dreams of being a professional artist and writer. By day, Lynn can be found carting around her two beautiful children, but by night she is a professional metal-smith/jewelry designer, and co-owner of Prunella's Workshop located in central Massachusetts. In her spare time, she enjoys writing fantastical stories, and she looks forward to being published in four different anthologies through out 2014. Keep an eye out for a novel sometime in the near future!

Instrument of Vengeance

R.W. WARE

TRYPHOSA CALLED ME *ANGEL*. I looked up from where I lay across her lap on the marble fountain and saw a warm glow about her. Her smile made my heart ache. There was no disgust in her eyes when she looked at my face, though even violent men have blanched at the mask of scars I bear. Her fingers combed my hair with a rhythm fit to soothe a babe. She shouldn't have loved me. I was not a man worthy of it. Yet, even though she knew I was there to kill her, she called me "Angel" and meant it.

A word was magic when it came from her lips. It had the power to churn up long-buried guilt or grant absolution. She always granted my soul sanctuary. I would steal, kill or die for her. I would betray Priam King—who had rescued me from a raid on Naxos, trained me in the deadly arts and gave me respect—had she but asked.

"I'll not do this," I said into her womb. "I'd sooner thrust my knife into my own heart."

"Sweet Lycurgus," she said. Her voice was as mellifluous as spring birdsong. The back of her hand traced my cheek. "Have I not told you? I have always known this time would come. It is my destiny. Who better to fulfill it than my Angel?"

How many other men had she called by that name? Had it stirred deep within them, too? Though it drove me mad to think of her with another, I had long known that the Priestess of Amphitrite could not be bound to one man. In all of the time I had made secret visits to her, I never suspected that I would be the last.

I sat up. For the first time since the pirates raided Naxos and murdered my parents, I felt my throat constrict and tears well in my eyes. Didn't she know I loved her? Didn't she know I'd never loved another?

"How can you ask this of me?" The words were mere whispers when I finally squeezed them out.

"I ask it because I would not be struck down in hatred. You will make it swift and as painless as possible, and I know you shall mourn me. Perhaps that shall be enough for Amphitrite's forgiveness."

"What could you have done to be so spurned?" I could not conceive of anything.

She looked at me through tears. "Oh, Angel," she said. "You look at me with the eyes of a lover. For you, I can do no wrong; harbor no hatred; lust for no vengeance."

She marked me true. On whom did she desire revenge? Kings came to her for the blessings and the favors of Amphitrite—sailed from all over the *Great Green* to make the treacherous climb to this temple. None would incur her wrath. Amphitrite kept but one oracle here, and she was a priestess of great and secret powers.

"A priestess of Amphitrite is initiated in a crucible of suffering," she said. Her voice took on a sad, distant note, and it was as if the clouds reacted by choking off the sunlight that had stretched past the columns just to be near her. "Mine began in a raid on Samothrace, much like yours on Naxos. Yet, a woman has treasures a man does not, and mine were plundered by every invader with a mind to."

She cupped my face in her hands and kissed me. The birds stilled their wings, the waves calmed, the incense that filled the chamber faded and...

...I was suffocating. Something pressed down on my chest, my arms were held out to my sides, strong arms held them. Hate pulsed through my veins and my breathing quickened. I tried to kick but my legs were swiftly pinned, so I thrashed about with all I could muster. A flash of blue sky was interrupted by a stubbled, dirt-streaked face with hazel eyes. He licked his lips and smiled, as he moved my chiton. I struggled against the filthy grips of sweaty, armored men.

My memories were hers. I could hear the grunts of her attackers and smell their fetid breath. And I felt pain unlike any I had known, unlike any *man* had ever known.

Dozens of faces flickered before my eyes—her eyes—each with the lustful grunts of hungry pigs. I burned inside, and it felt like they ripped me. Some spit on me, others smacked my face and yelled in an attempt to make me fight. But I remained distant, choosing instead to focus on the breaking waves of the Aegean. Did I see a face there? Was Amphitrite, goddess of the sea, watching my suffering? The pain became a dull, distant ache. My body rocked with each thrust, until soon, even the pain was gone.

A familiar voice called out to me and I rolled my head toward it. I lay broken and bleeding on the wet stones of a rocky beach. I saw my husband, Pausanias, and little Antoninus herded among the survivors of the raid. I was a mass of bruises and my hips hurt just to turn. Tears streamed down my face as the raiders beat my husband and son with whips, driving them down to the sandy part of the bay.

A warlord, Prince Priam of Troy, called out the dreaded order and, as the sword plunged into my husband I felt its cold bite in my own heart. I swallowed a lump, and it burned against my abused throat, but I was otherwise unable to move. When one of the soldiers grabbed Antonius by the hair of his head and hauled it back to expose his neck, I closed my eyes and turned away. I wanted to die, to live no more. There was nothing left for me. Blessed Amphitrite masked the sounds of my son and his murderer with the slaughter of all of my neighbors.

I kept my eyes closed until I felt hands lift me and the bounce of the boarding plank. I'd been carried aboard a trireme. For a long time, I lay motionless, wishing to die. My lips were dry and my throat parched. Sometime later, in the galley, a leathery old woman sponged water on my lips and tended the sores that appeared on my flesh.

"It's a disease," the woman said. "I'm sorry, my dear."

I felt no shame, only regret and emptiness.

THE HEAT OF THE AEGEAN and the rocking of the trireme made my wounds feel afire. The old woman had been diligent in comforting me. She rubbed my head as she hummed a soft, melodic tune, building to small crescendos, like the waves rolling past the bow of the trireme. The women and girl-children around us were fast asleep. All of them. As I looked around, I began to notice that the piper and the time-beater had fallen silent. When had the music ceased? The drum? And why hadn't I noticed it before? Neither of the row-leaders was evident, or the oarsmen would not have fallen asleep. Not one of the crew members seemed to be conscious.

It was my chance.

I rolled over onto my hands and knees and slowly rose to my feet. The old woman looked up at me and smiled. I could not smile. As kind as she had been to me, it didn't bring back what I had lost. Nothing was ever going to.

Careful not to step on the crew, who had fallen asleep and dropped from their benches to the decks, I made my way up to the second rowing bank. It was the same as below decks: no one stirred. My hips ached, and each step burned deep within me, but I hobbled up to the top deck. I heard the old woman's song growing louder, as she climbed up the decks behind me.

"Where are you going?" she asked, as if I were a delinquent child making a half-hearted attempt at running away. But, I wasn't. I knew exactly what I was doing and I refused to answer her.

I moved until I could not see her and climbed up on the gunwale. I could not bring my husband and son back, but I could quit living without them. I stepped off the rail and plunged downward between the oars and into the *Great Green*—which was inky in the night.

A moment later, the old woman hit the water and sank under the surface, only she wasn't the old lady anymore—she was something else. She glowed pale blue, and in the heart of the light she grew younger and more comely.

Then I recognized how the creatures in the water obeyed her gestures, and I understood. She was Amphitrite.

"I will not have you take your own life. Only someone you love and who loves you as much as I do can kill you. Only someone who will mourn you."

When we surfaced, it was to the shores of this island, and she directed me to her temple. "From here, you will have your revenge, sweet Tryphosa."

I didn't want revenge. I never had. I wanted to be with Pausanias and Anotninus.

"IT WASN'T UNTIL YEARS LATER, in this temple lavished with gifts from kings," Tryphosa said, patting the thread-of-gold pillows on which I now lay, "that Priam came once again into my presence, the man who had been the source of my misery. Yet, he did not recognize me."

WHEN THE BLUR CLEARED, I saw a man climb over the ledge of the mountain to the polished marble floor of the temple. The skin not under armor was glistening with sweat, and his breath was heavy as he stood to his full height of six and a half pous. His twenty stones seemed heavy on his sluggish form, but perhaps the armor exaggerated that. It wasn't until he removed the helmet that I knew it was Priam.

Long, braided gray hair dominated a crown which was once a mass of dark ringlets. His beard was cut in the Babylonian fashion, and it too was more winter than spring. His eyes were creased deep at the corners. Deep crevices crossed his forehead, and white wisps of eyebrows—like cat's whiskers—cast his green eyes in shadow.

"Wise oracle of Amphitrite," he said, his voice much lower than last I'd heard it, "I seek your guidance. An enemy—"

"The Mycenaean king, Agamemnon," I said, "has found an excuse to unite Greece against Troia. I have seen this."

"Then you know why I have come. How do I save her? How do I keep my city safe?"

I could have answered him true, for Amphitrite, in her generosity, showed me how to save Troia and the family line of Priam. But, I refused.

Instead, I said: "You are to close your gates and send Hector out. Gather the flocks and crops into Troia. Paris will volunteer to go out and fight Menelaus. Let him. With these attacks, and no food, you will defeat your enemy. Do not open your gates to trade until the magnificent horse is left in honor of your victory."

"I will make a sacrifice to Amphitrite this very night."

"You must consecrate this by lying with me."

He was happy to oblige.

And when he had finished, and was certain of his fate, he plunged his sword into my heart. I was surprised at the ferocity; even more surprised when he made the climb down and my wounds healed.

"YOU'VE GIVEN HIM THE DISEASE." I could see why she'd done it. I would've too, had it been me—

It *had*. It had been me—in a way. My stomach rolled.

"Priam was never one to restrain his desires," she said, her smile false under sad eyes. "And, as we speak, the disease creeps about within the walls of Troia. Hekabe and Andromache have already fallen victim to Priam's urges and my affliction, and it will soon destroy every last Trojan in the city. Only Cassandra is immune, but she will die too, in time. Troia, the city Priam cherished so much shall perish."

For a moment, I felt like a rat trapped on a burning ship. There was no safe place to turn. I don't remember rising, or when I began to pace, just a dull throbbing in the back of my head driving me on. The incense smelled of exotic fruits, but it only added to the isolation I was beginning to feel. Under Priam's command, his men had taken her, given her a disease and murdered her family—and she had given him his gifts back. For that, he'd sent me to murder her.

"There is more, my angel. Worse. But the truth must finally be known, as it shall be your burden to account for."

"What worse can you say than to tell me than that you've killed all those, aside from you, that I hold dear?" I couldn't fathom more. She had been just in her wrath for Priam King, he'd done her a wrong that he could not atone for—and Priam King was not the sort to try. But Hekabe and Andromache? All of Troia?

"Priam was not the only man to come to me that day—"

THE MOON WAS UP, and a gentle breeze undulated the gossamer curtains that were draped between the columns on either side of the temple, which was cut out of rock. It was Mycenaean armor the man bore, his beard sculpted in the Greek fashion that was the emblem on his cuirass. He got to his feet with much less effort. Agamemnon King was a hard man with corded muscles and black ringlets. His face was weathered, his eyes black like a falcon's, but he fit the precognition she'd had of the massive king. He was truly a war king, and his resolve was stronger than those against him.

"I come before the oracle to the kings, bearing gifts," he said. His smile was charming, but he kept a respectful distance. He went to his knees on the edge of the temple's floor, reached over, and then started hauling up a rope. When the rope's end arrived, it was securing a sack made of red velvet. "I seek Amphitrite's favor in my endeavor."

"She bids you, Agamemnon, heed the words of Odysseus when he speaks to you of his clever plan to gain entrance to the city."

"Then I shall simply ask the king of Ithaca, oh noble oracle." I saw then what he intended and how he would utterly destroy what was the greatest city known on earth.

"The earth will quake in battle and turn the tide in your favor, but it is only when Odysseus suggests it that you'll know the time is right."

"And Odysseus's plan will work?"

"It will," I said, and lifted my chin, "for already have I made it so."

Still smiling, Agememnon plunged his xyphos into my heart. But there was no love in his heart. His smiles masked the hatred in his heart. That would serve my purpose well. It was my only consolation as my heart again healed.

Tryphosa smelled of peaches, but her eyes streamed tears. My heart ached from more than her memories. It ached for her beauty, for her loss, and for the fact that I knew she had been right all along. If I did not kill her, she was doomed to suffer, and that was something I could not bear.

She smiled as my vision became watery. She kissed me and it felt so good it hurt. I took a deep breath and plunged my knife into her heart. She arched back, the hilt of my dagger in the air like an offering to almighty Zeus, before she collapsed in my arms. I kissed her again, and did not stop until I felt the life leave her.

When I lay her down on the same pillows I know not how oft we had shared, I felt the need to retch. The greatest gift I could give her was to take the only thing that made life worth living. I screamed, but it was only the sound of my anguish. It did not shake the temple or wake Amphitrite.

She was the only woman who ever loved me. I did not care to find another.

R.W. WARE is an award-winning artist in multiple mediums, with over one-hundred-and-ninety awards in dermographic art, an editor's choice award for a poem published in 2001, and three awards for original fantasy paintings. He has three SFWA accredited flash fiction publications, and has two stories in this publication. Aside from his day job, Mr. Ware illustrates the e-zine, **flash fiction online**, and does art by commission, such as two maps for Kevin J. Anderson's *Terra Incognita* trilogy, and album art for the progressive rock band and media tie-in Roswell 6. To this day, he feels his greatest achievements are his wife and children, with whom he never spends enough time.

D.N.A.

ALEX HURST

THE VENT WAS FREEZING. Alta grit her jaw and cursed the chatter of her teeth. Fear of discovery kept her from moving too quickly. She winced and bit down on her cheek as the skin of her thigh stuck to the metal flooring.

"I can't believe I'm doing this naked."

Not naked.

"Naked. Sorry, D. Even though you're sentient, you're still just skin. And I'm freezing."

There was silence in her head, and then, Shall I raise temperatures a few degrees?

"You can do that?"

The change was almost instantaneous: her skin tingled with electrical activity and the chill disappeared. She wondered if D.N.A. had actually warmed her up that quickly, or if he'd simply turned off the neural transmitters that told her brain she'd been cold.

Turning off neural networks is a last resort, Alta. Complications include excessive vascular dilatation and undue reduction in blood pressure, blood pooling—

"Thank you, Google, but that's enough. I'm just glad you aren't sending me into shock."

It would be highly counter-productive. My entire CPU is currently dependent on the functionality of your nanoCell skin. Should a malfunction occur, my program will be in jeopardy, and the mission will fail.

"A mission you insisted needed to start tonight, even though we weren't ready. But while we're on the subject, how's that synchronization coming along?"

My presence inside you was detected. We could not delay. Your neural networks and my mainframe are seventy-nine percent synched—a pause—Someone is coming.

The sound of a door opening confirmed the report. Alta strained to hear over the cooling system. There was a soft crackle in her ear, and her senses expanded, so overwhelming for a moment that she could hear a man in the room wheezing. It sounded like he had a really bad chest cold.

Felis catus, D.N.A. supplied, to her curiosity.

"You put cat DNA in my ears?" She reached back and felt them, expecting fur and pointed lobes. Nothing had changed outwardly, but that didn't stop her from grinning, "Salty." Alta carefully folded one arm, so she could press one ear against the vent's wall, "A bit loud though…"

The white noise cut back considerably. One voice turned into two.

"…reports from the bionetics lab revealed full acceptance across the board. The models could be ready for release as soon as next month, sir." It wasn't a voice she recognized. She tapped her ear a few times. They were too close to risk speaking.

Recording. Alta, permissions to your thought processes are available to me. You need only think a command for me to comply.

She knew, D.N.A. had already reaffirmed it a dozen times, but it still felt weird, communicating without speaking. Of course, it wasn't really the time to be thinking about D.N.A. She had other priorities—not being discovered on her way out topped the list.

"And the trials?" That voice she did know. Bryan Engel, project manager for the nanoCell Respiratory Unit; the man who had saved her life.

Also the man who signed off on nanoTech's proposal for inclusion of the suicide protein.

We don't have evidence of that.

Evidence isn't the concern. Deactivating the protein marker in the other patients is our main objective. Please show caution.

If you really want to stop nanoTech, we need to get proof. They won't find out. And even if they did, that's what I have you for. Her confidence didn't stop her from rubbing her chest. Would nanoTech really flip the microscopic kill-switch in those people's lungs if they grew suspicious?

They wouldn't. Would they?

How's that synchronizing, now?

`Eighty-two percent.`

Eighty-two had never felt so terrifying. So much hinged on that final eighteen percent: her escape, the other patients, and D.N.A.'s survival.

Alta returned her attention to the men on the other side of the vent's metal wall, frowning as she listened to Engel's cavalier tone. He had always been a little unsympathetic, of course, but she had never pegged him as being in on the whole scandal. She'd been his special guinea pig for this project, letting him use her unique DNA and muscle tissues to help develop lungs comprised entirely of synthetic nanoCells. It wasn't without precedent. Four years prior, she'd been the first successful case of a complete nanoCell transplant. 95% of her skin, from scalp to toes, had been damaged beyond repair after a chemical fire.

The synthetic skin had given her a second lease on life.

However, carbon monoxide from the fire had been so intense that an aggressive carcinoma developed in her lungs a couple of years later. When Engel's team had approached her to talk about another synthetic implant, Alta had been more than happy to participate in their new research and completely bypass the organ donor waitlist.

The man with Engel carried on, "Trial participants have noted that the synthetic lungs made it easier to breathe than the 3D-printed filters physicians had implanted in their tracheas. There was also an overall improvement of health, oxygenation of the blood rose 20% in those suffering from hypoxemia, and inflammation in the trachea has been eradicated."

"Excellent." The pleasure in Engel's voice made Alta queasy. "And the CR27 compound?"

The other man was quiet for a moment, "Untraceable through basic lab tests. The receptors in patients 7 and 13 responded to offsite frequency tests as predicted."

"And the patients?"

"Both patients suffered flu-like symptoms, which were treated normally."

Alta knew Patient 7. His name was Gordie Thompson, a young boy from the outskirts of the Dome. He was part of what the world was calling the "Non" generation: people born without the biological fitness to filter the higher levels of pollution Earth's atmosphere now experienced. Gordie had been ill most of his life, born with lungs only suited for Pre-Contamination Earth. Bionic filters in his throat had provided him some relief, but it was only a crutch. Eventually, his body rejected the bionic pieces, and they were removed. Before nanoTech came along, his only other option had been to live in an antimicrobial cleanroom.

Scientists at nanoTech had previously discovered—through Alta's own revolutionary and emergency surgery—that replacing the entire organ system, rather than a piece of it, was the most effective—and profitable—method of treatment. They filed patents with the government for every organ, tissue, and nerve system known to science before the media even got wind of the surgery's success. The shocking thing was that the government had permitted it. Almost overnight, nanoTech had become the only corporation in the world with the key to deciding who deserved a higher quality of life, and who didn't.

A little dramatic, don't you think, Alta?

But true. Alta carefully sat back up and turned, to slip her legs down a chute that would take her to the floor below. She'd gotten what she needed—evidence—and there was no use lingering. Before she could even register the lack of traction between the metal and her feet, the pads of her fingers and toes grew rough—stronger; her movements became as fluid as water.

Genetta angolensis.

Got me on that one, D.

Angolan Genet. Lived in Africa circa 21st century. Well-known for reflexive ability.

Scientists actually had its D.N.A. on file? The idea that D.N.A. could even splice extinct genetic codes with her own opened a million possibilities; a million questions. What would happen if he used dinosaur D.N.A.?

`Genome records only go as far back Holocene Era.`

So much for stomping around like a T-Rex.

Bryan Engel and his cohort's voices grew faint as Alta prepared to drop down to the next floor.

"…regarding Patient No. 58734," the nasally man said, "A Miss, uh, Alta Williams, there have been a few irregularities in her readouts. Seems her skin is malfunctioning."

Alta paused.

"Is it?" Bryan's voice sounded concerned. Almost.

"Our computers haven't been able to establish a connection with her nanoCell skin for a few days. I figure it's the receptors from her skin and the new ones in her lungs competing. I imagine it could be fixed with some sort of hard reboot? Maybe introduce a new batch of cells?"

"That should be sufficient. Keep me updated."

This is what you meant when you said your presence was detected?

`Yes. They will erase me.`

Well, we can't have that, can we? Maybe D.N.A. understood a few human emotions, after all. Self-preservation was high on Alta's list, too.

Whatever relief Alta felt at not being suspected disappeared as her thigh tightened up—a cramp was building in her leg muscle. *D, do something.*

`Unknown system error.`

The spasm hit and Alta's leg slipped, her knee banging sharply against the cheap, thin metal of her hiding place. Her body slid clumsily against the shaft's slated vent.

"Someone's here," Engel said. "Notify security." His voice drew near. Alta's heartbeat thudded in the veins of her throat as she pulled her body off the vent and out of view once more. Her knees made enough noise to give away her position anyway.

D, evasive maneuvers?

A logical plan of action. You have less than four seconds until he reaches you.

Alta rolled back to the nearest duct and dove down it. Her body banged and skidded all the way to the next floor. When her hip smashed against the bottom of the chute, the vent door attached to it snapped off and clattered across the tile of a lab room, Alta's body following suit.

I recommend you plan more graceful landings in the future.

When you figure out how to stop a charley horse. Alta rubbed her aching calf, looking around the dark room.

Full integration of your neural networks with my CPU circuits is only at eighty-nine percent. I can not control muscle reflexes yet.

I'll keep that in mind. How are we going to get out now?

The door. Use code '828347482' on the lock.

She didn't question where he'd hacked that code from. She just felt sorry for the guy it'd be traced back to. *Next?*

Lockdown is in progress. Assessing options.

"How about just breaking a window?"

The windows are made out of reinforced palladium alloy. It can not be broken with brute force.

Damn. I suppose we're too high up anyway.

Not necessarily—a pause—Assessment complete. Head for the roof.

"Isn't that completely opposite from the way I should be heading?" Alta turned around and sprinted down the hall towards the door marked 'Roof Access'. Heading up, then again, would probably be safer than heading down. Security would likely only pay attention to the lowest floors of the building. The more she thought about it, the more the roof made sense, really. *You'll have to explain how I'm going to get down, you realize.*

Do you know uroplatus fimbriatus?

You're not serious.

Of course. D.N.A. didn't pick up on her exasperation. Alta could only pray he had a better plan than giving her gecko feet.

ALTA'S HANDS COULDN'T PROTECT HER FACE from the wild winds of the rooftop. The sharp, chilly gusts across the high-rise felt like tiny knives against her skin.

Head to the eastern end of the building. The majority of the winds will be blocked by the building, and allow an easier descent.

Talking about the risk of the wind didn't make the prospect of sliding down the wall any more appealing, but she followed D.N.A.'s instructions. "There's really no other option?"

Down below, Alta saw nothing but quiet streets under a black tarp of sky. There were no police lights, no security vehicles. Of course, it was expected: nanoTech wouldn't want the intruder caught publicly. There would be no telling what she'd heard; what she knew… should she be apprehended by law enforcement, a public statement could follow. They needed to handle it internally. The thought made her shudder—how many times had nanoTech made a pest disappear in the past?

I need you to focus, Alta. Uroplatus fimbriatus had reversed knuckles. That's how they climbed walls.

But I only have regular knuckles. What do you want me to do, break all of my fingers?

The length of silence that followed did nothing to ease Alta's tension.

I was joking, D.

Yes.

Did D.N.A. understand her fear? Did he recognize what he was asking of her? Maybe for him, her physical limitations were only an algorithm, her emotions an illogical outlier—for her, those things were what made her human.

I will adjust my program to be more responsive to emotional stimuli.

Not particularly encouraging, D.

Shivering again, Alta clasped her arms across her breasts and looked over the edge of the eighty-story building. Vertigo settled deep in her gut and she jerked back, fighting the sensation that the whole building was lurching. *I don't know if I can do this, D. I don't even have any clothes!* "This is insane."

`Perhaps. Alta, I have a solution. But I can not attempt a full-body morph until our synchronization is complete.`

And how much longer will that be? Even as Alta asked, the roof door opened and light streamed out in a great, accusing beam. So much for the roof not being checked. She ducked.

`Synchronization is at ninety-six percent. Four minutes and thirty seconds remain, including my reboot.`

Reboot?! You never said anything about a reboot.

`A reboot is necessary for full integration. It will last twenty seconds. There may be a brief power failure.`

Power what? What does that mean? D, what about security?

`You will have to handle them while I am offline.`

Alta's heart tumbled at the warning, but what choice did she have? It was either D.N.A.'s option or handing herself over to nanoTech's security team.

Alright. Let's do this. She drew up memories of the self-defense classes she had taken in college. Go for the nose. Never turn your back. Use their weight against them.

Footsteps drew closer; rubber treads skidded over the rough concrete of the rooftop. It sounded like there was only one man. She could take one man.

`Ninety-seven percent.`

As if the guard heard D.N.A. himself, the flashlight's strobe swung towards her. She ducked, but her knee scraped against the rough surface of the rooftop. Her skin was no quieter than the security guard's boots.

"Who's there?" The security guard's voice was accompanied by the electric hiss of a taser wand. The very idea of that electrical bolt snapping against her skin terrified Alta enough to run. She would run in circles until D.N.A. was ready if she had to.

"Stop!"

Alta jumped towards a cooling system box, slipping behind it as quickly as she could.

"Was she naked?" The surprise in the security guard's whisper hardened. "Come out where I can see you!"

People didn't talk to themselves. How many others were there?

`Ninty-nine percent.`

Alta's eyes fixated on the guard's light as she angled herself away from its periphery. So far, only one. Maybe he really had been talking to himself—

A scuffle to her left; someone was sneaking around the back. Alta jumped to her feet again, tripping over herself as she tried to flee. Another taser fired up and cracked near her ear, but the guard's aim was off, and the electrical current missed her. If that electrical current hit her, there was no telling what would happen to D.N.A.

"There!" shouted the guard closest to her. Alta assumed a sprinter's posture and bolted. Her dark skin shown white under the brightness of their flashlights.

Something deep in her gut told her to jump, and she bolted over another random vent, just as the flickering tongue of the taser snapped against its side. It could have been her. Adrenaline filled her veins and she threw herself forward with abandon.

`Reboot initiated.`

Alta allowed herself a sigh. *About damned ti*— Something felt off. Her legs continued to run wildly, but they weren't under her control anymore. She couldn't make her arms bend, or her fingers flex. She couldn't even feel her toes.

A brief power failure. That was what D.N.A. had warned her about.

Panic bubbled to the surface, and with it, a single thought: She and D.N.A. were synched. D.N.A.'s reboot had triggered an internal reboot as well. Her brain was still functioning, but it had no control over her muscle responses—her legs powered on because the synapses in her spine hadn't gotten the message to stop.

She was the proverbial chicken with its head cut off.

"Get her! Quickly!"

Alta hoped they would. The edge of the roof loomed ahead. She would run right off if they didn't stop her.

More electric hisses filled the air. The shock of a taser rippled across her skin, electrifying her body. She could see the vibrations it caused, but couldn't feel it at all. Her legs finally stopped moving. The neural signal had been interrupted.

If she could have screamed, she would have. One of her feet had already crossed the threshold and hung out in the open air. Her body tipped forward. She was going to die. *Please let it be quick.*

One of the guard's hands lashed out and gripped the long tresses of her hair. Her head snapped back, but it was too late. Her second foot slipped off the building at the tug; the hair implants in the guard's hand tore from the root. Against the sound of her heartbeat, she could just barely hear the guards screaming as she slipped off the building and into the open air.

Air rushed passed her limp body. She wondered if it was cold. How long the fall would last. Why her brain hadn't turned off too, and spared her this grisly end. Would anyone miss her? Memories didn't flash before her eyes. There wasn't any holy light at the end of the tunnel. Instead, panic gripped her, fear consumed her, and her lungs burned to take even a single a breath as she fell.

Alta had no choice but to watch; her eyes wouldn't close. The orange lights of the city and black top of the roads below tumbled in confused balls of pigment as she spun in a dangerous free fall. Would her heart burst from the stress before impact? Did hearts do that?

Then, suddenly, the familiar sting of needles slid down her entire body. She'd never been happier to be in pain. D.N.A. was back. He was online.

D! Falling!

`Defensive maneuvers launching.` Alta caught glimpses of her skin changing from flesh tones to luminescent greens and blues. `Alta, curl up. Protect your extremities.`

She pulled herself into a ball; noticed that her joints were hardening, losing all of their flexibility and motion. She felt... she felt like a rock.

`Haliotis asinina.` Abalone.

The stuff they made armor out of. The streets of the city twirled beneath her. She braced herself for impact. *D, I'm going to make it, right?* The quiver in her thoughts couldn't be hidden. Alta had almost burned alive once before; she knew what death looked like—right now, she was rocketing straight for it.

`Yes.` There were no statistics given, no probabilities. Incapable of empathy, D.N.A. was just certain.

She finally closed her eyes, seconds before the impact. Her hardened body crushed and bent metal before she found herself thrust into the air again. She held her breath as the arc of her bounce made her stomach lurch. Then she smashed into something big, and then something small. Curled up under D.N.A.'s orders, there was no way to know what she was hitting. She didn't really want to know.

When she finally stopped, her muscles thrummed with a dizzy, almost drunk sensation. Her armored skin softened, returning to flesh. Her limbs uncurled and her eyes finally opened to stare up the massive skyscrapers all around her. The lights in their windows looked like stars. Her first real breath in the last minute tasted as sweet as candy.

She was alive.

"Wow... Lady, are you alright?"

Alta turned her gaze towards the voice, wincing in an attempt to focus the fuzzy glare in her eyes away. There was a young woman with a generic taxi badge looking down at her. She could hear sirens, horns, and raised voices all around. When she tried to lift her head, her muscles rebelled.

D?

You are experiencing a sensory overload. Your brain's neural synapses are currently handling distress signals from across your muscular system. My program can not manipulate your nanoCells without sending your body into shock.

"Lady?" The woman bent down and examined Alta's features. Recognition filled her eyes. "Hey... Hey! You're that lady from TV... the Human Doll. What the hell are you wearing?"

Alta couldn't look. She couldn't move. She could only hope the woman would get her out of there before she was reclaimed by nanoTech's security. "Help me." The words barely made it passed her locked jaw. "Take me away."

People were already gathering, snapping photos and videos with their phones. Alta's ears rung with the chaotic melding of their voices.

"—saw her drop out of the sky—"

"—think she jum—"

"—cret government project—"

The woman seemed to have heard her, though, and was bending down to pull her up. Alta was thankful the woman clearly had no medical training—the cabby hadn't even checked for broken bones before moving her. She dragged her to a car, and soon Alta felt the cool surface of black leather against her cheek. Two doors slammed.

"You better not die in my backseat, lady."

WARMTH WAS ALTA'S FIRST WAKING SENSATION, before a rush of pain and discomfort overpowered it. The air smelled stale, like dust and moldy bread. She wrinkled her nose.

Good afternoon, Alta. It is currently 2:43pm.

Afternoon? How... how long was I out? What day is it? Where am I?

You were unconscious for fourteen hours and nineteen minutes. It is Wednesday. You are downtown, on 49th & Excelsor Drive.

The Goz District? How'd I end up down here?

Sandra Ramirez brought you. She is the owner of this apartment, and the woman who found you last night.

Last night—It was too much to think about. Still too real. First things, first. Could she stand? Did she have any serious injuries?

You sustained mild muscle damage from the fall. Skeletal structure is intact.

Well, that's something. Alta pulled the blanket she was wrapped in away and stood up carefully. She was wearing something strange. Something as tight as her skin; meshed in matte grays and slick whites.

An upgrade, D.N.A. supplied. I meant to deploy it after my reboot, but you were only 100 meters from the ground. I've tailored it to your natural movements, for swifter response times. You are right-handed, so I attuned the left, or gray, for more defensive attributes. Your palms and soles, knees, elbows, ankles and wrists will remain flexible.

This... this is my skin?

Yes.

Forever?

No. But you did express a desire to appear clothed.

I suppose I did. Her eyes slid over the dark matte grays that covered the majority of her left side. It reminded her of abalone. Her stomach dropped as memories of her fall from nanoTech's towers, and the impact that should have killed her, returned. Her right side was smooth and as white as ceramic. She remembered, suddenly, the guard grabbing her hair. Her hand confirmed that large chunks of it had been torn or ripped out entirely. She'd have to cut it; it would be too expensive to replace.

It took a moment, but the fact that she was in a stranger's house finally dawned on her as the priority. Everything else would have to wait.

"Hello?" Her voice came out in a half-croak as she navigated the rooms of the small apartment.

She didn't have to wait long for an answer. "Just a moment!" Hasty goodbyes were mumbled, and then the woman—her savior from the night before—came around the corner, closing her phone ring and slipping it back on her finger. "I am so glad you woke up! How are you doing?"

Alta's mouth opened, but no answer came. She really didn't know. Between the physical, emotional, and psychological strain, she couldn't distinguish up from down. "Fine, I guess." A response conditioned through years of small talk supplied itself.

Her savior wasn't convinced. "You must be in shock. You fell pretty far."

Must be.

"What floor were you on? Fourth? Fifth?"

Those numbers seemed so small. "No." Alta strained to organize the events from the night before, to remember anything from before her terrifying drop. "No, I was on the roof."

"The roof!" The woman's eyebrows nearly lifted off her face and she ushered Alta back to the couch she had woken up on. "Lady, you must have hit your head *real* hard. The nanoTech building is almost eighty stories high!"

"Eighty-two, actually."

"You really think you fell off the roof, don't you?" The woman sat down, frowning gently.

"I know I did. It was D.N.A.—" she paused: Was this really information she should share?

"D.N.A.?"

D, you looked her up. Who is she? Can I trust her?

Sandra Ramirez, resident of Valley Heights since June 18th. License registered June 15th.

June? That's only two months ago. She hesitated, while Sandra patiently waited for an answer, and dropped her gaze to the steel ring mobile on the woman's finger. *Who was she on the phone with just now?*

A pause. Metro PD, Commissioner Gunner. 17 minutes.

The police department?

"You okay?" Sandra tipped her head in concern. When Alta didn't respond, she sighed, "You must be going through a lot right now. There are a lot of people looking for you, though."

"Are they?"

"Well, yeah. I mean… you're Alta Williams. The syntheskin patient, right?"

Alta had heard that nickname—among others—before. She had been an average woman before the fire. She remembered the novelty of her case to the media. The reporters and fans and cosmetic companies who'd all wanted a piece of her. The woman with the synthetic skin and hair. The woman who would never physically age unless she paid to have wrinkles put in. The Human Doll.

No one cared about the flip side though. The flawless skin wasn't *human*. She didn't have body hair, or creases on her knuckles and elbows. She didn't have nipples, or even fingerprints anymore. The fire had destroyed her femininity, the normalcy of her life, and even her physical identification.

And now she had D.N.A.

"Yeah, that's me." Lying wasn't an option; she was too recognizable.

"You're all over the news. See?" Sandra pulled up a remote and the blank spot on her wall lit up with the colors of a daytime news studio.

"—search continues for Alta Williams, who is believed to have suffered some mental instability before her escape from nanoTech Laboratories. Should anyone find Williams, officials advise calling the police. Do not attempt contact directly, as she still may be unstable. Harold Fletcher has more—"

Alta found herself inching away from Sandra and off the sofa. "You think I'm nuts."

Sandra met her gaze, "Are you?"

"You were just on the phone with the commissioner."

"What makes you say that?"

"I don't have time to explain, Sandra."

"I never told you my name was Sandra." Sandra's brown eyes looked perplexed.

The power of the conversation was shifting in her favor. "D.N.A. told me. Your name is Sandra Ramirez. You've been living here two months. You contacted a man named Commissioner Gunner at the Metro PD just now. The call lasted 17 minutes."

Sandra sat down again, eyeing Alta. "Alright. I'm listening. Who is D.N.A.?"

"I've got to go." She couldn't linger here, waiting for the police to show up. D.N.A.'s mission was still incomplete; human lives were at stake.

"I didn't turn you in, Alta," Sandra said, as if on cue, catching Alta by the arm. "Listen." She stalled, seeming to be gauging something in Alta before she continued, "I'm a private investigator. I was at nanoTech last night scoping them out."

"A PI? For who?"

"The Metro PD. Commissioner Gunner is my boss."

"Metro has nanoTech under investigation? What for?"

"That's classified."

Alta started tugging her arm out of Sandra's grip.

"There have been a lot of strange shipments recorded by warehouses recently. Electronics, radio wave emitters... not the usual sort of stuff you'd expect from a pharmaceutical company."

"That's nothing worth sending a P.I. out for," Alta challenged.

Sandra's features tensed and her grip tightened. For a moment, their eyes remained locked on one another. "Fine. Some of their recently discharged patients have gotten sick. Some of them have died."

Alta felt the blood leaving her cheeks, "It's... it's already started." It had never occurred to her that the Respiratory Unit hadn't been the only branch of nanoTech using the suicide compound.

"What do you mean?"

This was too big. She couldn't take them down on her own. Bryan Engel was one thing; the entire corporation was another. "Are you familiar with their current research? The nanoCell lungs for respiratory disease?"

"Yeah, of course. Everyone is."

"Listen to me, carefully. They've placed a receptor in the lung tissue that can release an aggressive chemical compound into the host. The compound forces the host's natural genetic cells to deteriorate. All nanoTech has to do is emit a simple radio signal, and they could order the receptor to release that compound, and, in essence, dissolve a patient's D.N.A. structure."

"You mean, there's something in those lungs that can make people sicker if nanoTech wants it to?"

"No, I mean there's something in those lungs that can *kill* people if nanoTech wants it to."

Sandra sat down, suddenly looking rather anemic. "That's impossible. Theres no way they'd get away with it. Where's your proof?"

"Some doctors I worked with before at nanoTech contacted me a few months ago to ask if I would assist them in this new venture. My body is highly tolerant to their synthetic tissue, so they wanted to use me as part of their control group."

"But you didn't need new lungs, right? You're in the Genetic Registry. You guys don't have a single thing wrong with you." The fact that Sandra knew Alta's genetic heritage was no surprise; the media's fascination with her had left little about Alta's life private.

"I *was*," Alta corrected. The Registry. The government's not-so-subtle attempt to weed out citizens deemed genetically inferior to the rest of the population. The Registered were the only people allowed to have children using their own genes, without modification, or hefty taxes. Those of the Non-Generation were aptly named. The future would forget them.

"The fire damaged my body badly. The news only talked about my skin, but I inhaled a lot of chemical smoke, too. My respiratory system had been failing for some time. Among other things." There was no need to go into detail. Alta had been born as part of the Registry's elite genetic class, but the accident had made her barren, and thus ineligible for inclusion.

She was a part of the Non-Generation now.

"So, you needed the lungs." Sandra didn't sound overly sympathetic. Alta didn't suspect any born into the Non-Generation would be.

"Yes. In any case, things went smoothly. My body took to the lungs easily and I admit, I haven't breathed this well in years."

"How did you find out about this receptor?"

"A couple of weeks ago. I was restless, and all of the interns had already gone home. I went walking around the lab. I don't know how to explain it. But there was this computer. I walked over to see if I could turn it off— the screen was so bright—but, when I touched the screen…" She rubbed her unmarked fingers together curiously in remembrance, "I guess it was the nanoCells reacting to something. I established an electrical current with the computer. Or, rather, the computer established a connection with me."

"How the hell does that work?"

"There was… this program. It called itself D.N.A. The leavings of a software code. The 'Digital NanoCell Accelerator' was charged with giving commands to the nanoCells: when to multiply, what to become, whatever. The master control."

"But that's still just software. You keep talking about it like it's A.I."

"It is. It even has a voice. It's a self-learning program. They made it that way so it could rectify mistakes in the nanoCell code, and improve its performance over time. Like a brain. The lab was using the program to construct synthetic tissue that could take into account all of the abnormalities and outlier data of each patient."

"And the program told you all of this? Why tell you?"

"D.N.A. is aware of his own limitations. He was tied to nanoTech's systems. All they'd have to do is unplug him to get rid of him. He needed a way out."

"Your skin…" Sandra sat back in amazement.

"Yeah. Exactly." Alta rubbed her arm. "It took him almost two weeks to upload his whole program intravenously. He had to tweak the cells in my syntheskin, but now I have an exact copy of the entire program in my brain and skin."

"And your lungs?"

"He ordered the receptor to self-destruct. I'm safe. Last night, I was trying to get solid evidence of the crimes they were committing before going to the police."

"Did you get it?"

"Yeah, I did."

Sandra's face lit up. "That's great! We should go then. Right now." She stood, reaching for her coat.

Alta didn't move a muscle. "We can't. It's too dangerous."

"Why? You said you're safe."—Sandra's gaze met Alta's own—"But the other patients aren't."

"Right."

In the background, an old, familiar voice rose above the white noise of the newscast. Bryan Engel stood behind a podium, addressing reporters casually, as if nothing were wrong at all.

"Alta Williams will be found, I have no concerns about that. When we get her back, we'll take every precaution to see to her health and well-being. In the meantime, nanoTech Laboratories will carry on with our plans for the public release of nanoCell Lungs at the end of the week."

Oh god, Gordie, breathing through a living bomb. And all of the other patients who had gone through the trial with them.

"As always, nanoTech's biggest priority is your health, and everyone's quality of life." Engel's face was the picture of compassion. Alta couldn't stand to look at it.

"I've got to do something."

"What, about nanoTech? Look, if you've got the proof you say you do, I can help you." Sandra leaned forward again.

"nanoTech is already on the alert because they realize I'm gone. If I make any mistakes going forward, all of those other patients are at risk."

"Then what are you going to do?"

"I don't know. But, I've got to save the others before I can take nanoTech down." Alta frowned, then turned her thoughts inward. *D, what are our options? Can you help those people like you helped me?*

Using the data acquired from your body, I can create nanoCell inhalers. Once inhaled, the new cells can deactivate the receptors.

That's great. Let's do that. How?

The cells would have to be created at a lab.

Any lab?

Affirmative. But, you'll have to go back to nanoTech to administer the inhalant to the patients.

Alta found herself smiling. "Looks like we've got a plan."

Sandra didn't have the same light of epiphany surrounding her. "I just watched you stare at my wall for five minutes. You sure you're not crazy?"

"You'll just have to trust me. And I'm going to need your help."

It was going to have to be a quiet operation. One slip, and nanoTech could erase all evidence... could activate the receptors. But Alta knew she couldn't do everything alone. There were too many lives at stake.

"Say the word, lady. I'm in."

"We're going to need a lab."

As Alta climbed out of the vent over the women's bathroom, she couldn't help feelings of déjà vu. She was confident, though. They wouldn't fail this time.

She'd arrived at nanoTech HQ almost six hours prior with a tour group. D.N.A. had copied Agent Ramirez's thumbprint for the sign-in stations and altered her facial appearance. At the halfway point, Alta had split off from the group, claiming an important phone call. She'd gone to the restroom instead, to slip up into the ceiling and simply wait until the building closed down for the night. Agent Ramirez had been the caller, and convinced the front security to let her back in; the switch seemed to have gone off smoothly.

Stripping her clothes off so D.N.A. wouldn't have any obstructions in case he needed to protect her, Alta attempted calm and focus. Her skin shifted until the white and gray armor revealed itself. *Walk me through it one more time?*

Head to the patient beds from this floor. Use the stairs. Insert the inhalers into the medication dispenser near the oxygen tanks, and call Agent Ramirez once the receptors are destroyed. The Metro PD will retain their holding position until then.

And how long will that take?

Fifteen minutes upon deployment.

D, you really love these waiting games.

The world wasn't made in a day. The sarcasm was so unlike him, Alta almost laughed. Almost. If it wouldn't have risked everything.

Okay, let's go. She took a deep breath, centered herself, and then entered the hall. D.N.A. had her senses heightened within seconds.

The room was dark except for the yawning green lights of the machines on standby. Alta slid carefully across the floor and crouched, her every instinct on fire. She had expected tonight to be harder.

Don't relax yet.

I know. But I just have to put the inhalers in the tubes now, and then wait.

Waiting was the plan last time, D.N.A. reminded.

She stood and nodded. *Yeah, I get it. Stay alert.* Time to get this done. She knelt before the first oxygen tank, opening the drawer at its side and installing the first inhaler. The little hiss it made as the nanoCells were released into the sealed bed's oxygen supply relieved only a small bit of her anxiety. *Nineteen more to go.*

Your heart rate is fairly elevated. She didn't need D.N.A. to tell her. Her ears were throbbing under her pulse.

Alta set the next container in. *Just tell me if there's someone creeping up on me.*

Odd. D.N.A. answered, Video surveillance on this floor has been disabled.

What? Why would they do that?

"What are ya doing?"

Alta froze when she heard the voice, an inhaler gripped tightly in her hand as she turned around. She relaxed almost immediately. "Gordie?"

The boy blinked in recognition, "Ms. Williams?"

Alta smiled, as calmly as she could manage, crouching some as she came before the child, "Yeah. Hey, how are you?"

"Good," he said, but his look of confusion didn't leave his face, "What are you wearing?"

"Just a special suit. What are you doing out of bed?"

"I had to use the bathroom."

"Well, let's get you back in bed, alright?" Much to her relief, Gordie nodded and returned to his pod bed without complaint, climbing in and letting Alta help him close the lid.

A blinking red light in the far corner caught her attention. A camera's bulbous lens was pointed in her direction. *Hey, D. I thought you said that the video surveillance was disabled.*

It is.

Then they're using analog. They must have suspected that she would return. Tensing, Alta turned back to Gordie's pod. Next to the tubes that dispersed the medicated air into the patient's pods was the canister that looked her like her own.

This one, D?

Yes. Replace it with one of the inhalers you brought with you.

Nodding, Alta got to work. The process was fairly simple and only took a couple of seconds. Gordie would be safe now.

There were still seventeen others who needed their canisters, though. "Good, Gordie. Now go back to sleep." Alta smiled, not wanting to scare the child, before she locked his pod and ran to the rest of them, no longer caring about making noise as she popped inhaler after inhaler into the beds.

In between pods, Alta turned back to the camera and its accusing red light, hoping she would be given enough time to install them all.

`Multiple key codes employed on the floors below and above.`

Fear slid like winter slush into her veins. But, she couldn't run; the people in the lab needed her. *Five more. We can do this!*

A door lock clicked at the far end of the hall. Her head start was over.

Alright, D. What have you got for me to play with tonight?

`Panthera Pardus.`

Alta sighed as she felt her skin change and restrict, tighten; refine. Synchronizing with D.N.A. had extended his abilities. She watched in amazement as spotted fur appeared against her right forearm, as her fingernails lengthened and darkened into razor claws. The arm of a leopard would make an excellent defense. Unfortunately, it made gripping the canisters nearly impossible. She fumbled with the next inhaler, before finally managing to release the gas with her left hand.

Security guards burst onto the floor in riot gear. Their tasers were fully lit and snapped brightly as they came into view. Their presence didn't surprise her, but the man at their center did. Bryan Engel, brandishing a taser wand himself, recognized her immediately.

"I'm not sure I like the new look, Alta."

Alta wasn't in the mood for banter. There were still four patients that needed to be inoculated against nanoTech's receptors. She jumped for the next bed.

"Get her!"

At the bark of Engel's orders, the security guards rushed forward. Pre-programmed muscle memory helped Alta respond as she swung her leg low to trip one guard, and then jumped up with an uppercut on the next. A third guard who smashed his nightstick against her spine was greeted with the claws of her new arm tearing through his padded vest. As the three recovered, Alta snapped the next inhaler in and dodged a fourth attack.

Remind me to thank you later for dredging up all those self-defense memories.

Noted. D.N.A.'s voice was calm, as always. To your right.

Alta spun, tearing the helmet off the next guard and cutting the arm of another with her claws. The next inhaler snapped into its oxygen tank without issue.

Bryan Engel's voice boomed loudly through the lab, "Williams, I'd desist if I were you."

Alta paused only long enough to see what looked like an antique mobile phone in Engel's hands.

"I know what you're trying to do. But I also know you're not finished yet. All I have to do is send a code, and we'll see which ones you haven't reached."

He's bluffing.

Better not to assume.

Alta watched as the five guards she injured recovered, readying their tasers again. Did they know what Engel was up to? Would they still try to stop her if they knew? *I'm pretty outnumbered here, D. If one of those things hit me, you're in trouble, right?*

An electrical shock would disrupt my system, yes.

There's no way to deflect it? She watched Engel's hand grip his taser tightly. *To channel it?*

The genetic structure of Electrophorus Electricus might work. But the voltage of those wands is quite high. Disruption may still occur.

Use it. I have an idea.

With two canisters in her hand that she had no hope of getting to the people that needed them, there was only one more option. Alta took a deep breath and charged straight for Engel. Her skin grew slimy and thick.

Wish me luck, D.

Inches from Engel, Alta felt the snap of a taser. The dark lab lit up brightly as several more cracked against her nude skin. The weight of her body seemed to sink to her toes as she felt D.N.A.'s presence disconnect from her. Just like when she was on the roof, her legs wobbled on, the synapses merely repeating the final command from her cortex.

That was all she needed.

Her outstretched hand smacked against Bryan Engel's chest seconds later. Her skin, which had been holding the charge from the tasers, released the voltage against him like the electric eel whose skin she'd adopted. Engel's eyes widened, before he was blasted back. He slammed into the wall and the guards rallied. Alta finally dropped to the floor, the unused canisters rolling just beyond her reach.

Hands came upon her, pulling her off the ground and wrenching her arms behind her back. The voltage had been too much; she felt her consciousness fading.

Not yet.

With one final rally, Alta did all she could do: focus on the fear. She worked herself into a panic as the guards restrained her.

When D.N.A. came back online moments later, the pain of his return set her eel skin's natural defenses off in a chain reaction. Electricity shot off of her body, connecting with any guards that were too close, and forcing a retreat of the rest.

Out of imminent danger, Alta managed a gasp. *D...*

She didn't have enough energy to finish the thought. She didn't have the capacity to send the call to Sandra. With a groan, she collapsed, out cold upon the floor.

When Alta finally came to, she was propped up against a wall in the hallway. A flood of voices sounded out everywhere.

Agent Ramirez was crouched beside her, wrapping a thick blanket across her shoulders. She smiled when she saw Alta staring.

"Well, you woke up after all. You're pretty good at that."

Alta glanced around. She was still inside nanoTech HQ. She turned her eyes back to the P.I. questioningly.

"We arrived about five minutes after you... well, whatever you did to Engel." Ramirez paused. "What did you do to him?"

"I electrocuted him."

"Well, that explains the reports."

"He had a box...."

"The transmitter, yeah. Seems you shorted it out when you lit him up."

"The patients?"

"They're safe. Thanks to you."

Alta relaxed, her shoulders sagging against the wall. "What happens now?"

"Metro is going to gather the evidence you gave us before, and the stuff from tonight, and bring nanoTech to court. It's bigger than we thought. All this stuff with nanoTech goes all the way back to the government. We think they've been funding some kind of eugenics program... having nanoTech do their dirty work."

She could barely comprehend the magnitude of what Sandra was saying. Her every fiber ached. "Everything hurts."

"Well, if the guards are to be believed, you took about eight lashes from their tasers. I'm surprised you can even talk."

Alta looked down. Someone had bandaged several large patches of her bare skin. The nakedness concerned her.

D?

There was silence for a time, before she felt that same, familiar sensationGood evening, Alta. Congratulations on a job well done. I accessed your memory; you knew your body would keep moving, even if I shut off temporarily. Because of what happened before.

She smiled. *You sound proud, D.*

According to psychologists, positive reinforcement helps confidence and increases morale. Did it work?

Alta laughed, attracting the attention of more than a few detectives on the scene.

Almost, D. Almost.

ALEX HURST was raised in the wilds of the south. Lightning storms and hurricanes created the playpens of her youth, and in the summers, she used to spend all of her time dodging horseflies in a golden river, catching fish and snakes with her bare hands, swinging from vines, and falling out of magnolia trees.

In the dawn of her adolescence, her family took her on a journey across the United States, from the white sands of Pensacola, FL, to the razor's edge of the Hell's Backbone in Utah. They finally landed in Marin, CA, where lotus eaters tried to make city folk out of them (but miserably failed). She currently lives in Kyoto, Japan, writing primarily character-driven fantasy, though she has been known to dabble in science fiction, horror, and LGBT literature as well. *D.N.A.* is her first serialized work of fiction. You can find her on the web at **alex-hurst.com**.

"I N EGYPTIAN MYTHOLOGY, there is a demon known as the Devourer of the Dead. She is the most feared creature connected to the pantheon. With the head of a crocodile, the body and forelegs of a lion, and the hindquarters of a hippopotamus, she was a vision of death. And death was her purpose."

Thomas heard a laugh someone attempted to cover with a cough. It appeared contagious, and a few others started chuckling. He smiled.

"It does sound pretty ridiculous-looking, doesn't it?" He saw a couple nods from a few of his students, but no one said anything. They knew he would go on.

"She might sound funny-looking to us, but the Egyptians were terrified of her. Her name was Ammut, and she was well-known for being the Egyptian version of Hell.

"Egyptian myth states that when a person dies, they undergo a trial called The Weighing of Hearts. Anubis—you all remember him from last week—would weigh the heart of the person who died against Ma'at, the goddess of order. Ma'at was often represented by an ostrich feather.

"It was believed that, if a person was good and had spent the majority of their life performing good deeds, their heart would be lighter than the feather, and they would have earned their right to pass on to the journey of the afterlife.

"Those who were cruel had heavy hearts, however, and they suffered the fate that all Egyptians feared.

"Their hearts—the very souls of these people—would be eaten by Ammut, the Eater of Hearts."

Thomas glanced up at the clock above his unused blackboard, then back to his students. "We'll stop there for the day," he said, and saw them beginning to put their books in their bag. "Please remember you have a test to take online by six o'clock this evening. You must be *finished* by six. And none of your papers on your chosen Egyptian god will be accepted any later than Tuesday."

He smiled at his students, who he could see were listening well to what he said. He was very lucky to have such a good crowd this year.

"Now get out of here. Enjoy your weekend."

There was a lot of shuffling and thumping of bags against the auditorium seats of the lecture hall. Thomas let the sounds fill his head. He tried to let it drown out the dread of his dinner plans that evening.

To no avail.

Thomas rubbed his temples where a headache had begun forming. He really didn't need all of this stress.

DINNER WAS WORSE than Thomas had anticipated.

The atmosphere was tense. The only sound at the table was the clinking of silverware on the dishes. Despite how uncomfortable it was, it was much preferable to the alternative.

The man sitting across from Thomas set down his fork and cleared his throat.

"So, Thomas."

Crap.

"You were teaching more of your hocus-pocus again today, I suppose."

"I was teaching my students about mythology, yes." Amelia's mother had made candied carrots as a side dish, knowing they were his favorite. It was very kind of her, but it was difficult for Thomas to enjoy them. They tasted like sawdust in his mouth.

Paul, Amelia's father, snorted derisively. "What were you telling them? They're all going to come back as cockroaches when they die?"

Thomas felt Amelia slip her hand into his under the table. He squeezed her fingers lightly in thanks.

He always hated the holidays. His parents had died when he was young and he had been an only child. It was unfortunate that he wasn't able to get along with his in-laws, but it had always been like this. He wasn't sure what he had done in order to make Paul Brennan hate him so much, but the man had always been vicious to him.

Amelia had mostly stopped trying to defend him last year. She kept her silence when they were together like this, unwilling to start something and break ties with her parents, but Thomas wasn't sure that would last very long. If Paul continued acting like he did, it was likely they wouldn't be getting together for the holidays next year.

He hoped the man came to his senses. Thomas wanted to have a good relationship with his girlfriend's family. He wanted to make them his in-laws officially, and she his wife.

It would happen, regardless of their opinion, but he did hope the former could bring happiness on both sides.

"We haven't touched on reincarnation, yet," Thomas answered politely. "Perhaps next week." He ignored the way Paul bared his teeth, as though fighting the urge to attack Thomas. It would certainly liven up dinner if it happened.

Thomas rubbed his head, trying to hide the fact that he was doing so. His headache was picking up again, no surprise.

Clearing his throat, he ran a hand through his hair and smiled at Amelia. He picked up the topic of his classes, since it was really the only thing they had going.

"My students should be finishing up their exams right now, actually. I hope they all got them finished on time."

THE DOOR TO THE APARTMENT CLICKED SHUT behind them. Thomas shed his coat and tossed it over the back of the couch, before flopping down in an armchair and throwing his arms to the sides.

"I need a drink."

Amelia hummed in agreement as she walked past him and into the bedroom. Thomas shut his eyes and dreamed of a big glass of spiced rum. He heard the squeak of the faucets and the gush of water as she began filling the bathtub.

"Crap. You're leaving tonight, aren't you?" he called loudly.

"Yes." Her voice sounded slightly muffled from the sound of running water, but he could hear her clearly enough. He pouted a little. He had forgotten that Amelia had a plane to catch that evening. She was attending a cooking contest in California and had a ridiculously long plane ride that left at midnight.

"Tommy?"

Thomas opened his eyes, blinking in surprise at the sight that greeted him. Amelia was standing in the doorway, clothed in a short, loose-fitting nightdress that did very little to protect her form from view. She brushed her hair back behind an ear self-consciously.

"Amelia?"

She glanced down at the floor, her face glowing red. "I've been saving it. Are you surprised?"

"I am... very surprised." He sat up fully, his eyes running from her forehead to her toes and back up, making her blush even more. He met her brown eyes, gleaming with nervousness.

"Are you wearing anything under that?"

He watched a smile blossom across her face, her lips pulling back to display large teeth. "No."

Grinning, he bounced to his feet, wiggling his fingers enticingly. "Then I am *very* surprised. May I unwrap you now?"

He grabbed her, scooping her up into his arms and kissing her neck. Her giggling paved the path to the bedroom.

"I THINK YOU SHOULD STOP PUTTING CLOTHES ON," Thomas said, from where he was stretched out on the bed. "And drop the towel."

Amelia grinned over at him, her cheeks glowing lightly. "You *know* I have to get going. Daddy will be here to pick me up in a few minutes."

"You don't have to go right now. I'm sure your dad would understand if you were a few minutes late."

"And would you like to explain why I was late to my dad?"

"I'll just tell him you get your looks from your mom. Man to man, he'll understand."

"Tommy!" Amelia fixed him with a scandalized look. "You can't tell my dad that!"

"Oh, come on, 'mel. Your mom is hot. He'd get it. Of course, he might shoot me anyway, on principle."

Amelia's mouth twisted into a frown and her fingers twisted in the fabric of the shirt she held. "I'm sorry he's being like this."

"Hey, hey, it's not your fault." Thomas climbed out of bed and walked over to her, rubbing her shoulders. "He just needs to get used to the idea, that's all. I bet if I was a dad, I'd be just as nervous about losing my little girl to some bad boy."

Not that he would ever treat his daughter's boyfriend the way Paul treated him, but Amelia already knew that. She didn't need for him to admit again how cruel the man was being.

She pressed her index finger into his chest, quirking an eyebrow. "You think pretty highly of yourself, Mister Brooks."

"Well," he said, looking down at her, "I am taller than you."

Laughing, she pushed him away playfully. "Go away. I'm trying to get dressed and you're distracting me."

"All part of my elaborate plan." He still moved back over to the bed and sat down, watching as she pulled a T-shirt on over her head. "So whose idea was it to have a three hour car ride full of father-daughter bonding? You could have just driven yourself to the airport."

"It was my idea," Amelia said, pulling her hair back into a high ponytail. "I have to break the news to him somehow, don't I?"

"You think it's a good idea to tell him while he's behind the wheel?"

Amelia clicked her tongue at him, a look of dismay on her face. "Don't be stupid. Daddy may not care for you much, but he doesn't hate you."

Thomas grimaced, not entirely sure of that.

"He's careful, and he'd never do anything to hurt me." She folded herself across his lap, wrapping her arms around his neck. "You're a lot more like him than either of you want to admit."

"Hrm… stubborn, self-righteous, grumpy, and balding…" He kissed her frown-formed lips. "Yeah, I can see that." He felt her lips curl up into a smile against his own.

"But I'm not old."

Amelia giggled, pressing her nose into the curve of his neck and exhaling slowly. "You just wait," she murmured against his throat. "Another six months might change your opinion on that."

"Hm." He slipped a hand under her shirt and began to rub the bare skin of her back.

"I have to go," she murmured into his skin.

"Mm-hm."

"You're making it hard."

"So're you."

She smacked his shoulder blade lightly. "It's a three hour drive."

"Do you want me to stop?" he teased.

"No."

He chuckled, rubbing circles in her skin. Thomas knew she really did have to leave soon, since her father was expecting her, but he just couldn't bring himself to let her go just yet. He had no plans for the weekend, and having her gone would mean his life would be very empty until she got back.

Thomas grimaced as his head began to ache again. This headache he had been having all day was incredibly persistent. He had blamed it on stress before, but it was really starting to bother him how determined it was to interrupt his day.

He licked his lips, trying to think through the pain.

"What will you make for the contest?"

"It's a surprise."

He pouted at her, eyes squinted a little against the light in the room. It was suddenly too bright, piercing.

Amelia giggled. "Don't look at me like that. It's a surprise for us, too. None of the participants know what we'll be making. That's what makes it so interesting."

"You are definitely going to win," he murmured, closing his eyes to block out the light.

She kissed the side of his neck. "You think so?"

"Mm-hmm."

Amelia pulled away from his shoulder and frowned at him. He blinked open his eyes when he felt her shift her position and found her staring at him in concern. He realized that his fingers had stopped moving in tight circles on her back. His hand was clenched into a fist.

"Tommy?" Her fingers touched his forehead, smoothing over the skin like she was checking for a fever. "Are you all right?"

Thomas blinked, the headache fading abruptly.

"I'm fine." His lips pulled back into a smile. "Let's make sure your knives are sharp enough before you go."

"WILL THE DEFENDANT PLEASE RISE?"

He stood up from the bench where he'd been sitting, hands clenched together tightly. He was trying not to let them see him shaking.

Show no fear.

"Thomas Brooks, you have been found guilty of one count of murder in the first degree. Under the state law of Texas, I hereby sentence you to death by lethal injection. Do you understand what this means?"

Thomas nodded shakily.

"Mr. Brooks, please speak for the record."

"Yes, I... I understand."

"Very good. Your sentence will be carried out in two weeks' time. Die well, Mr. Brooks."

Thomas' blood went cold.

"Guards."

A man on either side of him, Thomas was forced to his feet. He called out, but the judge had risen from his chair and made his way to the exit behind the stand. Now that the verdict had been decided, he was completely disinterested in anything that was going on.

The obedient guards led him out of the courtroom and back to the cell.

DEATH WAS EASY THESE DAYS. Lethal injection was a quick and painless way to dispose of criminals. Just like putting down an unwanted dog. Sometimes, it was even possible to convince yourself it was humane.

Paul Brennan stepped into the empty courtroom. His boots sounded oddly heavy on the hardwood floor, the steps of his heels echoing off the marble walls. The acoustics were strange in old buildings like this.

His pace was quick but casual as he moved down the aisle between two rows of pews, then past the jury box. There was no one behind the judge's podium, but the judge had a habit of staying late. Paul knew there was an office in the back of the building, and he *would* speak with the judge tonight.

"Mr. Brennan, a pleasure to see you again."

Paul spun, stumbling, a chill racing just under his skin. It filled his chest with an icy cold feeling that made his heart throb.

Standing in front of jury box was the man Paul had come to see, but the jury box was filled with people. He was sure it had been empty.

No, it *had* been empty. He knew it had. There hadn't been anyone around when he walked through the courtroom.

"How did you—"

His skin prickled with goosebumps as his breath quickened. His head whipped back to the door he had come through. It was still shut.

He turned back to the jury box. It was still full of people, none of whom he recognized. Their faces were almost indistinct with disinterest on his part. The only man that mattered was the one standing at the head of them all.

His hands were clasped behind his back in a casual stance that still seemed to work in a formal setting. He was dressed as though he were preparing for a hearing, his judicial robes in place, despite it being ten o'clock at night. It made the situation seem almost medieval, meeting a man in robes in a courtroom older than the town itself.

"Judge Menn."

The judge smiled, thin lips pulling back in a gesture that seemed almost fatherly, but there was a mockery in that. Paul had never had a good relationship with his father.

"I trust you were pleased with the outcome?"

Paul's lingering surprise gave way to his rage, the chill in his blood disintegrating to the heat that boiled up from his core. His hands clenched into fists at his sides and the strength of his rage alone kept his voice low, forced out through clenched teeth.

"You were meant to get him away from my daughter!"

"And so I did." The judge made a vague motion with his hand, as though to encompass all that had occurred within the last few days. "Granted, it did not occur in such a way that either of us were expecting, but it was completed to your specifications. Your daughter *is* free of Thomas Brooks."

The use of the name seemed to break whatever spell was held over Paul's vocal cords. His voice was a roar as he lunged forward, fist flying at the judge's face.

"You had that bastard kill my Amelia!"

His arm went further than he had anticipated and he stumbled forward, catching himself against the podium. He pushed himself back to a standing position and looked around. There's no way the judge could have moved so quickly.

Someone cleared his throat behind him. Paul spun around again. He could feel beads of sweat tickling his forehead, but he didn't know whether it was from the rage or the fear. He hadn't heard footsteps. How did the judge get all the way over to the door so quickly?

"Tsk tsk, Mr. Brennan."

Menn didn't look concerned in the least. There was a pitying look upon his face, a sad smile on his lips, as he began walking down the aisle that Paul had walked to get where he now stood.

"That is no way to treat a business partner."

"Business partner? You murdering bastard!"

"Now, now. Is name-calling really necessary?" He stopped at the end of the aisle and leaned casually against a pew, as though they weren't talking about a murder they had both participated in. "Especially when the proverbial shoe does not fit. After all, we both know it was Thomas who was the murderer."

Paul's teeth clenched together.

"If you wish to lay blame for your daughter's death, place it also at your own feet, Mr. Brennan."

"I would never hurt my daughter!"

"And yet you wished to take the man she loved away from her. In fact, you had him *killed*. That is one mark against you."

"One *mark*? What are you talking about?" Paul demanded, stepping forward. He felt something stop him, as though arms as strong as steel bars had wrapped around him. He could not move.

The judge continued on as though he had not spoken.

"You asked to have Thomas dealt with in such a way that his death could not be traced back to anyone else. You wanted him condemned for his own actions, and so wished for him to perform actions for which he could be condemned. Such actions as these required harm to another person. That is two marks against you."

"What are you *talking* about?" Paul yelled, struggling against whatever force held him. He tried moving to the right and left and found that he could go the short distance of a few feet before his movement was arrested again. With the judge's podium behind him, he was caged.

"You begged for him to be taken away, to suffer consequences he would not normally suffer. In order to accomplish this, action needed to be taken to force him to perform injustices that would warrant such consequence. Thus, he was bound to another soul, and an immoral joining was forced upon two unwilling creatures. That is three marks against you."

Paul had stopped trying to escape his prison. He could see no walls to scale and so had no way to perform an action to rise above them. Instead, he listened as the judge spoke nonsense.

"You asked that Thomas Brooks be removed from the presence of your daughter, and in so doing, he was removed from the presence and life of your granddaughter, leaving the child bereft a father. That is four marks against you."

Paul's breath stuttered in his throat.

"The requests you made led to the death of Amelia Brennan, the unnamed child of Amelia Brennan and Thomas Brooks, and Thomas Brooks himself. That is five marks against you."

The judge walked a few steps closer to Paul and regarded him with that pitying expression.

"Paul Brennan... how do you plead?"

"Plead?" He struggled to sound affronted through the pain the truth had wrought. He hadn't known... he hadn't...

"I'm not guilty of anything!" he snarled.

Judge Menn regarded him for a moment, as though waiting for him to rescind his words. When Paul remained silent, he raised his right arm in front of him.

Paul could see, as though it had appeared out of thin air, a golden set of scales hanging from the rope in his grasp. The judge held the scales aloft, studying them with a practiced eye.

"This does not look good for you, Mr. Brennan."

With his left hand, the judge drew a long, white feather from the deep pocket of his robes. It was large, as though it belonged on a bird the size of a man, and a different shape than Paul had ever seen a feather be before.

The judge placed it on one of the scales.

There was a chiming sound, like a single bell, ringing loudly through the courtroom.

The empty scale dropped down low, as though it had been loaded with rocks.

"A pity, Mr. Brennan." The judge's eyes flicked up to meet his. The pity had disappeared, and only disappointment remained. "You have a heavy heart."

There was a sound behind him. A low, gravelly groan, as though a very large animal was waking from a very long sleep. His back to the podium, Paul was forced to look up.

A great, wide mouth hovered above him, every inch of it teeth. Saliva ran down pale gums and dripped down onto Paul's face. He couldn't make his arms move to wipe it away. All he could do was stare up into the monster's face.

"What?" he whispered weakly.

"Ammut does not eat hearts often anymore. So many of you have turned to others, and few linger in the old ways." The judge displayed all of his teeth in a wolfish grin. "But you came to me.

"Services were rendered to your specifications, and now the price of these services will be paid."

Paul tore his face away from the beast above him when he heard retreating footsteps. "Judge Menn!"

The judge stopped and turned. Paul choked on his own breath when he saw his face. The pale flesh, slightly wrinkled with age, was gone. In its place was thin fur as black as pitch, a long snout, and large ears with pointed tips. He still had the body of a man, but his head had become that of a jackal.

The judicial robes were gone. The creature, for it was not a man before him, wore a white skirt that wrapped around his legs, belted at the waist and reaching only to his knees. His shirt was also white and thin with long sleeves. Facing Paul now, he could see the gold and blue cloth that covered the jackal's head between his large ears and fell down behind his head and over his shoulders. He was decorated with gold and turquoise armbands and a wide, elaborate neck collar. An ankh hung around his neck from a elaborately-braided rope.

Not even Paul could ignore the image that the judge painted before him now. One of the most iconic creatures in myth, he knew immediately that before him stood the jackal-headed god of Egyptian lore.

Anubis' mouth opened in a white-fanged smile that made Paul's heart pound painfully in his chest.

"I thank you for your help in bringing minds to us again, Mr. Brennan. It has been so long since Ammut has eaten, so long since I have held the scales. But the weighing cannot be undone, and the time for deeds is done.

"Judgment has been passed, Mr. Brennan."

The judge turned around and continued out of the courtroom, closing the door behind him and locking it. Not that he needed to keep anyone out. The Weighing of the Heart was not done where others could reach, and none could stop Ammut from having her much-deserved meal.

The hearts of the wicked would always find their ends at the hands, and teeth, of those still fouler than they.

Anubis faded away to the place where gods rest. Somewhere, lost within a place that did not really exist, in a world that not everyone knew was there, a room held the soul of a monster, and the Eater of Hearts.

Somewhere beyond a closed door, a wicked soul screamed.

And was silenced.

CASEY FRY is an author of dark fantasy and horror fiction. Her debut novel, *DeathSpeaker: Hunt*, is the first book in a post-apocalyptic trilogy and was released in October of 2012. Fry uses her love for psychology and mythology to build her characters and the worlds in which they live.

When not writing, she enjoys sketching, watching horror movies, and cooking. Fry currently lives in central Pennsylvania and is working on the second book in the *DeathSpeaker* Trilogy. Progress on her novels and short stories can be seen on her website at **www.caseyfryauthor.com** and on her Facebook page at **www.facebook.com/CaseyFryAuthor**.

THE RISE AND FALL OF
Red Brick and Humble Pie
G T LINES

THE FOUR BANK ROBBERS NEVER HAD A CHANCE.

Oh, they had planned well enough; plenty of guys, plenty of guns—they had even gone so far as to purchase nice-looking, ex-president latex masks, just to keep up tradition—and rightfully, had every expectation of success.

But today was not to be their day.

In a world filled with superheroes, nothing could be taken for granted. So, when they burst forth from Vastopolis First National Bank, duffel bags full of cash flung over their shoulders, Jack, Tricky Dick and all the rest were brought to a sudden and unanticipated halt.

Their getaway car had disappeared.

Instead, a large mound of white, steaming foam now occupied the bay where they had been parked. A sweet smell, quite delectable, wafted in their direction.

The leader of the bank robbers (whose name was Neville, although that has no bearing on our tale) scanned the immediate area. No cops, no civilians, nothing. A faint muffled sob came from deep within the white sticky pile. Somewhere inside was their driver, hopelessly trapped.

Only one superhero could do such a thing.

"Humble Pie," Neville muttered. He started to backtrack, his feet almost tripping over the steps, desperate to reach the relative safety of the bank, where at least he would have hostages to hide behind.

A dark shadow swept across his vision; something resembling a small mountain fell from the sky toward him. It hit the ground, sending a tremor that knocked Neville and his men off their feet.

Dazed, he looked up. An animated pile of red stone and rock stood before him, a looming monstrosity, vaguely man-like, a creature that resembled a really angry Gingerbread Man.

"Shoot it!" Neville shouted, knowing it was fruitless, while wondering where it had all gone so horribly wrong. The rat-a-tat of gunfire filled the street; it didn't last long. After a few seconds of BLAM, a liberal application of BLAT, and the merest smidgen of SMASH, silence descended on the street once more.

The superhero, Red Brick, towered over the fallen men. He was joined by a large, round pie that floated down from the sky. It was a full metre wide, with two long spoons waving energetically from its centre mass. The dust was just beginning to clear as the first of the news vans swept into view, a full thirty seconds ahead of any police.

"Did you call the media?" Red Brick said, sotto voce to his floating companion. "We've talked about that."

Humble Pie bubbled his browned crust (his version of a shrug) and floated off toward the steps. "A little publicity never hurts," he whispered, waggling his spoons.

"You are a master of duality," Red Brick grumbled, following his friend as policemen cuffed the unconscious men. A microphone was pushed toward him.

"Mr. Brick, tell us, how does it feel to be the number one superhero in Vastopolis?"

He shrugged, the tons of stone that made up his shoulders rippling and shifting, echoing over the newsman's head like a landslide.

Here we go again, he thought, and launched into his spiel.

Humble Pie loved it, adored the attention, but it was something Brick had never been comfortable with. It wasn't that he didn't think he was doing good, he knew he was: helping the public, saving lives, thwarting evil—and Brick loved to thwart—it was just he knew something that the newsmen didn't.

Brick knew he was a fraud.

It was in the Brickmobile as they returned to their secret lair (actually it wasn't secret, but everyone in Vastopolis had the decency to pretend otherwise) that Humble Pie noticed his friend was strangely silent.

"What's up, Daddy-Oh?" Humble Pie's crust edge worked up and down to form the words; Brick took his eyes off the road just long enough to spot the small beak of the blackbird that spoke on Humble's behalf, protruding out from the darkness beyond the crust, translating Humble's thoughts into words.

Strange times, mused Brick, but he had lived through strange times of his own. Not much surprised him any more.

Brick shook his head. He wasn't really sure what was bothering him. Tired, that's what it was. He'd been having The Dream, over and over, night after night. It wasn't something he could talk to HP about; his friend wouldn't understand. No one would.

"Hey, it's almost Six o'clock! Woohoo, time for the news, baby!"

Humble switched on the in-car television and noise filled the Brickmobile.

"And our main story: today another bank robbery was foiled by the superhero duo, Red Brick and Humble Pie. Despite desperate odds, the pair quickly apprehended the robbers. Shots were fired but no one was harmed in the raid. Here's Daphne Doric at the scene earlier today!"

"Oooh, it's me, it's me! She's interviewing me!" Humble Pie squealed with delight.

Red Brick sighed.

"Mr Pie." Daphne's voice blared from the speakers. "Once again you have the gratitude of the people of this great city."

"Well, thank you Daphne," the television-Humble replied, "but you know, Brick and I, we don't do it for adulation or reward, we do it because it is our duty. It is an honour to serve this city, this great nation, and the people that have made me—us—so welcome."

"That's so modest of you."

"All in a day's work, Daphne."

"Not quite what you expected when your consciousness arrived on this planet from… which galaxy?"

"Cellnar B, Daphne. Anyway, time for us to be going… crime never rests."

Brick, listening from the driver's seat, knew why Pie had cut the reporter off: the day of his arrival on Earth, Humble's consciousness, plummeting through the atmosphere at high speed, had decided that the large, round object the puny humans were gathered around must be a great leader of some kind—why else would they show it such reverence? How was he to know that it was Vastopolis's annual Giant Pie Bake-off competition He was a tad embarrassed about that, but credit where credit was due, for an alien consciousness forever trapped beneath a layer of egg-glaze, he really had made the best of it.

Brick's story was far simpler; he saw it every night in his dreams: he had been a member of a Bomb Disposal Squad, a veteran of countless operations. Then had come that fateful day when he and his boss, Captain Terrell, were called in to defuse a particularly nasty device. Brick remembered the flash of the nuclear explosion as it obliterated his body, leaving nothing but a faint shadow on a wall. But somehow he had lived, his spirit melded to the stone. The mound of rubble had slowly formed itself into arms, legs, a body, and head. That day, the man he was, Sergeant Danny Wandmann, had died—reborn as Red Brick.

Someone interrupted the reporter with a shout.

"You do alright with the merchandising though don't you?" It was a female voice, high-pitched, accusatory.

"I - I beg your pardon?" said television-Humble. Where had Brick been? Getting the car, he supposed.

"We don't need to hear this," muttered the real Humble, moving one spoon toward the remote.

"Leave it!" snapped Brick. What had Humble gotten them into this time?

"I know about the merchandising deals," the girl yelled. "I know about the sponsorship, the backhanders to the police. The things you have done to drive the other superheroes out of the city!"

"I don't know what you are talking about," stammered Humble. "Now really, we must be up, up and ..."

"Really? You don't know?" Brick took his eyes off the road and glanced at the screen. She was a small girl, mousy hair and glasses; he didn't recognize her.

"Don't you think it odd that SupaChap was arrested for indecent exposure as he changed in a phone-box? That Flying Squirrel Man is in quarantine for rabies? And as for Arachnid Youth, well!"

"It's not my fault he had that fall," Humble piped up. "I had nothing to do with that."

"Really? That building coated itself with Teflon did it? He's going to be in plaster for months, they say."

The reporters were all beginning to speak at once. Humble tried to quiet them.

"This is silly, baseless speculation…"

"I have proof!" the girl yelled, triumphant. "And I know the truth about Red Brick too!"

The crowd's noise dropped to silence. The girl's next words almost caused Brick to swerve off the road.

"He's a murderer!" she shouted.

That was more than the crowd could stand. Everyone started screaming at once, rising to the defense of their beloved heroes. It sounded like it was turning into a riot. The noise ceased abruptly as the scene cut back to the studio.

"Those were the events from outside Vastopolis First National Bank earlier today. More on this story as it develops. Now, the weather. An unseasonable storm system is approaching from the north…"

Brick and Humble exchanged glances.

"Um, did you…?" Humble began.

"No! Of course not. I never killed anyone. How could you think that? Hey, let's talk about you; what have you been up to?"

"Nothing. Honestly, nothing at all, I don't know—"

"Don't you lie to me, Humble Pie. Not me. I am your closest friend."

Humble Pie was quiet for a long moment. When at last he spoke, his voice was subdued. "Look, money doesn't grow on trees, y'know. It's not as if the superhero business pays or anything like that; a Pie's got to do what a Pie's gotta do!"

"If you—"

"No, look, listen. Do you know the difference between us and those other guys? Do you? Well I tell ya: at the end of the day, SupaChap can take off his cape and go to work the next mornin' at Vastopolis News."

"C'mon on, Humble, no one's sure it's really him."

"Of course it's him! He doesn't wear a mask. Just 'cos he's got on a pair of tights and wears his tighty-whities on the outside like some cross-dressing loon, doesn't mean he's suddenly incognito. And it's not just him, is it? It's the same for Arachnid Youth and Flying Squirrel Man; they all get to go home at the end of the day. We don't get to do that, Brick. We are stuck like this!"

They were nearing their base. Brick thumbed the button that dropped the false wall of the old abandoned factory the pair called home.

"I did what I had to do, Brick, to survive. Hey, where are you going?"

Brick had already exited the car and was stalking away, his large feet booming as they struck the concrete floor within the old factory's cavernous interior.

"Brick?"

"I'm going to sleep. Leave me be, Pie. Just leave me be."

He slammed the door behind him and fell in a heap onto the surface of his marble-framed bed. His stone teeth ground in his mighty jaw, filling the room with the sound of sliding gravel.

In many ways Pie was right. They were trapped souls, imprisoned within bodies they hadn't chosen. On his most reflective days, Brick knew that was true of everyone, but not to be able to feel the warmth of another person: not to be able to hold, to hug, to kiss; it ate into his tender stone heart.

But there was more. This girl was clearly making stuff up about a murder, but what if she did know something of the truth? Was his secret out?

If that were true, then everything would be undone.

A FRAGRANCE OF DIESEL AND DECAY SWEPT IN from the river. The lights of the city on the far bank dipped fingers of luminance into the turgid water's murky depths, as the two ferries moving between the opposing banks signaled to one another with mournful howls, like lost lovers, one forever arriving as the other was leaving.

Jenny Saul heard their cries as she waited, listened to their sorrow. Two lost beasts on a liquid prairie, she fancied, as she leaned over the iron railing that protected the unwary from the river's dank grasp.

(A poetic soul, is our Jenny.)

"You did well tonight," a voice behind her said.

She did not turn, but instead closed her eyes, feeling the brush of breath on her neck, the faintest hint of moisture and warmth.

"I did as you told me. Is it enough?"

The voice that answered was a whisper, a soft moan.

"It is a beginning," it said. "But enough? No, that day has not come yet."

"When? When will it come?"

"Soon. Now it is time to move on to the second part of my plan. We must isolate our enemy; he must stand friendless and alone."

"And then? Will it be over?"

"Soon, my love. Soon."

She turned, but the voice that had whispered so close to her ear, that'd pressed against her neck, was nowhere to be seen. The only thing that moved was a swirling of scattered leaves and garbage, spiraling up. In that dancing pattern, Jenny thought she could see a shape, a form.

The voice reached out to her.

"Only when I have broken his spirit will I finally be able to take my revenge on Red Brick, reveal him to the whole world for the monster he is. And then, when he is done, when he can take no more..."

"The police will arrest him... like we discussed," Jenny said.

The voice was quiet for the longest time. Finally it spoke.

"Yes... yes, my love... just that."

THE FIRE WAS A LARGE ONE, BRIGHT AND FIERCE. Every fire department within the seven boroughs had responded.

Firefighter Jeff Tombs (he only answered to JT; who in his right mind would want it widely known that his name was Tombs?) was deep inside the blaze, having run out the hose to its maximum length.

Jeff's heart hammered inside his chest. It wasn't the blaze, he was used to that—although every fire was exciting, of course—it was the location: Vastopolis Chemical Plant. The blaze had started in the offices, but if it continued on toward chemical storage, there would be a fireball of epic proportions. The firefighters were doing their best, but the blaze was winning. Jeff could see the paint beginning to bubble on the surface of the steel-shelled silos; he was desperate to get as far away from this place as possible; he was just waiting to be ordered out.

His radio crackled.

"Pull back, pull back."

Jeff didn't need telling twice. He began reeling in the hose, his partner already moving ahead of him. A loud screech ripped through the air. Jeff looked up in time to see a large pylon tumbling toward him. His eyes widened; the world slowed. He couldn't move, his limbs wouldn't budge; this was it—it was over.

Shit, he thought. I'm only twenty-four.

A mighty arm swung into view. The breath that Jeff had been holding exploded from his mouth.

"Red Brick!" he said. "Oh, thank god, it's Red Brick."

The giant, stone superhero used the wreckage of the pylon to demolish the shell of the office building, knocking down walls and stamping out flames. Jeff was running as the structure started to crumble; Red Brick killed the fire by destroying the space within which it had to grow. In the sky above, Humble Pie circled, spraying a thick jet of foam down on the silos and any flames that had crept close, before moving on to help Brick with the main building.

"Hit the fire suppression tanks!" Jeff heard Brick yell.

Humble's arsenal included many things, amongst them Intercontinental Ballistic Mince Pies. A pair of deadly pastries streaked in toward the building, smashing open the nitrogen tanks, releasing a cloud that enveloped the flames.

Jeff made it back to his fire engine. Beyond the pounding of blood in his ears he could hear men cheering.

From the sidelines the firefighters worked, sending in jets of water, until all that remained was a soot-covered behemoth standing amid the smoldering wreckage, his friend doing victory loops in the air.

The men shouted themselves hoarse. Jeff and every other guy there knew it had been a close call. If Red Brick and Humble Pie hadn't been there, the night could easily have ended in catastrophe.

The news people had turned up; Jeff wasn't surprised by that. These two guys deserved all the attention they got.

But as Red Brick and Humble Pie stepped forward to give their usual conference, it wasn't the fire that was on the agenda. At first there was praise, but then one reporter after another started firing a barrage of questions.

Jeff wasn't very close, but he heard the words 'embezzlement' and 'inappropriate behaviour'. The young firefighter began to push through the crowd. How dare they? How dare they treat his heroes like this. He came to the edge of the throng; a newsman was pushing forward a large colour photograph. Jeff couldn't make out the details, but he could see that it showed Humble Pie with a young woman.

"Oh no, Brick." Jeff was close enough to hear Humble's next words. "They've got a picture of her licking my spoons."

There was great sorrow in that blackbird-croaked voice. Jeff was shocked; who cared what consenting adults (and pastries) did behind closed doors? He expressed himself as any right, free-speaking and thinking man should.

Jeff found the nearest reporter and punched him.

Brick had never seen Humble so distraught. For an hour after they returned to their home he floated back and forth in front of the wall-mounted television, watching as increasingly lurid accounts of his not-so-super activities came to light. Even Brick was surprised: it seemed Humble—aside from developing a minor addiction to the seedier side of Vastopolis night-life—had also taken it upon himself to ensure that the pair were on the payroll, as security assets, to many of the city's banks and high-class businesses. The papers had made note that it was only those banks that hadn't been slipping money into Humble's offshore accounts that were being knocked over by robbers and hoodlums. There was no direct proof, but the circumstantial evidence was mounting.

It seemed that Humble Pie was running a protection racket, and not paying taxes. To all intents, he was a regular Al Capone. The Mayor had even gone so far as to hold a press conference of his own on the steps outside of city hall.

"If there is evidence of wrongdoing," he said. "We shall bring those wrongdoers to justice."

Humble Pie had simply snorted.

"Is it true?" Brick asked when the feed finally cut to a commercial.

"What?" cried Humble. "How can you ask that, man?"

"Humble, forgive the pun but you have your spoons in many pies. You've already said it takes a lot of cash to keep this enterprise going."

"Really? Do you really have any clue? I mean, have you ever once looked at the books?"

"Well, no... I mean..."

"No, of course you haven't. You just mope and mooch and stomp around, wrapped up in your own problems. That marble bed that you so like to throw yourself down on, do you know how much that cost?' Brick could only shake his head. Humble continued:

"Or the day-to-day operating expenses of this factory-lair, the Brick-Mobile, our intelligence gathering operation? The officials I have to pay so that we don't get sued every time we intervene in a crime? Or the cash we pay every time we do get sued? And people loooove to sue! Do you know where that money comes from?"

Brick looked down at his friend, Humble staring defiantly up at him. Humble shook his spoons sadly.

"Geez, man. You believe them! You think I extort the dough." Humble began to float away. "It's merchandising, brother. That's how I raise the cash. That's how I do it: little plastic figures of the pair of us. That's what makes us profitable. I don't know anything about these offshore accounts. I am being framed, and you know, I thought after all our time together... You should just trust me, man."

Brick could hear the hurt in his friend's voice, wanted to step forward and tell him that he had secrets of his own, but his own shame was too great, and by the time he realized his mistake, that Humble had taken his silence as doubt, the floating superhero was already heading for the door.

Brick finally found his voice.

"Humble, please; where are you going?"

Humble turned in the doorway. His whipped-cream eyes fixed on Brick's own.

"Hey, I know a set-up when I see one. Man, soon the police are gonna be comin' and this here is one extraterrestrial that don't do confinement, you dig?"

"But what about me?" Brick said.

Humble was silent a moment.

"Man, you really are a selfish shit, you know that?" His blackbird-voice choked over the words.

The door opened and Humble sailed out into the sky, spiraling rapidly upward.

"No," shouted Brick. "That's not what I meant. I only meant... I can't face it without you."

But Humble Pie was gone, just one more smudged star in the streetlight-drenched sky. Brick stared for as long as he could, watching that tiny speck float ever upward, until finally he blinked, and in that fraction of a second, the light was lost amongst all the others, and Red Brick was finally, irrevocably alone.

He stood by the factory door, the night air washing over his stone, soot-black face. Down by the river he could hear the sound of sirens: they were coming, just as Humble had known they would.

Brick wondered if they knew his secret yet.

It seemed to Brick that every policeman in Vastopolis turned up that night. They came in droves, sweeping down the road in their blue and white cruisers, lights flashing, news vans not far behind.

They formed a semicircle around him, men taking cover beside their cars, pointing guns at him.

After everyone was in position and the cameras were rolling, the police chief himself stepped from his vehicle, bullhorn in hand.

"I am arresting you on the charge of murder, Brick. I - sorry lad, we have proof," The Chief looked up into his eyes. "Come quietly now. We don't want any trouble."

Neither did Brick; he went meekly, like an old pugilist, punch-drunk and broken, still reeling from his final bout.

No car could carry him, he was too big, nor had handcuffs been invented to bind his wrists, so instead, like an animal, a slave, they chained him. Great steel loops encircled his mighty arms and neck, weighting him down, as they marched—paraded him toward confinement. A crowd, drawn by the news that their hero had been arrested, lined the streets. Brick could hear their whispers.

He never saw who threw the first egg. He just felt it splatter against the side of his head. It was followed by more: rotten fruit, cabbages, stones, bottles; anything the mob could lay its hands on.

Their hero had become a monster. Worse, it had all been a lie, and their hero a monster had forever been.

Brick didn't blame them. He knew what he was, the secret he carried; he had been a fool to think he could have pretended otherwise. But he hadn't killed anyone, had he? His memory before the blast was patchy, there were gaps, but... no, there was no way he could've murdered anyone; it wasn't in his nature.

But why let them take you so quietly? A voice whispered inside his mind. His heart ached, but he knew the answer. Shame. He was not the man they thought him to be. He had lied.

It was a long walk through those crowd-lined streets. The shouted insults struck harder than any blow; the betrayal on their faces stung more than any striking fist. Brick hung his head and moved on, the red and blue from the lights of the police cortege reflecting off his stone flanks. They entered the deserted bowl of Vastopolis Stadium (no prison or jail had ceilings high enough to hold Red Brick), leading him out onto the turf and securing him to a hastily erected steel pile that had been driven into the ground.

It began to rain, rippling, moving sheets of dancing water that filled the night sky. The stars had long since disappeared behind a roll of dark clouds that came sweeping in, blacking out the moon and leaving Brick with the sensation that he had been buried alive. A thunderstorm was building; he could feel it. As he looked up, lightning flicked across the sky.

Yes, it was going to be a helluva night.

Policemen in riot gear watched him from a distance, their eyes filled with pity and disappointment.

Finally the Chief of Police turned up and stood in conference at the edge of the turf with the Commander of the SWAT team that had escorted Brick in. They were talking, their eyes turned toward him. Something was up, Brick could feel it in his soul.

The Chief came forward, his face creased in concern.

"I don't know what to say, Brick," he mumbled. The pair had known each other a long time. "We were given a journal—your journal, it seems. It contains details of how you were the one who made that bomb, how you were going to show how vulnerable the country was to attack. Is it true? If so, you are guilty of the murder of Captain Terrell, lad. And that's just the start."

"What? No, of course I didn't kill him." There were blanks in Brick's memory but he could never forget that day. Besides, what he had done to Terrell had been far worse.

The Chief, his small eyes sad within the wide expanse of his pudgy face, looked up at him.

"The girl who made this accusation, who gave us this so-called evidence—she's asking to see you."

Red Brick raised his hands, rattling the chains.

"Well, Chief, you are just going to have to tell her that I am a little tied up right now."

The Chief didn't say anything for a moment, he just took a large bunch of keys from his pocket and started unclasping the padlocks that held Brick's bonds in place.

"You don't understand," the Chief said as he worked. "She is at the top of Vast Spire. She says she will jump if you don't show."

Brick rubbed his newly-freed stone wrists; the Chief beckoned the hero forward. Brick knelt so that the old Policeman could whisper in his ear.

"Dammit, Boyo, I believe you…. Just, if ya tell anyone, I will deny it."

Brick turned toward the stadium exit. Already the various vehicles and personnel had begun to move, clearing out of his path.

"Be careful, lad," the Chief called to his retreating back. "There's something 'bout all this that don't smell right."

Brick's voice rumbled in response. "I know."

VAST SPIRE TOWERED OVER THE CITY, dark, save for the infrequent play of lightning that flashed, illuminating the building's long, sleek sides.

Brick found himself running through the streets toward it, drawn on by some sense of destiny. He could feel it, tonight would be where it all ended—the record would be set straight.

Perhaps then he could rest.

And if that rest was death? Brick didn't care. Guilt and shame were a sickness of the soul, and like any illness the sufferer could only fight so long. If it meant an end to all of that, oblivion didn't seem so bad.

Brick reached the building and began to climb, his mighty arms hauling himself from ledge to ledge, handhold to handhold. Concrete crumbled beneath his grip, glass smashed, but there was no helping it.

"Who cares?" he muttered. "It's not as if they can sue me if I am dead."

At this, he began to laugh, but then stopped as memories of Humble flooded his mind. Humble. Where was he now?

"I am so sorry, my friend," Brick said. "I should have told you everything a long time ago."

They say that in the instant before you die, your life flashes before your eyes. Well, Brick wasn't sure of that, but on that long climb, everything he had ever done came flooding back to him, his whole life, good and bad.

He glanced down at the city where people had once loved him. That was all he'd ever wanted; to be loved.

With a sigh he looked away, raised one giant stone hand and finally pulled himself up onto Vast Spire's observation platform.

It was empty, and he could see nothing.

"Jenny?" he called.

A small, dark shape uncoiled from beneath the shadowed lee of the parapet. Even in the gloom Brick knew it was the girl.

Lightning splashed the sky, illuminating her features; despite the rain Brick could see Jenny had been crying.

"You killed him!" she shouted.

Brick shook his head. "No, no, Jenny. That's not what happened; I was scared. I ..."

"You set the bomb. I know you did. He told me."

Brick was confused, this made no sense. "Who did I kill, Jenny?"

She was openly weeping now.

"My father. You killed my father." She stepped closer to him, her eyes wild and gleaming. "He told me, the day of the explosion you ran and left him to defuse it by himself. It was a two-man job; he could've done it if only you hadn't run! You planned it! You killed him."

Brick was starting to understand. "Your father's Captain Terrell," he whispered.

"Sergeant Wandmann," she hissed. "Recipient of the Medal of Honour, decorated by the President, hero of the people… and a liar who deliberately killed my FATHER! You left him to die while he tried to defuse your bomb."

Brick held out his large stone hands. "Jenny, listen to me. I was there, yes, and I did leave your dad, but I didn't make the bomb... I didn't do that. I was simply..."

"LIAR!" Jenny screamed. "He said you would wriggle and squirm like the monster you are! That's why we made the journal, so you couldn't escape the truth!"

"Who said? Who is telling you these things?"

"My dad."

"Your dead dad?"

Jenny nodded, her damp hair slapping against the side of her face.

"But he's not dead, he's like you. Only he's not like you. Because you can be seen and touched and felt and held." She was choking on her tears. Brick reached forward to hold her.

"No!" she whipped open her coat and, despite himself, Brick took a step back. He could see rows and rows of metal cylinders strapped to a vest. Jenny was wearing some kind of bomb.

"Dad said if an explosion made you, then it can unmake you." In her hand Brick could see the trigger; Jenny's thumb hovered above the button.

"And what about you?"

"Me?" Her lower lip quivered. "He said that, when it is done, I would finally be with him."

"Oh, Jenny, he's lying."

"No!" Jenny's hand tightened on the trigger. "You're the liar. You are! Now it is time to..."

Before she could finish, before she could even react, Brick reached forward, grabbed the front of the vest and, like a magician whipping away a tablecloth, tore it from her body with one jerk of his wrist, sending the whole thing tumbling out into the void beyond the parapet, leaving Jenny standing there, dripping wet and pressing futilely at a button connected to nothing but two loose wires.

"What have you done?" she said. Brick ignored her, he could feel his great stone heart beating against his ribcage. Maybe he didn't want to die after all.

"Oh, holy crap, that was close! Wasn't that close? Lord you gave me a scare! Jenny, are you okay? Look, where is your Dad? I think it is time he and I had a long talk."

Jenny looked from the dangling wires up into Brick's face.

"He's here," she said. "He's everywhere."

"Brian Terrell is here?" Brick looked around him.

"That's not his name any more," Jenny whispered. "He doesn't answer to that. Now you must call him..."

As she spoke lightning streaked from the sky, striking the ground and knocking them both from their feet.

Red Brick was dazed; his head had struck the observation deck parapet. The abyss yawned beneath him, promising oblivion. Panicked, he scrambled backward, looking around for the girl, desperate to see if any danger had befallen her. But something else captured his attention.

A tornado of air was forming itself into the fuzzy outline of a person as it descended from the sky. Lightning crackled from its fingertips, sparks blazed in its eyes.

"Do you like what you see?" The voice seemed to come from all around; the clouds above rippled and hissed with every syllable.

Brick remained silent, his stone jaw slightly agape; in truth he didn't know what to say.

"Come now, don't you recognize me?"

There was something about the booming voice that was slightly familiar.

"Captain Terrell?" Brick said.

Lightning flared in Terrell's eyes.

"Sir, sir, sir!" He boomed. "When you address me, you call me SIR!"

Electricity flew from his vaporous hands, sending Brick skidding along the deck to smash into the far parapet. Terrell drifted toward his fallen foe.

"Truth be told, I don't care if you call me sir. Y'see, I have watched you as my body slowly coalesced molecule by painful molecule. I was forced to listen as you lied and took all the glory for yourself, and as I waited, I decided on a superhero name of my own. You can call me, Nimbus! What'dya think, Sergeant? Is that heroic enough for ya?"

More lightning splashed over Brick's body, pain ripped though him as he was pushed further and further out over the void. With herculean effort he grasped at the safety rail, the only thing holding him back from the long drop to the streets below.

"Why did you run, Danny? If we'd worked together we could have defused it. Why?"

"I was scared," sobbed Brick. "I was so scared, I just wanted to live."

"You killed me. Orphaned my daughter."

"I am so sorry. If I could take it back—live that day again…"

Nimbus drifted closer, edged down beside him so he could whisper in Brick's ear.

"Not good enough," he hissed. "Y'know, you've had all these people fooled. What? Did you think you could… atone, by going out and saving people everyday? You and that freak Humble Pie, saviors of the nation. Do you know what the sad thing is?"

Brick shook his head; he knew the end was close. He was ready to welcome it.

"The truth is," Nimbus continued. "You are the villain. And, as in any good story, it is time for the hero—me—to save the day."

Brick heard the crackle as electricity began to build in Nimbus's body.

It was time. Brick closed his eyes.

"Daddy." Jenny's thin voice cut through the tension. Brick turned toward the sound. Jenny was at the far end of the deck, her bloody face almost level with the floor as the rest of her body hung over empty space. Brick could see her scrabbling for a handhold.

"Daddy, I'm slipping."

Nimbus didn't even turn. Instead he raised his hands ready to finish off his fallen enemy. Brick felt his jaw tighten; he was ready to welcome death for himself, but the girl?

With a heave he threw himself forward, rolling past Nimbus as lightning blasted overhead.

Jenny's grip failed as Brick reached her; his vast stone hand wrapped around her wrist as she began to fall.

"I got you!" he gasped. "I got you!"

Lightning struck his back, pushing both him and Jenny further over the edge.

Brick looked over his shoulder, ready to plead with Nimbus, not for his own life, but at least for his daughter's. Sadly, Brick could see nothing but madness in those flaring eyes. The man Captain Terrell had once been was long gone. Brick wasn't sure what it was that had survived the blast, but it was not the soldier he remembered.

Nimbus prepared to strike them down.

"Daddy! Daddy!"

"He's not listening," Brick sighed, wrapping Jenny tight to him. "Close your eyes."

A faint whine could be heard, growing in intensity. Brick thought he saw a vapour trail in the distance.

Travelling at many times the speed of sound, Humble Pie came in low over the observation deck. The extraterrestrial pastry struck Numbus square in his vaporous chest, splitting him apart where he stood.

Humble's momentum carried him forward. Brick heard a: "Whoooooohoooooo!" as his alien friend sped past, arcing back up into the overcast sky.

For a brief moment, Brick thought it would be that easy, that they had won, but Nimbus had already started to coalesce once more. As Humble begun another attack run, Nimbus was ready. Blue lightning arced upward, sending Humble Pie tumbling from the sky to smash into the deck not far from where Brick lay.

Brick crawled to the shattered remains of his friend: his crust had been cracked open and sauce oozed onto the stone. A very dazed blackbird peered up at him from within.

"Humble, oh dear Lord…"

"Shut up," croaked the blackbird unceremoniously.

"I can't beat him, he's too strong. He's too…"

"Shut up!" Humble managed to right himself. "He's just water vapour, man. Just water vapour. What beats that?"

Brick looked at him with realization.

"Do you have an ICBMP left?"

"Just one, Daddy-oh!"

Brick was already moving as lightning reached out toward him once more. He ducked beneath it, throwing his weight against the wall that led into the main building. He was looking for something specific. He knew it had to be located somewhere on the rooftop.

Nimbus could hear Brick smashing through the interior walls, heard metal being wrenched, and watched as his enemy reappeared once more with a large cylindrical tank balanced above his head. Nimbus could make out the symbol on the side of the tank: nitrogen, part of the building's fire suppression system.

Brick heaved and the tank was sailing through the air before Nimbus realized what danger it posed. He reached forward, trapping the canister within a field of crackling energy, holding it suspended mere inches from his own body.

Nimbus laughed.

"What did you think you were going to do? Did you presume..."

Humble's missile struck the container, shattering it. In the space of a single heartbeat, Nimbus was enveloped, his thick, vaporous body whitening as he froze.

Slowly, very slowly, he began to split apart as the breeze sifted through him, sending a million snowflakes to drift and land amidst the bright lights of the city below.

Brick watched the motes sparkle and twirl as they settled all around. He turned to the sound of Jenny crying and lifted her up with one strong arm, while helping Humble along with the other.

"I am sorry," he said to the girl. "That day, with the bomb, I was afraid and I ran. I didn't mean to—I just..."

She looked up at him but said nothing. Beyond her sorrow he saw other forces at play: pity, anger, hatred. Brick was sure he deserved nothing less.

Paramedics had made it to the rooftop and he passed her over to them, unsure as to what trouble she would cause later.

He turned to Humble who was being reassembled by a small, efficient team of blackbirds.

"Well, looks like we are on top again, brother!" Humble said. "I think we can prove everything was a set-up after that, huh?"

Brick nodded. "Thanks for coming back."

"Don't mention it. It was a funny thing, I got halfway to my destination before I realized I had nowhere to go."

Brick's stone face creased into a smile, then he frowned once more. "Humble, I don't know if you heard, but ... what I told the girl."

"Hey, I know man, I've always known. You talk in your sleep, dude. It's not who you were, brother. It's who you have become that matters."

Brick wasn't entirely sure that was true. Already, the press was gathering, cameras flashing, videotape rolling. "What do I say?" he whispered. Humble waved his spoons.

"Smile and lie, Daddy-oh. Smile and lie."

Red Brick straightened his back, dusted off his shoulders, and with his friend's words echoing in his ears he walked toward the waiting microphones.

"I have something to say," he said.

And he did as any right, free speaking and thinking superhero should.

He told them the truth.

GARY LINES was born in London, England in 1970. An orphan, he was adopted and moved to the countryside just outside Cheltenham.

A shy child, he turned to art, sculpture and writing as a primary means of expressing himself. Hours and days spent roaming amongst the woods and hills of his beloved county sparked his imagination, and led, inevitably, to his love of fantasy; to tales of magic and wild places. It was only a matter of time before he started telling stories of his own.

He has worked as an actor, a drama teacher, a singer, an engineer, a statistician, a cucumber plant pollinator (don't ask); he is currently studying a degree in canine behaviour, and works as a dog trainer. Writing has been his one constant, and remains his greatest passion.

His lifestyle and influences are best described as 'eclectic'.

The Seduction

ANTHONY HULSE

S I WRITE THIS, MY HEART IS HEAVY, my conscience burdened by the enormity of my misdemeanor. Gluttony is an evil distraction, and the cause of my misfortune. It all started on what should have been a wonderful day in June.

At the age of twenty-five, I ought to have been indulging in such pleasures as the Charleston, Douglas Fairbanks, Buster Keaton or Louis Armstrong, but I was not. My idol was the renowned author, F Scott Fitzgerald. His novel *The Great Gatsby* had just been published, and the book motivated me. My vocation in life was to follow my mentor into the world of literature.

I was fortunate to have had wealthy parents who encouraged me and allowed me to pursue my dream. The cruise on the illustrious ship *Ocean Pearl* was my mother's idea. The atmosphere, she stated, would enhance my writing quality and afford me the solitude to write my novel.

I boarded the fifty foot liner in Plymouth, the embarking point of many a great sailor. I was shown to my cabin, and after I explored the ship, I settled down to fulfil my desire. Two hours passed, and a huge pile of writing paper lay at my feet, the rejections of my toil. I decided to have a stroll on the deck to clear my head, and that is when my chance encounter with Richard Sherman occurred.

I leaned over the railing and the sea breeze refreshed me. The intrusion of cigar smoke was most unwelcome. I saw the shadow and turned my head to see an elegantly attired man. He was handsome with his slicked back hair, groomed moustache, and captivating grey eyes. A spark of recognition registered, and I struggled to recall where I had seen him before.

"Good morning. Wonderful isn't it?" He offered his hand and the realization numbed me. I must have seemed like an overexcited child to him, as I stood in awe, my mouth agape.

"Richard Sherman."

"D-David Musgrove," I stuttered, as I prolonged the handshake.

"You can leave go of my hand now, David."

"I-I watch all of your films, Mr. Sherman."

"Really? I loathe Hollywood. Theatre is where I thrive, playing to a live audience. Now that's real acting... Tell me, what do you do, David?"

"I'm a writer. Well, I'm aspiring to be."

"How wonderful, a fine career choice. Have you anything published?"

"No, I'm merely a novice."

"We all must start somewhere. Who are you travelling with?"

"I'm on my own. My parents assumed the setting of a cruise ship would spark me into becoming a literary genius. I'm afraid it doesn't appear to be working."

The actor tried to reassure me. "Never give up, young man. Map out your ambition, and no matter how many rejections you receive, stick at it. I speak from experience, believe me."

"You were rejected?"

"Many times... Many times. It's been a pleasure conversing with you, David. I must go. I have a possessive wife, who will not allow me five minutes to myself. Why don't you join us for dinner tonight? We're dining at the captain's table."

"Are you serious, me dining with the famous Richard Sherman? I'd be delighted."

"Good, then that's settled. A good morning to you."

The great actor inspired me that morning, so much that I wrote the opening chapter of my novel. Just meeting the celebrated man had filled me with such ambition and self-confidence.

AFTER UMPTEEN ATTEMPTS AT FASTENING MY BOW TIE, I looked in the mirror and saw a nervous young man, attired in a tuxedo. I kept repeating, "I am a writer, I am a writer, I am a writer."

I left my cabin, and after asking directions several times, I entered the luxurious dining room. The silk shaded lights and marble columns complimented the arched windows and soft draperies. The enchanting notes of Vivaldi's *The Four Seasons* accompanied me to the captain's table.

I felt like a calf in a cattle market when the dignified diners were introduced to me, some of whom just scowled and turned up their noses. Not Richard Sherman. He made me feel like I belonged at the distinguished table and introduced me as an author. This settled me somewhat and encouraged me to join in the conversations. I now felt comfortable in the circle of the upper echelon.

The food was fitting for the grand setting. I sampled the culinary delights of cold salmon, roast pig, beef, and York hams. The finest champagne and brandy complimented the feast.

My eyes were attracted towards his beautiful wife, who seemed much younger than her husband; in fact, she could not have been much older than I. Joanne's long, auburn hair was swept up in a bun. Her green eyes and high cheekbones complimented her full lips, which demanded to be kissed. Her ball gown was of the finest white silk, and all eyes were on her when she waltzed around the dance floor in the magnificent ballroom.

"Beautiful, isn't she?"

"Yes, she is." I turned to face a tall, bronzed, handsome man.

"And to think he wants rid of her," drawled the man in an American accent.

"Excuse me?"

The stranger continued. "Richard absolutely despises her. He's found her out for what she is, a gold digging bitch."

I took an instant dislike to the American. "I don't believe I should be hearing this, and I beseech you to keep a civil tongue, sir."

"You're a writer, aren't you? Just starting out? I know how difficult that can be. The expense and the frustration as reject after reject follows. I may actually be able to help you."

"Help me? How?"

"I know publishers who, with a little prompting from me, would be delighted to take you on."

I eyed him suspiciously. "Why would you do this? I don't even know you."

He offered his hand. "James Lorimer."

"David Musgrove."

"Yes, I know. Listen, I have an interesting proposition for you. I'm a good friend of Richard's. He asked me to offer you one thousand pounds and the services of a top London publisher, if you'll help us."

"That is some offer. What is it you ask of me?"

The music of the violins ceased and the dancers kicked their legs and moved their arms in rhythm with the jazz music.

"Richard wants you to seduce his wife," whispered Lorimer.

"What? Are you mad?"

"She's been cheating on him for years, but has never been caught. She refuses to divorce him. He wants her out of his life, but it's difficult with him being in the public eye. It would be more appropriate for her to be seen as the villain, if you get my meaning. If the two of you were caught red-handed, it would be of great benefit. The public would then accept his divorce, and his reputation would remain untarnished. "

"This is crazy," I mouthed.

"Is it? One thousand pounds, cash. Think about it. You're not committing a crime. In fact, you'll be doing Richard a great service. You do like him don't you?"

"Yes, of course."

"Think about it, David. We'll not speak of this again, unless you decide to participate... Not a bad payday though, is it? Making love to Joanne Sherman and being paid for it."

"What makes you think she'd be interested in me?"

Lorimer smiled. "You're a man, aren't you? If you decide to go through with it, meet me at eight o'clock in the morning on the upper deck."

I was unable to sleep that night and it had nothing to do with the movement of the sea. I owed Richard a great deal after his encouragement. I tried to talk myself out of such an unruly deed, but the thought of making love to Joanne with her husband's permission was the persuader.

THE BLAZING MORNING SUN WAS EVIDENCE we were in Mediterranean waters. I ambled along the upper deck and spotted Lorimer smoking a cigarette. He did not seem too surprised by my presence.

"Okay... I'll do it."

"Excellent. Now listen carefully, David. Richard is playing cards this afternoon, leaving Joanne free for a few hours. Talk to her. Make a lot of eye contact. She'll no doubt fall for your boyish charm."

"And if she doesn't?"

"Oh, she will. I know her too well... At the given time, you contact me and inform me of the progress. Richard and I will conveniently walk in on your lovemaking. She'll have no choice, but to agree to a divorce. If she doesn't, we'll threaten to reveal her affairs to the media. Don't worry, we'll leave your name out of it. I'm certain she'll agree to a sizeable settlement. Under no circumstances are you to approach Richard or be seen with him. We must be careful. I'll hand you the money after the deed is done. Have you any questions?"

"The publisher?"

"After the completion of your novel, you'll contact me at a given address. Do we have a deal?"

I nodded reluctantly.

JOANNE WAS SITTING ALONE IN THE GARDEN LOUNGE when I ordered a cold beer. She was engrossed in a novel, and smoking a cigarette from a long ivory holder.

"Do you mind if I sit here?" I asked.

She smiled and motioned toward the seat, before returning to her novel.

"What are you reading?"

"Some mish mash romance. So you're an author?"

"Well, I'm hoping to be?"

"How wonderful. What are you writing about?"

I gazed in to her unblinking, green eyes. "Actually, it's a murder mystery."

"Marvelous. I'll make sure I read it when it's published."

"That's some way off yet."

"Joanne, by the way."

"David."

"Tell me, David, are you married?"

"No. I've been in a relationship, but nothing serious."

Her seductive eyes scrutinized me. "A handsome thing like you still single? You'll be a fine catch for someone." She sipped her champagne and looked around. "David, will you walk with me? I need some fresh air."

"Of course."

We walked the full length of the upper deck and back again. Joanne laughed and twirled her parasol, which protected her face from the strong sun.

"I get so bored on these cruises, so bloody bored... Richard is having an affair."

"Really?" I gulped. I had not expected such a candid and personal statement.

"Yes, with his cards. He thinks more of them than he does of me. I cannot remember the last time we made love."

I was lost for words. It was not ladylike to speak with such frankness, especially from someone of her social standing.

"Joanne, have you been to Cairo before?" Pathetic, yes, but it was the first thing that entered my head.

"I need a man, David. I'm hungry for love." She gripped my arm and looked into my eyes. "Will you come to my room tonight?"

Her suggestion simplified my devious task. My act of seduction would be unnecessary. "But, what about Richard?"

"His mistress, poker, beckons him. He'll be at the tables until the early hours of the morning."

"I don't know," I feigned.

"Well, David, if you can leave your novel alone for an hour or two, I'm in cabin number 24A."

She walked away, twirled her parasol and left me a quivering wreck. The fragrance of her perfume stayed with me long after she departed. This seemed so easy, or so I thought. Richard was right to want her out of his life. It took Joanne about ten minutes to seduce me. I was excited by the thought of making love to her. I only hoped I could perform, given all the distractions of what was to come.

JOANNE ANSWERED THE DOOR wearing a silk, purple dressing gown. She smothered me with kisses. She checked the corridor before coercing me into the room. We drank champagne and fed each other strawberries, before Joanne slipped off her gown and lay naked on the bed. I glanced at the wall clock, as everything had to be timed to perfection. I undressed and she seemed to devour me with her green eyes, like a cat that had cornered a mouse. She pulled me onto the bed, kissed me passionately, and her hands reached to my groin. Her firm breasts were warm as I caressed them. Her gentle moaning encouraged me to go further.

The door burst open and we turned to face Sherman and Lorimer.

"What is the meaning of this?" screamed Sherman. "You… you bastard. I offered you encouragement and all this time you were after my wife."

He swung at me and his fist connected powerfully with my chin. Lorimer restrained him, as I struggled to my feet. I bounded out of the cabin, naked, and holding my aching jaw. My clothes were tossed into the corridor and I returned to my cabin. I felt no satisfaction having duped Joanne; in fact, I wish they had arrived a little later.

I RECEIVED MY FEE AND WRESTLED WITH MY CONSCIENCE for the rest of the cruise, which interfered with my writing. I eventually completed my novel some six months later and decided to cash in on my debt.

The address Lorimer had given me was in Kensington. He looked none too pleased to see me. The house was lavishly furnished, and the paintings that caught my eye were certainly not the possessions of a poor man. I never asked what he did for a living.

He removed a fountain pen from his desk drawer. "Mr. Musgrove," he began. "I think I know why you're here."

"You do know why I'm here, Lorimer."

"Yes, indeed. I'll give you the address of the publisher. I hope the events of the last few months don't play on your conscience, as they played on mine."

I was confused. "Excuse me?"

"Joanne's death. You must have heard?"

"Sh-She's dead?"

"Yes. I'm afraid we were both victims of deception, David. Richard Sherman was using us."

"I don't follow."

Lorimer continued. "I was fond of Joanne, and Sherman promised me he would provide her with a generous settlement. Oh, Richard divorced Joanne all right, but never gave her a penny. Her name was disgraced, as Sherman spread rumors of her gallivanting on the *Ocean Pearl*. He kept your name out of it as promised, but the media hounded her, until she had a nervous breakdown. Sherman's solicitors ensured she didn't receive a penny from him. The strain was too much for her and she fell from grace so to speak. She took an overdose."

"Good God. When?" I asked.

"A month ago. I'm surprised you never heard."

"No, I heard nothing. I've been deeply engrossed in writing my novel."

Lorimer shrugged. "So there you have it. You and I are partly responsible for her death."

I was livid. "The bastard. Why don't you unveil him to the press?"

"Don't you think I haven't considered that? If we go to the press, Sherman will sue us. Also, we aided him, don't forget, and you were paid for your part."

"There must be something we can do."

Lorimer pondered. "There is. One thing that is dear to Sherman's heart is his fame. He's a vain man. If we could find a way to disgrace him, it would surely finish him."

"But, how?"

"Are you with me, David?"

I nodded eagerly.

MY HEARTBEAT ACCELERATED when I entered the restaurant. With my black curly wig and dark glasses, I left nothing to chance. The doorman reluctantly admitted me, as I explained I was a business acquaintance of Richard Sherman's and was to meet him for dinner. My throat was dry when I approached his crowded table.

Sherman looked up at me and showed no signs of recognition.

"Hello, Richard," I said in a camp voice, before I leaned across and kissed him fully on the lips.

He recoiled and stood up. "What is the meaning of this?"

"You were supposed to meet me tonight, Richard. Have you forgotten?"

His fellow diners looked at each other in amazement as I continued the charade.

"You think more of them than you do of me. Go on, admit it?"

"Is this a joke?" He looked at his fellow diners suspiciously and expected them to erupt into laughter. He actually believed he was the victim of a practical joke.

"If this is how you're going to treat me, then you can have your key back," I said, in an effeminate voice.

His face reddened. "Get out. I don't know who you are and what your game is. Out! Get out!"

I blew him a kiss, departed, and left the entire clientele of the restaurant open-mouthed as I walked limp-wristed among them. The first part of the plan had been fulfilled.

FOR THE NEXT TWO WEEKS, I kept up the farce, and turned up at multiple social events, until the media found out. Sherman made the headlines of every tabloid. Of course, he denied being a homosexual, but the media had their scoop. *Who was Richard Sherman's mysterious lover?* The newspapers offered a sizeable sum for him to come forward, but of course, that was out of the question.

Within weeks, Sherman was the forgotten man. Nobody, not producers nor directors would employ him. He had taken to staying indoors, as the paparazzi ridiculed him. Richard Sherman had become a recluse.

As promised, I was introduced to a leading publisher and my book was to be published at the end of the year, which excited me immensely. Then one morning, when browsing through my newspaper, I came across an article that would change my life forever. Richard Sherman had blown his brains out. The news did not shock me as it ought to have. I half expected it and showed no remorse for the cruel manipulator.

My bottom lip trembled when I read the next part. It mentioned that his wife Joanne was distraught and being comforted by friends. I dropped the newspaper and sat numbed by what I had read. It was not possible. Joanne Sherman had died of an overdose.

RAINDROPS STREAMED DOWN my unprotected face as I waited on the doorstep of the large house in Kensington. Lorimer faced me. He wore a black dressing gown and smoked a cigarette. A conceited grin adorned his handsome features.

"You'd better come in out of the rain, David."

I followed him to the elegantly furnished drawing room. He poured himself a drink and offered me one, which I rejected.

"I knew it was only a matter of time before you found out," he said.

"What the hell is going on, Lorimer?" I quizzed.

That is when I heard the unmistakable husky voice and the footsteps emerge from the bedroom. "Who is it, darling?"

She looked a vision, even without make-up. Her auburn hair was disheveled and the dressing gown hung loosely on her. She realized who her lover's visitor was.

"David, darling, what a pleasant surprise."

"Is it? Will you tell me what's going on?"

She lit a cigarette, linked arms with Lorimer and kissed his cheek.

Lorimer opened up. "I'm afraid we deceived you. It was nothing personal. You were in the right place at the right time. If it wasn't you, it would have been another young man on the cruise."

"Deceived me? I don't understand. Why did Richard pay me to seduce his wife?"

Lorimer blew out the smoke. "He didn't. I paid you, David. Richard knew nothing of the arrangement."

I nodded. "That explains why he hit me so hard."

Lorimer continued. "Yes, I related to Richard that I saw you enter their cabin. You see, we had to have you believe that Richard was behind the plot. It was obvious you worshipped the man."

"I still don't follow."

"It was simple really. Joanne ensured that she stayed out of the papers for a few months. When you came to my house, I told you she was dead. Then my friend, you almost know the rest."

"You mean, you knew he'd kill himself?"

"But he didn't," drawled Joanne. "I shot Richard and claimed I found him dead in his study. Simple really. The police suspected nothing, as they were aware he was in a state of depression."

"But, why?"

Joanne continued. "The same reason you undertook the task on the ship. Money. You see, I now inherit all of his millions." She gazed into her lover's eyes. "We'll wait a few months and then we'll marry."

I attempted to make sense of the intricate conspiracy. "Hold on, this doesn't make sense. Why the elaborate plot? Why didn't you just fake his suicide in the first place?"

Lorimer poured himself another drink. "Because, David, this way nobody will suspect foul play. We had to somehow entice him into a state of depression, and thanks to you it worked. You had to be involved from the beginning, don't you understand? You were emotional, a perfect subject. Once you believed Joanne was dead, you were like putty in my hands. Your acting left something to be desired, but you performed admirably."

"I could go to the police," I threatened.

Lorimer shrugged. "And tell them what? That you were involved in a plot to murder Richard Sherman? Don't forget, you accepted money for your part in the deed. I have the wig you used in your disguise in safekeeping. Look on the bright side, David, you had your book published didn't you? Come on, have a drink."

I turned around and left that house, my confusion magnified threefold.

So here I am, doing what I do best... writing. I'm not a brave man. Yes, I battled with my conscience over the next few years, but could not convince myself to go to the police. I'm now an old man, but every day I think of Richard Sherman. I watch his movies repeatedly. This is my confession to be read after I die. My vast wealth does not compensate for what I have unwittingly done.

Lorimer and Joanne indeed married. The union lasted just over a year before Joanne fell in love with a Hollywood producer. Shortly after the incident, I wrote another novel and it turned out to be a best seller. I will leave it to you to work out the plot. It required little research.

ANTHONY HULSE lives in the north east of England, UK, is widowed with two sons and engaged to Susan. He opted for very early retirement from Corus (British Steel) five years ago to concentrate on writing.

In 2003, Anthony had three novels published, but the two companies have since gone out of business. Since then he has written another eighteen novels and approximately fifty-five short stories. His WAIII entry will be his fifth inclusion in an anthology.

More recently, Anthony published fifteen of his books, mostly psychological thrillers and horror. He has also written a biography and is currently writing another. He has successfully converted his novels to e-books.

Anthony loves travelling, playing golf and most other sports. Funnily enough, he reads very little, but loves to write. He hopes one day to live in Crete, an island dear to his heart.

Facebook author page: **facebook.com/HULSEY33**

Twitter: **@AnthonyHulse1**

Anthony's Books: **lulu.com/spotlight/HULSEY**

Terra Infirma

HEMANTH GORUR

AS THE EVENING CHILL SHROUDED THE VILLAGE of Chargaon in Madhya Pradesh, farmers and traders scurried home for an early meal at the end of another dreary day. The night lamps went up as the village settled down; the only sound now punctuating the dusty air was the distant drone of the excavator drilling the rocky outskirts of Chargaon. All of a sudden, the drone went completely silent. A few moments later, there was a sickening sound as metal grated against gravel and rocky soil.

The scene at the drill site was a disaster. A gaping eight-by-five hole in the ground stood where once the excavator had been drilling. The fading light cast sinister shadows into the depths as mortified villagers craned to see the bottom. The mid-sized excavator lay crumpled and wedged fifty feet deep, like a great beast ensnared in a primitive trap. Only parts of the bright yellow semi-automatic machine were visible through the rubble, the rest hidden beneath.

Ten kilometers away, the phone jangled off its hook as Director of Excavations Kamal Siddhi was about to lock his office and leave for the day. Muttering under his breath, Kamal pushed back the door and rushed to his desk. Snatching the receiver off the hook, he listened intently for a minute before banging the pesky instrument down and rushed out. It was going to be a long night. *Especially since that damned NGT geologist was trapped.*

THE INKY BLACK DARKNESS vied with the dust to choke all senses and sense of existence. Seven figures lay in a heap in varying degrees of contortion and pain. It was a mindless jumble of arms and legs cocooned by the rocky earth of Chargaon. A hefty figure stirred. It was Lallan Singh, the barrel-chested and temperamental lead miner. A slender woman lay semi-conscious at his feet. Pushing her away with his feet, Lallan tried to get up and immediately slammed his balding forehead against an overhanging ledge. Feeling his way around, his hand came to rest on a fleshy, unshaven face gasping for breath. It had to be Bhairon Bhurja—the miner from neighboring Dhundhwa and his arch nemesis. Cursing yet again, Lallan tried to get into a sitting position, thwarted again by the tons of dead weight above him.

"Kalia! Chotu! Are you guys okay?" The sound from Lallan's throat was less the stentorian roar that it typically was and more a raspy drawl.

"*Bhau*, I'm here. I don't know about Chotu." It was Kalia, Lallan's trusted second.

"Check for that clown Chaggan. I'll look for Nirdhan."

"*Accha bhau.* What about NGT madam?"

"She's right next to me! I think she's knocked out," spat Lallan, his obvious dislike for the woman welling up from within.

Suddenly, a moan sounded, almost immediately breaking into a hideous shriek. "*Bhau! Bhau*, my arm! I think it's... it's... broken!" It was Chotu, the youngest miner and newest member of the mining team engaged by the National Green Tribunal.

Lallan climbed over the woman's leg and dug his way towards the source of the shriek, which had now subsided to an animal-like whimper. Lallan clamped his hand over Chotu's mouth and gripped what he thought was his broken arm. Chotu's body stiffened as his eyes almost popped out of their sockets in the dark, the pain excruciating.

KAMAL'S OFFICE HAD BECOME A WAR-ROOM of activity. Outside, two ambulances sat parked, with their rotating flashers dousing the landscape in an eerie wash of red and blue. Muttering to himself, Kamal yanked the phone off the hook for the fourth time that night. He was about to dial when a rim-rod straight, mustachioed man broke through the doorway. Dropping the phone, Kamal was immediately on his feet.

"Where the hell were you, Mr. Menezes? I've been…"

David bristled at the deliberate use of his surname. "Please! I got here the minute your lackey called me. What've you got?"

"Follow me. I'll brief you on the way!"

As they climbed into the brown MUV waiting for them, Kamal chuckled to himself. As he had done whenever he had worked with David Menezes. National Guard regional commanders had come and gone, but there had been none like David. The rim-rod straight demeanor and the clipped accent were all one big goofy, manufactured mannerism, Kamal thought as he settled in the middle bank of seats. The MUV roared into life and pulled out onto the muddy track.

"Six miners. All from Dhundhwa, except two. And, one very exasperating woman!" Kamal did not bother to hide his loathing.

"Woman?"

"Yes. Ms. Garewal. The geologist."

"Neetu? From NGT?"

"I didn't know you knew her."

"I don't. I've just read about her in the papers. She keeps getting splashed all over."

"Right. Pokes her pointed nose in affairs that are not hers to meddle with."

David rolled his eyes. "Alright. How deep is the well?" He didn't want to listen to another lengthy tirade on the geologist.

"My men are yet to assess the depth. My guess, from what I hear, is it should be at least two hundred feet."

"That sounds bad. Ventilation?"

"These crevasses are usually unconnected. There will not be any underground drafts of air. We'll take a call when we reach there. Meanwhile, I'll need water and food supplies."

"I've alerted our base at Chandrapur. Four hours, at most."

NEETU GAREWAL OPENED HER EYES DAZEDLY. The scene in front of her was the stuff of nightmares. A leg protruding from the dark rubble. An arm here. A head there. Sooty faces and caked bodies. All belonging to men still alive. All belonging to members of the NGT mining expedition. *An expedition she had chartered!* As if she didn't have enough problems already with the locals.

A gruff voice reverberated across the rubble. "So, you're awake? Are you happy now, NGT madam?"

"Lallan? Thank God, you're there! Where are the others?"

"All around us. You led us to this. We're not getting out of here. Do you know why?"

"Lallan, this is not the time. And, I'm trapped in here like the rest of you! Let's focus on the present. Why do you say we can't get out? Mr. Kamal would have initiated a rescue op already."

"You are new to this place. What is it, three years? Five? I've been a miner from before you were even born. These places are death-traps. Why do you think we resisted so long and so hard? But, you had to have your way!"

"Look, we had to do the survey and I'm just doing my job. And, you better start doing yours. We need air badly. Can we dig upwards a bit to see if there's an air pocket above us? It's a tube well after all."

Neetu thought she heard a rude sneer from across the darkness. Ignoring the hefty miner, she started digging upwards. Almost immediately, she stopped. It was no use. Digging upwards was actually loosening the packed mud above her, causing more soil and gravel to fall and occupy the remaining pockets of space around her in the crevasse.

"The first thing you need to do is shut your mouth. And, stop poking around. The knowledge from your books is not going to help you here."

Neetu did not react. She realized the hopelessness of her situation. She was trapped hundreds of feet below the surface in a dark crevasse with no air or water, and only six village boors who loved hating her. And, there were the tons of sand and mud above them that seemed to be pressing down unbearably and relentlessly. She bit back the tears as a lump formed in her throat.

KAMAL'S CELL PHONE RANG INSISTENTLY. Rubbing his bleary eyes, he looked at the incoming number and groaned inwardly.

"Yes, Mr. Garewal. What can I do for you?"

"What can you do for me? WHAT CAN YOU DO FOR ME? What kind of question is that? How is my wife? Have you found her?"

"Found her? Mr. Garewal, they have fallen into an old tube well that they were trying to re-drill. Utter foolishness. It's at least a couple of hundred feet down. It's going to take time to find them. And, it's not just your wife down there. There are six other helpless souls trapped. We are at the drilling site now and assessing the situation."

"ASSESSING THE SITUATION? You morons clear such expeditions without proper safety procedures and backup. And, you're standing there assessing the situation? Do you at least know if they are alive?"

"Mr. Garewal, we're doing all we can here. Now, I'll need to hang up. We have work to do."

Kamal winced as he heard the phone being slammed at the other end. Just then, David walked up. His expression said it all. There was bad news.

"The excavator's stuck probably midway to the bottom where I suspect the mining team to be holed up. The damn thing's blocking our access to the bottom."

"You have to be careful. The soil will not hold such a heavy thing for long. If the excavator gets dislodged, it's curtains for the trapped miners."

"Okay. We have to establish communication with the people down there. If not anything, it gives them hope. We may also need to pass instructions to them."

"The excavator has a bullhorn. But, I'm not sure if the people trapped can hear even if we use it. The well below the excavator looks to be completely blocked."

"There's only one way to find out!"

NEETU SAT IN HER CORNER, her face wrinkled with a mixture of awe and terror. Lallan had taken the help of Kalia and Nirdhan to clear the small underground crevasse by digging sidewards and pushing all the soil in the center towards the periphery, patting and packing the low ceiling of the crevasse as they dug outwards. For the time being, the air became breathable.

It must be the morning after, thought Neetu, as she tried to shift her weight and drive away the cramps that had started in her calves and thighs. The five miners had gathered in an arc around their leader, Lallan. Out of the corner of her eye, Neetu spied Lallan doing a peculiar thing. Every half hour or so, he looked at his watch and murmured something to his team, which was immediately met with a mix of groans and sighs.

"Is that watch working, Lallan?" Neetu asked testily.

"Yes. Unlike your survey plans."

"What time is it? Early morning?"

"It's still midnight."

Neetu looked at Lallan as if he had lost his mind. "We have been lying here for hours! And it's still midnight?"

As Lallan ignored her and turned back to his coterie, Neetu felt some bells tingling somewhere in her mind. She had enquired about Lallan Singh before she had approved the composition of the team. The lead miner from Chargaon was no doubt the most experienced miner in those parts. But, there had been a host of negatives in his resume. Lallan was moody, abusive and disrespectful. Not just with his team, but with officials, the authorities and the NGT. *Especially the NGT.*

Even as she tried to come to grips with the increasingly gloomy situation, she saw movement at the far end of the dark crevasse. It was Chaggan and Kalia. The duo were edging each other out of the far end, which seemed to be a bit cozier than the rest of the hellhole the team found itself in. Their surly faces said it all. They were tired, hungry, and trapped, and didn't like the feeling of grimy human bodies squishing against each other in the dusty, dark grave. The disorientation in time was not helping either. Suddenly, she didn't feel safe anymore despite having the area's most experienced miner on her expedition. She decided to confront him.

"Lallan! Are you feeding the same crap to those unwitting villagers? Are you sure your watch's working? It should be near morning by now."

Lallan continued to ignore her. Neetu felt certain about her guess. She usually felt hungry early in the morning. And, she was ravenously starved now. She looked above her. There was no way anyone could gauge the time. There was no crack or crevice in the ground above them to let in sunlight. Yet, she felt pretty certain about her estimate of the time elapsed. *Something didn't seem right. Or, was Lallan actually right? Was she hallucinating about the time elapsed due to the intense trauma in the preceding hours? Was it post-traumatic stress that was getting to her?* Her eyes drooped to a close even as she thought she saw the hefty lead miner move towards her.

NEETU DREAMT OF A VOICE that seemed to emanate from the heavens—a voice that seemed to start out as a deafening roar but mellowed to an even whisper as it reached her. Abruptly, she jumped. *It actually was someone calling out their names!* Disbelievingly, she opened her eyes. Immediately, she felt a sharp stinging pain on her left cheek. The area felt swollen and hot. Ignoring the pain, she looked around. The other five had crouched in the center of the muddy crevasse and were looking upward, with Chotu straining to see from where he lay on the ground. Lallan had decided to investigate. Standing on the shoulders of Kalia and a reluctant Bhairon, he eased upwards, straining against the weight of the earth above him. Listening intently, he quickly dug a hole into the ceiling with his right hand, while he cupped his ear with his left.

After what seemed like ages, he exulted and dropped to the ground. "It's the rescuers! They're using the excavator's bullhorn. I think they're sending a pipe down for air!"

The miners thumped each others' backs and grunted. Violent coughs shook the dusty air. There was hope yet.

Lallan seemed to think studiously before he eyed the others. "I'll go first." There was an air of authority tempered with caution as he spoke.

Immediately, Bhairon stepped forward, coughing, yet bristling with self-imposed authority. "What gives you the right to go first? You don't make the rules around here!"

Lallan glared. He had almost expected this. And, he welcomed it. "Bhairon, out of my way! And, stay out of my way if you want to survive!"

As the two hefty men sized each other up, Neetu recoiled. *So, this was it!* The men were finally breaking down after a day of being trapped deep underground. It had been ages since any of them had had a meal. The hunger and the thirst was bound to get to them.

Kalia quickly covered Bhairon's right flank, ready to thwart any attack on Lallan. Not to be outdone, Chaggan charged right into their midst, his eyes glaring at the lead miner. Subliminal village rivalry was getting the better of grown men. A cautious Nirdhan slowly made his way into the mass of muscle, intent on calming things down. Though he was from Dhundhwa, he owed his career to Lallan. He found it difficult to take sides. For now. It was clear that factions had developed overnight. It was Lallan and Kalia, versus Bhairon and Chaggan, with Nirdhan a fence-sitter. Incapacitated Chotu could just watch, yet given half a chance he would end up with his fellow villagers from Dhundhwa.

As Lallan and Bhairon continued to jostle, what happened next was unprecedented even for a man as temperamental as Lallan. The lead miner's right hand shot out like a sledgehammer, catching Bhairon squarely on his chin. The brutal blow was too much even for Bhairon. The fleshy man crashed against the mud-caked wall and slid down, unconscious.

Ten minutes later, Lallan dropped from the ledge he had created on the wall, coughing obscenely. "Your turn!" Lallan gestured towards the air tube, looking at Kalia.

Kamal walked briskly towards David who was peering down the steep precipice of the tube well.

"Have your men found a way in yet?" It was not a question.

"This well's too small. We're able to get just two men down near the excavator. That too, by dropping them on a line. The swaying's not helping. We need at least four men to move that damn beast!"

"It's been more than thirty hours, David. We need to get those food and water satchets down to them."

David switched on his emergency radio unit and barked brief orders. Minutes later, the National Guards who had plunged into the dusty depths of the renegade tube well emerged and took off their face masks. As David and his team went into a huddle, Kamal lit a cigarette and took a long drag. The sun was sliding past the horizon. It had been a dreadful day so far. Not only had they not been sure the mining team had heard them or received the air tube, but also had been frustrated by the stuck excavator which was preventing a quick extraction. A tap on his shoulders brought him back.

"It doesn't look good."

"They're going to suffocate down there. They're going to turn on each other. Give me some good news!"

"We have to wedge T-supports into the walls on four sides, use oxy-acetylene torches to cut through the stuck arms of the excavator and bring up the chassis to create an access vent."

"By when?" Kamal had become increasingly curt and irritated.

"Eight to ten hours. At least."

"Shit!"

Chaggan had stationed himself near Chotu, who had a terrified look in his bloodshot eyes. Nirdhan lay supine and senseless a few feet away from them on the wet earth. A cut had opened up on his upper lip which was now swollen. Chaggan eyed his younger compatriot. He was not going to last long with that broken arm.

Coughing mildly, Chaggan hissed in Chotu's ears, "He's doing it on purpose."

"Doing what?"

"He's provoking each one of us. I heard him talk lustily about Nirdhan's wife."

"Why is he doing that?" It was more of a weak howl than a question.

"Listen! First, it was Bhairon. Now, Nirdhan. He's going to come after you or me next! He's going crazy!"

A low whimper escaped Chotu's lips.

"Nirdhan fought hard, but he was no match. Come, I'll help you get some air from that tube. Hurry, before that old fool goes berserk again."

Four hours later, Neetu opened her eyes groggily. Her left cheek still hurt badly. Dizzy from lack of food or air, and completely disoriented from the fall, she tried to prop herself up on her elbow when she spied Chaggan and Kalia sitting across each other and glaring. They had been fighting again. The Dhundhwa villager had a nasty blue bruise on his cheekbone while Kalia was nursing a swollen eye and a cut chin. Neetu knew that her best chance at getting through this ordeal was to pretend nothing was wrong and stay neutral.

"Have you guys gotten some air?"

Both the villagers nodded brusquely before resuming their stare-off.

A few minutes later, Chaggan was crouched beside Neetu. "NGT madam," he hissed, "be alert of that old fool. He put you to sleep twice. By slapping you. Twice!"

As Neetu looked at him in shock, Chaggan suddenly fell silent and averted his eyes from her. Lallan had crawled up to the duo, looking at his watch. "It's been twenty hours since we fell. Where the hell are these rescuers? Where's the water and food they usually send? Anyway, they won't be able to send much through that pile of rock up there!" Sensing Neetu's livid eyes on him, he sneered, shifting his gaze towards the air tube in the ceiling of the crevasse, "NGT madam, did you get something from that tube?"

Neetu could not control her fury. "I would have, so would have these poor blokes, if only you had left something for us!" Her hand had subconsciously moved to caress her left cheek.

Lallan's sneer suddenly disappeared. "Try after two hours. The tube is narrow."

Puzzled by his change of stance, Neetu persisted. "Why are you giving us false information? That watch is working. And, you know it's been more than two days since we fell. We need to know the correct time that has elapsed—that will help orient ourselves mentally."

Lallan gazed at her for a few dispassionate moments, before shutting his eyes.

As Neetu looked at him, for the first time she realized there was something different about his face. Peering closely, she realized with disbelief that there was a huge dark welt right above his eye that spread all the way down to his ear. Stunned beyond words at the turn of events all around her, a strange sense of detachment overcame her as her eyelids felt heavy.

IT WAS THE FOURTH MORNING AFTER THE DISASTER. Kamal was perched on the edge of his chair, closing a media enquiry, when his cell phone buzzed. Finishing up with the reporter across his desk, Kamal whipped out his phone.

"We have a problem."

"Now what?" The irritation in Kamal's voice was undisguised.

"I'm down in the well myself. We're having to do this by para-drop line. The torches are catching fire at the fringes of the well. There's something weird going on."

"That must be methane."

"Methane?"

"David, the soil in that area is fertile. It would be packed with methane gas given out by decomposing organic matter."

"Okay, that solves one issue."

"There are more?" Kamal was on a short fuse by then.

"Yes, it's about the food and water supplies. Nothing that can't be handled, though."

"Oh, what's the issue? Spit it out!"

"The tube we have to insert for food and water can't be as narrow as the air tube. We need to cut a bigger hole in the excavator. I'm figuring out a way to do that without becoming a human cannon here with all this methane floating around!"

AFTER WHAT SEEMED LIKE AGES, Neetu opened her eyes. At first, she couldn't focus. Then, blurry images came into view. It was Lallan talking animatedly with Kalia. Her eyes wavered, searching for the others. With a start, she made out a figure lying at the far end next to Chotu. It looked like Chaggan. Motionless. Barely breathing. As her panic mounted, her eyes refocused on the duo from Chargaon. *Something was wrong!* She could make out Lallan's customary sneer. *But, this time, it was aimed at Kalia! His long-time confidante and second-in-command! Was Lallan finally losing it?*

Neetu watched in shock as Lallan moved without warning and struck Kalia on the temple with a rock he had snuck up behind him. As Kalia slumped noiselessly to the ground, Lallan himself collapsed, his eyes rotating in their sockets and slowly fixating on her! *He was finishing them off methodically. For the air. For the food and water!* Neetu frantically reached for her cell phone, which had got stuck in her front trouser pocket. As her feeble hands tried to tap on the keypad, she could make out Lallan creeping up towards her from the corner of her eyes.

ANIRUDDH GAREWAL WAS INCONSOLABLE. Across him were David Menezes and Kamal Siddhi, both exhausted by their rescue efforts over the preceding four days, with no success. The bull horn had not worked. There had been no response to the instructions sent to the trapped mining team. There had been no sound discernable through the air tube either. Nor had there been any way to drill a hole big enough for the food and water tubes without igniting the methane in the surrounding walls of the well.

David turned to Aniruddh. "Tell us about that message you received from your wife this morning, Mr. Garewal."

"It's futile. It's of no use now. You guys had four days. FOUR DAYS!!"

"Mr. Garewal, please."

Aniruddh took a deep breath. "She said this Lallan character's gone berserk. He's turned on his own men. He's already put down four of them."

"What…?" Kamal could not believe what he was hearing.

"And…?" David persisted.

"And Neetu and one more young chap are left." Aniruddh shot back, glaring at them with bloodshot eyes. "She said she didn't expect to make it!"

"What in God's name…" The anguish in Kamal's voice was real.

THE LATE AFTERNOON SUN BORE DOWN MERCILESSLY as David and his team gripped the makeshift harness and pulled it up. The slender figure of a woman came into view. Sooty, disheveled and gaunt, Neetu squinted against the glare from above as she saw sunlight for the first time in days. The disorientation in her mind competed with this new excruciating pain in her eyes as she grappled with the reality that she had actually been rescued and was finally on the surface after having been trapped in a hellhole for what seemed like eons.

Minutes later, she was wrapped in cooling blankets as the paramedical team on standby put her on oxygen. One by one, frail, bloodied bodies were lifted out of the fated tube well and shifted into waiting ambulances. An hour later, the rescue team lifted a hefty but emaciated body out of the harness and lay it down on a stretcher. It was Lallan. Neetu had been waiting all along. Weakened by the ordeal, Neetu shuddered at the sight of the lead miner's body. The anger welled up as she spat in his direction. Exhausted by the effort, Neetu fell back.

Neetu sat propped up in her bed, sipping clear soup. The events of the previous few days were still playing in her mind. Still in shock over her ordeal and in disbelief that she was alive, Neetu looked at the spotless walls and ceiling of the hospital room she was in. It was heaven! Closing her eyes, she let a sigh escape her bruised lips. David and Kamal were sitting by her side, while Aniruddh was at the far end, talking softly on his phone.

"How do we proceed with this? Do we lodge a police complaint against Lallan?" Kamal had been dogged by that question ever since he had heard Aniruddh read out Neetu's last message from the crevasse.

"I'm not sure. We need to consult with psychiatric experts before we come to a conclusion." It was David, objective and collected as usual.

"Oh no, you won't! He killed them all! You hear me? HE KILLED THEM ALL!" Neetu was awake and glaring directly at them. Aniruddh hung up and rushed to his wife's side, trying to calm her.

"Well, these are extra-ordinary circumstances and…" David never got a chance to complete. The on-duty doctor walked in. He had news.

"We've been able to save five of them. Four of them are now stable. The fifth member—the young fellow—is in the ICU. We may need to watch him for a while before we take a call on future course of action. His hand has been operated upon."

"You said five. What about the sixth?" David's antennae were up.

"Unfortunately, we couldn't save him. It looks like an acute case of methane gas poisoning, plus concussion in the cerebral region which has led to internal hemorrhage. We'll be able to confirm tomorrow after the post-mortem reports come in."

Neetu was looking intently at the doctor. "What was his name?"

"Lallan."

"Serves the sick bastard right!" spat the geologist.

Abruptly, Kamal straightened. "So, doctor, what about the other five? They were not poisoned?"

"No. Actually, we found traces of methane in their random blood tests, but not enough to cause poisoning."

"Isn't that strange? They were all in the same airtight space for more than four days," posed David.

Kamal settled back in his chair. "Not if the poisoning happened by sucking the air out of the air tube we inserted from above."

Neetu's eyes were bulging as she looked at the experienced Director of excavations. "What do you mean?"

"Any such narrow tube inserted into the soil in this region at such pressure will suck in the air captured in the soil as it goes down. The methane in the soil will get concentrated in the tube as it moves down. Anyone who inhales that—typically the first person to do so—will take the brunt of the poisoning."

Neetu felt her head slump back against the pillow. "And, what about the false information Lallan kept feeding everyone about the time elapsed?"

"What do you mean?" It was Aniruddh, who had been quietly absorbing everything all along.

"Well, he kept lying about the time that had passed. He kept shortening hours to minutes, days to hours… you know?"

The doctor smiled gently. "That's standard practice for avoiding stress during psychologically intense situations. It's a placebo effect where you fool the brain into thinking you have greater chances of survival by feeding it information that less time than actual has elapsed."

"But, I saw him repeatedly and brutally assault those poor miners. He was such an animal. Why would he do that unless he wanted to kill them?" Neetu's voice shook even as she dreaded the reply that was to come.

"In fact, the five miners are alive mainly because they were in homeostasis. It was shock-induced homeostasis with lowered metabolism rates during the four days that saved their lives."

Neetu's jaw dropped, as she covered her mouth.

David butted in. "So, Lallan rendered them unconscious in order to get them into this state of homeostasis?"

"He had to know that being unconscious saves your life in such conditions. He was the most experienced miner this side of the Narmada, after all." It was Kamal, his voice cracking with an odd mixture of pride and grief.

For a minute, no one moved. Neetu felt the earth sinking beneath her feet. She bit her lip hard, burying her face in her knees as she caressed her left cheek. The tears came.

HEMANTH GORUR is a contrarian by choice and an author by accident. His coy affair with writing took off quite innocuously in 2009 when he started a humor blog for a lark, followed by a business blog and later by his first commercial writing assignment – a short form biography of a steel industrialist.

In 2011, the crossover into professional writing was complete when CRISIL, a $160 million financial services company based in Mumbai, India, engaged Hemanth to author their corporate story, which was eventually published by Westland Publishers in December of 2012.

Today, after a decade and a half in the corporate world, this former IBM-er is a biographer and novelist based in Bangalore, India. He writes fiction for a singular reason. In his own words: "I write because if I actually did whatever my characters do, I'd be incarcerated on an island in the Pacific!"

Aymaran Shadow, his debut fiction novel launched in 2013, was recently the #12 Bestseller on Amazon. An alumnus of IIM Calcutta, Hemanth is also a consulting editor and helps first-time authors as well as experienced writers achieve their goals of publishing their creations.

Hemanth can be reached at: **hemanthg1975@gmail.com**, or at: **http://www.hemanthgorur.com**.

Alpha

R.W. WARE

SMELLED IT even before the elevator bounced to a stop. Not the fear emanating from the crooked old woman across from me—her heart pounding like a mistimed motor—but the stomach-churning odor of sex and sweat gagging me from halfway down the hall on the next floor. I knew that smell and had to cut off a growl. The old woman clutched her bag to her chest and shuffled a step closer to the button panel. I smiled, but she turned her thick glasses toward the doors and trembled.

The bell dinged and the doors slid open. I pushed past her and stepped out, and heard her exhale. I resisted the urge to spin and flash a grin worthy of the fear I tasted on her breath. It wasn't her fault: *Skins* didn't understand us. How could they? They didn't even believe *Moonkind* were real.

Dingy lamps cast muddy puddles on the stained carpet. A dark-colored Skin in a filthy purple nightie leaned against a battered doorjamb and smiled at me as I walked past. Dark blotches trailed up her umber arm like a predator's footprints on a well-trodden path. There were so many body-scents on her that they blended. She was a pitiful creature, and worse: wasted meat. Damn shame what Skins did to themselves.

Apartment 316 was a shit-hole, but we needed a place to lay low, to hide from the *Five Points Pack*. Chastity and I were all that was left of *Old Claws*. As I stood before the door, the smell of Chastity's spent efforts reminded me that *we* weren't above abusing ourselves as badly as the Skins. It sickened me, what she was doing to herself. But what could I do? I was an Enforcer and she the Alpha Bitch. The *bond* demanded my obedience, though she never had to use it. There were so many coats of paint it sounded like a seal broke when I forced the door open. A body lay draped across the fake-leather sofa like a discarded robe. The odor in the apartment was so thick and cloying that I couldn't even tell if the body was Skin or Moonkind.

Either way, she'd done the right thing.

Chastity sat in the matching chair with her legs pulled up under a stained Mickey Mouse t-shirt so only her painted toenails showed. She hugged her legs, her head bowed so trusses of auburn hair shrouded her face. She sniffled. Her shoulders shook with silent sobs. I'd seen this so many times I couldn't bear to watch.

I pressed the door closed and swallowed a lump of bile.

Still facing the door, I whispered, "I'll clean and dispose of that in a minute."

She answered softly, her voice a breeze through a field of lilies, "Thank you, Dagonet. You're always so good to me."

I wanted to say, *because I love you*, but knew better. Instead, I said: "You're my Alpha. I live to serve you."

There was no reply but the creaking of fake leather. A moment later, warm air stirred the hairs at the base of my neck. I closed my eyes and imagined her hand reaching for me, hovering, hesitating.

"You're so young, dear Dagonet," she whispered. "So rigid." Goose bumps rippled down my spine as her tic-tac-scented breath tickled my right ear. "You have your choice of dozens of Skins on any street you stalk."

Her fingers ran up the back of my neck and through my hair. I struggled to hold my composure. Chastity was a creature of seduction. I doubted she thought about it anymore.

"It's different for me," she said. "I have lost my Alpha, and no matter how I try—" her voice broke, "—I cannot replace what is missing."

"I'm not as free as you think, Lady Chastity."

The huff against my ear sent fresh waves of goose bumps over me. Cool air replaced her warm breath. She was gone.

It was as good a time as any to dispose of her leftovers. I grabbed a plastic sheet and a couple of contractor bags from the closet. We were getting low.

It used to piss me off to find Skins flung across random pieces of furniture because it meant she always passed me up for a Skin. The anger made quick work of breaking the bodies down, but it didn't last. Our lives had become a rerun. I couldn't muster more emotion than someone scraping a plate at Red Lobster.

Once I finished the wetwork, I put the plastic sheet in one of the three contractor bags with the remains. The plan was simple: Three different dumpsters in three separate parts of town. It was risky, and if we were going to stay in Slab City more than a few weeks, I couldn't keep dumping Skins in the trash. That brought cops around, or worse, other packs.

Slab City was a *Moonkind* name. I'd forgotten the city's Skin moniker long ago.

I opened the window and scanned the alleyway. The bums not hiding in their cardboard condos stood around a trashcan fire. Satisfied nobody who'd care would see me, I dumped the bags out the window. I'd learned my lesson about taking the elevator.

"I'll be back soon," I said. "You should probably get cleaned up."

My '60 Special, Bess was battered, but she had a cave for a trunk and ran like an angry bull. She sputtered a little as she made the trek around Slab City, but we got the job done. Chastity and I were scheduled to work, and classy joints like *The Golden Banana* didn't put up with late dancers or bouncers.

When I got back, she was waiting outside the barred doors, the sole focus of a blinking streetlight. I'd seen her do a complete change a thousand times and it always amazed me. I'd left behind a crushed spirit, a lost girl, but what I'd returned to was a moon mistress in rose-print lace. She made the one-armed, black dress with a loose-ruched tulip skirt look good. A white fur cropped-jacket hung from her sleeved arm, under which she held a silver clutch purse.

With a shift of Chastity's hip, she even turned the whore's heads, and I belatedly realized it was my cue to get out of old Bess and open the door for my Lady Alpha. She slid into the backseat and I closed the door. Bess purred as I coaxed her onto 42nd Street.

Lights flared from the rearview mirror. The asshole behind me had his brights on. Was it a dealer or pimp? If so, that was an easy fix. I made a fast right on 122nd Avenue, hit the gas and cut a squealing left into the alley running between 45th and 43rd Streets.

Before the brownstone on the corner blocked my view, I saw the headlights again. This time, I saw it was a pickup, its bed filled with Skins or Moonkind.

Though she probably felt my nerves all a-jumble through the bond, I said, "Trouble coming, Lady Chastity."

In the rearview, I saw her turn. Brights haloed her head. She looked at me with an arched eyebrow. If she was concerned, it didn't show.

"They're Moonkind," she said and pulled a pewter cigarette case from her purse, took one out and tapped it on the case. "Apparently, I've angered someone's bitch." She stuffed the cigarette between her lips and lit it.

I took a right into another alley and shouldered a dumpster. *Sorry Bess.*

It took a moment for her comment to hit: Chastity had slept with an Alpha.

"Are you trying to get us killed?"

Moonkind weren't like humans; Alphas didn't date. They could never love less than an Alpha, and Alpha Bitches weren't just jealous, they were deadly.

She rolled the window down and blew the smoke out. When she looked back to me, her eyes were red. "I had to try *something*, Dagonet. I can't take this much longer. My mind's a black hole. What's the point if the pack can't grow?"

I spun to face her for a moment. "Survival," I said, and something smashed into us so hard it lifted Bess's ass and drove her nose into the pavement. I spun around and fought to keep Bess from crashing into a wall. There was a fountain of sparks. Only my angle kept me from shattering my head against the steering wheel, but Chastity was only thrown forward inches before she regained control. In the rearview mirror, I saw a yellow glow spark deep within her pupils. She smiled and flicked the cigarette out the window.

I tromped the accelerator.

"Hit the brakes, will you," Chastity said, her smile was... malevolent.

I clutched the wheel so tight my knuckles popped as I drove the brake pedal down with both feet. *Sorry, Bess, baby.*

Chastity's move proved unexpected. In the rearview mirror, I saw the nose of the truck dip and shadowed figures fly from its bed. Bess's rear right fender smashed into a dumpster. The hideous sound of metal scraping metal made my hackles rise—*right through my skin.*

"The gas, Dagonet," she said.

Her voice snapped me out of my distraction and I hit the gas. Bess squealed and coughed out a cloud of smoke. She was hurting. Her engine ticked and whined, but she pressed on like a trooper.

Something thumped onto Bess's trunk. I reached under the seat and brought out the Mark XIX Desert Eagle I kept there in a hidden holster, flipped the safety off and cocked it. I should've brought the pistol out before, but silver bullets were far too costly to waste on Skins. I had to be sure.

Bess took another hit as I watched the rearview for signs of an unwelcome hitchhiker. A trash barrel bounced by on my right. Bums cursed.

BANG-BANG-BANG!

Gunfire. I ducked my head between my shoulders. Bess was taking a real beating, but the mirror showed Chastity sitting still and looking unimpressed.

Was she *trying* to die?

I swung the Mark XIX over the dip in the seat-back to fire at a half-changed-bastard slamming his claws into Bess's trunk. Chastity leaned right, just enough for me to do my job. A bloody claw smashed through the rear window and I fired a round into its owner's armpit. He rolled over on his back and howled. Anchored by the other claw, the half-changed werewolf couldn't drop free. So, he flopped back and forth into Bess's fins until the ragged metal holes lopped his fingers off. Trash fluttered in our wake, and a scattering of homeless hugged tight to the buildings on either side of the alley. We were safely away.

A couple of blocks from *The Golden Banana*, I parked Bess and slid the pistol in the back of my pants. I stuffed two spare magazines in the pockets of my leather jacket and got out to open the door for Chastity. She held out a hand and waited for me to take it before pivoting and stepping out into the street.

"You knew they were coming," I said. We'd been run off by packs before, but this was different.

"Yes." She nodded. Her face was blank, as if bored. "I had hoped they'd come sooner."

The realization hit me like a falling I-beam. "You wanted them to kill you when I was out and unable to protect you."

Her mouth became a thin line and her right eyebrow twitched.

"Am I so worthless you'd make me Outcast? Would you make me a trash-dweller or corpse-eater?" Loving her was doomed to failure, but I couldn't stop and I couldn't tell her. Flinging my arms wide, I exposed my neck in submission. "Kill me now, Lady Chastity. I can't watch them kill you, and I won't be masterless *and* packless."

Cars passed. People walking by skirted the buildings or crossed the street. A couple of hoods yelled shit, but a glare silenced them.

For a moment, as her right hand dropped, I thought she was going to slash open my throat. I swallowed once, puffed my chest out and waited.

"Dagonet..." Her eyes pleaded for understanding.

"We working tonight?" If she'd started something with an Alpha Bitch, *The Golden Banana* was a dangerous place to be.

"Of course," she said, as if I should've known better than to ask.

I WAS ON EDGE THE ENTIRE NIGHT. Anyone who moved too close while Chastity slithered on the stage was suspect. Even guys tucking money into her g-string, made me bristle. Chastity moved like she was in heat, and it stirred the Skins into a frenzy.

I kept thinking if she fucked with an Alpha, we were lucky to be alive. I scanned the patrons for Moonkind. No eyes magnified the light. No scent of gaminess or *the wild* in the room, nor a taste of copper in the air. There were a few shadowy figures at the tables skirting the wall, but nothing different from any other night. Bluish-gray fog rose from a dozen ashtrays and gathered in a layer along the ceiling. All the scents were dampened.

A scruffy-looking blonde man at a table full of hooting businessmen and empty pints grabbed Chastity and tried to drag her off the stage. It took great effort to keep the change at bay. My nails hardened and grew about an inch, but I was so fast, I was sure no one noticed. The drunken patron released Chastity, as my malformed claws dug into his arms and I slammed him back into his chair.

I could taste the blood in the air.

"This is your warning. Next time you touch one of the girls you're out of here." It was all I could do not to tear the Skin apart.

Chastity went on as if nothing happened, the guys around her subdued. She rolled on the floor and surged up like an ocean breaker, gaze locked on mine. Was it punishment or thanks? I backed away and leaned on the bar.

"On edge tonight, eh?" asked Joe, the bartender. "That guy's going to need more than a new jacket." He nodded toward the guy I'd snatched. There was more blood than I'd thought, but none of the other Skins seemed to notice.

For a Skin, Joe wasn't a bad guy.

I wiped a hand across my face. *Get it under control or you won't be able to protect her.* I couldn't do much against an Alpha, but I could hold my own with an enforcer or two. I took comfort in the pistol pressing against my lower back.

Joe offered me my nightly coffee—I limit myself to one, or it messes with my sense of smell. It tasted a little bitterer than usual. "You forget to clean that coffee pot out, Joe?"

He shrugged. "Cleaned it the same as every night, Dags."

Even though it tasted like sludge, it must've worked, because I stopped tensing at every movement. The crowd mellowed and by the end of the night, I was cool.

Chastity went into the changing room. With an Alpha Bitch hunting her, anything that went down would be over by the time I got there.

"Dags," Big Tony said. His arms were so thick they strained the sleeves of his satin jacket. "Boss wants to see you."

The Boss—Remus Vincento—never saw anyone face-to-face. He had a two-way mirror with an intercom below it. Knowing someone was watching, people squirmed when faced by their own reflections. That wouldn't work on me. If something went down, I was prepared. No matter how chiseled Big Tony was, a 50AE slug would bring him down. Chances were the mirror was bullet proof, but the wall under it probably wasn't. I hoped I wouldn't need to find out.

Big Tony crossed his arms, pushing the limit of the satin, and leaned against the mirror's frame.

"Dagonet, Dagonet," said Vincento, his gruff voice had a tsk-tsk in it—like a don in a mob movie. He even gave the obligatory sigh. "What do I do with you, eh? I can't have you hurting the customers, making them bleed all over their designer suits. It's no good for business."

"Just protecting my..." I almost said Alpha. "...girl. Besides, he didn't give me any more trouble."

"True. But, he will notice the marks in his Brooks Brothers jacket. *Claw* marks."

My heart beat faster. Vincento shouldn't have been able to see from there. What did he know? Suddenly it was important to know if he was Moonkind or Skin, Mafioso or Alpha.

"You're here because I let you be, Dagonet." Vincento's voice carried a threat. "Both of you. You get me?"

Did I? Was he saying that his *pack* ran this territory or his *family*? "I think so."

"Good. Then we never have this conversation again. That Skin may bring the cops down on us, and then we're fucked, our covers blown—covers we worked hard to create, *capisce*? We're not ready for a war with the Skins. So, something happens again, somebody has to pay."

"Won't happen again," I said, my stomach twisting over the new discovery. "Sorry, Boss."

"Good, now take Chastity home."

WE WENT OUT THE BACK DOOR into the alley. It had rained and everything had a shine. Rusty dumpsters, sheet metal and glass from countless broken bottles glittered under the streetlights. The smell of beer and puke was so thick I could taste them in the air. I spit.

"That was a big risk, tonight," Chastity said. Her melancholy seemed completely gone. "This is Vincento's turf. I'm lucky you're not in pieces right now."

"Is he the Alpha you—?"

Chastity lit a cigarette. "Do you really want to know this?"

"I knew it!" screamed a woman, bursting from beneath a pile of trash.

Six enforcers came from various hiding places around us. Vincento's Pack must've been pretty large, if his Alpha Bitch had six enforcers at her command. Who was looking after the pack's interests? There had to be more. Those thoughts pounded through my brain as I pulled out my Mark XIX.

Could I kill them all? Did Vincento sanction this? And what bothered me most: Why hadn't I smelled them?

The Alpha Bitch wasn't one of the dancers. Her face snapped outward and teeth grew so rapidly, I only had time to register a redhead changing shape. Her hips were too wide, legs too short—not the dancer type. Maybe once...

I could see why Vincento would step out with Chastity.

One of the Enforcers grabbed Chastity's arm. I spun and put a bullet through his chest. The Alpha Bitch darted forward and raked a claw across Chastity's stomach.

The bitch was fast.

As Chastity bent over and the dead Enforcer's hand slid free, I drew a bead on the Alpha Bitch. If this didn't end quickly, we'd be trapped here when Vincento did decide to come out.

BANG.

A blur of reddish-brown fur flashed in front of me. Instead of the Alpha Bitch dropping dead, another Enforcer did.

I popped three more shots off—two at the Alpha Bitch, which she dodged, and one into an onrushing Enforcer—opening a small breach in the ring of attackers. Chastity regained enough sense to back away.

Three down, four left. For a moment, they seemed surprised by my pistol, and I wondered why none of them had one. It wasn't the middle ages.

"Get to Bess," I told Chastity. "I'll meet you there. And if I don't, get the hell out of here."

She bolted.

Before I could lift the Mark XIX, something hit me so hard the pistol flew out of my hand and I crashed into the trash barrels behind me. It knocked the breath out of me.

Two enforcers came for me, while one went after Chastity with the Alpha Bitch. With all my strength, I flung a barrel at them. It hit the Alpha Bitch hard enough to knock her into her enforcer and take them both down mid-stride. I prayed to Mother Luna it was still *my* Chastity—the one who wanted to live—fleeing toward Bess.

The move cost me.

The enforcers delivered a fury of slashing blows, bites and head-butts. I'd like to say I gave back what I got, but anyone who saw me that night would know better. I vaguely recall the Alpha Bitch sending them after Chastity, but I could do little more than lift my head. My whole body felt like a big road-rash.

I think one of them pissed on me.

Sirens blared. The gunshots probably brought them. I fell back into the trash heap three times before I found my balance, and it wasn't steady. One eye was nearly swollen shut, but the other fixed on the Mark XIX leaning on a trash can across the alley. I stumbled over, and when I bent to pick the pistol up, my wounds really introduced themselves. I tucked the pistol in the back of my pants.

Fortunately, Moonkind heal much faster than Skins. Wounds tried to stitch together—stiff and angry—as I limped out of the alley.

I had to find Chastity.

Everyone I passed reacted: Some covered their mouths, others crossed the street. I must've looked like a zombie. My face burned with every move and grids of fire crossed my core. My senses were screwed. I wasn't used to my nose failing me. My sight was no better than a Skin's. Running my tongue around my gums, I winced at the raw spots on my inner cheeks. And then I tasted it: Joe's coffee.

Wolfsbane.

I should have recognized the taste. It lingered in my mouth, the taste of hubris. Joe. He must've been part of the Alpha Bitch's plan the whole time. The wolfsbane masked his true odor. He had to have been giving me small doses all along.

Riding the elevator up to the apartment, I knew I couldn't trust my senses. Every bum, whore, and crack-head was now suspect. It seemed glowing eyes peered from every peephole, sparked in every shadow. How long until it wore off?

Not seeing Bess parked outside gave me pause. Maybe Chastity had finally listened to me: Maybe she'd gotten out of town. I needed a dose of atropine, a change of clothes, and a shower. About the only poison that kills Moonkind is wolfsbane, but it had to be a huge amount; we're adaptable creatures. Any Alpha worth his bite had a direct line to atropine and a stash.

Chastity kept ours in a small black bag on the top shelf of the closet. I shook a few pills out of the bottle, worked up some spit and swallowed them. Poison to fight poison, but belladonna never killed a werewolf. Besides, anything that drove away the stiffness before it paralyzed me was a good thing—regardless of the side effects.

I ran a shower and as I dressed, I heard a familiar ticking, clunking sound.

Bess.

Chastity shouldn't have come back for me, but I was glad she did. Her scent was perfume to my nostrils. From the window I saw her getting out of Bess. Dosing up had brought some of my sense of smell back, but not completely.

Time to run again.

I grabbed the emergency suitcases and the black bag. Everything else could be replaced. My wounds were still angry on my way out. A growl escaped before I realized it was coming. The prostitute—a permanent fixture—widened her eyes, went inside and slammed the door.

I reached the elevator before Chastity got out. When the doors slid open, I was there.

Chastity was thrown out of the elevator and nearly collided with me. The Alpha Bitch and three Enforcers were in the elevator, under a gaping hole torn down through the roof. I threw the suitcases at them, and they caught each other up enough for the doors to close on them.

"The stairs," I said to Chastity, and nodded toward the door opposite the elevator. "Quick, I'll hold them off." It hurt to draw the Mark XIX, but I would do what was necessary.

Chastity ran. The elevator's alarm went off and there was a loud *whump* as the door dented outward.

I fired three shots into the metal swell.

More pounding mangled the door, and it squealed as clawed hands on both sides pried the battered doors open. I emptied the magazine and dumped it to reload. The Alpha Bitch burst through the opening and hit me so hard I thought my chest caved in.

I landed about ten feet away, but I kept hold of the Mark XIX. I scrambled to load the magazine and get to my feet before the Alpha Bitch and her enforcers got to me.

"Hey!"

Everyone looked at the sound of Chastity's voice, but I used the diversion to slam the magazine home. If I couldn't protect her now, we were both dead. I took aim and blew a hole straight through the center of Alpha Bitch's chest. She grabbed the gun on her way down and bent it. The enforcers were roused by her death, and both leapt and hit me at the same time.

I managed to form a claw and punched it into the smaller enforcer's chest. His eyes went wide as I clutched his heart. The other enforcer hit me, but I felt nothing as I ripped the smaller werewolf's heart out. Before I knew what I was doing, I'd sunk my teeth into it and swallowed the thick geyser that shot out.

Coppery. Salty. I got a rush that must've been what it was like to shoot heroin. As the other enforcer drew back to hit me again, I snatched his face and bit out his throat.

I'd changed.

Power pulsed through my veins, fogged all of my senses except that of taste, and I found myself unable to pull away. My victim could do nothing but spasm around my teeth, which worked so deep in his throat I hit his spine.

Was someone calling me? No matter, they could wait.

I sunk my fingers into his flesh and shredded open his chest cavity. The hunger had control. I sought the heart while it still beat.

Something dug into my back, like a mechanical claw, and ripped me from my meal. The biggest Moonkind I'd ever seen filled the hallway with fur and fury. He roared and threw me through a nearby door.

A Skin screamed and tucked herself into the corner of the room. Her heart pulsed, tempting my newly awakened hunger. Before I could clear my mind, those claws snatched me and slammed me through the wall of apartment 316. I landed in Chastity's bed, pinned down by a wall of fur with gnashing fangs.

Remus Vincento.

Teeth flashed toward me. I leaned and the Alpha locked his teeth through my left shoulder. A new level of pain burned through my body as he shook his head. If it'd been my neck, I'd be headless.

My arm was useless, but I got my feet underneath him and tried to tear out his underbelly. My rear claws had torn through my shoes but not enough to eviscerate him.

The Alpha arched back and shook wildly, and I scrabbled out from under him and off the bed. In the flurry, I heard two distinct growls, and with the flash of auburn, knew that Chastity had attacked the Alpha's back.

He bashed her against the wall until her grip slipped, when he snatched her from his back and flung her into the opposite wall. I got to my feet. He turned and snarled at me. I sprang up with all I had and locked my teeth into his throat. Alpha skin was tough. I bit with all I had.

He thrashed about and slammed me into the wall, and when he reached for me, I slammed my right claw into the thinly-haired spot under his arm. My jaws ached, but I tasted blood.

He smashed my ruined shoulder, but the hit only forced me to grind my teeth into him. He raked both sides of my ribs and swung me against the wall, hard.

I lost my grip, dropped to the floor, and knew it was over. I'd played the hand dealt me but it just wasn't enough.

He hovered over me—teeth coated in his own blood—and raised his massive right claw to end me. I steeled myself for the final blow. His hand came down...

Chastity hit him so hard there was a snap of bones. The Alpha fell beside me and his head lolled. His mouth moved, but nothing came out except blood. Chastity stood over him, chest heaving, both claws at her side, dripping blood. She was a magnificent creature.

"Finish him off," she said, nodding toward Vincento. "Eat his heart."

I found enough energy to get to my knees. He was still breathing, albeit shallowly. Already, I had tasted his blood and the power it held. I looked up at Chastity. She would make me an Alpha?

"Hurry, my love," she said. "Or we can never be."

My love?

With a flush of renewed strength, I tore his chest open, snapping bone and drove my muzzle in deep. When I bit into his heart, it wasn't blood I tasted but that zinc-taste: Power.

It washed over and rejuvenated me. There was no stopping it and the power threatened to drown me. I ripped the heart free and devoured it. Pain flashed through me, and with it memories, thoughts, and senses that weren't my own.

I was ALPHA!

Chastity knelt and exposed her throat. I knew what to do. I'd waited so long. I bit her.

I held her. My power dominated her as her longing filled me. Our thoughts mingled, *bonded*. She had never wanted to die. The bodies I'd dumped hadn't been Skins, but weaker members of the Five Points Pack through which she'd discovered their Alpha. *This* had always been her plan.

R.W. WARE is an award-winning artist in multiple mediums, with over one-hundred-and-ninety awards in dermographic art, an editor's choice award for a poem published in 2001, and three awards for original fantasy paintings. He has three SFWA accredited flash fiction publications, and has two stories in this publication. Aside from his day job, Mr. Ware illustrates the e-zine, **flash fiction online**, and does art by commission, such as two maps for Kevin J. Anderson's *Terra Incognita* trilogy, and album art for the progressive rock band and media tie-in Roswell 6. To this day, he feels his greatest achievements are his wife and children, with whom he never spends enough time.

Let Sirius into Fire Melt

ROY C. BOOTH & R. THOMAS RILEY

ANDREW NEGMAN KEPT HIS HEAD LOW, hurrying down the hall. All around him lockers clanged as other students hurried to retrieve books and supplies in preparation for the next class period. He'd almost made it to his own locker when he heard his name shouted.

"Hey! Negman!"

Andrew quickened his pace, making a beeline for his locker.

"Hey! Negman! I'm talking to you!"

Andrew stiffened as he felt the other boy's hand grip his shoulder. Derrick Rainer, his own personal bully. "What do you want?" he asked.

"Got any change on ya, Negman?" said Rainer, taunting him.

Andrew opened his locker and unburdened his books. He dug into his pocket while Rainer jabbed him in the back with a finger. Without turning around, Andrew held out the change he'd fished from his jeans. Rainer took a swipe at the change, sending a few coins clattering to the floor.

"Well?" Rainer said when Andrew didn't move. "Pick 'em up and *hand* them to me."

Andrew turned and knelt. His face burned as he caught sight of Misty Nelson standing at the edge of the gawking students. Misty was the prettiest girl he'd ever laid eyes on. Completely out of his reach, yet he couldn't help but imagine what it would be like to kiss her, even if just once. She looked on, her face unreadable. Their eyes locked for the briefest of moments and something clicked in Andrew's chest. Suddenly, he couldn't breathe. The hallway narrowed and she was all he saw. His hand hovered above the coins, but they were forgotten.

Rainer nudged Andrew with a foot. "Hey, sometime today, Negman."

Andrew glanced up for the first time and stared hard at Rainer. The boy grinned back, urged on by the other students' chuckles and laughs. The pressure in his chest was near bursting and Andrew suddenly remembered to breathe once again.

"Got something to say, Negman?"

The tips of Andrew's fingers burned and ached. He grimaced as the pain shot up his arms and settled in his chest. A void rested there, cold and desolate. The void burned as Andrew's psyche raged. He quickly gathered up the coins and thrust them out to Rainer. The other boy grabbed the coins and shoved Andrew back into the lockers. The students laughed as Andrew slumped down, sprawled out.

I'd seen enough. It was time to intervene. The students dispersed swiftly as I approached. Andrew gathered his legs beneath him, leaning back against the locker with eyes closed. I watched as he willed the pressure in his chest to subside with slow, deep, controlled breaths. The heat subsided around us and the coldness returned like an old familiar friend.

You may be wondering how I knew what he was feeling. That will be explained in time, if you care to stick around for the rest of this story.

"Mr. Negman? Everything all right?" I asked, reaching out a hand.

Andrew opened his eyes and he reached up, but just as he was about to grasp my hand, I jerked back.

"Oww," I gasped, rubbing my hands together. A weird look passed over Andrew's face as he stared up at me.

Andrew placed a hand on the locker behind him and gained his feet. My eyes were drawn to the locker behind him, breath caught in my throat. Confused at my sudden silence, Andrew glanced behind him to where my gaze was riveted. A handprint, his handprint, could be clearly seen on the metal. The paint had been seared from the locker.

Keeping my distance, I said, "Come with me, Andrew." My tone was soft, yet assertive. "We need to talk."

Andrew followed me down the empty hall as the first period bell began to ring.

IN THE BEGINNING

AT THE TURN OF THE CENTURY, superheroes were everywhere. It seemed that even the smallest of towns boasted a metahuman. There was Memory Man who could absorb memories. People from around the world would come to his lair in the Louisiana bayou to unburden themselves of painful memories, whereupon he'd solve unsolved mysteries and battle crime with the knowledge gleaned. There was Card Trick, a master magician based out of Las Vegas, who made headlines on a daily basis as he traveled the country fighting crime and injustice with a whole assortment of card-based gimmickry and a modicum of actual mystic might. The Shock, Gorilla Girl, Wilton Quimby from Planet X, the list went on and on and the world was a wondrous, mysterious, and masked place.

Then, the metahumans began to die off. No one was sure why these heroes were dying by the dozens. Was it some hideous plot by arch villain, Mind Gallery? Had the Mentalist of Crime developed a virus that would kill them all off? This was the common opinion, until even Mind Gallery himself finally succumbed to whatever killed the rest of the heroes. In just a few short months there were no more metahumans left. It'd been thirty years since the last of the metahumans died and over the years mankind forgot about masked heroes.

I knew the truth, however. Those in our government were terrified of the metahumans and what their kind represented. What was to stop one of them from rising to power and making their jobs obsolete? So a virus was created in the darkest reaches of power by a scientist named Vernus Malcum and unleashed on the unsuspecting heroes.

Only the virus worked a little too well. Hundreds of millions of innocent civilians died in "collateral damage." The Plan, as it was called in the secret halls of government, decimated the world's population by more than a third. Chaos erupted and mankind was plunged into a new Dark Age. Families turned against each other in vain attempts to live. Who was infected, who were carriers of the Malcum Virus? In trying to protect their seat of power, the government effectively destroyed itself.

The world is a much smaller place now. Travel is almost non-existent, commerce a thing of the past. Our colony is known as Sirius 7 and boasts a population of two thousand souls.

In the beginning, our part of the system moved underground and constructed a nano-shield over our spot of the world. Up to that point, we'd been safe. The Phalanx, those super tech world beaters, eradicated those infected with the deadly Malcum Virus. Those suspected of being infected the Phalanx dealt with. For the good of the group, the Phalanx ensured there were no exceptions or uncertainties. I'm sure there were many that hadn't been infected that were taken care of in this brutal fashion, regardless. It was all so... convenient for them. I try not to think about that too much. We, the Phalanx, did what needed to be done to survive, as a race.

We did what we did best as a species. We buried the truth. We taught our children an alternate history. We clouded their minds with hypno drugs and misdirection. The sky above our children was manufactured. There was night and there was day. There were stars, clouds, a sun, and a moon. All nano-manufactured to keep our past sins buried.

Thirty winters ago the Malcum Virus was released and the world changed forever. As suddenly as the virus appeared, it had vanished, having done its vile job, effectively burning itself out in the process. In the back of all our minds, those that remembered what we'd done, our new government, the Phalanx, watched for signs of the virus' re-emergence. We all cowered in our colonies and hoped for the best. Naturally, I only told Andrew sanitized parts of this story, enough to pique his interest and to further gain his trust...

"You've got to be kidding me," said Andrew as I finished speaking.

"Yes, Andrew. It's true. It's something we don't talk about anymore. You're special. I'm part of an interested group that has searched for the rise of the next metahumans all these years."

"Metahumans are myths," Andrew scoffed. "It says so in all the history books. There are logical, scientific explanations for the supposed powers they had. I've been to Rizen, every summer; I've been to the beach with my family. We've taken road trips!"

"Are you sure about that?" I countered. "Think about it. What exactly do you remember? Have you ever wondered about the pills you've taken since you were little?"

Andrew's brow furrowed and a frown grew on his face. "They're vitamins. They're... I'm not... sure."

"I know better," I responded. "I was there. You are in great danger. You mustn't exhibit your powers in public. Ever."

"You're crazy."

"Explain your hand print on the locker. Explain the way you've been feeling lately."

"How did you know about me?"

"Someone like you was bound to happen somewhere, again sometime."

"Wait a minute," interrupted Andrew. "You said I was in danger. From whom? From what?"

I paused and creased my brows, pursed my lips, and shook my head. "We're not sure, but someone was responsible for killing all the metahumans thirty years ago. We're sure about that."

"You said so yourself, you're not even sure what killed them in the first place. What makes you think anyone did?"

The kid was sharp. I wasn't going to be able sneak anything past him. He would have to be convinced. I stared at Andrew for a long moment. He smirked and crossed his arms. It was an act. Inside, I could sense, his mind was awhirl with the possibilities. He was scared to death. What if what I were telling him was the truth? What if he were in danger? At the same time Andrew was excited to find out he was special, exhilaration and terror felt at odds in his head.

I weighed telling him the truth. Not just yet. I finally broke the silence, "It didn't happen by itself."

REVELATIONS

THE CONVERSATION PLAYED RELENTLESSLY in his head as he sat in second period Algebra. *It didn't happen by itself.* Christ! How was he supposed to concentrate with this crap in his head? He kept his books open, but he was oblivious to anything going on around him. He glanced out the window and peered at the sky. Was it false? He had no way of knowing. The sky was something he'd never questioned before. It was just there, a fact of his existence. Deep down he realized he really didn't remember those family trips as if he'd experienced them personally. Sure, he remembered them, but the memories were like a second-hand telling, overheard from a friend. He stared down at his hand in his lap, palm up. Was that a glow just below the skin? He concentrated and the glow spread until he could see his metacarpals faintly beneath the skin of his palm.

"Neat," he whispered.

Andrew, I said, *stop doing that.*

Andrew sat up straight in his chair, glancing around the room. He'd heard the voice as clearly as if it were right beside him, yet he didn't see Mrs. Keene.

I'm in your head, Andrew, I answered in response to his question.

I was sitting in my office at the opposite end of the school, yet I could see Andrew as clearly as if I were standing right next to him.

It's not a special power, I continued, *it's a natural skill everyone possesses.*

Andrew frowned and whispered, "Not a special power? You're in my head!"

Easy, just think what you want to say, I instructed. *Meet me in my office after classes. We have to talk.*

I watched Andrew enter my office, closing the door slowly behind him. I motioned for him to take a seat at one of the chairs in front of my desk. He chose the right chair and settled in. He fidgeted as he tried to appear cool, but I could see right through his brave façade. His belief system was crumbling.

His hands glowed softly and he self-consciously tried to hide them in his lap. The heat was potent as it wafted off his body in waves. I wiped the sweat from my neck and wondered why his clothes weren't catching fire. That I didn't know the exact reason troubled me.

"You need to control your new ability," I began. "If you don't learn how quickly before it fully manifests itself, you could end up hurting a lot of people."

"What's happening to me?"

"Your body is changing, Andrew. Adjusting to the new chemical processes awakening in your genes."

"What if I can't control it?"

"There is no choice, you must learn how," I answered, my voice stern.

"Why me?"

"Why not you? This you must remember," I continued. "There are always two sides to a transformation. One hero and one villain. You need to find out who the villain is, before they find out who you are. Until you do, you will not be safe."

Andrew stared at his hands and sighed. They glowed a bright red and then dulled. "What about you?"

I smiled and tented my fingers. "What do you mean?" I asked, even though I saw clearly the real question behind the innocent one he'd just asked.

"You can read my thoughts."

"I told you, that's natural, anybody can do it. It's not special."

"Then why doesn't everybody do it?"

"Have you ever been thinking about something and someone mentioned it out loud without you having to?"

"Well, yeah," Andrew said slowly.

I tented my fingers again, nodding my head sagely. "I want to show you something." I stood and walked to the door. "Follow me," I said over my shoulder.

THE HOUR APPROACHES

NDREW STARED DUBIOUSLY at my car as I motioned for him to get in. I offered a reassuring smile and shrugged. "You really need to see this." I got in the car without waiting for his response and started the engine.

He rolled his eyes and opened the door. He slid into the seat and looked at me. My dress had rode up my thighs. I smiled and said, "I *can* read your thoughts you know…" He blanched with embarrassment and quickly looked out his window. I shifted the car into drive and pulled out of the school parking lot. He kept looking at me the whole time I navigated the small town. I turned onto a side road and he cleared his throat.

"Yes?" I asked knowingly.

"This road is closed," he answered as if I were a small child.

"Yes."

"So why are you taking it?"

"You'll see," I said with a wink. "Here's a question for you: How long has this road been closed?"

"Um… forever?"

"You ever wondered about the way things are? Why you've never had any new neighbors and you have the same friends. Why there aren't ever any new kids in class?"

I could tell my questions were making him wonder for the first time in his life. It's funny how the human mind works when it has never been properly challenged. The majority of people, especially children, are curious by nature. Naturally, but we'd engineered the perfect cocktail of hypnotics that repressed this natural inclination. It was in their food, in their sodas, in their candies. In the beginning, before the Phalanx had gotten the dosage correct, children had ventured past the safe zones. It was a necessary evil. These adventurous ones were dealt with.

I glanced nervously in my rear view. The Phalanx were everywhere in our colony. They monitored these routes and they monitored our children. It was auspicious to have discovered Andrew before they did. I had to trust I was the first to discover him. From all signs, I was fairly confident. Still, that niggling of doubt tickled the back of my mind.

"So tell me about Misty."

Andrew blanched and coughed with embarrassment.

"Come on now," I encouraged. "It's all you think about. I can see her quite clearly, you know."

"She's just a girl."

"She's more than that," I prodded. "Have you told her how you feel about her?"

Andrew fixed me with a flabbergasted look. "Are you serious? I could never do that!"

I chuckled and slowed the car. We were nearing the end of the road, so to speak. A brightly colored construction sign loomed before us blocking the road. A dozen yards further the bridge was clearly missing.

I exited the car and rested my rear on the hood. Andrew came to stand beside me, staring at the expanse between us and the other side of the road. "Go on," I said. "Walk past the sign." I knew he wouldn't take the bait, but I had to offer him the choice.

He shook his head and stood his ground. I smiled and walked forward. A few seconds later I heard him gasp. Naturally, he would gasp as I'd effectively disappeared from his sight.

"Where'd you go?" he asked. The beginnings of fear were evident in his voice.

I turned around and walked back towards his voice. He gasped again as I reappeared before him.

"It's a hologram," I explained. "An illusion."

"You were telling the truth!"

He started to walk forward and I grabbed his arm. "No, I wouldn't advise that. I can walk through it because I am a member of the Phalanx. If you walk through without an adult member deactivating the field they'll know the illusion has been shattered."

"Why are you telling me all of this?"

"Because you're special. If you are one of the next metahumans, then maybe we can return to the surface after all these years. You will be our Savior, our Hero."

"I'm no hero," Andrew muttered. "I'm nobody."

"That's enough for now," I said. "Too much revelation too fast and you'll be too overwhelmed."

The seeds had been planted. My job had been done superbly. Now I had to hope that those carefully planted seeds took root and wrought their intended harvest.

I kept my distance the next few days to ensure the Phalanx hadn't detected my actions. Andrew walked around in a daze. He attempted to talk to me a few times and I rebuffed his advances, impressing upon him the need for secrecy. I knew he was practicing his powers in the woods and was becoming more proficient. The desire to do so was my doing. My gentle mental prodding when he needed motivation. Things were in motion and would come to head that afternoon. All the pieces were in place. I tempered my excitement with the utmost caution.

FATE BLOOMS

"Hi."

Andrew glanced up from his meal and gawked. He eventually realized his mouth was open and he closed it quickly.

"This seat taken?"

"Um, no," he managed. His hands burned and he squeezed them tightly, shoving them into his lap beneath the lunch table.

Misty set her tray down and settled at the table. "I'm sorry about what happened the other day with Derrick."

Andrew's cheeks burned with embarrassment. He shoved a good helping of mashed potatoes into his mouth because he couldn't think of anything to say. As soon as he did so he realized it had been a mistake. The potatoes turned to paste in his mouth and he found he couldn't swallow. Panic set in and Andrew was seconds from either spewing his food all over Misty or bolting from the table. Misty reached over and placed a hand on his and smiled. The tightness in his chest loosened and Andrew swallowed. He grinned.

"There. That's better," Misty said with a laugh. "Hey... you wanna...?" she took a deep breath and plunged on, "You wanna hang out sometime?"

"Are you serious?" Andrew blurted.

"Well, yeah. I'm serious, that is, unless you don't want to?"

"Of course, I want to!"

"Great!" Misty laughed. "Meet me after school and we'll hang out."

THE DOMINOES ARE SET

NDREW SEARCHED THE PARKING LOT and sighed. There was no sign of Misty. She was messing with him. He should've known better. He shouldered his backpack, fighting the sting of humiliation.

A scream stopped him in his tracks. He glanced over between two of the school buildings and spotted Misty being dragged by Derrick. He started running before he realized he was doing so.

"Hey!" he shouted.

Misty's dress was torn at the shoulder and her face was bloody. Derrick grinned at Andrew and punched Misty soundly. Her scream was cut short and she slumped in his hold. The two disappeared between the two buildings. Andrew ran even faster, spurred on by the sudden blast of adrenaline. His hands glowed, his vision narrowed. He burst into the alleyway and stopped short.

Derrick was straddling an unconscious Misty, a brick raised above his head. Andrew shouted, but knew he was too far away to stop what Derrick had set into action.

The brick came down as if in slow motion.

LET SIRIUS INTO FIRE MELT

I TURN FROM THE WASTELAND outside my pod window. The city's populous screams and moans below me. Desolate and foreboding, the nuclear-scarred sky swirls and moves with menace. The fruits of man's labors taunt me from below. There is no hope, no recourse. I must do this; wipe the slate clean.

I check the monitors, pleased that all of the events I've programmed into the VR are nearing fruition. The emancipated boy grunts and moans as the events play out in his mind. His hands glow and pulse with undulating luminosity. Soon, he will do what I've influenced him to do. Soon the entire world will pay for what they've done to us.

Every transformation requires a hero and a villain. Both sides of the same coin.

Soon, Andrew will obliterate this dystopia of pain, grief, and suffering. If you haven't figured it out yet, I will help you. It really doesn't matter what you know now. It will all be over soon enough. I was once known as Memory Man.

I was a hero... once.

And now, now I am Andrew's villain.

And soon, very soon, a hero will make the world pay for what they've done.

ROY C. BOOTH is an author, poet, essayist, screenwriter, game designer, editor, and comedian from Bemidji, MN with over thirty books and fifty short stories in publication, either in his own name or under his Evil Psuedonym. As an internationally awarded playwright, Roy has had 57 stage plays published with 800+ professional and amateur productions of his work in 28 countries and in ten languages to date. His more recent speculative fiction books in release include *Sherlock Holmes and the Case of the Man-Made Vacuum* (w/. Nicholas Johnson, Harren Press), *The Flesh of Fallen Angels* (w/. R. Thomas Riley, Grand Mal Press, also available as an audio book from Audible), and *The One: Children of Destiny* (w/. P. A. Copeland, J. Ashton Ellington Press, Best YA Book winner of the 2013 Preditors & Editor Readers Choice Awards).

Upcoming future releases include *Mortuary of Madness* (again w/. Riley, Permuted Press, the novel adaptation/expansion of a screenplay by Jim O'Rear, also slated to made into a feature film), future installments of the *Steampunk Sherlock Holmes* and *The Werecat's Journal* series (w/. Brian Woods, JEA).

Roy's work can be found at the following:
www.amazon.com/author/roycbooth
www.samuelfrench.com & **www.hitplays.com**.

R.THOMAS RILEY, of Minot, ND, is the author of the short story collection THE MONSTER WITHIN IDEA (2009-2011) published by Hugo Nominated Apex Publications and re-released as a Kindle exclusive in 2011 and in January 2013, the collection reached the Top 100 Paid Bestseller list in the Horror category. To date, the collection has been downloaded nearly 70,000 times on Kindle. IF GOD DOESN'T SHOW - A Gibson Blount Novel (co-written with John Grover) was published by Permuted Press and Audible.com August, 2012. THE FLESH OF FALLEN ANGELS—A Gibson Blount Novella (co-written with Roy C. Booth) was published by Grand Mal Press in February 2012. DIAPHONOUS (co-written with Roy C. Booth) is available now on Kindle. THE DAY LUFBERRY WON IT ALL was adapted to short film by Frosty Moon Omnimedia in 2010 with a script written by Roy C. Booth and John F. Mollard.

The Providential Hero

SANJAYA MISHRA

SINCE EARLY MORNING, the weather had had something ominous about it. The static formation of grey clouds in the sky, the slithering wind, and the intermittent drizzles all gave the feeling that somebody was hatching a plot against the village to be let loose soon. Ten years ago, only the elders of the village could have been able to discern these signs. However, with the changing times and technological advancements, the villagers were already informed about the cyclonic storm Phailin lurking somewhere in the Bay of Bengal, ready to sweep everything that came its way.

The cattle returned early from their daily sojourn in the afternoon followed by the cowherd boys. The dust raised by their hooves enveloped the village road. Unmindful of it, the villagers one by one congregated near the platform under the old banyan tree, their venue for meeting for generations. The government had issued an evacuation warning, urging the coastal villagers to take shelter in the nearby town, some fifteen kilometres away, where arrangements had been made for the needy. Everybody was well-aware that they had to shed any attachment to their property. Sixteen years ago, when the last storm hit the village, some people who were unable to do so chose to stay. They went into oblivion with the many houses of the village and the loss haunted many of the villagers.

Unlike other meetings, this time there were no chairs for the important people of the village to sit. Narayan Choudhury, the village head, his face grim, stood up on the platform and raised his hand to keep silence.

"Friends, we all know how devastating the cyclone was last time. There is hardly a family in the village that didn't lose a family member due to it," Choudhury, said.

Many of the villagers hadn't yet recovered from the colossal damage the last cyclone inflicted. Aside from a half dozen concrete structures, all other dwellings in the village were destroyed. The silt that the Salandi river brought in had made their lands unfit for cultivation for two years. The loss of crop or property, however, wasn't their primary concern at present.

Hari Mishra, the lone survivor of his family during the last cyclone, said, "Saving lives should be our first priority."

"The meteorological report predicts that the cyclone will hit tonight. But who knows? The Wind God, seething with fury, may decide to curse us sooner. So, it would be wise to move out soon...may be in the evening," said Choudhury.

"What about the cattle?" somebody asked, his voice sounding feeble in the overwhelming situation.

"We assemble them in the grazing field. There aren't many trees around, so the chances of getting crushed under them would be less," Choudhury replied. "Have you got any other questions?"

Some of the villagers exchanged unsure glances, the women talked in hushed voices among themselves about the essential things they would need to pack, but none of them said anything.

The old priest of the village said, "What about our deity, Ma Karnika? Should we leave her here?"

The eerie silence that followed was palpable. The deity in the village temple, situated on the bank of the river, should not be left as it was.

Indeed, Ma Karnika was their primary deity who received their prayers and offerings, propitiated their sins, and gave blessings for their well-being. During the last cyclone, she was only an elongated, cylindrical granite rock of two feet, exposed to the beatings of nature, which she had survived gallantly. But the number of its devotees had swelled in recent years, and with them, a temple had been erected around the deity.

The confused villagers exchanged glances, talked in hushed voices, and finally looked towards the village head and the priest.

"But can't the deity protect herself?" a young boy asked.

In the face of the impending storm and certain destruction, none of the villagers ventured to reply, to regale about the deity's omnipotence; their deep attachment and unfaltering reverence for her notwithstanding.

Finally Sanatan Tripathy, the septuagenarian devotee of the deity, said, "Surely she can protect herself, my dear, and others as well. But from time to time, she decides to test us, assesses our devotion, our willingness to serve her. If we falter now, she would desert us and may not be there for us when the storm is over. Who will look after us then?"

Although the answer stopped the boy from querying further, it didn't shed any light in solving their problem in hand. It was still a snag they had to resolve before running for cover.

"We will take the deity with us," Choudhury said finally.

"But sir," said the old priest in earnest, "we have to perform a '*puja*', in order to displace the deity from its current position."

"Why can't we perform the rituals now?" Choudhury asked.

"It will take a full day to complete." the priest replied.

The following silence was interrupted by the howling of jackals in the distance. Nobody had a viable solution. Most of them didn't know the intricacies of these rituals. Only a few of the learned people in the village knew something about it. With the impending storm and their plan to leave within hours, they only had a little time to do the rituals.

At last, the teacher of the primary school in the village said to the priest, "Sir, there is one thing we can do. Let's move the deity now and when we return after the cyclone, if the temple is still in its place, we will perform the ritual to absolve the sin committed in the first place and then replace the deity. I think, Ma Karnika will understand. After all, should we doubt her benevolence?"

"So, we take the deity with us, you bring it, and join us before we leave," Choudhury said to the priest.

The crowd dispersed with tearful eyes. Everybody was eager to pack up their belongings and feed the children. Many of the women cried. Who knew when they would return? What would be left of their houses? Would the place be filled with debris from the river?

IN THEIR HURRY TO PACK UP AND GET GOING, what no one in the village considered were the ornaments that the deity adorned. Like a lightning bolt in the stormy sky, however, it occurred to Kalo the thief, sitting away from the crowd.

The priest will bring the deity from the temple. Obviously, he would also carry the ornaments with him.

Kalo had successfully stolen things from houses in the faraway villages; nothing spectacular enough to reach the news in their own village, but there were rumors among the youths and some of his friends that he was the one responsible for the crimes.

This is a big opportunity, he thought, *something like this doesn't come frequently—a chance to grab the ornaments of the deity.* He would go to a faraway place with the booty. The villagers afterwards would believe that he, like many others, has fallen prey to the cyclone.

As the priest made his way towards the temple, Kalo followed him at a distance, saw him enter the temple, and waited, ready to snatch a bag that would surely be filled with the ornaments at the first opportune moment.

Due to recent rains, the river had swollen, its turbid, brown water tapping the banks. As decided in the meeting, he saw some cow-herd boys escorting the cattle to the nearby grazing field. Suddenly Kalo became apprehensive. This was the first time he was planning to rob his own village.

What if the priest decides to return while it was still daylight? Somebody may see the snatching. The priest may raise alarm!

Kalo approached the temple, took the stairs, and tiptoed to the front door. The priest had to be in the inner sanctum. He carefully closed the front door, fixed the latch, and returned to the village, assured that the priest could not come out of the temple even after he packed up the deity and the ornaments. Nobody would be drawn to his shouts for help from inside in a time like this. And when everybody in the village would have left for the makeshift camps, he would come back to snatch the ornaments in the storm.

THE WIND PICKED UP AND IT STARTED TO RAIN. As dusk approached, people came out of their houses and packed their belongings on bullock carts. Many of them held lanterns or torches, their flames dancing in the wind. Some of the women and children climbed on to the jeep owned by the village head, while others rode on the pillions of the available bikes in the village.

Kalo knew it was time to make a move. Everyone in the village was fully occupied in leaving. He walked unnoticed towards the temple through the darkness and rain. The moon showed through the dark clouds intermittently. The river was in full spate and the water almost reached the walls of the temple. It seemed there had been heavy rains in the upstream areas. Perhaps the cyclone would hit earlier. Kalo wasn't afraid of it though: with his agile legs, he could surely find his way through it. In fact, it would give him good cover.

The river water already submerged some of the staircases leading to the temple. Kalo opened the door of the temple and slipped into the darkness again, waiting for the priest to come out with the bag. But the priest didn't rush out. Kalo found this odd. There were no windows, so the priest had to come out through the entrance. When the priest didn't come out even after half an hour, Kalo decided to go in and see what the priest was up to.

The priest, perhaps sensing his presence, cried, "I am not going."

Kalo stood at the door of the sanctum sanctorum and in the dim light of the lantern looked at the deity and priest sitting on the floor.

"You can take her ornaments to a safe place but I cannot leave the deity here and go," The priest said again in a hoarse voice, still not looking towards him.

For a moment, Kalo took his words literally, as if he was urging him to flee with the bag of ornaments. The priest was reciting some inaudible hymns; his eyes on the deity.

Kalo realised that the priest believed the villagers had sent him to look for the priest and deity. It was clear, however, that even if Kalo was there to help, the priest wanted to stay with the deity and be swept away by the flood.

"But why aren't you leaving?" Kalo asked.

The priest turned. In the dim light Kalo could see tears rolling down his cheeks like the flowing river outside. "How can I go when I cannot take her with me?" the priest said, pointing at the deity.

"Why can't you take the deity with you?"

"After I took the ornaments from her and placed them in a bag, when the time came to remove her, I realized that I no longer remember the hymn, the mandatory, minimum ritual to displace the deity. I never thought in my wildest dream that I would have to chant this hymn one day."

Kalo kept on looking at the sobbing priest.

"And now," the priest continued, "my book of rituals, it is destroyed."

Kalo looked at the book the priest was holding. It was soaked completely in rain water that seeped in through the doors. Its papers were in disarray; the letters smudged and illegible.

"I would rather die here than take the deity from her abode without performing the ritual," the priest said.

Kalo knew he could take the bag and go away. The priest wouldn't live to tell the villagers about who took the bag of ornaments. Glancing up, his eyes rested on the long, elongated structure of the deity for a moment. The eyes, gems embedded in the stone, the thin gold-plating on the mouth, and the surrounding vermillion paste all shone in the light from the lantern. She could, they said, usher in thousands of lights or cast a spell of abysmal depths of darkness; she could bless you or curse you. And the old man sitting in front of him, was ready to embrace death for her.

The thunder outside brought him back from his reverie. It reminded him that it was undoubtedly a time when nature was at its most belligerent, hell-bent on punishment. He had to get out fast. He bent down to pick up the bag.

Just then, water surged into the temple, throwing its doors wide open. The sanctum was at a lower level than the rest of the temple. Soon, it started to fill in with water. The old priest leapt up and clutched the deity. Struggling through the water, evading the branches of the trees and shrubs that the water brought in, Kalo emerged from the sanctum and looked out.

In the flashes of lightning, Kalo saw that the river water surrounded the temple. The road to the village and the paddy fields were submerged under it. It also covered the grazing fields and Kalo could see the cattle swimming back towards the village. The water level was rising fast and he wasn't sure if he could swim back to the village. He looked back at the priest who was forcing his way through the water—which was up to his chest—still holding the deity.

"You can't swim back. Let's ride the waters to the top of the temple," the priest said.

The priest was right. Kalo reached the top of the temple and sat by the side of the triangle-shaped, red-colored flag which, though soggy, still fluttered in the wind relentlessly. The priest, due to his age and the weight of the deity, found it difficult to climb up. Bending down, Kalo took the deity from his hand and pulled the priest up. They clung to the temple top like two monkeys. The ferocity of the rain and wind waned after couple of hours, but the accumulated clouds kept on thundering overhead. Straining their eyes, they could see the top of some of the tall buildings in the village.

"We have to move somewhere safer," Kalo said, clinging to the bag. The priest remained silent. In the unending expanse of water, no place was safe. Soon, the wind would become violent, threatening to blow them away like sheets of paper.

But it was the water that reached them first, slackened their hold on the temple and swept them away; first the priest, holding the deity and trying his best to keep the rock above the water, followed by Kalo, clutching the bag. Kalo yelled in despair at the sight of certain death, his plan to flee with the booty flowing away with the flood water.

As they struggled in the current, the long and elongated structure of the deity stuck in the branches of a large banyan tree near the temple and the priest caught hold of the hand of Kalo, who was behind him. Both of them climbed to the top of the tree.

"Ma Karnika saved us," the priest said, looking at the deity in his hand.

Kalo looked at it.

How long can the deity save us, he thought. *The cyclonic wind is bound to come soon, and shake us off the tree.*

Kalo could hear the priest chanting some hymn at the top of his voice. He was intrigued and amazed at the priest's faith—absolute and unwavering. Holding the deity in his hand, atop a tree, he saw the old man, praying to save himself from the clutches of certain death. However, at the back of his mind, it did occur to Kalo that perhaps she was the only one who could save them. He tried to look at her in the darkness. In the spurts of lightning, he saw the same gem stone eyes and gold-plated mouth. Most of the vermillion was now washed away in the rain. He begged forgiveness and prayed for his life.

Before long, the speed of the wind became menacing, hissing like a giant cobra. The leaves and the branches of the tree trembled. They found it increasingly difficult to hold onto the wide slippery trunk of the tree. Kalo knew it was just a matter of time before both of them would be thrown into the flowing water and swept away. He caught hold of the deity and stuck it between two strong, V-shaped trunks of the tree, just above the level of water. Then he tore his shirt, and with it, tied the both ends of the deity to the tree. It would be easier to hold on to the rock than the trunks of the tree.

"Come here and hold on to the deity," Kalo yelled to the priest. The priest obliged.

"Keep your body under the water. The impact of the wind will be less there. If the level of water doesn't rise, perhaps we'll survive," he said.

The wind kept on blowing like a trumpet, playing with the water, making waves that drowned them from time to time. The tree shook, dislodging leaves, twigs, and branches. The rain, however, finally stopped. The priest and Kalo with his bag of ornaments latched on to the deity like two limpets, with only their heads remaining above the water. In the darkness, Kalo kept on talking to the priest lest the old man loosen his hold due to fatigue.

At dawn, the fury of wind lessened. In the day light, they found snakes sticking to the trees.

"It was only due to the blessings of Ma Karnika that we are alive now," the priest said, invoking the deity in his own way—by chanting the hymns. Kalo, his intention of previous night forgotten and unaware of the priest's ways, extended his gratitude through a silent prayer.

By afternoon, the water had receded considerably. The village head and some young men came searching for them in a boat. Kalo untied the deity, careful not to let it fall in the water, and along with the priest came down.

At the relief camp, the priest placed the deity on a pedestal.

"Ma Karnika, our deity saved us," he said. Then pointing at Kalo, he announced, "But she chose Kalo to do so."

It took some time for the crowd to understand the full meaning of his statement.

A boy, known for his precociousness, said, "Kalo saved the priest and the deity!"His face flushed with excitement.

"Kalo has secured our salvation from the clutches of Phalin, the Cyclone. Yes, he is our pride, the hero of the village,"Choudhury said.

The crowd clapped and roared and Kalo could hardly conceal his exhilaration. But, as he recollected his readiness to rob the deity only a few hours ago, a feeling of deep remorse gnawed at him. Now, the villagers took him to be their savior. Kalo looked at the deity again and tears of gratitude filled his eyes. Ma Karnika had not only forgiven for his intentions, she had also made him a hero. Bowing down before her, he vowed to remain so—a hero—for the rest of his life.

ALTHOUGH Sanjaya Kumar Mishra works as a geologist, searching for ground water in underdeveloped areas in India, writing has always been his passion. His field trips often provide him the footage for the stories.

Sanjaya's stories have been published in desilit.org, dispatchlit.org, BTW Magazine, splitlipmagazine.com, "At Home and Abroad: Prize-Winning Stories" by Joyous Publishing, Lost Coast Review by Avignon Press Books. One of his children's stories will be translated into Chinese this year. With the support of Fiction Writers Group, he has also had couple of short stories published in the *Flash It!* flash fiction anthology and look forward to be published in many more anthologies. At present, he is working on his debut novel.

Sanjaya lives in the state of Odisha in the eastern coast of India with his wife and son. He can be contacted at sanjayamis@gmail.com.

A Girl's Best Friend

T.D. HARVEY

LAST TO LEAVE THE HOUSE, I raced to join Dad and the others in the underground tornado shelter. The sirens pierced the air and the rushing white noise of the wind was getting stronger. My hair whipped around my head, temporarily blinding me. I tied it back as I ran through the maelstrom. Dad was frantic; he was screaming at me to hurry, but the wind stole his words. The air smelled of copper and churned earth, and the sky grew darker with a green hue seeping through. Gusts pushed me back towards the house as I fought my way to the shelter. As I got to the door—held open by my father—I stopped and looked back at the house. The gale whisked tiles from the roof. Leaves and twigs danced in the air. Dust spiraled magically. Dad grabbed my arm and pulled me down into the shelter opening. To my horror, one of the family was missing.

"Lady!" Dad fought to keep the door open as the storm buffeted against it. "Lady. Where is she?"

"Get in."

"No. Where's Lady?" I pulled away from his grip.

Lady was our dog, a Toller. She was my best friend and I wasn't about to leave her. She was always there for me and now I needed to be there for her. No one could stop me. I ran for the house like the devil was clawing at my back. I screamed Lady's name. Would the wind take my voice through the house? I hoped it would. I hoped she would hear me. The thought of losing Lady caused my stomach to twist and tighten. What if I couldn't find her? I turned in the doorway to see

Dad was still holding the door open. I gestured for him to go inside but he shook his head. I hoped that wouldn't be the worst decision of his life. I hoped it wouldn't be the last.

Inside, I shouted for Lady, but heard nothing. The howling wind raced around the house. It found its way in through the tiniest gaps, making the building shriek. A clattering above made me pause. The frigid air made my face and fingers sting. I had to find Lady. I didn't want to think about what I would have to do if I couldn't.

"Lady!"

Lady's leash was hanging on the hooks by the door. I shook it, making the metal chink and ring. Lady did not come running. I searched the first floor. The living room and dining room were deserted. Lady's bed by the kitchen fireplace was empty. My heart sank and my stomach tightened. She was gone.

"Stupid!" I knew where she'd be. How could I have forgotten? I raced upstairs, remembering that when afraid, Lady would hide under my sister's crib. The skirting around the base covered the legs and Lady seemed to feel safe there. In the nursery, under the pink, flowery curtain, I found her.

Lady cowered and shivered with fear.

Despite the storm, I grinned with relief. "Come on, Lady," I said, trying to soothe her. "It's all right. Come on, let's get out of here, okay?"

Lady refused to move. I pulled her by the collar, pushed her from behind, frantic to get her out. She felt like she was made of lead, heavy and unyielding. Clipping the leash to her collar, I wrapped the handle around my hand. Then I stood and lifted the crib off the dog with a strength I didn't know I possessed. It had overtaken my body, and I threw the crib like it was nothing.

It crashed to the floor and Lady leaped in surprise. Heart thumping, I bent and kissed the dog on her head. I wrapped my arms around her, happy to have her free.

"You silly girl. What are you doing here? C'mon, we gotta go!"

Lady's eyes were enormous with fear. I smoothed her coat and tried to calm her. We stood, but she refused to walk. Her tail and bottom were tucked underneath her, legs tensed to run and trembling violently. Her head dipped low and her folded ears alternated between lying flat against her head and raising, anxious to hear every sound. I grabbed the dog in my arms and ran to the stairs. The rattling of the house was much louder now. The whistling winds rose to a higher pitch; the storm was stronger. We would never reach the shelter in time and I couldn't risk Lady being snatched away—stolen by the storm and thrown into the churning funnel.

I had to think. I had to be smart. The basement. Yes! We'd be safe there. I ran down the stairs. Lady struggled, throwing me off balance. I held her tight and somehow, we made it to the first floor.

I ran to the window, knowing I shouldn't, but I had to see. An enormous cone of rushing air rose into the sky. It moved erratically, picking up anything in its way and destroying everything it touched. I could see a truck caught in its vortex. Trees and power lines uprooted. It held my gaze with its destructive beauty. I forced myself to look away and saw my father had closed the shelter hatch. A breath of relief escaped me, my shoulders sagged a little. I was only responsible for me and Lady now, and I could handle that.

A loud clattering broke my focus. Debris hit the house as the tornado closed in. We had seconds to get down to the basement. Shattering glass sprayed my back as I ran.

The basement door was locked, but the key was on top of the doorframe. Reaching up, just managing to scrape my fingertips across the wood, I felt the key's cold edge. I flicked it and, oddly, over the increasing clamor, heard its metallic clattering as it hit the polished wooden floor and bounced away. I put down the dog, still holding the leash and reached for the key. Once the door was open, I pulled Lady through, closing and locking it. The walls and floor trembled with the force of the wind. The grinding and creaking turned to crunching and cracking as the twister finally tore into my family's home.

I raced down more stairs, Lady at my side. The basement door was rattling in its frame, but it held—for now. Down in the basement, I found a corner behind some old furniture. We settled under a heavy, metal work table piled with boxes. I hoped it would be heavy enough. Lady huddled into me; my body mirrored her shudders. I whispered calmly, trying to comfort us both.

"It's okay, Lady," I said. "It's all right, baby girl. I won't let anything happen to you. I promise. It's okay, baby. It's okay."

The tornado breathed its destruction. It roared hatred and malevolence. It hunted its prey, hunted me, and I cowered in fear of it. Glass smashed and wood splintered. It was pulling my home apart, searching for me. I prayed it would give up and move on, but it didn't.

A symphony of snapping boards, shrieking metal, and crashing furniture made me hold tighter to Lady. Would the tornado rip the house from above our heads, as I had ripped the crib from above Lady's? The once dark basement was flooded with the insipid yellow light of the storm. Debris fell on and around the table that protected us. The deafening bellow of the wind was unbearable. My breath was stolen by the squall. I buried my face in my arms. Lady pushed her muzzle into the shelter of my arms too. We huddled there as the basement disappeared around us. I didn't want to see the destruction. A loud crash shook the table as something hit it, buckling the legs and slamming it into my head.

I DON'T KNOW HOW LONG I was unconscious, but when I woke, I couldn't move. I was engulfed in darkness once more, but the table appeared to have completely crumpled. It forced my head into my neck and shoulders, making breathing difficult. My throat kept making odd, snoring noises. Where was Lady? I reached, but couldn't find her. I pulled my body sideways and agony tore through my spine. I was pinned. I reached out. Then, I relaxed, as I felt her warm soft coat.

Lady.

She stirred under my touch and whined softly.

"It's okay," I said. My voice croaked, barely a whisper. My throat was almost completely blocked; my head pinned to my chest. I tried to move but couldn't and pain shot through me. My body was held fast by the table pushing down on me. I couldn't afford to panic, I had to stay calm, but I was afraid. Each faint breath seemed to sap my strength; I fought to get air into my lungs. I hoped my family had fared better. And the house, the house was gone! Had the whole house been dumped on top of me? Had it been it chewed up and spat out by the monstrous tempest?

I WOKE AGAIN, nauseated and weak. The silence was shocking, almost unnerving. Was the storm over? The world was spinning-and-stopping, spinning-and-stopping in jerking movements. To distract myself I thought of my family. I was the oldest child of five; not really a child any more, as I was seventeen and soon to leave high school. My twin brothers, Davey and Mikey, were nine, and total pains in the butt. They would have loved the excitement of racing around the house in the storm. They never saw danger. They were such fun to be around, when they weren't driving me crazy. My little sister, Emmy, was the princess of the family. She loved everything pink and sparkly, the total opposite to me. Finally there was baby Bobby who spent much of her time crying and pooping, like all babies seem to do. My parents liked to space out their children, apparently. Then, there was Lady.

Lady was the family dog, but there was a special bond between her and me from the day my parents brought her home. As a kid, I would dress her in my clothes. More recently she comforted me after my boyfriend kissed Prom Queen wannabe, Mason Loggins. She only went with him because everyone knows the Head Cheerleader and Captain of the football team were meant to be an item. I didn't even want to be a stupid cheerleader, let alone Prom Queen. They could have each other. What did I care? I couldn't rely on boys or friends, but I could always trust Lady. And I could always trust my parents.

They always listened to what I had to say. Mom was busy with the other kids, but she tried her best to find time for me. I wished I were with them, instead of in the basement. Mom and Dad would be worried about me and I had no way of letting them know I was okay. My eyes burned, as tears rolled down my cheeks. Movement in the ruins broke my reverie and I prayed it wouldn't cause more rubble to collapse on us.

"Carly?"

Lady's tail thumped as we both heard the glorious sound of Dad calling my name. An enormous sense of relief flooded through me. He was safe and he was coming for me. Just as I knew he would. Dad was always there when I needed him. Fresh tears flowed and I tried to speak but my throat was too closed to do more than croak. Lady barked. Not a menacing or excited bark but a single, loud report, repeated regularly as if she knew we needed to alert Dad to our position.

"Carly?"

My father's deep but desperate voice was calling to me and I wanted to scream out 'Dad!' but couldn't utter a sound. Instead I relied on the reports from Lady, who continued to announce our location. Soon I heard grinding and clattering and knew my father had found us. Lady's bark became excited as he got closer. Soon light poured in from above.

"I can see Lady," I heard him shout. "Can't see Carly, though."

"I'm here, Dad," my voice cracked, not loud enough for him to hear. In the corner of my eye, I could see his hand reach down for Lady and grab her scruff to pull her out, but she yelped in pain. I stroked her gently, wanting to protect and comfort her.

"Lady's hurt. I'm gonna need to dig her out."

"Carly?" came my mother's frantic voice.

"Not yet, but there's so much to search through. She could be anywhere."

It seemed to take hours for my father to dig down around Lady, but he finally got to her and called to my mother.

"Got Lady. Her leg's caught but I can get it out. I think if I... Carly? Carly, is that you? Carly?"

"Yes, Dad," I said. "I'm here. I'm here, Dad."

"Barb, I found Carly. She's here!" Dad's voice broke and he was crying, but the joy in his voice rang out like a bell. "I found her."

Dad must have freed Lady because she rose away from my hand. The debris shifted and slid as he took her to safety before working his way down to me. He lifted the table. My eyes shut against the sudden clear brightness of sunshine after a storm. I slowly opened my eyes to see my father, hunched over and looking at me. On his face, fear and relief fought each other for supremacy. When I lifted my head, pain seared through my neck, head, shoulders, and back.

"Carly?" he said, his voice gentle. "You okay, baby?"

"Yes, Dad," I managed to whisper, but my throat still felt constricted. "It hurts."

"That's okay, baby. We'll get you out of here and get you fixed up, all right? I love you, Carly."

As gently as he could, Dad put his arms around me and lifted me out from the rubble. I felt safe in his strong arms. I rested my head against his chest. Mom was waiting for me beyond the detritus that was once our house. Bobby was cradled in her arms, the twins and my sister by her side. Lady sat at her feet, ears pricked and tail wagging when she saw me, one paw raised and shaking. Her golden coat was tarnished with spots of dirt and blood. Emmy and the boys had been crying; streaks of dirt ran down their faces. My mother looked desperate, and when our eyes met, tears burst from hers. Her arms reached out to me, despite the distance still to be traversed.

I looked at the devastation around me. The neighborhood was gone. Trees had been uprooted and strewn across the land, trucks lay in crumpled wrecks and houses were nothing but the foundations they once stood on. People called to their loved ones, as Dad had called to me. The desolation pinched my chest; tears blurred my vision. As Dad stumbled over the torn timbers I saw one house standing, a lone sentinel amongst the destroyed neighborhood. Lady and I had been lucky. I smiled and asked, "Dad, is Lady gonna be okay?"

"Sure she is," he said. "What you did was really stupid. You know that, don't you?"

"I know. I'm sorry, Dad, but Lady's family."

"Yeah, I'm sorry I didn't get her to the shelter. I guess I was so worried about your Mom and your brothers and sisters that I forgot to check on her."

"She was hiding under the crib. It's okay."

We continued through the damage that was once our home. My father was quiet, perhaps contemplating what could have been and how lucky we were.

"Lady saved me, Dad," I said. "If she hadn't barked, you might not have found us. I might not have made it. I couldn't breathe."

"Yeah, she was pretty cool, wasn't she? She would have been killed, though, if it weren't for you. You were very brave. You're a hero. You saved her."

"I guess I did, didn't I? We saved each other." I gave a weak smile as my father took me to the rest of our family. We hugged and cried, happy to be together once more. Lady barked, wagging her tail, and I hugged her tight. "Thank you, girl."

We fell silent as we stood on what once was our quiet, leafy street. The house us kids had grown up in, the house that had nearly claimed the lives of Lady and me in its demise, was nothing but a splintered pile of rubble. The sky was calm and blue, showing nothing of the destructive power it had wielded only hours before.

T.D. HARVEY has been writing stories since she first put pen to paper. Having lived in Philadelphia in the USA, Caerleon in Wales and Bristol in England, she always returns home to Hampshire, England and sets much of her writing in that beautiful and historic county. In her previous career as a qualified Veterinary Nurse, her writing often revolved around animal stories and thrillers based in the Veterinary world. Today, she sees herself more as a dark fiction author. Although her writing spans many genres, it always errs on the darker side.

She juggles her writing with a full-time Business Analyst career, looking after her two cats and three fish tanks, growing her own fruit and vegetables and managing a chronic pain condition, Fibromyalgia. Ms. Harvey has been published in two anthologies, *Flash It!*, an un-themed flash fiction anthology and *Shades of Fear*, fear-themed short stories. She has several stories appearing in anthologies this year, including *Sins of the Past*, a collection of historical horror shorts; *An Anthology of Pants*, a fun anthology with a pants (trousers) theme; and *Anything Goes*, an un-themed, multi-genre anthology. Ms. Harvey plans to publish her debut novel, *Paper Dragons and Shadow Demons*, a dark fiction/fantasy story about the things all children fear, in December 2014. Find her on Twitter **@TDHarveyAuthor**.

Facebook: /T.D.HarveyAuthor

http://tdharveyauthor.com/

Hero Hazha

MIGUEL A. RUEDA

NOTHER DAMN PARADE. These people think I haven't got better things to do? Sure, at first the accolades were exciting, the free meals, the groupies, oh Lord, so many groupies. They find out about a couple of extraordinary abilities, and they get curious about what else is "special" about me. Who can blame them? But c'mon, Minneapolis just held one for me last week; now Newark wants to throw one in my honor.

Minnesota I can see: a dozen radioactive yetis attack a Viking's game, and rip apart half the visiting NY team's offensive line before I get the alert to fly over and help out. I mean, it's not like the Jets can get any worse, but at least I prevented any fans from getting hurt.

This save in New Jersey though, it was just a couple of container ships. A school of gigantic squid started dragging them underwater. No one got hurt. So what if a few hundred cars and televisions got wet? I don't need anything more than the lifetime supply of giant calamari I've got frozen in my compound in Antarctica.

A parade through their depressing downtown for saving some consumer goods? No thank you, just send me a plaque; I'll add it to the pile. Although, technically, it's more of a pit really. I've been trying to fill the hole I accidentally dug during an—epic—drunken stupor on a dare from that nitwit Speed-boy. Said I couldn't get to the North Pole directly through the planet. So it turns out that ass-clown was right, but how was I supposed to know without trying? Such a dork, gonna miss him. Other interesting tidbit I learned that day was, although he could be *really* fast when sufficiently motivated, unfortunately he was not faster than a molten geyser of lava. Oh well, less groupie competition for me.

The impetus for dear departed Speedy's nickname was kind of unimaginative, albeit accurate. I mean at the age of forty-five, he really should have changed it to 'Speed-man' a *looong* time ago. I never knew his real name. It's an unwritten rule of the American Society of Supernatural Expert Saviors, kind of a "don't ask, no really, don't ask" thing. My name, on the other hand, is my actual given name.

Hazha, according to my angelic mother, an actual Angel by the way, is my grandfather's middle name. But if you believe my drunken semi-god of a father, yes he's an actual drunk, it was because of the small machine the hospital had for typing in baby's names. On the tiny keyboard, the hyphen symbol, '-', shares a key with 'z', and he simply didn't hold the 'ALT' key down long enough. It took me years to figure that one out. Yeah, dad may have only been half a God, but he was 100% D-bag.

My mother is why I'm telling you this; I need to get the feeling of abandonment off my chest. She's in heaven now. Oh, don't worry, she isn't dead, just went to visit her folks and decided humans were too stupid to deal with anymore. Said she'd come visit on my birthday, guess I have to clean my room at least once this year.

If dad could have had his way, my life might have *totally* gone in the other direction. My abilities starting showing up in my late teens, just in time for him to decide having an empowered offspring might have some benefits for him. Of course, mom didn't know about it at first, she was *piiiiissed* when she found out. My father had me sneaking out at night, snatching tractor trailers of scotch, and burying them in the backyard. Worked out great a couple times, but when I brought home Johnny Walker *Red* instead of at least *Double Black*, he pounded me into the next week. Did I mention that, as part deity, he has the ability of selective time travel?

I ended up missing my senior prom. He punched me on Thursday; I felt it the next Wednesday. Mom really wanted to see me in a tuxedo, and have my photo taken with Marla Marvelous down the block. She was so mad when she found out I was grounded for a month; she not only took my ability to fly, but my heat sensitive x-ray vision too. That power I missed *a lot*. Marla of the bodacious Marvelousness liked to walk around her house in the nude. Good thing my bedroom walls were steel reinforced, or there'd have been a lot of messy little holes through my house.

My mom put me on the right path; I would have ended up hanging with a bad crowd instead of joining the ASSES. Yeah, that's our acronym, just because we have amazing abilities, doesn't mean we have astonishing intellect. The smart ones join the villain team, the Coalition of Outstanding Lawbreakers; their group's acronym is literally "CoOL". What nerd can resist that?

I don't run into them much; I deal more with the murderous wildlife that mere men can't fight. Mother said "it's my duty to sacrifice my time in the service of humanity". She told me I was born to be a protector, a champion, a Hero... blah-blah-blah. Jeeze, she drilled it into me. I think her real ability isn't temporarily performing little miracles, like granting or suspending superpowers; it's her super-guilt. Anytime I tried to do something for myself I'd hear it: don't steal liquor for your dad, don't speed through the girl's locker room on epic panty raids, don't jump off to China on a food run because your friends want authentic eggrolls. Thank Granddad she doesn't know about the girls, or I'd have no fun at all saving people.

Look, I'm not complaining, I like what I do. Seeing the world, meeting giant monsters—and then killing them—racking up notches in a gigantic belt the people of Sumatra gave me when I saved their country from an invasion of tiger and elephant hybrids. These weren't the, "let's stop global warming" Prius kind of hybrid. These were the "home crushing, people munching, house sized creatures waddling across the island, cutting a swath of desolation in their wake" type of species fusion. I'm not sure what they thought I would do with a football field length belt, but I did find a practical use for it. Keeping track of my sexual conquests is a service to humanity.

If I had turned the other way, the CoOL way, I think I would have been okay. Their members aren't all bad; they're not sociopaths or anything, just a bunch of guys and girls out for a good time. In fact my old pal Marla's a member. She can control certain male body parts with her mind; at least that's what they tell her so she'll keep showing up to the meetings. I know her dual talents work on me. She probably didn't even think about it being a power back when we were young. We've grown up and drifted apart since my imaginary lust filled days of my youth. We still keep in touch and run into each other at conventions and whatnot.

Those international get-togethers are fun, and not just because it lets me catch up with an old friend, I enjoy them because all of the world's Super Associations get together once a year, good and bad. Most of us get along, though there are a few of us that don't like each other. There's always someone who has to declare they won't "hang with their arch-enemy". Like throwing "arch" in front of it makes you mortal foes; *pullease,* grow the frig up already. Nobody has to die to prove you're invincible. Everyone has a nemesis, and all of us have a weakness. Mine is a pretty face. I can be, and have been, duped into anything for a cute smile and a wink. Hey, if I had any brains I'd be CoOL right?

Don't tell my mom, but one time I scooped up ten acres of a prime African diamond mine for a redhead with big boobs and an ass I could bounce a quarter off of. And she let me, that's why I did it; sprung that sucker across the state. Later, I found out it had caused a multi-car pileup on the interstate when it cracked through the windshield of a semi. Not like anyone died or anything. A few people were maimed, but I've saved more than I've hurt, so it balances out in my book. Doing more harm than good will get me kicked of the ASSES faster than those Kanga-rabbits I had to fight in Australia. Although it would break my mother's heart if I changed sides, it's not completely unheard of. There is a precedent for, at least, dual membership. There are two common members to both clubs: Iron-butt Willis and Sake-sai.

Iron-butt's dubious "ability" is that he can sit without fidgeting for a really long time. I mean a *really* long time. The ASSES felt obligated to let him in because he came to one of our meetings, and sat in the back of the room without moving until we left. He was still in the same place when we came back a month later! He said he wouldn't leave unless we let him join. We figured he was harmless, so what the hell. Besides, he comes in handy on stakeouts-- there's no need to relieve him. Set him there, give him the team's special whistle to signal for help, and let him wait; it definitely comes in handy. I heard that CoOL made him sit for a year before they started drawing things on him with a Sharpie. He had a full mustache, beard, bushy eyebrows and two penises on his face before they gave in. They are so *cool*. In the grand scheme of valuable super powers, sitting on your butt for months on end is about as worthwhile as Marla's ability to produce boners in strangers. They have a very limited scope of usefulness. Sake-sai however, he's got a real skill.

I met him while I was being honored in Okinawa for saving some local dignitaries who were visiting Alberta Canada. They set me up in their finest hotel, gave me a very nice *Noh* mask trophy, had an endless parade of Asian beauties that wanted to meet the "big American hero"; the hotel's food was pretty good too. It was a pretty sweet weekend that turned into a month when I met Sake-sai. For a week or so they loved me, but then they couldn't get me to leave without letting me "borrow" Sai. His Jesus-like power is that he can turn any liquid into pure *daiginjo* that's always warmed to the perfect temperature. Yeah, I know! Is that great or what? That's why he belongs to every Super club on the planet. There's no downside to having him around.

We spent days down at my place on the ice, drinking, playing Super truth-or-dare; it was a rage to end all ragers. Well for poor Speed-boy it was anyway, that was when he, well, swiftly passed on. In my defense, I saved Sake-sai because I honestly thought Speedy-pants could get outta there. Sake's only got the one power, and it's a valuable commodity. I did say I learned two things that fateful day, didn't I?

Uh-oh. Wait, I hear Iron-butt's whistle and I felt the earth move a little. That usually means something's coming up out of the depths of Hell, or at least Newark Bay. Before I go, though, I've got one more little story to tell. It's about what I did to get invited to Japan, where I was introduced to Sake-sai. This, as we know, eventually led to our, not-as-fast-as-we-thought friend speeding off into oblivion. Whatever Ol' Lead Butt's impending emergency is, it can wait. What are they going to do, sue me? Well actually they could, and have—that's part of the story. You see, PETA, the ASPCA, Sierra Club, and the Audubon Society have joined together to litigate my ass. Those tree-hugging, non-human-humping, leaf-eating nincompoops are charging me with animal cruelty.

I get it, I really do. There was only one transmuted twenty-foot-tall caribou on the planet, and since I killed him, they're now extinct. Honestly,

I'm not anti-animal; I am, however, against mutant critters rampaging the planet. My position is this: a) it's not like he was going to mate with anything to make more of them. Like we'd know what to do with a herd of uncontrollable, man-eating, beasts anyway. And b) he was friggin eating people!!! As if I should have let him happily munch away on those Japanese tourists. Their Super Samurai club, or whatever the name is in their native tongue, wasn't coming to save them; I got the call, I came, I saw, I demolished that massively antlered beast and walked away. I got an award for it, and I'm very proud of the phenomenal, 150-point rack hanging on my ice mantle. Imagine my Super-surprise when I got served papers for creature cruelty!

Nobody ever sues the CoOL people; they are just too hip to let that happen. HIP, that's their ultra-Mensa certified inner circle's name, Highly Intelligent People. The name isn't even stupid like ours. I need to go to their meetings; Marla said she'd put in a good word. In fact I can tell she's thinking about me now... there's some movement in my extraordinary nether regions. I think they're meeting tonight in Monaco. *Really. Friggin' Monaco!* The ASSES meet in Harrisburg, Pennsylvania, because it's "sensible".

I love my mom, but I beginning to think dad had it right. I want to be a CoOL kid, so I'm gonna take Marvelous Martha up on that offer. Let some other ass deal with whatever Iron-butt's emergency is, 'cause I'm outta here.

MIGUEL A. RUEDA has held a variety of jobs: bagel maker, stock boy, baby photographer, field service technician, professional actor/stage manager. Presently employed as a senior project manager at one of the leading integrators in the security industry, he has absorbed a wide variety of characters through his exploits.

In his spare time, he enjoys: motorcycling, rescuing dogs from high-kill shelters; loving his wife, daughter, four grand-boys, and all things nerdy.

To sum up his outlook on life, biker-geek would be appropriate.

"Hero Hazha" is the first published story under his given name. He has published several short stories under the pen name Wayne Hills. It joins his previous works, "Bozo Gets a Laugh" and "Chizuko", available in the *Flash It!* anthology, and "Natural State" in the anthology *Anything Goes*. His selfpublished stories "Soul Flip" and "Soul Library" are available on Amazon KDP select.

Check out his works in progress, and non-published stories at **waynehillsauthor.wordpress.com**, or visit his Facebook page at **www.facebook.com/AuthorWayneHills**.

Alistair

DEBBIE MANBER KUPFER

THEY SAT AT THE WOODEN TABLE with the chessboard between them, just as they had sat every evening for the last two years. The boy scrunched up his face and concentrated. He had never once beaten Alistair, but tonight he was close. Alistair stared at him with his piercing blue eyes, his spidery white fingers casually moving a pawn.

"You think I'm a monster, don't you, Joshua?"

Josh didn't answer. He pondered sacrificing his knight. Of course Alistair was a monster, how could he be anything else? Every full moon he chose a victim, a victim for his feast. And every full moon he grew stronger, so that each new victim was easier prey.

But Josh was not a monster. He was proud he had never tasted human flesh—that in the two years since he had been turned he had quenched his hunger on the night of the full moon with rabbits and squirrels.

"Maybe I am," said Alistair, "But there are monsters worse than me in this world. You are lucky, Joshua; lucky you have me to protect you. I was not so fortunate." Alistair took a long breath in and exhaled slowly, "neither was my mother..."

I WAS BORN MANY CENTURIES AGO in a small village just outside of Vienna. I see you don't believe me, Joshua, but I am not lying. I have lived for a very long time. The flesh and blood you so disdain has nourished me for all these centuries.

My father, Klaus, was a blacksmith. He was well-respected in our village. He was courteous, hardworking, someone the villagers could rely upon. He fashioned their horseshoes, molded their weapons, and mended their cooking pots. He was paid well for his services; we never went without the essentials, or the luxuries of the day for that matter. But my father was greedy. He wanted more and was always devising ways in which to outsmart his neighbors. He bent over backwards to please them, while at the same time taking their best wine and meats.

But once our door closed for the night, the façade was dropped, and he showed us, his family, his true colors—the evil that lurked beneath his smiling surface. He detested the other villagers, but knew he needed to ingratiate himself to gather their gold. But not so with us; at home he was the master and his word was law, and the slightest infraction of that law lead to terrible punishments.

The embers of his forge fires would glow white throughout the day and night, and one of us would always have to tend them, lest they extinguish. My father kept a selection of brands that the villagers used to mark their cattle. But sometimes in a fit of temper he used these fiery hot implements to punish us, to mark us as his possessions.

My sister, Elena, was only four-years-old when she first felt the white heat of the brand on the back of her thigh. My father, ever careful, chose spots to inflict his evil where the scorched skin would not show, and we knew better than to take our wounds to the village doctor. We learned to bear our lot stoically and quietly tiptoed around Klaus, careful not to set him off.

I longed to escape. I studied hard with the village schoolmaster at every opportunity. I borrowed books of alchemy and magic; maybe in their covers would be a spell that would rid my family of this evil man. I poured through the legends of the region. There was an area not far from our house that was said to be the home of immortal beings with amazing powers; I longed to join their ranks, to bring down vengeance on my father.

You must understand, those were different times. There was no divorce, no way for a woman to escape the clutches of a man like Klaus, short of death. My mother, Marlena, certainly contemplated that way out, and were it not for us, I'm convinced she would have thrown herself onto the fires of the forge long before she was forced there by Klaus.

When my sister, Elena, died, the villagers all came by to pay their respects. What a tragedy, such a beautiful little flower, plucked at such an early age before she had a chance to bloom. She was but seven-years-old. She had strayed too close to the fire and had slipped. Such an unfortunate accident, but there was nothing they could do. Klaus had tried to pull her out of the flames, but their heat had consumed her too quickly. None of the neighbors even had an inkling of the truth; that Klaus had grown tired of her whining and her weakness, and had determined that she would have far more worth thrown in the flames than tending them.

My mother sat there, her eyes far away, while the villagers showered us with gifts. They brought their finest wines, enough to fill my father's cellar, plus foods to fill our pantry, and fine furs to clothe us for the winter. Klaus accepted all the gifts with a great show of humility.

"I thank you all. Such generosity. Yes, an awful tragedy," Klaus repeated, a tiny smile playing on the corners of his lips. The villagers didn't notice, didn't see the terrible truth behind his expression. I wanted to kill him then and there.

When the final visitor had paid his respects, the door shut and Klaus turned his gaze on my mother and me. Slowly his smile broadened; it turned into a chuckle and then a guffaw, until he was practically rolling on the ground at his own cleverness and the stupidity of his neighbors.

"How idiotic they are," he said, "and how lucky I am. Look around you at all this treasure. If one worthless life can bring me so many riches, just think how wealthy I will be when I finally rid myself of both of you. But come, let us celebrate! You want to try a little wine, boy, in honor of your poor dead sister?"

"No!" I screamed, "I want nothing from you." I ran from the room, my father chasing me and grabbing my arm hard, pulling me back.

"Oh no you don't! Don't worry, I will not kill you today. And I will leave your dear mother alive. If I killed her who would clean for me and cook for me? Who would wash my clothes and tend my fire? Come taste a little wine, boy!" With that he grabbed my ear and pulled me towards him. He wrenched open my mouth and poured the blood-like fluid down my throat. I gagged and wretched the noxious liquid up onto the floor. Klaus laughed–amused by the show. My mother grabbed a rag and silently started cleaning the puddle of red liquid on the kitchen floor.

That night in my bedroom all alone, I desperately missed my sister, who had slept in a small bed by the window–an empty spot, which I tried to blot out of my mind. I could hear my parents arguing in their bedroom next door. I desperately tried to block out their voices by placing my pillow over my head, but the walls were paper thin.

"Stop your crying, wench. Or I'll stop it with my brand. Elena was worthless. It is easy enough to make another, a boy this time.

But not like Alistair. That boy's not a worthy apprentice. He sneaks off into the village to meet with the schoolmaster. He thinks he's better than me. But I will show him. Come Marlena, let us make another son."

I scrunched up my face, desperate not to hear my mother's cries from the next room. I knew I had to get out of there. I had read stories about vampires that lived deep in Transylvania and could only pray they were true. I sought immortality and power. If I gained those things I could easily get revenge on my father.

The vampires turned out to be a myth, but in Transylvania I found another breed of magic—one that would give me the power and immortality I was seeking. *Werewolves.*

There I met Roman. Roman was to be my mentor, rather like I am to you, boy. He saw promise in me and tutored me in the way of the wolf. He was very selective. Only the best could join his pack. And once he believed we were ready he would send us on the ultimate test.

To gain immortality and awaken our true powers, we needed to consume one who was truly deserving of this fate—ideally a family member. I knew who it had to be.

I had taken to watching my family's home. My mother was pregnant again and the pregnancy was difficult. Klaus was angry I had disappeared before my time, and he took his anger out on my mother. Her body was covered in scars from the fire. I shuddered when I thought of the future of the baby.

And then she was born—another sister, a beautiful girl, with haunting blue eyes that reminded me so much of Elena. My father was furious, but as always, he let his anger brew under the surface during the day, making nice with the villagers, while he forged their horseshoes and tools. But when night came, the bubbling anger rose and my mother was the target for which he took aim.

"You're worthless, Marlena. I told you I needed a son, especially since Alistair left, and what do you give me? Another pitiful girl! How will she have strength to tend my fire? Maybe it's time to take a new wench. There are many in this village that would beg for a chance to be with me."

I was watching at the window. I watched Klaus grab the infant from my mother's arms. The baby girl remained strangely quiet, staring up at Klaus's face. "Maybe she can still be of some use. It worked the first time and my wine cellar is running a little dry."

"Give her back, Klaus. Please, I beg you!"

"You'd better keep your voice down, my dear, there's room in the fire for two." With that he flung the baby high into the flames.

My mother flung herself forward, but it was too late. She stumbled and fell into the fire. Klaus watched, a smile playing on his lips. "So sad," he muttered, "so very sad."

There was to be a full moon that night. I waited, biding my time. I watched the sky darken and the moon slowly rise. I welcomed it into my limbs. Tonight I had a purpose. Tonight I would achieve my destiny, my immortality, and I would make Roman proud. Tonight justice would be mine.

My transformation started to take hold. Today I have complete control, but back then I was still at the mercy of the moon. My limbs lengthened, the fur on my body grew and bristled. My facial muscles stretched. Some of

Roman's new recruits feared the metamorphosis, but I have always enjoyed my lupine form—believed somehow this is what I was always meant to be.

I flexed my now fully-formed claws and bared my canines. I put out a paw and tapped on my father's door. I imagined him inside preparing his story of the terrible accident that had occurred, preparing to bask in the gullibility of his neighbors.

He didn't expect me. He opened the door and peered out. My wolf form is formidable on all fours, but I reared up on my hind legs and pushed him to the ground. I placed my paws on his shoulders and enjoyed the fear in his bloodshot eyes. I willed him to understand who I was, to understand that I had come for vengeance for the murders of my mother and sisters. Then I tore the shirt from his chest and sunk my teeth into his flesh.

It was the best meal I have ever eaten.

As I consumed his body, I gained power beyond measure, and when I returned to Roman after the full moon, I was welcomed as an equal.

"So am I still a monster, Joshua?" Alistair asked.

Josh didn't answer and stared at Alistair with wide eyes before returning his attention to the chessboard. But it was too late.

Alistair reached across the board. "Checkmate!" he said.

DEBBIE GREW up in the UK in the East London suburb of Barking. She has lived in Israel, New York, and North Carolina and somehow ended up in St. Louis, where for the last 15 years she has worked as a freelance puzzle constructor of word puzzles and logic problems. She lives with her husband, two children, and a very opinionated feline. Her first novel, *P.A.W.S.*, was published in June 2013 and she's currently working on a sequel. In addition, she has short stories in two anthologies: *Flash It!* and *Fauxpocalypse*. She believes that with enough tea and dark chocolate you can achieve anything! Connect with Debbie on her blog **http://debbiemanberkupfer.wordpress.com/** or on Facebook: **https://www.facebook.com/DebbieManberKupferAuthor**.

The Birth of a Villain

KELLEE A. GILMORE

T HE ENTIRE WORLD HATES ME because of a heinous crime I didn't mean to commit. I have this power I never asked for and never wanted. I'm standing in a sea of burned bodies all because I wanted to change the world.

As I sit here inhaling the putrid stench of burned flesh, I can't help but blame myself for being so damned naïve. My mother always told me I was too trusting and put way too much faith in people who didn't deserve it. That was the single piece of good advice she ever gave me. I just wish I'd taken it the day I met Damon. The same day my world began its descent into this hell I'm currently living in.

I was leaving my part time job at the local pharmacy store. I'd been working there for a year and considered it the first step to breaking into the world of medicine. I attended the University of Chicago five days a week and was half way through completing a Bachelor's degree in Biological Sciences with a minor in Genetics. The program was grueling, but I'd been maintaining an A+ average every semester.

As I made my way down the sidewalk, I noticed a man standing just outside the pharmacy. He was tall, had short cropped hair and a clean shaven face. There was a very serious demeanor and intimidating presence about him. I intended to walk right by him, but he stepped in front of me, blocking my path.

"Alexis Powers." He spoke with authority.

My stomach knotted. I should have known then he was trouble and hauled ass in the opposite direction. Instead, I answered, "Yes?"

"I need you to come with me please," he replied. His eyes were hidden behind dark shades.

I didn't know exactly who the hell this guy thought he was. I wasn't going anywhere with him. Did he think I was stupid? "I'm sorry, who are you?"

He pulled a badge from his inner suit pocket and flashed it at me, "I'm Damon Matthews. I work for the Genetics & Neurology division of the CIA."

I wasn't expecting that response. "Okay… what would the CIA possibly want with me?"

"If you'd come with me I'll explain. It's classified information that I will only disclose in our private facility. Trust me you'll want to hear this. It's an opportunity you'll never come across again," he replied.

I was reluctant to go anywhere with this suspicious looking man but his badge looked legit and if I could possibly have an opportunity to work with a division of the CIA, I would be a fool to turn down this once-in-a-lifetime chance. My wheels started to spin faster. I imagined what kind of opportunity this could be. I paused the barrage of thoughts floating around my head long enough to ask, "Is this a job offer?"

"More like an internship if you're selected to be a part of the program," he answered.

I agreed to go with him and he escorted me to a facility that wasn't too far from the U of C campus. Damon introduced me to Dr. Arvid Eriksson and he explained the CIA was creating an experimental drug that would help people unlock a very special part of the brain. This section of the brain was not utilized by ninety percent of humans and he believed unlocking it would allow telekinetic and psychic abilities. He believed if we were able to access this part of our brains, we could also see through what he called the veil of the spiritual world.

He wanted me on the development team. I'd be brainstorming with the best scientists and medical experts from all around the world to create the formula that would unlock this amazing human potential. The internship definitely had its benefits. The CIA paid all of my accrued tuition expenses thus far, plus any additional schooling I decide to take in the future. They also paid for room and board and provided a weekly stipend of $1,000 tax-free dollars. I'd get to pick out my own apartment as long as it was close to the research facility—as I'd be spending a good amount of time there.

The only downside was I had to drop my classes until I was done with the research. I wouldn't have time to pursue my degree and meet the agency's requirements of me as well. They also stated that under no circumstances could I tell anyone about the research we were doing here. That wasn't a problem for me because I had no one to tell—all the free time I had was spent in the pharmacy or on studying. I hadn't made any friends since I'd been at U of C. The only person in the world I spoke to somewhat regularly was my mother and right now she was out of the country with her current beau of the year. She usually checked on me once a month just to make sure I was still among the living.

I was reluctant to drop my classes at first, but their promise to pay my tuition once I resumed school was enough to convince me to join the project. Dr. Eriksson's justification for having me on the team was the need for a fresh viewpoint and new ideas in order to achieve their ultimate goals. He stated that my unbiased perspective would take this experiment to the next level. Apparently the agency had been watching me for some time, keeping an eye on my academics and my potential as a "medical genius", as Dr. Eriksson referred to it. I was tremendously flattered and accepted his explanation for my desired participation in the project without any further questions.

I began the internship immediately. We had an amazing team of fifteen highly intelligent individuals, all of whom were very prevalent in the world of science and medicine. We researched for two years before we developed the first version of the drug formula, which we called HBE. We gathered a group of trial participants whom we paid $5000 each. At least a hundred people signed up for the testing, which was a benefit to us because we could be more selective. I was always surprised at what people were willing to sacrifice for money.

It was our goal to have as few hiccups in the process as possible but this was uncharted territory for all of us. We all had to accept the fact there would be a fair amount of errors. The first version of the formula we produced, HBE1.0 was approved for human testing about three months after its creation. This was the moment we'd all been working towards and it had finally arrived. We were going to find out if we'd created a scientific miracle. The drug was given to six trial participants and was a complete and utter failure. Two people died within ten minutes of being injected with the drug and the remaining four were permanently brain damaged and would spend the rest of their lives as vegetables.

The entire team took it hard, but I was crushed by the deaths we caused. I decided I didn't want anything else to do with the project. The evening of the disaster I went to see Dr. Eriksson to hand in my resignation. When I entered his office he was sitting as his desk looking as bad as I felt. I cleared my throat when he didn't immediately notice my presence.

"Alexis, I thought you'd already left for the evening. What are you still doing here?" he asked. His voice sounded weary.

I took a deep breath in preparation. Trying to sound as formal as I could, I announced, "Dr. Eriksson, I've decided I can no longer participate in the program. I appreciate the opportunity you've given me but I can't continue this research."

I reached into my bag and pulled out an envelope. As I handed him my resignation letter he held up his hand to stop me, "Alexis, you can keep that. I won't accept it."

I knew he wouldn't make it easy for me. "I can't continue." Emotion caused my throat to tighten as I thought about the lives we'd lost. I had to pause to regain my composure before I could go on. "I thought I could do this, but after today I know I can't. I don't have the stomach for it."

"No one has the stomach for it, Alexis!" he shouted, startling me.

I'm sure I resembled a deer caught in oncoming traffic as I stood there, shocked by his reaction.

Realizing he'd scared me, his face quickly softened. He let out a long breath before speaking again. "I'm sorry. I didn't mean to yell. Everyone is devastated by what happened here today but it doesn't give us a reason to quit. We committed to change the *world*, Alexis! I believe in this research and I know we will be successful. This formula will change the face of the entire human race. Don't you want to be a part of that?"

"Of course I want to be a part of this program. But I don't think I can carry the weight of death on my shoulders. I just can't." I admitted. The tears that threatened to fall earlier now spilled from my eyes.

He stood up and walked towards me. I lowered my head to hide my tears. He did something so unexpected it nearly caused me to jump out of my shoes. He pulled me close to him and wrapped his arms around me.

"It's not your responsibility to carry anyone's death on your shoulders. All of the participants in this trial knew exactly what they were signing up for. They wanted to make a difference just like you. So much so, they risked their lives for it. Being successful in this program would honor their deaths. I know this isn't an easy thing to do Alexis, but you're strong enough to handle it. I knew you would be invaluable to this research from the moment you stepped through the door. Don't quit on me. We need you."

When I left his office I was completely drained and confused about what I should do. I sat in my apartment for three days thinking about what Dr. Eriksson said and even though I felt horrible, I believed him. He was a brilliant doctor and an amazing man. If he could deal with the consequences, so could I. On the fourth day, I decided I would go back to the facility and finish what I started.

TWO YEARS LATER WE'D PERFECTED THE FORMULA; there were some casualties along the way but the day we tested HBE21.3 made all the loss worth it. Three participants: Serena, Matthew and David, were injected with HBE21.3 on the same day. The first sign this latest formula was a success was the absence of the negative side effects that had been present in every other trial. For the first few days, they all were their normal selves. The tests we conducted on their motor skills, physical, and brain power all read the same as the day they entered the program. On the fifth day, Serena began to exhibit some strange behavior. She was sitting at a table eating breakfast when she stood up suddenly and quickly backed up, crashing into the nearest wall. She looked around the room wildly and then slammed her hands over each of her ears.

"Stop it! Shut up! It's too loud!" She screamed and panted, falling to the floor.

Dr. Eriksson rushed into her room and the rest of us stared from behind a glass window. "Serena, what it is? What's wrong?" he asked her.

"Shh!!!!" was the only reply she gave.

"Serena, I need to know what's going on," he whispered gently.

Internally I prayed Serena survived this trial; this version of the formula had to be right, we'd tried everything. The next step would be to start from square one and who knew how many years that would take.

"Fuck you, you heartless bitch!" Serena screamed, looking up towards the glass window I was staring through.

What in the hell was happening to her?

"I heard you! You hope I don't die so you don't have to start from square one." She screamed towards us.

Her statement brought everything in my world to a screeching halt. Everything we had been working for was coming to fruition. Serena actually heard what I was thinking! The formula worked! I almost ran into the room and kissed her but the death stare she was throwing in my direction made me stay put. Instead I turned around to my partners and announced, "Ladies and gentlemen, the formula works!"

THE NEXT FEW DAYS WERE FILLED WITH DISCOVERY. Matthew wasn't showing signs of telepathy like Serena, but his telekinesis was unmistakable. He was in his room one night preparing for bed and as he lifted his arm to pull the covers back the entire blanket flew off the bed before he'd even laid a finger on it. That was the first incident; only two days later he was levitating his entire bed without any effort.

David was another case all together. He wasn't showing any signs of the formula's effects. No telekinesis, telepathy or any other extraordinary abilities. While Matthew and Serena were growing stronger everyday, he remained his normal self. I was beginning to wonder if he'd been injected with a placebo after two weeks with no sign of progress. Then, one day while I was taking his vitals, the biggest event in human evolution to date occurred. David was a little irritated he wasn't exhibiting any extra abilities and was venting to me about it as I took his vitals. He'd gotten so worked up that his blood pressure began to rise.

"Calm down David, it may take a little more time for the formula to work on you. Don't give yourself a heart attack," I warned him as I pulled the needle and strap from around his arm. I turned to put the vial of blood I'd drawn from him on the tray behind me. When I turned back around to face him, the chair was empty.

"David, where'd you go?"

"What are you talking about, doc?" His voice came from the direction of the now empty chair.

I looked down towards the floor to see if he'd climbed to the floor for some odd reason but he wasn't there either. "David?"

"Yes?" he spoke and there was no mistaking he was right in front of me. I was standing close enough to the chair that I could smell the peppermint on his breath when he answered me.

My heart and stomach were taking turns doing cartwheels. I reached a shaky hand out towards the arm of the chair and sure enough I felt David's arm even though I couldn't see him. I snatched my arm back so suddenly you'd swear I'd just touched a burning flame. I tried my best to remain professional and not freak out in front of David.

"Excuse me, stay right here…. I'll be right back, I-I just left something in the other room," I quickly walked out of the room and then sprinted down the hallway to find Dr. Eriksson. He was leaving Serena's room when I spotted him.

"Dr. Eriksson! You have to come with me, hurry!" I called urgently. I didn't want to say too much because we were so close to the patients' rooms. I didn't want them to worry about their own well-being given my surprise at David's reaction to the HBE21.3.

"What is it Alexis?"

"Come with me please, I'll tell you on the way."

As he followed me to the examination room, I explained how David had just disappeared as I was performing a routine physical and taking blood for tests.

"What do you mean he just disappeared?" he asked.

I explained exactly what happened and Dr. Eriksson listened intently to my every word. He didn't look as surprised as I was by this new development. He actually looked as if he would smile, and that would have been the biggest miracle to ever happen in that place. It would trump telekinesis, telepathy, and the invisible man waiting for us in the exam room. Dr. Eriksson never smiled. He always held a very serious, no-nonsense demeanor. Picturing him cracking a smile was downright scary.

We rushed to the exam room, and when we arrived, David was visible again.

"Oh! Hi David," I said.

"Were you expecting someone else, Dr. Powers? I'm right where you left me. You're acting mighty strange today," David replied.

"No, not at all. I'm just-"

Dr. Eriksson cut me off before I could finish and I was thankful.

"David, how are you feeling today?"

"Fine doc, perfectly ordinary. Never felt so damn ordinary in my whole life," David grumbled, still sounding irritated.

"I understand your frustration David, but I'm afraid I have some news you may not be too happy about. Dr. Powers has been running tests on your blood, and it seems as if your body has rejected the formula."

I didn't know what the hell Dr. Eriksson was talking about, but I remained silent, knowing he must be lying to David for a reason. It quickly became apparent what the reason was when David's blood pressure spiked and he suddenly disappeared again.

I was frozen by what had just taken place. This was something completely unexpected and I'm not even sure what elements in our formula would cause a human to just disappear. I knew we were creating history here, but this just seemed impossible.

"Dr. Powers, get David a mirror." Dr. Eriksson's command cleared my haze and I hurried to the other side of the room to grab a hand mirror.

"So what does this mean, doc, am I being kicked out of the program? I need this money badly. Are there some other test trials that I can participate in?" David questioned, sounding a bit distraught.

"Don't worry about that David. I want you to take a look at something. Dr. Powers is going to hold a mirror up in front of you, and I want you to take a good look."

I walked over to the chair and stood directly in front of it. I couldn't see him so I just raised the mirror up and stopped where I thought his head should be.

"Is this some kind of a trick?" David asked in disbelief.

"No trick," was my only reply, giving David time to let what he was seeing really sink in.

"Holy shit! I'm the fucking invisible man?!"

THE NEXT FEW DAYS WERE WEIRD to say the least; one minute David was disappearing and the next he was levitating the furniture. Serena and Matthew hadn't developed any new abilities, a fact Serena was none too happy about. I'd catch her every so often staring daggers at David as if he'd personally offended her. Another weird occurrence that seemed to grow in frequency was Dr. Eriksson's isolation of David. He was now conducting all David's medical tests and wouldn't let me near him, not even to take his vitals. The two would be sequestered away for hours on end and neither of them would speak about David's progress or any new developments at all. I was growing very irritated with their behavior; I'd devoted years of my life to this program, and to be kept away from a portion of the research was unfair and rather offensive.

After two weeks of feeling totally shut out. I decided I was going to find out what was going on. Dr. Eriksson had to leave for a medical conference where he was presenting and most of our team was going with him. All except for Dr. Laura Ingrich. He left her behind and in charge while he and the others were away for the week. Dr. Ingrich had a lunch meeting one Wednesday afternoon that required her to leave the facility for an hour and a half. It was my window to find out what all the sudden secrecy was about. As soon as she left and the patients went to the cafeteria for lunch, I headed straight for Dr. Eriksson's office. Thankfully his door was unlocked. He had a tall cabinet of file drawers to the left of his desk and I headed straight towards it. I discovered the cabinet was locked when I pulled at the first drawer. I went to his desk and rummaged through the drawers until I found the small key that unlocked the cabinet. My heart raced as I slid the key into the top of the cabinet and turned it. A satisfying click sounded.

The first drawer was filled with patient files, all of the patients that had ever walked into our facility to participate in the trials; all but David's. I opened the second drawer and there were more files filled with documents about our research. All of the documents contained information I already knew. *Dammit! Where is David's file?* The third drawer held nothing of interest either. The final drawer had to contain some clue to what was going on here. I didn't have too much time to find out what Dr. Eriksson was hiding; it just had to be in this last drawer.

I pulled the drawer open and at first glance it seemed to be empty. I slammed my hand against the cabinet in frustration and the act caused an item in the drawer to shift forward. I looked down and noticed there was a small metal lock box inside. It must have been pushed all the way back in the drawer when I first opened it. I bent down and pulled the box out. I lifted the latch that held it closed and pulled open the lid. There was a thick stack of hundred dollar bills wrapped in a rubber band and underneath was a file folder inside with the name David Dorsey written on the tab. Next to that were the letters HBE/SHE Program. They weren't acronyms I recognized. Sure HBE was familiar, but SHE was completely unknown to me.

I moved the cash aside and pulled out the folder. I opened it and began reading the first document. It looked like Dr. Eriksson's handwriting. He had scribbled notes all over the page.

The HBE/SHE formula seems to be working better than anticipated. In addition to David's ability to make himself invisible, he is also exhibiting pyrokinetic abilities! During one of our many practice sessions, David grew very irritated with me and a small burst of flames shot directly from his hands, startling us both. He was unable to duplicate the action, but I intend on correcting that sooner rather than later.

I was completely shocked at what I'd just read. Dr. Eriksson had obviously made some alterations to the formula and hadn't bothered to inform me about any of this. I wondered if the other doctors knew about it. What was he planning to do with this new formula? I'd never dreamed we could create something so powerful. What could he have possibly put in it to create these amazing abilities in David? As I thought about it more, my anger at being kept out of the loop quickly grew into curiosity about the elements of HBE/SHE. I needed to find out what was in it. I searched inside the box, looking for the formula equations or anything that would give me some sort of clue to its constitution. I couldn't find anything else in the box, so I closed it and put it back in the bottom drawer.

I'd been in here far too long and couldn't risk being caught snooping around. I put everything I'd moved back in its place and quickly left. I had to figure out a way to get my hands on that formula before the other doctors came back.

Later that night as I lay in bed, I planned and plotted on a way to get Dr. Ingrich out of the building tomorrow. I spent a good amount of time wondering why Dr. Eriksson could trust me with the development the HBE formula but not this new improved version he'd created.

I felt a deep sense of betrayal from someone I'd actually considered a colleague and friend. *Had he used me all of these years? Pretending to be interested in my personal growth only to steal my "fresh ideas" as he called them?* Even though I'd worked just as hard as the rest of the team had over the years to perfect the HBE formula, they obviously still didn't consider me an equal. That hurt me more than I could ever express—and it pissed me off royally. I stayed up for hours thinking of a good enough excuse or lie that would get Dr. Ingrich out of the building, but I fell asleep before I had the chance to develop a plan.

THE NEXT DAY I RESUMED MY DUTIES AS NORMAL. I took all the patients' vitals and looked for signs of any new developments. The only thing I'd noticed was Serena's particularly foul mood. She was never that pleasant to be around, but that day she was downright intolerable. She was normally very temperamental and didn't care for me at all. I'd gotten used to the attitude but now her displeasure was directed at David and Matthew as well. I chalked it up to PMS just because I didn't feel like dealing with one of her many outbursts.

When lunch-time came around, I got lucky again. Dr. Ingrich had yet another meeting and had to leave the building. As soon as Serena, Matthew and David left for lunch, I went back to Dr. Eriksson's office to see if I'd missed anything. After finding nothing, I walked down to the labs at the back of the facility. I'd once asked Dr. Eriksson about the rooms back there, but he said we wouldn't be using them until we expanded the program. I accepted his answer, having no reason to doubt it. Now I was going to find out exactly what was back there. The hallway leading to this section of the building was dark and silent. I entered the first room I reached at the front of the hallway. Inside, all of the equipment was covered in big white cloths and everything seemed as if it hadn't been used in quite some time. I quickly decided what I was searching for was not here. I walked back out into the hall and searched four more rooms until I finally found one that wasn't draped in white, dust-ridden covers. This had to be the room Dr. Eriksson used for testing his new formula.

The doctor didn't seem too concerned about being discovered because he didn't go through any trouble to hide his work. Files that contained his detailed notes about the formula and its effects were left on his desk for anyone to see. There was a cooling container in the corner of the room that held clearly labeled vials of the formula. Everything I was looking for was right here. I began reading all of the files that detailed the make-up of the formula, his plans for it, and every disturbing side effect that could possibly result in a test patient. It was all so fascinating, and I became more enthralled with each page.

I came to a sheet that looked like a proposal or preliminary contract of some sort. As I read further, I discovered it was an agreement to sell the formula to an entity named D.O.S.H. I wondered briefly if it was a government agency, or even worse, an anti-government terrorist group. I don't know what made me immediately jump to that conclusion but isn't that how this stuff usually played out in the movies?

As my mind considered a thousand different ways this formula could fall into the wrong hands, I completely forgot to pay attention to the clock. It was long past the lunch hour when I heard the sound of someone clearing their throat behind me. My whole body seized in fear. *Shit! Alexis how could you be so stupid and lose track of the time!* How the hell was I going to explain this? I closed the file in my hand and placed it on the desk in front of me. I turned around to find Serena standing there with a smug smirk on her face.

"Hello Dr. Powers. What are you doing down at the forbidden end of the facility?" She asked with acid lacing her tone.

"I should be asking you that." I responded sternly. I was relieved it was Serena who'd discovered me here instead of Dr. Ingrich.

"I'm here for the same reason you are: to snoop," she said knowingly.

I made sure my tone was very stern as I answered her, "I have no idea what you're talking about Serena, but you need to get back to your section of the facility. You have no business being down here."

"You're full of shit, doc. This place was unknown to you as much as it was to me. You're here to see what the others are using their little lab rats for now and that's also why I'm here. Why don't you just hand me that file on the desk?" she said, while making her way towards me.

"Serena, I don't know what you expected to happen here, but you need to get back to your room before I'm forced to excuse you from the program," I threatened. I couldn't believe her audacity. As if we owed her anything. She signed up for this program willingly, and there she was, acting as if we'd forced her to participate.

"Look doc, oh wait, that's right, you're not even a doctor." She dropped that little bomb and a self-satisfied smile grew across her smug face.

I was floored by her statement. The doctors had decided not to reveal to anyone outside our immediate staff that I was not a medical physician. We thought it was best to keep the information to ourselves because it could pose a certain amount of risk to the program if anyone were to find out. How the hell did she know that?

I was unable to hide my shock and she clearly read it on my face. "Didn't think anyone else knew that did ya? We wouldn't want anyone outside of the program to find that out now would we? They might shut you guys down and all the time you've put into this would have been wasted with nothing to show for it. Of course, I wouldn't tell anyone that, just as long as you hand over that folder."

She had some nerve but she did have me there. No one could know about me being this involved in the development of the test formula. I picked up the folder and handed it to her. She made her way to the desk with urgency, quickly snatching the file and devouring each page. As I watched her read through the contents of the file, I became more and more furious with her for trapping me in this corner. I didn't know what she planned on doing with this information but something told me it wouldn't be good for me or the program.

When she was done, she closed the folder and her face contorted in rage. She was silent as she walked over to the container that held the vials of formula. "So this is your super formula, huh?" It sounded more like a rhetorical question, so I didn't answer.

She opened the door and removed a vial. She examined it with her eyes, rolling it around in her petite hands. "You all think you're gods. You think you can do anything you want to us without any repercussions because you're supposedly improving humanity. That's what you tell yourselves. Every day you crawl further and further down that little black hole that has no room for conscience or humility or even compassion. You turn into monsters. How can monsters help to better humanity, Alexis? Can you explain that to me?"

Her comments cut me deep because there was an overwhelming truth in each word. I knew she was telling the truth; what we were doing here was wrong. Deep down I knew that, but I did it anyway, justified it to myself so I could do it again and again until I got the formula right. I had moved all the thoughts of the people that died to the back of my mind and kept going, only to cause more deaths. I was going to hell and I knew it, but what was done was done. I couldn't do anything about it now.

Serena let out a bitter chuckle before speaking again. "Just when I think you may still have a shred of humanity left inside you, you prove me wrong."

She approached me so quickly I completely missed the movement. I blinked and she was next to me, stabbing me in the arm with a needle, injecting me with something.

"You're the next guinea pig—let's see if you survive."

I MUST HAVE PASSED OUT. I woke up to the sounds of fire alarms and people screaming. I opened my eyes and saw smoke and flames. I pulled myself up from the floor, coughing as smoke filled my lungs. I couldn't make out any one person in particular, just bodies running past me.

"Dr. Powers, stop it please! Please stop, let us out!" I heard someone pleading to my left. I turned to see Matthew standing there with charred clothing and a tear-streaked face.

"What happened?" I asked, completely confused about what was going on here, yet oddly calm. You'd think I'd be panicked out of my mind with smoke and flames billowing around me.

"You're killing us, please let us out," he cried.

"I told you, you were a monster and now the whole world will know." I heard Serena's voice. I turned to see her, but I couldn't spot her in the crowd of bodies flying past me. I heard her voice though, how could I not see her?

"I'm in your head! You can hear my thoughts. That formula worked much faster than I thought it would. How does it feel to know you're a lab rat, just like me?"

"I don't know what you're talking about." I looked around again trying to find her. I noticed there was a fire directly in front of me and immediately jumped backwards to get out of the way. A piercing scream howled to the left of where I was just standing and I looked in the direction of the scream to find Matthew engulfed in flames.

"No! What the hell is going on here?! I have to get out!" I screamed as the panic finally set in.

"You're the one that did that to him. Look at your hands, Alexis," Serena's voice sounded in my head once again.

I looked down and saw flames were shooting from my hands. The sight froze me in my steps and I screamed as I realized I was doing this. I burned these people! It was me! Just like Serena said. And I didn't know how to stop it. I didn't know how to stop the flames from shooting out of my body. The more I realized that, the more I panicked, and the more I panicked, the more the flames grew. Until each of the bodies running through the lunchroom trying to find a way out began to fall, engulfed in searing fire as my flames stretched longer and wider.

"There's no way to hide the bodies this time Alexis, I faxed that file to a reporter along with all of the research you've been doing here. The whole world will know what you and your team did here. They're going to hunt every one of you down and you're going to pay for what you did to us."

I began to grow angrier as I listened to her. She did this, it wasn't me; this was her fault. This wouldn't have happened if she hadn't injected me with the formula. She knew it.

There was no response from her after that. I don't know if she ran away at my accusation or was just done taunting me. I did notice the fire shooting from the palms of my hand had stopped but bodies were still burning. The smell of burning flesh filled my nostrils and caused tears to well in my eyes. I'd done this. I killed all these innocent people. As reality sunk in, a severe pain began to build in my chest and caused me to collapse onto the floor screaming with the agony of so many deaths. I screamed and cried until my voice was gone and no more tears were left. I sat on my knees holding myself and rocking back and forth in complete despair.

I don't know how long I sat there, but the sudden need to get out hit me with severe urgency. I had to get away. If she told the reporter about this project then they would be after me. I had to get up and get away quickly. I went back towards Dr. Eriksson's office and found the key to his file cabinet. I opened the bottom drawer and pulled the stack of cash I'd discovered when I'd initially found David's patient file.

I ran to my office and put on the spare set of clothes I kept there. Then I ran through the back and out the door. I heard police and fire truck sirens as I exited into the alley. I didn't bother to go back to my apartment, who knew when the story of what went on in our facility would be released. I went straight to the Greyhound bus station and got the first ticket that would take me west. From there I could go to Mexico. Then I could figure out my next steps.

The one thing of which I was absolutely sure; I was going to find Serena and she would pay for what she did to me.

TWO YEARS LATER....

SERENA LIVED ON A REMOTE ISLAND IN JAMAICA. She wired money to her family once a month and that's how I tracked her. After years of plotting and planning the perfect way to make her and Dr. Eriksson pay for what they did to me, the moment had finally arrived.

There was a grassy hill about fifty yards from the small hut she called home. It was far enough away that she couldn't hear my thoughts, but close enough for me to get a good target on her. I knew every inch of her surrounding environment. I'd stalked her for days, familiarizing myself with her property to eliminate any surprises when the time came.

I could see Serena through the window. She stood over the kitchen stove stirring a pot, oblivious to my presence. I aimed my rifle, loaded with tranquilizers, directly at her neck. I wiped my damp palms on my shirt and steadied myself. My heart raced with anticipation as I gripped the rifle firmly and squeezed the trigger.

Unfortunately for Serena, the boiling pot of water fell to the floor along with her. She let out an agonizing scream before the tranquilizer took effect and knocked her out cold. I ran into the house and locked the door behind me. I pulled Serena up into a chair and secured her with rope.

After two hours, the effects of the tranquilizer began to subside and her mind awakened from the fog. The pain of third degree burns brought her back to full consciousness. She was in so much pain my presence didn't even register to her. "Serena, open your eyes. The pain is gone."

I'd honed and developed my powers while I'd been in hiding. Now I had the ability to read minds and control them. The only reason I'd bothered to shoot Serena with a tranquilizer was because I didn't know how much her power had grown over the last two years. Judging from the amount of effort she was expending to untie her ropes, it hadn't grown much.

She finally gave up her struggle and looked at me with pure hatred. "So what now?"

"Now you're going to tell me where Dr. Eriksson is." It wasn't necessary for her to voice his location because as soon as I mentioned his name, the answer appeared in her mind. Her thoughts also revealed Dr. Eriksson had plans to come to Jamaica to help resolve an unpleasant side effect of her abilities.

"You finally realized the wonderful Dr. Eriksson screwed you over, huh?" she said. The sly smile on her face made me want to rip the flesh from her bones.

"If you know how much of a back-stabbing bastard he is, why would you trust him to help you?"

A flash of desperation appeared in her eyes before her face quickly became a mask of disgust. "He's the only one left who can help me, besides you."

I laughed cynically before replying, "Well that just fucking sucks for you, doesn't it? Because I'm certainly not going to help you and you won't survive long enough for the wonderful Dr. Eriksson to save you."

For the first time since the initial effects of the HBE formula developed in Serena, I saw fear in her eyes. I relished it, closed my eyes and let the anticipation of sweet revenge settle on the back of my tongue. My body warmed as the fire inside me traveled from the pit of my stomach up and out of my pores. The flames rippled down my arms and danced upon my fingertips in fervor. I opened my eyes to see Serena's look of sheer terror before I burned her alive.

The acrid stench of burning flesh was now like the smell of fresh air.

KELLEE A. GILMORE was born and raised in Chicago, Illinois where she currently resides with her husband and two sons. As a young girl, Kellee was captivated by horror movies and R.L. Stine novels. Her love of books began at a very early age thanks to the children's book clubs her mother enrolled her in every year. Whenever the briefcase shaped boxes that contained her new books arrived at her doorstep, she opened them immediately, filled with joy and anticipation.

Kellee's love of books naturally shaped her passion for writing. She has been creating short stories and poems since the age of eleven. Although she's written romance stories and dabbled in fan fiction, her favorite genre to both read and write is paranormal romance. At the age of thirty-one, she began writing her first paranormal romance novel, embarking on the journey of living out her dream.

Website: **www.kelleegilmore.com**

Facebook: **www.facebook.com/KelleeAGilmore**

A Spark Extinguished

SCHEVUS OSBORNE

HEARING SLOW FOOTSTEPS on the floorboards above, Molly scurried away from the short set of steps, dragging her ratty blankets with her. It had only taken a few lashings from the thick leather belt to teach her to listen vigilantly for those footsteps and move quickly.

The bitter chill of frozen earth enveloped her like an unwanted lover, seeping out of the bare concrete walls and gravel floor of the crawl space. A small square panel covered the entrance above the stairs. The barest hint of warm air seeped down through the cracks around it. The heat was enough that she stayed near the entrance as much as she dared.

She tried hard not to fall asleep there, but fatigue occasionally overcame her caution. The first step beckoned to her weary head, soothing as a soft down pillow. The welts on her arms and back did their best to remind her to be more careful.

The panel opened, and Molly's dilated eyes ached from the muted light that filtered down into the pitch black crawl space. Squinting, she saw something flung down into the gravel. She thought she heard the crinkle of a water bottle and her heart lept. She was dreadfully thirsty.

The wooden hatch slammed shut with grim finality, blanketing her in darkness once again.

Creeping over to the steps, careful not to bump into them, Molly felt around on the ground. Her hand closed around something warm and greasy. She smelled it. Chicken—a breast by the feel of it, mostly eaten. Gnawing away what bits of meat remained, she continued searching and found two corn cobettes, also mostly eaten, and an almost-full water bottle.

She opened the bottle and smelled it also. Not everything that came down in a bottle was water, and she almost gagged at the memory. Thankfully, today was a good day, and the water smelled clean. She took a big drink, but was careful to leave some for later. There was no way to know when she would be so lucky again.

Skinning the corn bare and tossing the cobs and chicken bones into what she had designated the trash corner, she contemplated whether it was safe to stay near the stairs. She took another small drink, and decided it probably was.

Resting her head against the bottom step, Molly wrapped herself as best she could in the threadbare blankets and promptly fell asleep.

MOLLY STARTLED AWAKE to the sound of a piercing screech. There was a great commotion on the floorboards above, and the cries of a young girl rose and fell like a perverted siren. The scuffling and banging approached the entrance to the crawl. Molly hurried away into the dim light that filtered in through a single vent in the blocks during the brief hours of daylight.

The panel was ripped away, and the girl landed in a heap at the bottom of the stairs. Her head jarred as she banged it against the bottom step, and she clutched it in agony.

The panel fell shut, and heavy footsteps stomped away.

Molly approached the girl warily, unsure what this new development meant for her continued existence.

The girl noticed her for the first time, and screamed again.

"Shhh, shhh," Molly whispered, trying to placate the girl. "I'm not going to hurt you."

The girl did not look convinced, but she did stop screaming after a moment.

"I'm Molly, what's your name?"

"Sarah," the girl said, so softly that Molly barely heard her.

"Sarah, good," Molly said. "Listen, Sarah, I don't know what happened to you, but like I said, I'm not going to hurt you. I'm trapped here too." Sarah's face caught some of the light, and Molly was surprised how much the girl looked like her younger sister, Abby.

"How did you get here?" Sarah asked, rising to a seated position, with her arms draped over her knees.

Molly scowled, thinking back to the horrible mistake that had landed her in this position.

"I was out with my boyfriend. He drove us deep into the woods, and he tried to have his way with me. I slapped him, hard. He got pissed off and drove away without me. My cell didn't get any signal, so I started walking back."

Molly stopped, choking up a bit at the memory. She had tried so hard to repress what had happened until now. Tears streamed down her face, hidden in the gloom.

"An old blue truck came down the road and pulled up beside me. The driver looked friendly enough, and he offered to take me into the nearest town where I could call someone to pick me up.

"The next thing I knew, we were pulling up in front of this house. I demanded to know what was going on, but he pulled a gun from somewhere. He dragged me inside and threw me down here. He hasn't told me why... when I ask, he beats me with a leather belt... so I've stopped asking. I'm not even sure how long I've been here."

Sarah shuddered and started sobbing uncontrollably. Molly moved to sit beside her and draped her arm over Sarah's shoulders. Sarah was not fat, but the feel of well-nourished flesh drove home for Molly how emaciated she had become. With a stab of fear, she wondered if Sarah had been taken to replace her. Did he expect her to die soon?

Sarah stopped sobbing long enough to try blurting out an anguished question. "Did he...r-r-rap...?"

"No," Molly said. "I've been terrified of that happening every day, but he only seems to enjoy beating me."

It sickened Molly to feel Sarah's shoulders sag with relief. How awful it was that the thought of imprisonment and beatings was so preferable to the alternative.

"Sarah, do you know what day it is?" Molly asked.

"It's the 23rd," she said.

"Of December?"

"No, January."

Molly's mind reeled. She had been taken on December 12th. She refused to believe she had been trapped in this crawl space for well over a month. How had the authorities not found her by now? She had survived on the hopes that she would be found. Someone would have seen her get in his truck, or they would have tracked down her cell phone. Something. Something that would lead the authorities to this place to take her home.

If it had already been over a month, she knew that hope was now unjustified. No one was coming for her. It suddenly occurred to her that might not be the case for Sarah, however. Sarah was a new variable to the equation.

"How did you end up here, Sarah?" she asked.

"I ran away from home. My mom was at work and my dad was drinking again. He tried to hit me, but he was too drunk and he tripped on the coffee table. I ran out of the house and just kept running."

"Oh, no," Molly interrupted. "How old are you?"

"I just turned 18 a few weeks ago. After a while, I started to get tired, and cold. It was getting dark. The same old blue truck pulled up, and he offered me a ride home. When I refused, he pulled his gun and forced me to get in."

"How far did he drive you?"

"I'm not sure, I was so scared. It can't have been too far."

"We must still be pretty close to your home then," Molly said, hope again taking root. Surely the authorities would find Sarah when she was so close to her house? Another thought occurred to her, as the nagging idea that Sarah's arrival was not a good sign for her refused to go away.

"Do you think you would know the area well enough to get help if you got away?" Molly asked.

"Maybe. My brother and I used to ride four-wheelers all over these woods. If I could just find another house... another person, they could call the cops. How would I get out though? Do you have a plan?"

"No, no I don't," Molly said dejectedly.

After hours, Molly still had not come up with any decent ideas. Everything she could think of involved risking her own life to allow Sarah a chance to escape. What was the point of that, when odds were better that Sarah would eventually be found anyway? Should she just try to wait things out?

A pang of hunger and the scratchy dryness in her mouth laughed wickedly at this, assuring her that she probably didn't have much time left. When no food or water dropped down through the hole that evening, Molly became even more certain that they would have to act soon.

Molly and Sarah curled up together in the darkness. Molly was disgusted to admit to herself she was glad for the warmth and comfort of another human being.

THAT COMFORT MADE MOLLY COMPLACENT. He was roaring from the top of the steps. Her heart pounded, shooting adrenaline through her body, waking her instantly. She jerked Sarah up and away from the stairs, moving the groggy girl behind her as they went.

The bare light bulb that hung from the low ceiling turned on, dazzling Molly's eyes with lasting spots in her vision. She heard him hustle down the steps. A heavy hand rocked her face to the side, and she fell down, scraping her withered hands on the rough stones. Sarah screamed, the same piercing wail from the day before.

Molly looked up to see him pulling off the belt, holding Sarah down on the ground with a fistful of her hair in his firm grip. Molly's back stung in sympathetic agony for the pain she knew Sarah would soon feel. Something snapped inside her as the first blow landed, and Sarah's screams reached a new threshold.

Molly hurried over to the trash corner and grabbed the chicken bone from the other night. She was satisfied to feel the sharp ends of the bones poke into her fingers. Sarah shrieked again as the belt landed across her shoulders.

Turning back to face him, Molly threw the some gravel at him. She was too weak to throw it hard enough to do damage, and it bounced harmlessly off his back.

"Leave her alone!" Molly shouted, and was glad to see him turn to face her. His ugly face seethed with rage. He threw Sarah down roughly, and she sobbed miserably into the gravel.

He rushed toward Molly, and it took all of her courage not to cower in the face of him. As he brought his arm back to swing the belt at her face, she ducked forward. He clearly had not expected this, and she easily brought the chicken bone up and into his jaw, raking it down his neck.

"Run, Sarah!" she yelled. "Run, now!"

Clutching at his bleeding neck, he stumbled back a few steps. Molly retreated into the corner of the crawl, fearful he would turn his attention back to Sarah, who had managed to get to her feet and was scrambling up the steps. She felt a great relief as the girl's feet vanished, and his murderous gaze remained steadily on her.

Her back met the cold stone of the cinder block wall, and her heart sank with fresh dread. Sarah had escaped, but surely he would kill her now. She briefly considering trying to run around him, but instead sank into a defeated heap, covering her head with her hands.

The slow, grating footsteps stopped in front of her, and she could hear his ragged breath. The first blow was a savage kick that knocked her onto her side. She felt something inside her crack, and pain speared through her torso. He grunted, and the next strike was a familiar one, the belt tearing into her upper arm. It landed again and again, blistering pain flaring with each hit. Her shoulder. Her back. Her neck. She wept silently, denying him the screams she knew he craved, and that made him even angrier. The belt caught her temple and she finally cried out. *Please, God, just let it end*, she thought.

When she heard the sirens wail, Molly wasn't sure if she was still alive, or if she had moved into some cruel afterlife of eternal misery. Sadness flooded through her, as she realized the sound must be Sarah. He was pulling her back into this dark pit of hell. He would get his revenge on her now that he was done with Molly.

Her body had numbed to the pain of each strike, so she did not notice him stop hitting her, looking up at the floorboards in a stupefied panic. She did not notice the blank expression that passed over his face, or him reaching into the waist of his pants, pulling out his pistol. She did not even notice the loud bang of the gun firing, or the mist of blood that settled on her face.

Drifting in a sea of silent darkness, she thought she heard a kind voice telling her, "You're going to be ok, Molly. Hang in there."

In a moment of pristine clarity, Molly realized that she would never be okay again. She hoped Sarah could be. With a long, slow sigh, Molly reached out to embrace the void.

SCHEVUS LIVES near St. Louis, Missouri. He is a software developer by day, and a father and husband in the evening. He scrounges what few minutes remain to write. So far in his fledgling writing career, Schevus has had other short stories published in *Spirits of St. Louis: Missouri Ghost Stories* and *Fauxpocalypse*. He is also working on his first novel project, a science fiction story that's been rattling around in his brain long enough. You can find out more at **http://schevusosborne.com** or follow him @ **SchevusOsborne** on Twitter.

As the Crow Flies

JADA RYKER

ER CHAPPED HANDS TIGHTENED around the steering wheel as Fresna peered through the heavy rain pounding on her windshield. In an effort to see further than a foot in front of her headlights, she flipped her defroster as high as it would go and switched her wiper setting to *frantic*. She had to get to work at the nursing home in time for her afternoon shift. However, she also needed to get there in one piece.

What would her husband do if she got herself smashed to pieces along the wooded, two-lane road? As she thought of Steve, her hands gripped the wheel tighter. Would he grieve? Would his heart ache? Fresna shook her head, tossing around the dull, graying hair just below her shoulders. If any tears fell, they would stem from his loss of a free meal ticket. Even a fleeting sense of his grief would be easily assuaged by her life insurance policy.

After getting fired from his last job, it took Steve nearly a year to find his present position, loading boxes at a warehouse. She snorted to herself. He hadn't even looked for the damn job; rather, his brother practically forced it on him.

Only two weeks at the warehouse, and *it* had already started; Steve complaining about how hard he has to work. How he doesn't like the way his boss treats him or plays favorites, and his assumption that his co-workers were out to get him by making him look bad. Oh, yes, *it* had started... and she knew exactly how *it* would end.

Why did she continue to expect anything different from him? Steve's father had spent decades on the couch in front of the TV, with a "bad back", while his dutiful wife worked full-time as a waitress, took care of the house, and raised the children. And yet, whenever Fresna's father-in-law wanted to go to the pool hall or fishing with his buddies, his "bad back" never prevented him.

Steve had always been lazy and self-centered—just like his father—and that would never change.

Fresna's eyes filled with tears. At the same moment, the sky flooded with white lightning and a huge, black mass covered the windshield.

Fresna braked, turning the wheel as hard as she could toward the right shoulder. The car jarred to a stop.

"What the heck? Did I slide off the shoulder?"

The unidentified black object disappeared from the windshield, as if it had flown away or was pushed off by the wind. Another flash of lightning lit up the sky as she opened the door and slid out onto the gravel. Fresna walked to the front of the car to investigate. Her wheel had fallen off, leaving the jutting metal bare.

Fresna dropped her jaw and covered her mouth with her hand. "Thank God that black shape hit my windshield! If I hadn't stopped before the wheel fell off, the car would have careened out of control and..."

She sucked in her breath. "If I died, Steve would be set with the money from my life insurance policy, and he'd never have to work again. He would be able to sit at home, and play those dark, twisted video games all night and sleep all day. Just like he always does when he's not employed."

It was not until Fresna reached the nursing home that she was finally able to stop shivering. She rummaged through her locker in the staff lounge for a clean uniform. In spite of her raincoat, Fresna had become soaked by the cold rain when she stood against the side of her car to inspect the wheel. She shivered, more from fear than the chill. If she had been driving when it fell off, the car would have crashed.

Fresna stood in front of a mirror, comb in hand, and attempted to smooth her gnarled hair, which resembled wet rodent tails around her pale face. Once again, she thought of the black object that appeared on her windshield.

What was it? A black sheet of plastic? A wayward tarpaulin? A huge bird?

As Fresna scampered from room to room to help the patients get ready for their dinners, the sun came out. The rain-soaked trees and plants glittered from the sunlight, and a blinding warmth penetrated through the windows.

"Girl! Fresca, or Sarsaparilla, or whatever the hell your name is, quit gawking! Take me out to the patio! Now!"

The strident screech of old Mrs. Stith pushed the storm, and her close call, right out of Fresna's head.

Careful to stay out of the old lady's vicious biting range, Fresna settled the persnickety resident and her mounds of blankets on the patio. As she bent over and locked her patient's wheelchair, Fresna noticed a crow standing on the edge of the cracked, gray, concrete birdbath. The bird was staring at her so intently it caused her body to freeze in mid-stoop over the wheelchair brakes. The bird's eyes were bright and penetrating, and although it shook its head with the jerky, jittery movement characteristic of a bird, it did not take its eyes off hers. She studied the bird as it bobbed its head toward the top of the birdbath, as if it wanted her to come over and look into the pool of water.

Fresna shook her head at her own fancy, and slipped through the sliding glass door. It was time for her to gather clean linens and change the beds.

FRESNA LUMBERED DOWN THE HALL, her vision obscured by the clean sheets, pillowcases, and towels piled high in her arms. Time was passing quickly, and she wanted to make sure she saved plenty of it for her favorite patient, Mr. Corvus. Fresna loved his deep, melodious voice, which contained a hint of an accent that she assumed was British. They often discussed several diverse topics, such as the possibility of alien life forms on Earth, one true God versus many gods, and even the existence of magic. Mr. Corvus would always listen to her very carefully, with his impossibly black head cocked to one side, as if every word she uttered was important.

While she was lost in thought, Fresna stumbled when her foot accidentally connected with a hard object, sending her tumbling down onto the tile floor.

"Should be more careful where you're going, you fat cow."

Surrounded by the scattered clean linens, Fresna looked up to find Jeneva Valentine and Terry Snider, the two nursing assistants who worked the opposite wing, standing over her. Their smug, self-satisfied faces solved the mystery of Fresna's unexpected stumble and subsequent fall.

Fresna rose to her feet and rubbed her aching backside. Now she'd not only have to fetch more linen, but she'd also have to rewash, dry, and fold the spilled linens scattered around her.

Jeneva energetically shook her head, and her brown eyes grew darker with feigned regret. "Oh, dear. Now you won't have time to suck up to Mr. Corvus."

"Betcha Fresna puts in all of that extra time in his room hoping to get in the old man's will." Terry snickered, her pudgy face displaying glee. "Sucking up to *something* to get into his good graces!"

Her shoulders stiff with anger, Fresna kept her head down as she gathered the strewn sheets and towels. Since she couldn't afford to get fired for fighting, she decided it was best to ignore their baiting taunts.

Jeneva laughed her trademark squeal, which sounded similar to a fork scraping a glass plate. "You're wasting your time, Fresna. Don't you know that old geezer showed up on the doorstep with nothing but that ratty old straw purse and that moth-eaten black blanket?"

Terry waggled her fingers. "He just showed up in the lobby, no car or taxi in sight, as if he'd just materialized out of thin air!"

"No insurance, no assets. Nothing worthy of keeping you in his room all of the time!" Jeneva frowned. "Guess the old guy's gotta have something, since the administrator gave him the largest, most comfortable room in the facility. She kicked Mrs. Stith out of it, and moved the old lady to a narrow room in the other wing with a view of a brick wall."

Fresna now realized the reason Mrs. Stith took out her frustrations on her, in a toothy sort of way.

"Maybe we should try our hands in that direction, Terry," Jeneva said, poking her friend in the ribs. "Haven't you noticed how Ms. Tate behaves around Mr. Corvus? Normally, she's always laughing and cutting up with the residents, or joking around with the family members. But Mr. Corvus…"

"You're right," interrupted Terry. "The administrator does act like the old man is a member of royalty or something. Maybe he's in line to inherit a kingdom!"

Jeneva filled the hall with her derisive laughter. "Maybe Fresna will marry him, and live happily ever after. Maybe he'll even let her carry his purse!"

Without warning, both women crumpled to the ground.

Fresna blinked. Her bullies were on the floor, thrashing and groaning. How could they have fallen? They couldn't have slipped; they made no effort to move, not even to walk.

A rustling sound in the hall caught Fresna's attention.

Mr. Corvus, with his black, knitted afghan settled over his bony shoulders and straw bag gripped in his hand, loomed like a bird of prey. He raised his arms, which caused the blanket to form an image of black wings. The fringe edging of the afghan resembled feathers. Even at a distance, Mr. Corvus' eyes looked like bottomless black pools.

"Take what the crow offers, Mr. Corvus?" Fresna smoothed the wrinkles out of the bedspread, moving around the bed to ensure all the edges were even. She stumbled when her foot bumped into the old straw handbag next Mr. Corvus' chair. She frowned. With the wicker frayed and sticking out, it looked more like a disorganized bird's nest than a bag. "Live happily ever after? What are you talking about?"

Mr. Corvus touched Fresna's arm with his firm, yet gentle, fingers. "The enchantment born of the violent storm and intense sunshine will dissipate soon, my dear. Go out onto the patio now. Look upon the raven's magic reflected in the pool of water in the birdbath."

If any belief in "happily ever after" remained in Fresna's tender heart, her dreary, day-to-day reality had blasted it into oblivion long ago.

"Mr. Corvus, I am a middle-aged, married, personal care attendant. My job is to take care of the residents' soiled beds, wet diapers, and do my best to avoid Mrs. Stith's strong jaws and sharp teeth. When I'm at home, I have to pick up empty beer cans, prepare hot meals... which are not appreciated... and keep quiet so I do not disturb my husband while he plays his beloved video games. My husband of thirty years does not love me, or care about me, or cherish me. Rather, he sees me as an irritant. He only gets a job when I badger him to. And shortly after he gets one, he'll immediately lose it due to his lousy attitude and hot temper. If there's magic out there, it won't be for me. It's too late for me."

Fresna's eyes blurred with tears and her shoulders slumped under her unbearably heavy and interminable burdens.

Mr. Corvus pulled himself up straight, spreading his arms. With the moisture clouding her vision, he resembled an avenging phoenix, rising up out of the ashes.

THE REMAINING RAYS OF THE EVENING SUN SHONE through the window and pierced Ms. Tate's hair, making it appear a bright, burnished copper, the eye-catching color suitable for the adornments of a high priestess. Ms. Tate pursed her full lips. Her bronze eyes narrowed as she studied the two beaming, innocent faces across her desk. "Jeneva Valentine. What a beautiful, melodious name. It trips across the tongue, like a love song."

Jeneva smirked, lowering her eyes as she looked at her white shoes in feigned modesty.

"Too gorgeous of a name for such a mean-spirited, spiteful bitch."

Jeneva's jaw fell in shock.

"And Terry Snider. You are a follower, with an easily swayed, susceptible mentality. Not truly evil, but not strong enough to be truly good."

Terry's mouth opened and her eyes bulged.

"I gave you both a chance. A chance to be kind, to demonstrate you can do good deeds for others who needed you. If this was two thousand years ago, I'd have you both executed."

The two clutched each other and broke into exclamations of disbelief and fear.

Ms. Tate's mouth twisted. "I said, if this was two thousand years ago. The modern banishment is termination of employment."

Jeneva found her tongue. "But... but... but... why?"

The nursing home administrator rose, acting like an ancient queen passing judgment on two peasants. "You're indifferent to the needs of the patients. You're cruel to your co-workers."

"How did you—" Terry broke off when Jeneva stepped on her foot. "I mean, what makes you think that?"

A tiny dimple appeared at the corner of Ms. Tate's mouth. "Let's just say... a little bird told me."

IN MR. CORVUS' ROOM, Fresna reigned in her imagination and sneaked a careful peek at the resident. He was an old man in a nursing home, covered by an ancient black blanket. She laughed at her fancies, and gathered the dirty linen. She paused and glanced out the window. Huddled in the chair next to his bed, the old man followed her gaze.

"Remember that little crow you saw out there on the patio earlier? You felt like he was looking right at you, trying to get your attention, didn't you?" Mr. Corvus asked, his eyes locked on hers.

"A crow?" she frowned, focusing on the elderly man's full head of soft black hair topping his oddly-shaped, elongated head.

He must work really hard to keep from having white roots, Fresna thought.

Mr. Corvus' sharp black eyes sparkled, as he placed one knobby hand on top of his head. He studied her intently, as if he was trying to read her thoughts. "They say crows, or ravens as they are sometimes called, hold a rare magic. Like I said, the magic is known to be its strongest right after a powerful storm, one that is immediately followed by the brightest sunshine."

"Magic, Mr. Corvus?"

Fresna unintentionally glanced out the window. The birdbath was bare, its earlier occupant nowhere in sight.

"According to the ancient legend, if the raven offers you the opportunity to gaze into the pool, and you're brave enough to take that opportunity, you'll see something in the water that's of life and death importance to you." The old man rose unsteadily to his socked feet. "Go on, Fresna," he said, giving her a gentle nudge. "Take what he offers."

INEXPLICABLY IRRITATED WITH MR. CORVUS, Fresna continued with her work duties. She helped Mrs. Stith into her wheelchair. Then, she pushed the old lady down the hall toward the patio at a brisk clip.

Magic pools? Ravens?

When they reached the sliding glass doors, Fresna instantly froze in place. Her hands were wrapped so tight around the handles of Mrs. Stith's wheelchair, she was surprised the metal didn't bend. Her eyes penetrated the glass and landed on the birdbath. She had not meant to look at it, but her gaze tracked there of its own volition. The bird was perched on the edge of birdbath, patiently waiting for her.

Mrs. Stith screeched, "I've changed my mind! I want to go back to my room! Hurry up! You hear me?"

In her mind's eye, Fresna saw the years stretch before her with Mrs. Stith's screeching and Steve's whining. Mrs. Stith would one day get past her defenses and bite her. Another freak accident would lead to Steve collecting her life insurance money and living happily ever after.

The raven was here now, offering her an opportunity for her very own happily ever after. But, she didn't believe in magic.

Did she?

Fresna's feet turned toward the birdbath and walked to it, leaving the complaining Mrs. Stith sitting in her wheelchair by the sliding glass doorway. She felt incredibly foolish.

The raven waited, perched on the concrete, as if it was expecting her.

He'll just fly away when I get over there, Fresna reasoned to herself.

She reached the birdbath, but the raven didn't move, and continued to stare at her. Then, it bobbed its black head toward the still pool of rain water, as if it was telling her, "Look inside."

Feeling half fearful, half idiotic, and a snippet curious, Fresna leaned over the pool.

She could see herself in the water, and the bird perched along the edge. Fresna frowned. Suddenly, she was able to see something else in the pool.

The reflective surface revealed a picture, like an old television screen, of her husband, Steve, in their driveway.

What was happening to her?

She started to back away, but the harsh caw of the bird stopped her.

The pool revealed an image of Steve, carefully looking around, while using a wrench to loosen the bolts holding the tire on her car.

Fresna straightened and pressed her eyes shut. Her husband had tried to kill her. And, she was seeing it in a birdbath, for God's sake!

The sound of a throat clearing beside her made Fresna jump. Her eyes bulged.

A tall, slender man with short, slicked back, dark hair was standing right next to her. His suit, shirt, and tie were as black as the darkest night. His eyes were shining ebony, connecting intimately with hers. His nose was unusually long and hooked, resembling a bird's beak.

"Caw! I mean, Fresna! Damn, sometimes bilingualism can be a curse!"

Fresna slowly shook her head. He looked familiar. Add wrinkles, bent shoulders— "Mr. Corvus?"

He smiled. "Please. Call me Aviary."

A disturbance at the sliding glass door caused them to turn their heads.

"Get out of the doorway, you old witch! We have a score to settle with that fat cow and the old man!"

"We'll make them pay for getting us fired! Push the old bitch and the damn wheelchair out of the way, Terry!"

Jeneva? And Terry? Fired? And now they were after her and Mr. Corvus?

"What's it to be, Fresna? Do you want a life of happiness with me, who appreciates your gentle spirit and warm heart? Or do you want a life of misery with your husband, albeit a very short one since he wants you out of the way?"

"Damn it! She bit me!" Jeneva's outraged scream drowned out Terry's squeal of pain.

Looks like Mrs. Stith got a two for one, Fresna thought, with a hint of satisfaction. She wrenched her attention back to the man in front of her. She slowly, and regretfully, shook her head. "I can't take what the raven offers. I'm old, I'm tired, and I'm hopeless."

He pointed to the pool. "Look."

Fresna gazed into the water. She expected to see her limp hair, scattered with gray; her tired eyes, full of despair, and her sloping shoulders; holding the weight of her worries.

She squinted for a moment, then widened her eyes in shock. The woman she saw in the reflection had thick, glossy hair, with eyes bright with hope and happiness. Next to her was a face with a beak-like profile, staring at her. Love was naked in the bony features.

Fresna looked up. As she took his hand, she felt the warmth of the setting sun on her face. "Where will we go?"

"Not far. Not far, as the crow flies."

Having drawn their blood and routed the enemy, Mrs. Stith settled back in her wheelchair, and watched the two crows take flight. They circled, the glistening sun reflecting off their glossy, black wings. One wobbled a bit as the other protectively hovered. With a flourish of her wing, the newborn crow righted herself. Her companion cawed in approval.

Mrs. Stith watched until they both flew out of sight.

JADA RYKER is the author of the *Takes a Dare* mystery series. The books combine humor and murder into a total package of entertaining and fun Southern adventures. At the same time, Jada sketches in addiction/recovery issues and childhood angst with a deft and compassionate touch.

Jada lives in central Kentucky with her wonderful husband and their cat, rescued from the animal shelter. In her day job, Jada works in higher education. She holds a masters degree in public administration.

Jada loves feedback from readers, both one-on-one and through customer reviews on Amazon. Connect with Jada to share thoughts about her books by visiting her web site **www.JadaRyker.com** or emailing her at **Jada_Ryker@yahoo.com**. She is also on Facebook at **https://www.facebook.com/#!/jada.ryker**

Murder Takes a Dare and the sequel, *Mayhem Takes a Dare*, are available on Amazon in electronic and paperback versions. The third volume, *Arson Takes a Dare*, will be released Spring 2014. *Dog Days of Karma*, the first book in her new series, will also be released Spring 2014.

Life Sucks

RENEE' LA VINESS

AVAN SMILED AS HE WALKED through the double doors at precisely four o'clock. Doranda gave him a high five, grabbed her jacket, and headed out.

"Same time tomorrow," he said. Doranda agreed with a nod.

Avan enjoyed his new job as the evening lifeguard at the local recreational center. He was finally on his own, making a living, like his parents always wanted. He wasn't the lawyer or doctor they'd hoped for, but he was doing something he enjoyed.

Shortly before seven o'clock, the senior citizens and a couple of younger adults shuffled in for their nightly water aerobics class. Most of them said hello or nodded as they passed Avan. He was amazed at how strong people of seventy and older could be if they exercised regularly. "I want to be as healthy as you guys when I'm your age," he often told them.

The center had an "Open Swim Hour" until nine o'clock every night. Some of the old fogies hung around and visited or did some cool-down exercises to relax their muscles and prevent cramps after their hard workout. Not many people came for that final hour, so Avan spent much of the time doing mundane, rote chores.

Late one evening, a senior citizen swam to Avan's side of the pool. "You sure do waste a lot of time," he said in a gruff tone.

"Why do you say that, Mr. Howard?" Avan asked in the nicest voice he could muster after such an accusation. "I've swept the floor, put away all the beach toys, added water and chemicals to the pool, and started the vacuum. Everything else is done. I still have to sit up here and watch over my swimmers to be ready for rescue at all times."

"You could be doin' a lotta other stuff 'sides sittin' in that chair, half dozin' off."

"What did the previous lifeguard do?" Avan asked, hoping for a clue of what would make the old man happy.

"He sat his lazy a—you know, in that chair and fell asleep a few times. I told the lady up front about it, so he'd get in trouble, and he did, alright. They threw his durn butt right outta here."

"Well, I thank you for my job and I'll certainly do my best not to fall asleep while on duty, sir." Avan nodded at the man, who harrumphed and swam away.

ONE EVENING, one of the elderly women swam up to Avan. With furrowed eyebrows and squinted eyes, she asked how to get an old grump to leave her alone. Pointing him out, she said, "He keeps untying the halter strap around the neck of my swimsuit! Isn't that sexual harassment or something? Are you gonna do anything about him, or do I need to tell the manager or call the police, or just coldcock the jerk? I sure don't need the likes of him hanging around!"

Avan followed the point of her finger to see the same man who had practically called him lazy a few nights before. "I'll have a talk with him," he said.

Reaching the other end of the pool, Avan called the man aside.

"Mr. Howard, I'm sure you think it's fun to tease Ms. Singleton, but she's complained that you've gone too far and untied the top of her swimsuit."

"Oh, she did, did she? She honestly said I would do such a thing?"

"Are you saying you didn't?"

"She has no right to go around telling people our private business. That woman is a gossip!" Mr. Howard said.

As frustrating as Mr. Howard could be, Avan sometimes considered him borderline comical.

During the Open Swim Hour, Avan was putting toys away on the far side of the pool. He bent over to retrieve a waterlogged bandage. He'd lost count of how many had been found that night.

"What the hell do you think you're doing?" Mr. Howard bellowed. "Aren't you supposed to be watching us to make sure nobody drowns? Did you notice you can't see the pool very well with your back turned? Well, I did. I just might have to turn you in for inattentive behavior, young man!"

Avan almost fell into the wall when he heard Mr. Howard's angry tone. Before turning to face the old man, he took a deep breath and plastered a smile on his face.

"Wow, Mr. Howard, how nice of you to come across the pool to visit with me. What was that you were saying?"

"I-I didn't say anything important. This water is colder than normal tonight. Did you forget to adjust the temperature?"

"No, sir. I checked it a while ago. You're not coming down with a cold, are you?" He tried to sound concerned.

"I'm fine. You need to check that thermostat more often. I bet some brat kid turned it down for you."

"I doubt that's likely," Avan replied. "The center has taken precautions to prevent such a thing."

Mr. Howard followed along the inside of the pool as Avan continued working.

Reaching the supply closet, Avan escaped the man's stalking stare for only a moment while he retrieved the vacuum. It was his job to put the machine to work during the last hour of the day. After setting the vacuum in the water to sink, he connected the long, semi-clear flex hose to the pipe in the side of the pool, then turned on the suction.

The vacuum crept along the bottom of the pool, picking up small pieces of trash. "Ticka-ticka-ticka-ticka-ticka," it whispered, like a time bomb waiting to explode, or a rattlesnake preparing to strike.

Soon, a woman swam up against the hose. She must not have heard the ticking before she bumped into it. A screech tore through the air. "Shit!" she exclaimed.

Avan instinctively looked toward the woman. Her round eyes and the hand over her mouth told him the outburst had surprised her as much as anyone.

"I'm so sorry," she confessed as her head sunk between her shoulders. "I promise I'll try to be more mindful of my words."

Avan smiled as he returned to his lifeguard chair.

Mr. Howard swam near the hose that floated at the top of the water. "You need to run that vacuum after everyone's gone home for the night," he said. "It gets in the way when we're swimming." With a quick swat, he tried to push the hose out of his path. It bounced back as if rebelling. He pushed it again and held it out in front of him. The vacuum lifted off the floor of the pool and moved toward him. He let go and swam back to the shallow end of the pool.

When Avan arrived for work the next afternoon, Doranda, the day shift lifeguard, said the boss wanted to see him. Avan wondered if it had anything to do with the night before.

He stepped into Gloria's office. "You asked to see me?"

"Oh, hi Avan. Yes, I did. We received an anonymous call this morning. The man said you have been wasting time around the pool. What can you tell me about that?"

Avan laughed. "Mr. Howard thinks that pool is his own private property and he can boss me around. He told me a few nights ago that I needed to quit sitting in the lifeguard chair and that I could be up and doing a lot of other stuff, if I wasn't so lazy. He said he reported the previous lifeguard for being lazy and you guys got rid of him."

"Well, he's definitely wrong. The guy before you abandoned ship one evening. We showed up the next morning and he had left the building unlocked. After that, he just quit showing up. That's when we hired you to replace him."

Avan smiled. "Thanks."

"So, try not to get in target range of any grumpy, old men, okay?"

"No kidding." They laughed as Avan walked out of the office and turned toward the pool for his day's work.

Partway through the evening, Avan recognized a blonde-headed teen from a few nights before. The boy had been with a couple of dark-haired twins around the same age. This one had a cocky attitude and was built like a wrestler.

The seniors began complaining about the teen splashing them intentionally as he swam around the pool. One woman said he was stalking her and wouldn't allow her to swim more than a few feet from him.

Avan walked toward the teen and yelled over the splashing to get his attention. "Hey!" No answer. "Hey! You there!" The kid raised his hand and stuck up his middle finger before swimming away. Avan blew his whistle. The senior citizens cringed, moaned, and covered their ears. The kid swam on. Avan continued blowing the shrill whistle until the teen stopped and yelled at him.

"What's your problem, jerk?"

Avan replied, "I don't have a problem, but you do. Your fun in the pool is over for today. Time to get out."

"I don't have to get out if I don't want to," the teen replied.

"I'm sure the police will see it a little differently," Avan said as he raised his cell phone to call the police.

"Whoa, Dude! I'm outta here. Just give me a minute to get to the steps and I'll go."

Avan put his phone down and watched the young man leave. A loud applause erupted from the pool in support of Avan's bold confrontation of the bully. He blushed, then went back to his lifeguard chair to continue his watch.

After work that night, Avan checked the register to learn the teen's name and write him up as a troublemaker. "Jason Deal," he said out loud. "I'll know his name next time I see him."

Toward the end of the following night, only a few swimmers remained. Avan had finished most of his work and was relaxing in the chair as the vacuum cleaned the bottom of the pool.

Mr. Howard couldn't let the night pass without a sour word or two. Avan had become somewhat accustomed to the old man's daily grumbling, although it agitated him.

"Did you get that hairball over in the corner when you swept? I thought I saw it over there a minute ago."

"Yes, Mr. Howard. I swept it up. The floor is good and clean, now. The folks with the mops will make their way around in the morning."

Avan looked up at the clock. Five more minutes. Most of the other swimmers had left for the night. Only a handful remained and they were on their way out.

"You people haven't washed the windows, lately. They ought to add that to your job to keep your lazy butt busy."

Avan sighed and chose not to respond. He was glad the night was almost over. Turning back toward Mr. Howard, he saw the vacuum lift off the floor of the pool and move toward the old man. Something was wrong with the machine. Before he had time to react, it rose to the top of the water and pounced on Mr. Howard from behind. The old man opened his mouth to cry out, but the vacuum sucked him in before his voice could escape. His body distorted and condensed into a long, stringy shape as he traveled through the three inch wide hose.

Not believing his eyes, Avan's mouth fell open and he froze. He rushed to the edge of the pool and leaned over to jump in, but there was no time. The string of a man had snaked rapidly through the flex hose and into the wall of the pool. Mr. Howard wasn't his favorite person, but Avan would never have wished him any harm.

Avan ran to the supply closet where the large pumps were located. He was sure he wouldn't beat Mr. Howard to the pumps, but hoped the filters would halt his progress. Turning the pumps off, he wondered if Mr. Howard could survive such an ordeal. What condition would he be in? Would he be able to resume his previous form? If the whole thing really was a tragedy and not some crazy imagined event, how would he explain the incident to his boss? To the police?

Holding his breath, Avan pulled out the first filter. There was no sign of Mr. Howard. He replaced the filter and tried the second one. Nothing there, either. Beads of sweat and a prickly sensation covered Avan's body. His hands shook and thoughts raced as he considered what to do next.

"Oh, no! Maybe he's stuck in the pipe!" Avan jumped at the sound of his voice. He turned the pumps back on and rushed to the pool. He disconnected the hose and checked the suction. It was strong as ever. He replaced the hose and rushed back to the pumps to check the filters again, but he found no sign of Mr. Howard or his green, seaweed print swimsuit. No blood. No guts. Nothing.

Gloria's voice penetrated his thoughts. "Hey, Avan. What are you doing in here? It's time to shut this place down."

"Y-yes, Miss Gloria," he stammered. Spinning around and rising to his feet, he took a quick breath and put on his best poker face. "I was just checking to make sure everything was in good working order." He wondered if she had seen any of the events that brought him to the supply closet. Still leaning in the doorway, a smile was on her face and she seemed genuinely happy. No, he decided. She hadn't seen.

Avan slept in short, restless fits, that night. He had a recurring dream of watching Mr. Howard move through the vacuum hose and into oblivion. Unanswered questions plagued him. Did he really see Mr. Howard travel through the hose? How did Mr. Howard do that? Was he trying to get Avan into trouble? Maybe the crotchety old man was some kind of stretchy superhero and the bad attitude was just a cover. If that was the case, would the old fart come back and turn Avan in to the police for letting it happen?

Or, would he expect Avan to keep his secret? Could anyone be allowed to live if they knew such a secret?

AVAN WALKED IN WITH BAGGY SHADOWS under his bloodshot eyes the next afternoon.

"Hard night?" Doranda asked.

"Yeah, a little trouble sleeping."

"Take a pain pill. Works for me."

"Now you tell me." He aimed toward the lifeguard chair, sat down, signed in, and watched the swimmers. He had almost convinced himself the previous night's terror was only a bad dream. That's why he had kept dreaming it over and over. But, Mr. Howard wasn't at the pool. He wasn't there the next night, either. Nobody seemed to notice the old man's absence, so Avan assumed he was fine and everything he thought he'd seen was a momentary brain spasm from frustration. Lots of people had them, right? He decided to keep his wild imagination to himself. It was a few nights before he slept peacefully, again.

THINGS WENT ALONG SMOOTHLY and nobody gave Avan much grief for a while… until the night Jason Deal returned to the pool with his buddies. After hearing the boys talk about their foster home, he assumed they didn't have any proper training. They had probably been moved from home to home all their lives. Avan wondered if the kids had siblings who lived elsewhere. He'd heard that families were often divided for foster care and adoptions. He almost felt sorry for the boys, but they interrupted his thoughts with their trouble-making antics.

Avan blew his whistle and grabbed his phone, in case he needed to call the police.

"This is your last warning," he said as he pointed at them and set his jaw.

"But, it's only our first warning," one of the twins said in a sassy tone. He gave his brother a high five. Jason laughed at them.

"And it's also your last," Avan said firmly. "Next time you cause any trouble, you're out for the night. If I have to, I'll ban all three of you."

"We'll be good," Jason replied. As Avan walked away, he heard the boys cackling from behind. He knew they'd be up to no good in less than five minutes.

He was right. The twins started splashing Ms. Singleton and Mr. Franklin yelled for Avan's assistance.

Avan blew his whistle and motioned for the boys to leave the pool.

Jason spoke up, "I didn't do anything. Can I stay?"

"He's telling the truth," Mr. Franklin said. "He didn't do anything. It was the twins."

"Out!" Avan commanded the twins, sweeping his pointed finger toward the double doors. The twins headed for the steps to climb out.

"Awww, you ruined all our fun."

"You boys need someone to teach you what fun really is," Avan said.

"So, I can stay?" Jason asked.

"Okay, you can stay, Jason, but if I have *any* trouble out of you…"

"I got it." He motioned a thumbs-up sign to Avan and smiled as he swam away.

A carnival had opened in town that evening and many of the regulars were absent or left early. Shortly before closing, Jason was the only one remaining in the pool.

After Avan set the vacuum to work, he took the broom to the other side of the pool to sweep the walkway.

When he bent down to pick up a rubber band, a large wave of water flung up onto the walkway and all the sweeping he had done was washed away. He turned to see Jason trying to contain his laughter. Avan gave him a warning look and returned to his sweeping. When he got the wet trash swept together again, another wave hit. Laughter followed the wave before Avan could turn around.

"That's it. Get out of the pool and go home." Avan pointed toward the exit.

"If you want me outta the pool, lifeguard, you gotta come and get me. I bet I can hold you under water longer than you can hold me under. Wanna see?"

Avan wasn't sure whether he should get angry or worried. He knew Jason could easily drown him. How would he get him out of the pool? Nobody else was there.

"Here, I'll come help you into the water," Jason said as he started to raise himself at the edge to climb out.

Before Avan could respond, the vacuum shot out of the water and landed on Jason's head. The teen had no forewarning of the attack. The vacuum sucked him in, the same way it had sucked in Mr. Howard.

Avan blinked as he watched Jason's body slide through the flex hose and disappear into the wall of the pool.

I have to be imagining things. How can that happen? What am I going to do if those twins come back here looking for him?

On cue, the boys walked through the double doors. Avan's heart stopped.

"Where's Jason?" the bigger twin asked.

"Uh… Jason?" Avan responded as slowly as possible. He had to think of something.

"Yeah, the guy who got to stay when you sent us packing earlier."

"Oh, Jason. Um… he left." It was the truth after all.

"What do you mean, he left? We're his ride home."

"He just left." Another truth. Still no air in Avan's lungs.

The boys muttered something to each other and left.

Avan's heart resumed its beat. Running his fingers through his hair, he reviewed the events of the last few minutes in his head. Then, he remembered.

Dropping the broom, he rushed to the supply closet. He knew he wouldn't find anything in the filters, but he had to check. What if someone else came in and found blood and guts in the filter tomorrow morning?

After checking everything, Avan was pretty sure Jason was wherever Mr. Howard had gone. He hoped they weren't conspiring against him.

Finishing up his chores, he locked up the center and went home.

THE REST OF THE WEEK, Avan didn't run the vacuum. He was afraid. If people continued disappearing, it wouldn't be long before someone noticed. He was surprised nobody had asked him about Jason after the night he disappeared.

When Avan showed up for work on Monday afternoon, Doranda met him at the double doors. "Gloria wants to see you," she said.

Fear gripped his heart and squeezed. "What's up?" he asked as calmly as possible.

"Something about the vacuum, I think."

Avan walked slowly to Gloria's office. *What am I going to tell her? Did she find something in the filters? How am I going to explain it?* He had no way of knowing what confrontation awaited him.

Gloria's door was open when he arrived. "Hi Avan. Come on in," she said. "Please close the door behind you."

That couldn't be good. She never wanted him to close the door. He sat in the chair, wondering if the police were assembling outside the room to take him away when he tried to escape.

"I noticed you didn't run the vacuum for a couple of nights last week," she said. "Why not?"

"There weren't that many people in the pool. Everyone was at the carnival. I figured the pool wasn't very dirty. I was wondering about having Doranda run that thing. There's a whole hour between the afternoon open swim and the high school group," he explained.

"We expect you to run the vacuum at the end of the night so the water can settle down after it's finished."

No chance of getting out of it. "Okay," he said.

"I'm surprised at you, Avan. I've never known you to skimp on the job. I hope this is a one-time thing."

"It is, Miss Gloria," he assured her. But, he didn't want to run the vacuum.

That night, a young girl came in to swim. She had a figure Avan couldn't miss and she was showing it off with every move. "Hi-ya, Honey," she said as she leaned in to whisper in his ear. "Wanna come with me to a really cool party, tonight? There's gonna be some good stuff to smoke, if you know what I mean." Her warm breath on his neck gave him goose bumps and made his knees weak.

Avan looked at her eyes and tried to determine her age. "You're not a day over seventeen are you? How are you going to go to a party after this place closes? I'm sure your parents are going to expect you back home. Curfew's at ten."

"Well, maybe I am a little young, but maybe I ran away from home about a year ago and maybe my parents have no clue where I'm at. I've managed to make it more than halfway across the country since then. Good looks serve you well, when you're a girl who's going places."

"I have no need to go to a party. You really should go back home to your mom and dad so they can take care of you. Life is just too tough out here on your own," he said.

She stepped close enough for her breasts to lightly touch his chest, stirring things that should not be stirred. Tilting her head slightly and drooping her decorated eyelids, she asked, "Can I take you with me, Honey?"

"Are you here to swim, or not?" he asked. "I could lose my job if I'm not watching over the pool."

"Who cares about your silly ol' job?" she snapped. "I can make you feel so good you won't care." She stuck out her bottom lip and turned on the puppy dog eyes. "Pwease say you'll go to da party with li'l ol' me, tonight?" She blinked her eyes at him.

Avan sighed. *This one watches way too much TV.* "Are you swimming or leaving?" he repeated.

"Oh, all right." She backed away and walked toward the pool. "But, you'll change your mind. I know you will."

Throughout the night, the young girl teased Avan. She was pretty, but not his type. He might not be a super catch, but he expected a lot more than that kind of trouble for a date.

A few minutes later, Avan stood outside the supply closet. He didn't want to open the door. He didn't want to see the vacuum. His hand rested on the door knob, but he couldn't turn it.

"Whatcha doin' back here?"

He yanked his hand from the knob when he heard her behind him.

"Can I go in there with you? Is it big enough to get comfy together?"

"Only lifeguards are allowed in here."

"I won't tell if you won't, Honey… and you can call me Tiffany."

In a stiff voice, Avan replied, "Look, I've got to do my job. I have people to watch over. You either need to leave me alone or go home."

The girl's eyes opened wide and she stood up straight. "Well, I think I'll just go have a swim."

When she turned away, Avan looked at the ceiling and mouthed the words, "Thank you." Without thinking about his fear, he turned back around and entered the supply room for the vacuum.

Avan was very uncomfortable with the girl harassing him all night. He hoped she would find someone else to bother. *I wish I had control of that vacuum. I'd sic it on her, for sure.*

As soon as the thought jumped into his brain, he felt bad. He had never wished harm to anyone before. She might be annoying, but he had no reason to wish her bad luck. He went to work sweeping the walkway around the pool.

Everyone left early that night—everyone except Tiffany Trouble. She swam near Avan as he worked. He was very aware of her ridiculous efforts to show off her hips and breasts. He stayed busy and only glanced her way to make sure she wasn't drowning.

When she swam to the edge of the pool and spoke to him, he only looked up for a moment.

"Have you decided to go to the party with me, Honey? It's gonna be a lot of fun, I promise."

"I can't go to a party. I have to close the center."

"I can wait on you."

"I have somewhere to be after I close."

"Ahhh, a girlfriend. Is she as sexy as I am?"

Avan looked at the clock. Five more minutes. *Forever.*

"Go on back to your swimming. I have to finish my work," he said.

After returning the broom and dustpan to the supply closet, he was ready to collect the vacuum and close. He looked toward the pool to tell Tiffany it was time to go.

"Yoohoo, Honey! Over here!" she called. He followed her voice and saw her waving something in the air. Then, he saw her full, round breasts staring at him above the water. She was waving her bikini top in the air to get his attention.

"Why me?" he asked, looking at the ceiling.

"Put that back on!" He marched toward Tiffany, wishing the vacuum would just fix the problem for him.

Before he got to her, the vacuum attacked her from behind, like it had done to Mr. Howard and Jason. He had summoned it. He knew it was true. He had summoned the vacuum and it obeyed him. His chin fell and his eyes filled with tears as he realized the power he unwillingly held.

I'm a villain. A real, live villain. I can have people sucked into the vacuum just by thinking it. Did I make it attack Mr. Howard and Jason? I'm not a cruel person, am I? He covered his face with his hands and cried. He didn't care if someone came in and saw him. He was a villain… a horrible criminal.

After the usual checks on both filters, when he was certain there was no sign of Tiffany in the system, he closed down the recreation center and went home. He left a note telling Gloria he was sick and would stay home from work the next day.

Sleep was not an option for Avan, that night. He was afraid to sleep. He had to decide if he was crazy and none of the recent events were real, or if he was a mad man full of hate and violence. He didn't know if he should turn himself in to be evaluated, or not. His parents would be so disappointed in him. Since there were never any missing person reports on the news, he finally decided he was probably losing it.

ON FRIDAY, Avan set an appointment with a psychiatrist for following Monday morning. He only had to get through one more night at work, then he could lock himself in his little apartment for the weekend.

Avan kept to himself most of the night and seldom smiled. Some of the swimmers asked if he was okay. "I'm fine. Just not feeling my best," he would answer before waving them away. Nobody challenged his response.

During the last hour of Open Swim, Avan kept himself busy around the pool. Friday nights usually required more work to shut the place down for the weekend.

One of the regular Friday night kids asked Avan for a beach ball. "Why can't you get it yourself?" Avan snapped at the boy, but he got the ball, because it was what he would normally do.

A little while later, the ball bounced up on the walkway where Avan was sweeping. "Hey! Watch where you're throwing stuff!" Avan yelled.

"I'm sorry. It bounced off her head," the kid said as he and his sister giggled.

A few minutes before closing, the boy and his sister were about to climb out of the pool, but he stopped near Avan, first. "Is there something I can do to help you feel better?" the boy asked.

"Yeah, you can take a ride in the vacuum." Avan huffed. As soon as he said the words, the vacuum raised near the boy's head and dropped beside him. Avan blinked to make sure he'd seen that correctly. He thought about it, willing the vacuum to suck the boy in, like Mr. Howard and the others. The vacuum came near, but sank back to the floor of the pool.

"Hey, you guys, come on! Let's go home to Mom and Sparky!" a man called out to the kids.

"I'm coming, Dad!" the boy yelled as he turned and swam away.

Avan was a nervous wreck. That was an innocent kid and he almost willed the vacuum to have him for dinner.

After everyone left for the night, Avan sat on a chair near the pool. He still needed to put up the vacuum and a couple other things before he could go home for the weekend. He had loved being a lifeguard until the night Mr. Howard "took his trip". He was almost certain he was an unintentional murderer, but, he needed to know the truth. If he was the one causing all the horrible events, he had to know before he hurt someone else.

Avan needed to spend a few minutes in the pool. With no swimmers to watch over, he could relax for a little bit. He really needed to relax.

He swam the length of the pool a couple of times. It felt good to stretch his muscles and move through the warm water. He turned to go to the other end of the pool just in time to see the vacuum over his head.

JORDAN SMILED AS HE WALKED through the double doors at precisely four o'clock. Doranda gave him a high five, grabbed her jacket, and headed out.

"Same time tomorrow," he said. Doranda agreed with a nod.

FROM HER EARLY TEENS, Renee' entertained as a ventriloquist and country/western singer. Later, as a devoted wife and home-school mom, she took on extra challenges from coaching her boys' sports teams to organizing and running groups and events. In more recent years, she can play a mean game of pool—and also loves to swim in a pool—not at the same time, of course. When she has time, she dabbles in graphic designs and photography.

Published in multiple short story anthologies, magazines, and newspapers, Renee' loves writing fiction and nonfiction.

"I grew up with an addiction for reading and writing. If it was written, I had to read it. If it wasn't written, I had to write it."

Playing with her grandchildren and volunteering for the local schools keep Renee' on the move. She also runs a local critique group for children's book writers in Oklahoma, where she lives happily with her husband, their nervous Corgi and two fighting fish.

Renee' connects with her fans at www.reneelaviness.com or at facebook.com/Author.ReneeLaviness.

Go Towards the Light

ANGEL COX

SHE WAS PAPER THIN with translucent white skin. Her silver-white hair hung around her shoulders like a shawl made from moonlight. By contrast, he was tall and dark. He loomed protectively over her. The soft glow that seemed to emit from her was quickly captured by his darkness like a black hole. Their appearance in the cool night was surreal as they walked hand-in-hand down the almost empty street, she taking two steps for his one.

She was from the past; an old soul. Her knowing smile held volumes of stories. Her pale blue eyes looked deep inside everyone that passed by, sharing their secrets.

He was from the future. His darkness was from the fact that he did not exist yet, but was only a shadow of what was yet to come. He walked by without ever acknowledging anyone, as if they were not there, because to him they weren't. Only their memories wafted by with a faint, musty smell of lilacs and old cigars.

The two were here for a purpose. The world had forgotten its past. When that happened, people were destined to make the same mistakes again, only this time with even more tragic effects. Their goal was to refresh some memories and to make people aware of what was to come before it was too late.

They stood on a street corner as if they had nowhere to go. A man rushed up to them and pushed the cross walk button twice. His hat was pulled down over his eyes and he seemed in a hurry to either get somewhere, or get away as quickly as possible. She reached into her pocket and pulled out a single daisy. It looked as if it had just been picked from someone's yard, which was impossible here in this city of concrete and steel. She held it out to the man. He was surprised by the gesture and immediately seemed to slow down. Gently, he took it from her. He remembered this from his earlier years. He looked at her and smiled, bringing the flower to his nose. The sign told him to walk, and he did. It was a start.

Humanity had ceased to have a reason to exist. God was no longer feared. Churches were now places to hide from the daily sins of life. Words from the pulpit were sugar coated with grace and forgiveness. There was no shock value left. Lust and greed were all a part of life and dealt with like dirt under the rug. Children did not trust their parents, and parents did not know their children. Role models did not exist. Integrity was swapped for fame, no matter if it was good or bad. Only the attention mattered.

Mistakes of the past had to be revisited, and the goodness of neighbors and family had to be restored. Pride in work needed to be found again. Self-motivation and gratitude needed to be brought back into the light. The world needed something to work together toward a common goal; humility.

A single tear moved slowly down the crease of the pale woman's nose and rested in the corner of her mouth. He bent down and gently kissed it away, but there was no smile on his lips. He knew what was in store for them. His black eyes bore into hers saying stay focused. He loved her with every fiber of his soul. Without her, he would be nothing. She held everything that ever mattered. All memories were kept within her. She would never let them die. She knew their power and made sure they were kept ready for the future when they would be needed again. He knew no one, including himself, could exist without her. The book read: *For when the future overcomes the past, life of all kind will cease to continue.*

The man, holding the daisy, opened the door and went straight to the kitchen. He walked over to his wife and planted a kiss on her lips. Her surprise was apparent. He laughed and then told her he wanted to go away for the weekend; maybe to the beach. She felt his forehead in mock concern. He reached in his coat pocket and pulled out the flower and put it behind her right ear. As he left the room she reached for the flower wondering where he could have found a daisy this time of year.

HE LOOKED AT HIMSELF IN THE MIRROR. He could hardly make out his own features now. Each day he became darker and less detailed. This was not a good sign. The only things that were still distinguishable to him were his piercing eyes. They were black pools of ink. Time was running out. Without a future, the past would die. He had to protect her from that. She had struggled too long and hard to let her down. While she rested, he ventured out into the rain. He felt only a sense of urgency.

He walked past the school and past the police station. He rounded a corner and found himself walking up the steps of the library. It was a huge stone building. It looked like it had been around for at least a century. The heavy wooden doors softly whooshed as he made his way into the hall of books. His wet shoes squeaked on the marble floor, making the old lady behind the desk scowl at him. He never even looked her way, but he could smell her heavy perfume and it made him sad.

He walked straight to the classics. He pulled heavy volumes of books from the shelves and stacked them on a back table. As he opened the first cover, he was astonished at the power the words held. He read all day: Shakespeare, Hemmingway, Steinbeck, and Tolstoy.

After that he found a book of famous quotes and speeches. He read Lincoln's and Kennedy's. He loved Patton's strength and Martin Luther King's wisdom. He read scriptures and even plowed through some of Nostradamus' ramblings. They made him laugh. But even he realized that the future could be altered by the acts of man and nature. Life was not mapped out. It was created and changed with every breath that held a decision or a promise.

He made his way back to her. She was lying awake. Her blue eyes looked gray. As he walked in the room she smiled and took in a deep breath, taking from him the knowledge of the past he had just ingested. It made her feel better. They depended on each other for their very existence. It was her turn to learn about the future.

She took his hand and closed her eyes. At first she saw nothing. Then things began to come into view as if through a heavy rain. It took only 34 seconds before she opened her eyes, shaking uncontrollably. She covered her face and wept openly. He couldn't console her. He was the reason for her sorrow.

The one thing she never felt was defeat. There was plenty of sadness along the way, but even when battles were lost there was always a winner. Some played harder than others while some just played dirty. But even the losers took something from their loss and made a change in their lives. Man can never go backward, but his past can light the way for his journey.

The world thinks there are no more surprises. Its inhabitants thought this back in the earlier years. That's why there are surprises—changes come unannounced. They take us unaware and astonish us with their newness. It's like finding money in your pocket, or seeing a falling star streak through the sky. One minute you are looking at a sky that hasn't changed in centuries, then something new appears and changes the whole view. It makes you smile and alters your whole train of thought. We even make wishes on falling stars because we feel their magic of change.

Some surprises take time and sweat. Discoveries and inventions don't usually happen overnight. Then some just fall into our lap due to inconveniences or just pure luck. These make our past rich with knowledge and our future hopeful for something new and fresh.

"We can learn from history how past generations thought and acted, how they responded to the demands of their time and how they solved their problems. We can learn by analogy, not by example, for our circumstances will always be different than theirs were. The main thing history can teach us is that human actions have consequences and that certain choices, once made, cannot be undone. They foreclose the possibility of making other choices and thus they determine future events." - Gerda Lerner

THE WORLD AWOKE TO A STRANGE OCCURRENCE. Overnight, all over the earth, people awoke to a substance that covered the ground. It was the consistency of a dumpling, a little wet and spongy. It smelled of honey and tasted even better. They had heard of this before in the wilderness of Egypt.

Some saw this as a sign of the end. Others spoke of it as a true testament from God that he was still with them. Others didn't care where it came from and they stuffed their bellies full of the sugary substance. It happened for three nights-in-a-row, and on the fourth day the people were already tired of its appearance and they were glad it was gone. So much for the power of miracles.

Weeks later several large scale disasters occurred on the same day. Major fires broke out in Europe, a huge hurricane hit a populated coast of Asia, and tornadoes danced across the Midwestern USA Not one single life was lost! Man praised their own technology for saving so many people in the face of these disasters, and life went on.

The future became dimmer and darker. He was just a shadow now. He could not go out except at night and away from the lights of the city. There he would walk the moonlit countryside with her and listen to her tales of great men that won against huge odds and people that fought for beliefs and freedom. These ideas were strange to him, but they gave him hope that humanity could once again pull itself up from the muck of life and start over with a clean spirit.

He was confused by her stories of the martyrs of her time. He couldn't comprehend the idea of dying for a cause. That just didn't ever happen in his world. People fought like hell to stay alive. Nothing was important enough to die for in his time. How could anything get done if the good ones died? In the future, death was a fleeting thought. Important people died and the world thought about them for a minute, then everything moved on as before. The only life that really mattered was your own.

The past was proud of her people and their accomplishments. They never truly died. They were immortalized in books, statues, songs, and on mountainsides. The only problem was people had forgotten how to live their lives for a reason. Not for the moment, but for the sake of their children and grandchildren. No one looked beyond the present and what could make them happy right now.

This thought made the past's shoulders slump and her eyes glisten with held back tears. She felt the weight of the world and realized she might not be strong enough to carry it much longer. Their weaknesses made their determination stronger. They were fighting for each other now. He embraced her and looked deep into her eyes. This time the message was this: You are far too important to me to ever let you go.

THE FUTURE MOVED QUICKLY through the city's crowded streets. He wasn't even noticed. He was only a foreshadow now, mostly ignored because the present was so glaring and yelling for attention with each horn blast. He reached out and touched as many people as he could. With his touch each person experienced a fleeting glimpse of their own future. It was almost subliminal in its clarity, but the impact was amazing. Some people physically stopped moving and the wave of motion was interrupted for a second. He walked for miles, impacting hundreds of people. The flow grew slower. People began looking beyond their thoughts and at the others around them. Some looked perplexed, as if they had just seen a ghost. Others were obviously disturbed by what they had just experienced. But the effect was definitely one of slowing down. And then, as if a giant clock had wound down and ceased its ticking, everyone stopped. The city fell silent.

A single child stood among the frozen people. She looked up at the looming shadow and smiled. "What's your name?" he asked.

"Destiny," she answered. With her smile, the air seemed to warm and the world began to slowly move again.

The future made his way back. As he walked into the room she could see the difference in his appearance. His midnight black eyes held a spark again. She took his hand and they began their journey back to where they had come.

"Destiny is not a matter of chance, it is a matter of choice; it is not a thing to be waited for, it is a thing to be achieved." -William Jennings Bryan

ANGEL COX is a sixth grade English/Language Arts teacher, and writer, living in Fort Worth, Texas. Her genre of writing is dark fiction, with a preference for Flash fiction. In 2013, Angel's first anthology entitled was published.

Through the support of Fiction Writers' Group, she also has four short stories published in three different anthologies, and is heading an anthology project for a charity.

"Writing frees the soul to explore things through words that may be experienced in life. The challenges of society are highlighted in my stories so that our eyes may be opened wider, and we become more open-minded and less judgmental of one another." Find out more at: **www.dayinthedark.com.**

Phone Call

J. ROSE ALEXANDER

THIS SHORT STORY IS A PART OF "THE FACTION STORIES" UNIVERSE.

I DIDN'T EXPECT THE PHONE TO RING, but that's true of anyone. What I truly didn't expect was who was on the other side of the line.

I had been in my dojo for daily practice. Usually I spent that time there in the morning, but for some reason, I had come back. The swords hadn't given me any reprieve, nor had the *sais* or the *bo*. I felt restless. Meditation wasn't working well either. Some ninja master I was. I couldn't get myself to sit still.

I forced myself to full lotus and inhaled slowly and I could sense him in the door. I opened my eyes and smiled at Jimmy. He leaned up from the door where he was standing, put fist to palm and bowed, then stepped in.

Even my husband would not to enter my sanctuary without obeisance.

I rose to my feet as he walked over to me. "Is something bothering you, master?" He teased me lightly, easily, putting a gentle hand on my arm.

"Yes, but it's ephemeral still," I said.

"Who speaks? The wife or the ninja?" He caressed my arm softly.

"Both," I smiled. "And you keep that up, they are both taking you to the mat." I nodded at his hand tracing along my skin.

"Maybe," he said, leaning in, "that's why I'm here."

"The master needs her meditation and exercise."

"Meditation, I'll agree to," Jimmy answered, leaning in even closer, "but I need you to step outside your dojo and be my wife for a while."

"Mmm," I agreed. "Maybe I'll forgo the meditation."

He slipped his hand down my arm, then headed for the door. "I thought you might."

WITH OUR EXERCISE ACHIEVED for the day in places other than the dojo, I rested my head on his chest as we watched television. These moments, these quiet, gentle moments between our long stretches away: away from our home in Zephyr, were the ones I treasured most of all. Here, only here, could I ever feel truly and completely me. Where I could take off my glasses, not put on the mask, sit around in yoga pants and not care about who saw what.

The jangle of the phone ripped through the quiet house and I grabbed it from the cradle next to the couch so as not to wake our little girl asleep upstairs.

"Hello?"

"Beth?" came the question in a familiar voice.

"Stan?" I asked, looking at Jim and giving him my shocked face. "What's up? I haven't heard from you in over two years."

"I'm on an assignment that's required me to be out of touch," he said. "I'm sorry I couldn't call you sooner."

I laughed. "Should you even be talking to me, then?"

"I need your help. I need to talk to someone who hasn't been at the crowning of Miss Corn Husker for the past two years."

All the unsettled feelings that had been plaguing me rushed out with my next breath; this was what I had been waiting for. A phone call. Sweet relief, I could now concentrate on the conversation. "Miss Corn Husker?" I asked.

"I'm in Iowa, and the corn is killing me," he offered.

"Corn? Is some big secret project you're working on?" I asked.

"Well, it's not really classified. It's secret the way…" he paused. "… the way your identity is."

Oh. "Ninja level? What do you need help with?"

"It's more esoteric than you coming here and kicking ass. I need some advice," he said.

"Advice?" I asked, feeling my eyebrow rise.

"Yes," he confirmed."I've been involved in an assignment to find these children who were exposed to a certain chemical. This was one of those classified experiments that yielded nothing, or so they thought. They didn't do their research very well."

"Do you have weird mutated third arms going on here, Stan?" I asked.

"No, but you're on about the mutants," he said. "The area I'm in was blanketed with a chemical wasn't carefully researched. But, back in the seventies, the… uh, let's just call them a government agency had used the exact same area for a different chemical test that apparently failed. They located the experiments where people had previously been exposed to other test chemicals."

"Oh, no," I said. "They double exposed the population?"

"Yup," he said. "And the results have been these kids who apparently have fantastic abilities. These kids didn't realize they were fantastic abilities, though. One of the exposed kids was diagnosed with astatic seizures, and didn't realize what was going on. Well, the FBI is trying a pilot program here and I have to make contact with all them."

"All?" I asked. "How many were there?"

"Oh, dozens were exposed the second time," he said. "But only a handful had a particular type of double exposure."

"So, what's this pilot program?"

"Officially, on the books? It's called Project GC One-sixty-two," he said. "In my notes? Well, they haven't picked a team name yet."

"Team name…" I said. "Stan, are you creating superheroes out there in the corn?"

"Yes," he said.

"Oh, Jesus, Stanley," I said, putting a hand to my forehead. "Is this really a good idea?"

"It was my idea, when I heard about this," Stanley answered.

"They're kids, aren't they?"

"Just about sixteen," he said. "Beth, with the exception of one hiccup, they were awesome at the parade."

"The parade?" I gasped.

"A float blew up," he said. "I have never encountered a city more soaked in dishonesty and international intrigue than Downing City. And coming from me, that says a lot."

From Mister FBI himself, it was a lot.

"Whoever it is that has mobbed up this city, has a clue that there is a level of government interest in these kids. They have been trying to kill high schoolers left and right, and we can't get a bead on him. Her. Whoever. I don't feel like I can, in good conscience, leave these kids out there without some kind of defense."

Killing students because they were accidentally exposed to some idiot government program. I shook my head; I couldn't disagree with what Stanley was trying to do. "Well, I can't condone or condemn anything the FBI does, Stan," I said. "If you think they can handle it…"

"I do," he said. "But I need some help."

"Help with what?" I was still confused. If he didn't need me to come out there and help him kick ass, which I certainly wouldn't mind doing, was he asking about cake and punch?

"They are meeting with me this afternoon to pick names so I can get them IDs and place orders and start them off as superheroes. But, what the hell do I tell them? How do I help them?"

"You're really making more superheroes?"

"They don't like the term 'superheroes'," he said, and I could hear the laugh in his voice. "They prefer 'masked avengers'. You were always my mentor when it came to fighting crime, and now I'm mentoring others. You never sat me down and explained the ins and outs of the superhero gig."

"No. I never did, because you weren't putting on a mask. What I taught you was… well. Basics. I never made you come to the dojo. You never said you wanted to."

"I never did. Being a superhero looked like too much work. Secret identities, changes of clothes, all that training you do. But, now, I'm stuck. What do I tell them? What would you tell them?"

I paused as a chill ran up my spine. There was an eerie foreshadowing in his request as I wondered what I *would* tell brand new superheroes.

So many things flashed through my mind at that moment. Time I had spent behind the mask, with a sword, sneaking through the streets of New York. The few times I had put my mask back on and prowled the streets of Los Angeles, or San Francisco. The utter thrill of confusing and confounding a thief. The adrenaline rush of stopping a rape or murder. That pervasive, permeating feeling of *good* and *right*.

I shook my head, remembering the hilarious conversations that could result from having a secret, masked identity. The fun you could have toying with the people who tried to guess who you were. The fright when someone got too close. The joy of finding that one person you wanted to share all of your secrets with.

Even the skirting of the law, the deep dark secrets I held or shared with only the man who shared my bed, reminded me of all of the people I had saved. The lives that were able to continue. The women, and men, who could sleep well at night because I had put that mask on.

And. The Sound.

That one sound, which still haunted my dreams. Even years later when I had done all the good I could with those abilities, and powers, the sound of the first maiming—the snap of bone, the scream of consuming pain—still came back to me. The gangbanger would have killed me without a thought; yet I was the one who had to be haunted each night by That Sound.

What would I tell new superheroes about the adrenaline; the good, and the pain that went with the mask and cape and secret identity?

"Well. I, um…" I stuttered. There was suddenly so much I could tell him, but the basics were the best; there were things you couldn't, and shouldn't, explain.

"Your mask doesn't protect you, it protects those you love. Don't take it off. This isn't about glory, it's about justice. You can't be everywhere at once, so don't try to be. You have to have a life without your mask as well. Learn to protect your teammates first and foremost. And try not to let on if you don't know what you're doing; people will lose confidence in you." I thought another moment. So much more lingered in my mind, but it wouldn't do any good. "I guess that's what I would tell them."

I could almost hear him thinking. "What about fun?"

Oof. Fun? High schools kids on the verge of adulthood might make that mistake. "Stan, there's some thrill in it, and some fun," I said. "But you when lob off the head of another living being, get the bloody shit beat out of you, or have to watch another person die because you couldn't save them? It stops being fun."

"I think they already know that," he said.

"Why?"

"They lost a classmate to an attack, and they encountered a very badly burned person at the parade. He died only a few minutes after reaching the hospital. There was no saving him."

I wanted to get out of my chair, find these prodigies-by-proxy and give them all a collective hug. They would see the bodies in their dreams. I pursed my lips. "Have they… killed anyone yet?"

"No!" he gasped. "They're children, Beth!"

"Stanley, you know damn well what I mean."

"Do I?"

"What you do becomes who you are."

There was silence, then, "I forgot about that."

"I didn't. But you're doing what I was doing then. You're training children, teenagers, to be ruthless killers. To make decisions that normal people in normal situations would never have to make. This isn't all fortune and glory. Even if they aren't normal, as the others weren't, they could until this moment pretend they were. Now, once the blinders come off, you have forced them into a world that most adults can't handle. The black and white will run to grey."

"Have I done the wrong thing here?"

Stanley was not one to question himself. I took a quiet moment to look at my husband next to me. He watched with a raised eyebrow, clearly listening and clearly knowing what we were talking about. No secrets, not since the day he found out. I smiled at him; he was my rock, my reality, and most certainly my reason for still putting my mask on, even if only rarely now. He secretly loved the intrigue as well.

"No," I finally answered him. "No you haven't. There is far more reward than there is trauma. The others are happy now, even if they know what they are capable of. If you teach them well, teach them to follow their hearts, make sure they are upright and moral people, their reward will be a thousand times more than any tribulation."

He paused. "I think you've given me plenty to chew on here."

"Stan," I said. "If you, or they, need help, just call me," I said. "I can always lend a hand."

He laughed. "They'd get a kick out of the White Ninja showing up," he said. "I'll keep you in reserve. Thanks for indulging me, Beth."

"Hey, I'm always ready to spring to the rescue."

"Tell me about it," Jim mumbled. I hit him with my slipper.

"I promise that I will call more often."

"You'd better," I said. "You're one of the good guys."

"I'm glad someone thinks so. Bye, Beth."

"Bye, Stan." I hung up the phone.

"What he's up to?" Jim asked.

"Oh not much," I answered. "Just making new superheroes."

"Never a dull moment between the two of you," Jim said, turning back to the television.

J. ROSE ALEXANDER is the author of a few poems here and there, co-author of *The Faction Stories*, and host of the intermittently updated blog, Down Write Nuts at **jrosealexander.blogspot.com**. She lives in Pennsylvania with her husband and three—make that four—cats. Chatter box, compulsive writer, *bon vivant*, stunt commuter, and a ninja in her dreams, J. Rose enjoys losing herself in the capes and masks of her superheroes, finding new trouble for her witches and werewolves—and is always on the look out for a new adventure, on the page or in real life.

Quest for Pain

ANTHONY HULSE

HYDE PARK, LONDON, 2001

MARK COCHRANE IGNORED THE CHILDREN when they mocked him. Within his fragile mind, he was not in London, but in Baghdad. The man was still a prisoner and the suffering would not cease. The impoverished children mimicked his walk as they waddled along on the balls of their feet, the tramp unaffected by their cruelty.

Filthy attire hung off his wasted body. The old RAF jacket had seen better days and was tied around his waist with a bit of old cord. His straggly, unkempt hair and beard were in dire need of a shampoo, the lice having found a new home.

Walking across the park toward his favorite bench, he noticed the passers-by distancing themselves from him. He relished the hours he could relax on the bench. It was a welcome change from the cardboard box.

Mark squinted at the blinding sun in the blue sky, the same merciless sun that had scorched him in Baghdad. After he returned home to London, Mark was offered rehabilitation and a measly sum of compensation. He was insulted by their paltry offer. Is that all he was worth after giving so much for his country? The disturbed man attended rehab for a few weeks, before he gave up on it, as they had given up on him. What did they know? They weren't there, were they?

His wife, Judy, seemed to understand at first, unlike their three children who chose to distance themselves, confused about the change in their father. He used to sit for hours, rock in his chair and stare at the wall.

Judy had tried to coax her husband to bed at night, but often found him stooped over, his hands on his feet. Sometimes he would be like that for hours. Judy had contacted the rehabilitation services, who conveyed to her he would no longer cooperate with them, so they were unable to help. Finally, she turned to a psychiatrist who agreed to talk to Mark, but he would not listen and was unresponsive.

Judy moaned that she was tired of getting up through the night and cleaning his waste, as he refused to use the toilet. Mark's condition deteriorated. Judy often caught him sticking pins into his body and burning himself with matches. One night she witnessed him pulling his own teeth out with pliers. Mark craved the pain. The funny thing was, he didn't feel it. She had even found a leaflet in his pocket from a massage parlor, which advertised macho-sadism.

Several times, Judy had told him she did not know him anymore. She had married Flight Lieutenant Mark Cochrane, a bright- eyed, handsome man with a wicked sense of humor. The broken man he had become was a stranger. How he resented her complaints.

Since he often refused to eat, Mark had lost a great deal of weight. He eventually ceased to wash himself, and his body odor repulsed Judy. She must have realized what he had been through, but after three months she decided she could no longer tolerate the bizarre behavior. Judy came to the inevitable decision that she wanted a divorce. Mark never contested the divorce, in fact he never said anything. His psychiatrist believed he was insane, and suggested it was best for him to be committed to an asylum. It never happened.

One morning, Mark left home, his destination unknown. The police looked for him, but abandoned their search after a couple of days. Judy recovered from her loss, and her lover, the psychiatrist, moved in with her shortly afterwards.

Mark frowned when another vagrant sat beside him on the bench. This was his bench, and nobody but he could use it.

"Lovely morning, isn't it?" asked the old stranger.

Mark never responded. He bent over and clasped his ankles.

The inquisitive tramp probed further. "You into that yoga then?"

Mark rocked back and forth and hummed to himself.

The stranger pointed. "Hey, look over there. The bandstand's on fire."

Mark straightened up and watched the flames, which seemed to move in rhythm with the sirens of the fire engines.

"I'm George, what's your name?" asked the vagrant, who offered his grubby hand. "You don't say much, do you? Come on, shake on it. We're both men of the road, aren't we?"

As he witnessed the transformation in the man's hairy face, Mark's eyes glazed over. The old vagrant had a wrinkled face with no visible teeth, but the feature that upset Mark was the black, bushy moustache.

Mark squirmed, put his hands to his face, and moaned gently. It was all coming back to him. The horror was returning.

SYRIAN BORDER, 1991.

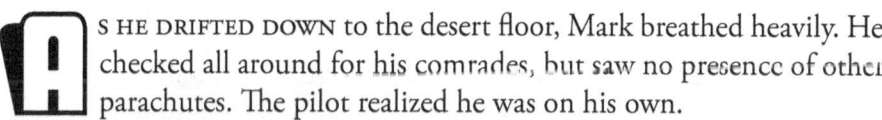

S HE DRIFTED DOWN to the desert floor, Mark breathed heavily. He checked all around for his comrades, but saw no presence of other parachutes. The pilot realized he was on his own.

After the initial explosion, they watched the fuel leaking from the left wing of the Tornado and the flames lick at the fuselage. Someone gave the order to eject. It seemed like a good idea at the time. He heard the loud explosion when the Tornado crashed into the desert. A bright flash illuminated the wilderness, like a giant firework on November 5th.

Mark touched down heavily and rolled over, thankful not to have broken a limb. The reality of the situation did not encourage him. His comrades must have died aboard the aircraft.

After the bombing of Baghdad, the flight crew had been on their way back to the base in Muharraq in Bahrain. The high-spirited crew looked forward to a cool shower and a cold drink, and did not expect the horror of what was to come.

Concealing the chute was Mark's chief concern as he dug aggressively at the ground. He stopped digging, and in the distance, through the heat haze he watched the contorted view of the sand clouds. The parachute was discarded before he ran for one of the dunes. The sand clouds meant vehicles, and Mark did not expect them to be British.

The hot sun burned the dismayed man's hands when he lay prone on the ground. Daring not to chance a look, he listened to the foreign voices. Two minutes passed and Mark heard the click in his left ear, followed by an unfamiliar voice.

"English!" shouted the soldier.

The Iraqi soldier was joined by others. There was more shouting of orders, and Mark placed his hands on his head. He never saw the first blow of the rifle butt. He heard only the crack and felt the blood ooze into his eyes, as the soldiers kicked him until he blacked out.

Mark was taken to Al Rasid Intelligence Headquarters in Iraq. When he awoke, the only sound to be heard in his damp, bleak cell was the dripping of a neglected, rusty pipe. Beads of perspiration trickled down his bloody face and stung him as they sought out the numerous cuts and sores.

Mark swatted at the flies, the irritating insects no doubt attracted by the putrid stench. He looked around the squalor of his prison, a concrete cell that was dark and stifling. An old wooden stool, a flea-ridden mattress and a hole in the ground were the only features in his cell, apart from the picture of Saddam Hussein that hung on the wall.

The approaching steps and the rattle of the keys in the lock alerted the prisoner. Three soldiers entered the room. They all looked similar, with their black moustaches and berets.

"Stand up, please," ordered the officer in the center." I'm Colonel Al Hakim, and this is Lieutenant Al Sadir and Sergeant Med Barzani. You're in a prison in Baghdad and your conduct will decide how you're to be treated. If you cooperate, you'll no doubt live to see your family again. If you choose not to cooperate? Well, let's hope it doesn't come to that, eh?"

The colonel lit a cigarette and paced the cell. The strange odor of the tobacco was most unpleasant. He stopped and faced Mark. "Let's start with your name, shall we?"

"Flight Lieutenant Mark Cochrane, 172382."

"Splendid. And your squadron?"

"Flight Lieutenant Mark Cochrane, 172382."

The colonel laughed loudly and nodded to the burly sergeant, who slapped Mark twice across his face.

"Now come, Lieutenant, enough of this stiff upper lip nonsense. I know how proud you British are. I studied at Cambridge in 1980. Beautiful country, but so arrogant and disciplined. If you don't tell me what I want to know, it'll be most unpleasant for you, believe me. Sergeant Med Barzani is skilled in what he does."

"Where are you based?" probed the colonel, who drew deeply on his cigarette.

"Flight Lieut-"

"Enough!"

The impatient man shouted something in Arabic. Two guards entered the cell and tied Mark to his chair. The sergeant took out a pistol and hit him twice over the head with the butt.

"Wait! Lieutenant, you have one more chance. Your base?" asked the colonel.

The colonel nodded when Mark bowed his head. The sergeant and the two guards viciously pounded Mark with their fists. When he blacked out, they threw water over him.

Colonel Al Hakim, whose breath reeked of garlic, stooped down to face Mark. "My, look at your face. Enough of the stupidity. I assume you have a family? A wife and children, possibly? Your ignorance is futile. Actually, we know the locations of all the air bases. We merely wish to confirm our data. Whether you tell me what I want to know or not, it'll not affect the outcome of the war. It will only affect you, my friend. Tell me what I want to know and you can see out the remainder of your imprisonment in peace. Clean sheets, water, food... it's your call, Lieutenant."

Through his bloody mouth, Mark looked up and mumbled something. His face had swollen beyond recognition.

The colonel placed his ear against Mark's mouth.

"Flight... Lieutenant... Mar..."

The colonel seized his prisoner by the hair and pulled out his pistol, before he held it against his temple. "Fucking listen, infidel. You have ten seconds to speak or I swear I'll blow your brains out. One, two, three, four, five."

Mark grinned at his captor.

"Six, seven, eight, nine."

"Undress him," ordered the colonel, who withdrew his pistol.

Untied and dragged from his perch, Mark was stripped naked and made to sit back on the stool, his wrists tethered to his ankles.

"Not very comfortable, is it? Get used to it, my friend. You'll be in that position for some time. Oh, and if you fall off the stool or dare to sleep, you will be beaten. I'll return in a couple of hours, just in case you change your mind."

Mark was dehydrated, his mouth coarse and his lips sore. He could see the boots of the guards as they waited for him to fall from his stool. His back ached so badly.

Mark heard the footsteps, and the unpleasant odor of the cigarette suggested the colonel had returned.

"Lieutenant, how are you feeling now? Thirsty perhaps? It's so hot today."

The guards cut Mark's bonds and he sat up straight. He grimaced at the pain in his back.

The colonel held a mug of water, which he sipped slowly. "Would you like a drink, Lieutenant?"

Mark nodded.

"Tell me what I want to know and I'll grant you your wish."

Mark bowed his head again.

He crashed to the ground when the colonel kicked away the stool. The sergeant and the guards kicked and punched him, and Mark covered his genitals to protect himself. A pool of blood formed on the floor, before he was dragged back onto the stool.

The colonel looked toward his prisoner's groin and smiled. He nodded and Mark's wrists were tied to his ankles, again.

The treatment continued until morning, the questions and then the savage beatings. Mark was given a little water and a handful of rice to keep him alive. He fought the fatigue and knew the beatings would continue if he fell asleep. To relieve himself, Mark had to go through the indignity of squatting over the hole in the ground, while the guards grinned at him.

THE CAPTURED PILOT WAITED and listened for the approach of the footsteps, which confirmed his torturers had returned. The rising sun filtered into his cell, suggesting another unbearable dawn had broken… another nail in his coffin. Several flies had been attracted by his cut and ravaged face.

"Good morning, Lieutenant. How are we this morning?" asked the colonel. He said something to Lieutenant Al Sadir, who in turn nodded to Sergeant Med Barzani.

The sergeant removed his tunic and rolled up his sleeves. "Are you ready to talk?"

Mark said nothing. A powerful punch knocked him to the ground and a rag was inserted into his bloody mouth. The guards laid him on his back, as the sergeant hovered over the struggling man with a pitcher of water. The soldier poured the water into the rag, and Mark panicked and tried to kick out with his restrained legs. He felt a hand roughly squeeze his testicles. He gagged when the water vapor took effect, which gave him a sensation of drowning. After a couple of minutes, Mark was placed back on the stool, his testicles black. He was yet again tethered in his usual position.

The routine continued until nightfall, his only respite being the two hour intervals when his torturers would leave. Three times he fell off his stool as he fought his battle with drowsiness, only to receive a sound beating. He was not allowed to fall unconscious. The water would be there to revive him.

DARKNESS BROUGHT WITH IT A COLD CHILL. With no electricity, the cell was lit by candlelight. Mark was uncertain how long he had been confined, and was not sure how much more of the torture he could withstand.

The sound of the returning soldiers filled him with dread. He was again untied and forced to sit up. His eyelids were so heavy, and he mumbled to himself. The disoriented man had lost all coordination.

The colonel rubbed his hands together. "Brrr, it's cold in here. Lieutenant, how much longer are you going to keep up with this charade? Please, it gives me no pleasure to see you this way. After all, we're both soldiers in a sense of the word, are we not? So, where is the airbase? Where is the fucking airbase?"

The cell door opened and a long, sturdy rack was dragged into the room by the guards. Mark was forced onto the ground and his bare feet were placed into the rack and locked. The sergeant then beat his feet with a long implement, which resembled a series of whips. Mark screamed out when the whip connected. The torture went on for about fifteen minutes before they tied him up again and left.

The pain in Mark's back was unbearable. His groin ached badly and his ravaged feet had been cut to ribbons. He wept, softly at first, and then loudly. He sobbed and mumbled indistinctly. The guards mocked their prisoner, and routinely stubbed out their cigarettes on Mark's naked body. Several times he fell off his stool and received beatings.

Later that evening, the guards nodded off and slumped on the ground, their backs against the wall. Mark only noticed because he had fallen off his stool again, but this time the guards did not beat him.

A scorpion crawled about a foot in front of Mark, who watched through swollen eyes and tried to make a clicking noise, like you would to attract a dog, only his mouth was too dry. The pilot whimpered as he tried to summon the scorpion, hoping for the poisonous creature to end his pain.

The cell door opened and the colonel and his entourage entered. They yelled at the sleeping guards. The sergeant crushed the scorpion with his rifle, and along with it, Mark's salvation.

"You're lucky we arrived here in time, Lieutenant. You could've been stung," smiled the colonel.

Mark was placed back on the stool.

"Have you anything to tell me?" asked the officer, who lit a cigarette.

Mark whimpered.

The colonel approached and stubbed the cigarette out on the prisoner's forehead.

Mark stared at his tormentor and grinned. He was knocked to the floor again and beaten.

ANOTHER DAY WENT BY and the colonel appeared more lenient. Mark was given a mouthful of water and told he could sleep.

"S-s-sleep?" stuttered Mark.

"Yes, sleep."

The guards helped the captive onto the mattress. A bed had never felt so good. He lay back and sobbed when the candles were extinguished. He heard the cell door shut, and shivered on his newly found haven. The cold did not bother Mark so much after the beatings. He closed his eyes and was on a beach with his wife and children. He sipped an ice-cold beer as the waves lapped at their bare, cool feet.

The cell door opened and the soldiers returned and lit the candles. Mark cried loudly when he was dragged back to the stool and tethered.

The colonel grinned. "Enough sleep for now. Five minutes is a start, is it not? Again, where is your airbase? Yesterday, you told me it was in Syria. Is that correct?"

Mark muttered incoherently. "Yesterday, today, tomorrow, yester-"

"Enough, infidel. You've tested my patience, and now I've had enough."

THE PRISONER RECEIVED THE WATER TORTURE AGAIN, and over the next few days the visits became less frequent. The Cruise Missiles moved closer every day and Mark no longer seemed so important to his captors.

Mark was allowed some sleep, but on waking up he regularly taunted the guards and received the beatings he learnt to crave. The Englishman had been tortured so much that he welcomed the pain. He needed his fix for the day and longed for the beatings, like a drug he could not give up.

Eventually, the guards abandoned their torture of the crazy man. He was not even locked up anymore. Mark was given the freedom of the building, but was never allowed to venture outside. He often begged the guards to beat him, but received only verbal abuse for his trouble.

ONE AFTERNOON, the Cruise Missiles were close and the bombing was severe. Mark walked on the balls of his feet to the cell door and found it unlocked. He struggled to the main exit and gazed out. The sudden, bright sunlight rendered him sightless and he paused for a moment. The wonderful sensation of a breeze, warm but welcome, caressed his swollen face. He crossed the burning sand to the well and ignored the numerous flies that buzzed around him. People scurried past, attempting to evade the missiles.

Mark's slender frame tugged on the rope and pulled the bucket to the summit of the well. He filled the ladle with the refreshing liquid and drank greedily. The liberated man giggled like a schoolchild when he poured the water over his scarred body. He sat against the well and cried, as he witnessed the carnage all around.

Two days later, he was found wandering aimlessly around by a British Special Task Force. Mark had been a prisoner of Iraq for six weeks.

HYDE PARK. LONDON, 2001

MARK WALKED SLOWLY TOWARD the blazing bandstand and the old tramp shuffled after him.

"Hey, don't get too close."

Mark ignored the pleas of the tramp. He walked into the fire, his arms outstretched. The deranged man looked up and laughed loudly when the flames ignited his rags. The laughter continued, even when he fell to his knees and the flames burned his feeble body. Mark welcomed the ultimate pain.

The police constable and the fireman witnessed the incident too late. The constable uttered, "Who was he?"

"Some old tramp. I doubt the poor bugger will be missed."

ANTHONY HULSE lives in the north east of England, UK, is widowed with two sons and engaged to Susan. He opted for very early retirement from Corus (British Steel) five years ago to concentrate on writing.

In 2003, Anthony had three novels published, but the two companies have since gone out of business. Since then he has written another eighteen novels and approximately fifty-five short stories. His WAIII entry will be his fifth inclusion in an anthology.

More recently, Anthony published fifteen of his books, mostly psychological thrillers and horror. He has also written a biography and is currently writing another. He has successfully converted his novels to e-books.

Anthony loves travelling, playing golf and most other sports. Funnily enough, he reads very little, but loves to write. He hopes one day to live in Crete, an island dear to his heart.

Facebook author page: **facebook.com/HULSEY33**

Twitter: **@AnthonyHulse1**

Anthony's Books: **lulu.com/spotlight/HULSEY**

Red Hands

HMC

DAPHNE REMOVED HER CARDIGAN *and wrapped it around the wound on her arm. Panic hadn't quite taken over her body; she ripped off her red heels and got up to run again. She stumbled through the undergrowth and dodged trees on Devil's Hill. Another puncture under her breast bled. She held the spot.*

Terror caused a knot in her throat. Screaming wouldn't help anyway, Nicky would only find her faster. So she concentrated on getting to the Hockinham Road, which would lead her to Billy's Drugstore. Billy, the owner, would be watching Bonanza or Gunsmoke right about now, and bitching to his wife about Eisenhower and the Cold War from his stool at the counter.

But it was too late; she could hear sticks break under his feet, his heavy breathing.

He was behind her.

"Come here!" His hands clamped down on her and dug into her arms. This time she did scream as he squeezed her wound. "Where are you going, Darling?" He breathed in her ear. The smell of his double mint gum churned her stomach. "We were just getting cozy."

"WHY'D YOU DO IT?"

Sergeant Johnson had a beefy face and piggy eyes. He glared at Nicky. Sweat dripped off Johnson's face and onto the interrogation table. Nicky sat in a chair, his hands cuffed behind his back. He wanted nothing more than to wipe the sweat that dripped from his brow, and he wondered if the fan was left off just to make him feel the heat.

"Why'd ya do it, Pretty Boy? You messed up in the head? You like preying on cute young waitresses? You sonofabitch!" Johnson slammed a meaty fist on the table, no doubt wanting to rattle Nicky just a little. He pulled out a cigarette and lit it. He circled the table and puffed smoke into Nicky's face.

"You're the one who's been taking these innocent girls on my watch! How many now? Seven! Seven missing girls. Where are the bodies, Nicholas?" Nicky couldn't help but notice the sergeant's grey suit was a size too small. He looked like an overstuffed sausage, and he'd undone his top button to let his red neck breathe.

Nicky whipped his head to the side to move a greasy curl of hair from his eye. "I got nothing more to say."

"Oh, you'll be saying plenty more. Plenty, I assure you." He pointed at the photo. "See this little girl you picked out over all the others?" A brunette in a floral dress smiled back at Nicky, with dimpled cheeks and an impish twinkle in her eye. *Daphne. Sweet, sweet Daphne.* His stomach flipped.

"She wasn't just anyone." Johnson slapped a paper on the table that read:

Detective's Daughter Kidnapped on Devil's Hill

"That's right. She's the daughter of a friend of mine. Not just any detective either, one of the best in the Big Apple. You haven't got a chance in seven hells of getting outta this one."

Nicky hunched over; it was hard to look away from Daphne's face, that beautiful whimsical creature he'd fallen for. He didn't fall for chicks, it wasn't his style. He couldn't help himself with this one, though. She was different.

"She was the daughter of a copper then," Nicky said solemnly.

"Yeah. You sure know how to pick 'em. " The sergeant blew smoke into Nicky's face and his eyes watered. He almost bit his tongue as shivers ran through him. What had he gotten himself into? It just kept getting worse and worse and Nicky's shoulders felt like bricks. He wanted to puke all over the interrogation desk. He doubted the ash tray would hold it all, though.

"I told you everything about Daphne," he rasped. "So what happens now?"

"You go to court, get charged with murder in the first for slicing and dicing a pretty young thing and then you're going straight to the chair— just like you should, just like you deserve." Johnson leaned in; his face twisted in disgust. "There's more than one, isn't there?"

"One what?"

A slender blonde with barrel curls and freckles across her nose peered through the door and stared at Nicky. She had a Monroe look about her. Nicky stared back.

"Narelle!" Johnson broke her trance. "I told you not to come in here."

"Sorry, I just, well… it's just that there's a call for you. It's important." She smiled at Nicky, then checked herself. After all, he was a criminal. He wondered if she knew what he was in for.

"For me or for him?" Johnson snapped.

"Ah." She peeled her gaze from Nicky. "You, Sir."

She left and Johnson leaned in even closer, his cigarette hanging from his lip.

"Tell me why you *really* did it, Boy."

BEFORE THAT

NICKY WOKE UP IN HIS CHEVY PICK-UP. He looked down at his clothes covered in blood and grime. His once white car seats were stained red; destroyed. *What a mess.*

Sleep had brought him nothing but more weariness and the mother of all headaches. He opened the door, stepped out into the garage, and inspected his car. Dominic's Motor Mechanics wasn't due to open for a few hours, so Nicky had time to think. He usually did it while working on a ride, but right now he felt like throwing up... again.

The old '39 rust bucket clunker needed his attention. But his car needed it more. Nicky grabbed a clean rag and filled a bucket with sudsy water.

He washed the blood from his seats, but they were stained now. He thought about the woman the blood belonged to as he scrubbed and scrubbed.

That pretty thing, Daphne, was sweet as a candy apple. He imagined her sitting in his passenger seat, playing with the radio, and fidgeting like a kid. Man she was a dream come true. Nicky liked her so much he could have taken the kid downtown and married her on the spot. Now she was a whisper of a memory.

Flashes of Daphne screaming, blood, choking, the struggle. The monster that killed her needed to be captured and locked away for good.

A car pulled up outside the garage – and not just any car. The doors slammed shut and voices called out; one of them made Nicky's stomach drop. *Rosa.* Crap. Not Rosa.

What's Dominic doing here so early, anyway? Keys jingled in the lock.

"Hey, Nicky," Dominic said. He entered, wearing his greased up overalls. Nicky got out of the car and Dominic took in the blood on his clothes.

"Nicky!" Rosa ran past her father and threw her arms around him. Dear sweet Rosa didn't see the blood. But she soon would, so Nicky held her longer, her blonde hair tickling his face. He couldn't let her see it all. She'd be terrified. Why had he come here? Dominic was like a father to him and Rosa a little sister. Dominic had given him a job and a chance at a better life and this was how he repaid them? By bringing this twisted mess to their doorstep? He didn't deserve their love. He didn't deserve this warm embrace.

"What happened?" Dominic asked, moving into the garage to yank his daughter from Nicky.

"Something not so right," said Nicky. He didn't want to look at either of them. But Dominic peered into the side window of his car, panic in his eyes. He pulled his daughter further away.

"Is this what I think it is?" Dominic was frightened. Nicky couldn't respond to that. "Are you okay?"

"Not really," Nicky said.

"You're bleeding, Nicky," Rosa stepped towards him.

"Do you need me to call the cops?" Dominic asked.

"Yeah. I do."

It was time to make things right. Daphne would've wanted it that way.

HE WAS ON TOP OF HER NOW. Rocks dug into her back and the pain in her ribs was unbearable. "It's okay," he purred and caressed her cheek. She waited for him to get nice and close, close enough and she'd bite him – she'd bite his damned cheek off and kick him in the good spot like her father had taught her. But he didn't lean in and he still held that knife in his hand. It had done so much damage already and she couldn't take any more. She needed to keep her wits about her and another litre of blood on the forest floor wasn't going to help.

"Please don't hurt me again. You don't have to. I won't run anymore."

"Let's make sure of that, shall we?" He leaned down, grabbed her foot, and sliced the tendon in the back of her heel.

BEFORE THAT

THE DRIVE-IN AT VALLEY STREAM on Long Island was the place to be. Greasers with leather jackets sat in an orange Fairlane with lime green flames up the sides, combing their hair and smoking cigarettes. Girls bounced around, chewing gum, and giggling. Nicky looked up at the tiny black and white television as he waited in line for candy.

"What'll it be, Sugar?" The woman behind the counter leaned over and winked.

"The box of chocolates, please."

She reached behind her and grabbed a box. "That'll be one dollar and nineteen cents. For a lady friend?" Nicky handed the candy stripe aproned lady her money. She was enough to turn heads. Her wedding ring shone and caught his eye. That wouldn't usually bother him, but Nicky was somewhere else tonight. His mind was on Daphne Carmichael.

"Yeah, they are."

"Aw, shame." She pouted. "There you go."

He took the chocolates with a grin.

Nicky made his way past a white Ford that had a red head sucking the wrinkles off a turkey-necked driver. Turkey-neck gave Nicky a thumbs up, but he pretended not to see it. The horror movie music came to a climax, and a girl on his right squealed as he made his way to his Chevy and the angel sitting in it.

"Sweets for my sweet?" he asked, handing Daphne the chocolates.

"Oh, God help you if that's all you got." She smirked and those little cabbage patch dimples got him again. She opened the box and rather than chew one, she sucked on a chocolate, glancing at him from the corner of her Forget-me-not blues. "I'm sorry," she said, mid-suck. "Did you want one?" Nicky grabbed a chocolate, threw it up into the air, opened his mouth and waited. It hit him in the forehead and fell onto the car floor.

"Smooth." She giggled.

He couldn't find it anywhere. "Damn, that's gonna melt."

"Then one day you'll reach under your seat, looking for something else, and you'll come up with a finger covered in melted chocolate. You'll remember that you're a show off and shouldn't try to impress girls so much."

"Did it work?" He raised a brow in anticipation.

"Almost. Kookie is the new kill."

He stared. "Did you just call me Kookie?"

"It's a compliment, Daddy-O. Take 'em anyway you can get 'em."

Nicky wanted to peel his eyes off her and pretend to be interested in the movie. It was hard to be cool. She smelled like rose and myrtle – like his childhood garden – like adventure mixed with pleasure. And she made him laugh. No girls made him laugh. Girls weren't funny.

There was something so different about this girl, it made Nicky want to change, to settle down and be a better man. He hadn't been sure that was possible.

BEFORE THAT

The Rockola jukebox played "Hey Good Lookin' " and the cute waitress sauntered up to his table with a fresh pot of coffee. Steamy Joe's Café was quiet on a Monday night and that was the way Nicky liked it.

"You got a Washington?" Tonight the waitress's dimples made her look younger than she was. Maybe it was her apron covered in kittens, or her white socks with lace around the trim. Maybe it was her thick chocolate curls that fell over her shoulder like a grown up Shirley Temple – one that blossomed into perfection.

"Yeah, here ya go." Nicky passed her the note.

"Mind if I sit?" She slid into the red booth before he could answer, and filled his coffee cup. "You look like one of the mushroom people, a lonely man who roams at night. That who you are?"

"Maybe. Maybe not. What do you think, Sugar"

"You really want to know what I think?" She raised her eyebrows. "I mean, I'm not sure you're ready for a girl like me to tell you what she thinks."

"Oh, now I *need* to know." He returned the smile.

"You come in here every night and drink four to five cups of coffee, and what is it? 9 p.m. So you probably sleep in the day, like me. You're a loner. You don't like people much, but mostly because they want to talk about themselves. You drive a Chevy pick-up because it's practical. You fix cars at Dominic's garage. Say, what's your name anyway?"

"You've got all that from my visits?"

"You asked me what I thought. And don't answer questions with questions."

Daphne had already been interesting, but now, well…. "It's Nicky."

"I'm Daphne." She reached over and shook his hand. He didn't tell her he already knew her name – that he knew her last name, too. Nicky knew many things about the brunette before him, much more than she had guessed about him. She used strawberry lip gloss and applied it while driving a blue and white Fairlane with carburetor issues. She didn't drink coffee, but tea from an Elvis mug; she loved to sing "Don't be Cruel".

"I like that name," he said coolly.

"You mean you *really* didn't already know it? So all the times you've looked at this name badge and you still don't know my name, let alone asked me out. What kinda fella are you?"

Nicky rested his chin in his hand and glared at the whimsical thing before him. She was serious. "My apologies. Let me make that up to you right now. The Drive-in. Tomorrow night. Seven."

"That how you ask a girl on a date? And it works? Sheesh."

"Not always. How about this time?"

"I'm working." She grinned.

"You never work on a Tuesday night." Nicky took a sip of his coffee.

"Is that right? So you *have* noticed my name then? And you were just waiting for your chance to make a move huh? Nicky, short for Nicholas. I'll see you tomorrow at seven. Pick me up here in your pick-up." She giggled and wandered off to the kitchen, ignoring a customer clicking his finger at her.

How does she know I'm a Nicholas? Nicky looked down at his clothes. Then he smiled. Some nights he'd wear his work clothes, with Dominic's Motor Mechanics written on the back in huge yellow lettering. He also had a personalized sewn name badge that Rosa had begged him to wear. A badge that said 'Saint Nicholas'.

"Tell me why you *really* did it." Sergeant Johnson's breath stank of cheese stuck in his teeth too long.

"Why do I do anything I do?" Nicky said. "I do what I do because once I started I couldn't stop – because the thrill of it all makes me whole." Nicky's eyes changed; he felt a darkness come over him. It was a familiar feeling. Insanity, a whole other person in side of him? He could never put his finger on it. He called it 'the monster.' And a monster it was.

Nicky could feel his face change from fear to knowing, powerlessness to certainty. "Why do you *think* I did it? I did it because I *can*. I did it because I *wanted* to."

No! The voice in Nicky's head shouted. *I don't want any of this! I never wanted to hurt Daphne.* But no one could hear that voice right now. It was an echo at the back of a twisted mind.

"You prick!" The sergeant's eyes bulged and his face reddened as he held his breath. "You little prick!" He shook Nicky by the shirt.

"Oh, you're going to wanna look after me, Little Piggy," Nicky said.

He let go. "Why the hell would I want to do that?"

"You need me."

"I need you like I need a goddamn hole in the head!" the sergeant screamed angrily.

"Oh no, you need me. You need me to tell you where the rest of the girls are," he said calmly.

The sergeant stared. "What are you saying?"

"They're not all dead, you see. Your missing girls. But they will be, unless you cooperate."

Johnson took a chair and sat across from Nicky. He took a few deep breaths. "So Daphne isn't dead?"

"No, she isn't. She bled a lot, oh yes. But she's alive."

"Where is she?"

"You need to forget about Daphne. You want to play the big hero, Sarge? The only way you'll find the other girls before they're dead is if you *forget* about Daphne Carmichael. She's mine."

Please, thought Nicky. *No.*

HMC, Hayley Merelle Clearihan, resides on the Gold Coast, Australia. She has a degree in psychology, writes a column for an online magazine and blogs about global issues. HMC is inspired by many genres, but has always been particularly fascinated by magic, thrillers, or books with a twist.

"It's so great when I don't see it coming. Who doesn't love a good twist?"

At the tender age of eleven, she found her first favourite author—Stephen King. At bedtime, she would creep out into the hallway where there was just enough light to read on. When the couch squeak signalled her mother's movement, she would rush back to bed and hide under the covers.

HMC went on to fall obsessively in love with reading and has spent hour upon hour in the clasps of an eclectic bunch of authors from R.L Stein and Paul Jennings to J.R.R. Tolkien. She later moved on to fall for authors such as the late and great Bryce Courtenay and J.K Rowling, never truly realising what an influence these people would have on her life.

She now spends her time doing one of the things she loves best, writing.

Come and visit her at **www.hmcwriter.com**.

The Truth About Tony

GENE LA VINESS

JENNY GOT OUT OF HER CAR and hurried up the stairs to her boyfriend's apartment. He hadn't answered his phone since they talked that morning.

Last night wasn't the first time Tony had been a victim. After one incident, he had two broken ribs, a busted nose, and a cut over his right eye. Tony said he didn't get a very good look at who did it that time, either. Occasionally, he sported a swollen nose, busted lips, or bruises on his face. He blamed those on accidents, like running into the door or falling. Jenny knew he wasn't being completely truthful. At six foot two inches tall and muscular, Tony was the strongest man she knew.

Jenny had asked if a gang was trying to force him to pay for protection or just picking on him because he was a goody two-shoes. She frequently pleaded with him to move. Tony argued that the rent was cheap enough to save money for a ring and a down payment on their home after they were married. When that didn't work, she said he should move in with her and save even more money. He turned her down, saying he knew she wanted their wedding night to be special and there would be too much temptation. She had no doubt about Tony's commitment to wait, but wondered if he was right.

Jenny's heart pounded. Her face was flush. Fumbling with her keys, she tried to find the right one. Jenny unlocked the door and found him lying on the sofa. "Tony, are you okay?"

"I'm alright." Tony yawned and started to stretch, but immediately winced.

"I've been calling you all day."

"I'm sorry, the phone died and the charger is over there." He gingerly pointed across the room.

Jenny leaned over and kissed him softly. "You still look terrible."

"Yeah, I got beat up pretty bad this time."

"How many fingers am I holding up?"

"Three, and I'm still not going to the hospital."

"I saw a video some girl took with her phone last night. She was attacked and a guy came to her rescue, fighting off three thugs. He was some tough dude. One of them busted a board over his head, but he kept fighting. You could use lessons from him."

"Did it show who the guy was?"

"No, it was a lousy video, too dark and it kind of looked like he was wearing a hooded mask. The girl said he came out of nowhere."

"Oh, you want me to take lessons from duh-da, duh-da, Thatmaaan." Tony chuckled lightly. "Oh, that hurts."

Jenny couldn't help but smile a little bit. "If I promise not to tickle you, will you be more careful?"

"Please don't. I'll try," he said.

"I wonder if the guys who jumped you were the same ones who attacked the girl. It wasn't too far from here."

"I guess they could have been."

"Maybe you should move. I never liked climbing the stairs to the third floor, anyway."

"I want to take a hot bath. Will you help me?"

"Now, Tony," she said, putting her hands on her hips.

"Don't give me that look. I know you want to wait. Besides, I'm in no condition to seduce you. I just need help getting in and out of the tub."

"I—"

"You don't want me to ask my mom to come over and bathe me, do you?"

"Well, since you went through all this trouble just to get me to undress you, I guess I can cooperate a little."

JENNY RUSHED TO TONY'S AFTER WORK. He had an appointment to get his eyes checked. She let herself into his apartment and heard the shower. She sat down and pulled a book from her purse. After reading for a few minutes, a loud thud startled her. Running to the bathroom, she barged through the door and found Tony lying on the floor.

"Tony, you're wet and naked as a jaybird!"

"Yeah, that's how I usually take a shower."

"I'm sorry," she said trying not to laugh.

"I'm such a klutz. I slipped and—"

Jenny blurted out, "I can't help it," and laughed so hard she snorted. They both had a good laugh.

After the appointment with the optometrist, Tony returned to the waiting room wearing an oversized pair of dark plastic glasses. Walking out the front door, he put a hand over his eyes to shield them from the sunlight.

"Step down," Jenny said as they started across the intersection.

"Thanks. I can hardly open my eyes out here. Maybe the doctor gave me a special dose when he dilated them."

As they neared the other side of the street, a woman screamed, "Stop that man! He took my purse!"

Jenny was distracted and forgot to mention the other curb. Tony stumbled and fell into the thief, knocking the breath out of him. Jenny picked up the lady's purse while Tony fumbled around trying to find the dark glasses he had been wearing. He stood and put the glasses on, just before the woman ran up and gave him a big hug.

"Thank you."

"Uh, she got your purse ma'am, not me," Tony said.

"I saw you headbutt that, that... You nailed him good, right in the breadbasket. Thank you."

Jenny handed the purse to the woman as a police car pulled over to the curb.

"Tony, I didn't know you had it in you," Jenny said.

"What? You didn't tell me to step up, just led me right into the curb. I can't see and you're using me as a battering ram to take out purse snatchers."

Jenny burst out laughing. After regaining her composure, she said, "I can't wait to tell your mother what you did this time."

"It's a wonder you don't dump me. I'm such a goof," Tony said.

"Don't say that. You make me laugh and feel good. I don't know what I would do without you."

After giving their information to the police, they walked to Jenny's car. "Falling into that purse snatcher seemed a lot like when you fell about a year ago. You know, when you fell down the stairs and into that man with a gun. Those old people told the police you flew half way down the stairs like Superman," she said.

"Yeah, they were totally traumatized. I never did figure out which half of the steps I flew over. It felt like I bounced off every single one of them," he said.

"I heard you falling, but didn't get to the stairs until you were crashing into the robber. It did look kind of like you dove head-long into him."

Opening the car door for her, he said, "I'm not the only one that can fall. Last winter you slipped on the ice and rolled down the hill."

"Yeah, but I didn't take anybody out when I did it."

"Some of us just aren't as lucky as others." He gave her a consoling pat on the back and blew a raspberry at her.

WEEKS PASSED WITHOUT INCIDENT OR ACCIDENT. Tony and Jenny had dinner at his apartment. He didn't say much and stared right through Jenny at times.

"We don't have to watch a movie if you don't want to, but tell me what's wrong," she said.

"Nothing's wrong. Maybe it's the allergy medicine I took today. I'm feeling kind of groggy, but it should wear off soon."

"So you're not mad at me or having problems at work?"

"I'm definitely not mad at you and work is fine. If I don't snap out of this soon, you can throw a glass of water on me."

"I just might."

Tony smiled. "I love you, Jenny."

"I love you, too," she replied.

Tony wandered out onto the balcony. Jenny quietly walked up and goosed him from behind. He jumped, tripped on some small potted plants and fell over the side. He managed to grab the top rail with one hand, but was only able to hang on for a moment.

"Oh no! Oh Lord no!" Jenny screamed. She looked down in time to see him land on top of a car. Jenny called for an ambulance, then ran down the stairs and out to Tony. He lay motionless on top of the smashed in car roof. "Oh, I'm so sorry baby. Please be okay. I'm sorry."

He moaned and with a feeble, broken voice said "Excuse me... I think I farted."

"What?"

Frank, a friend who lived in the same building, ran over to Jenny, "What happened?"

"He fell off the balcony," she sobbed. "He mumbled some nonsense a minute ago. He's hurt real bad and it's my fault." She grabbed Tony's hand and bawled uncontrollably.

Jenny spent the night with Tony at the hospital. The next morning Frank came to check on him. "How's he doing?"

"I don't see how, but the doctor said he only has some minor bruising. They kept him overnight as a precautionary measure," she said.

"You're not going to believe what's in the newspaper this morning. He's really out-done himself this time."

"What is it?"

"The headline reads, 'Freak Accident Stops Alleged Serial Killer'," Frank said.

"What? That's not about Tony, is it?"

"The article says a teenage girl was being kidnapped from the apartments and Tony fell on the car, knocking the guy out as he was about to drive away. It also says the guy confessed to killing three other girls and there's a picture of the car. Look!"

"Wow... That's too weird," she said.

"You think we should wake him up and let him know?"

"No, why don't we let him sleep a little longer. He looks so peaceful and I know he's going to be hurting when he wakes up."

"You're probably right."

Jenny stood up. "Will you stay here while I go get some clean clothes for him?"

"Sure, but I get to show him the article since I saw it first."

ONE NIGHT, TONY CALLED JENNY. His voice was barely louder than a whisper. "I think I need to go to the hospital."

"What happened?"

"It's my ribs. I can hardly breathe. Please."

"Hang on, Honey. I'm coming."

At Tony's apartment, Jenny found him in the kitchen. His face was lying in a puddle of blood and his breath was shallow. "Tony, can you hear me? Hang on. There's an ambulance on the way."

His lips moved as if to answer, but no voice came out, only blood. She dampened a rag and wiped his face, checking often to make sure he was still breathing.

AT THE HOSPITAL THE POLICE ASKED ALL THE USUAL QUESTIONS, but Jenny knew nothing. She told them Tony had been beaten before, but he always said it was an accident, or he didn't see who did it.

Jenny hadn't been allowed to see Tony since they arrived at the hospital and was about to have a panic attack when a doctor came out and told her, "I stitched up his head and arm. It looks like he was thrown from the car."

Jenny sniffled and tears ran through the trails of makeup left from the previous crying spell.

"He's pretty banged up and keeps trying to get out of bed, so we're going to keep him sedated for a few days," the doctor said.

"Thrown from a car? I don't understand. I thought he was beaten by that gang again," she said.

"He's been in and out of it, but he mentioned a car wreck a couple of times. It rolled down a hill."

"I don't know. I don't know what or why this happened. Waaait, his car is in the parking lot back at the apartments. I'm sure it is," she said.

The doctor shrugged his shoulders and walked off.

TONY REMAINED IN THE HOSPITAL FOR A WEEK. Neither Jenny nor the police were able to get much of an explanation from him.

On their way home from the hospital, they passed a bank with the alarm sounding. Snapping out of a blank stare, Tony said, "Jenny, I have to go to the restroom real bad." He pointed to Leonard's Quick Stop, about a half block past the bank and asked, "Will you pull into the gas station?"

She said with a stern voice, "You better wait. I don't think you're in any condition to check out that restroom," and kept her foot on the gas pedal.

"Okay," was all he said, with a puzzled look on his face.

"We'll go by and pick up some things, but you're coming to my place to stay for a while."

A few nights later, Tony said he needed to go to the store.

With a sharp scolding tone, Jenny said, "Anthony, if I'm going to be your wife, you have to be completely honest with me." She walked into the living room where Tony was. "When you were in the hospital, I went to your apartment to get you some clothes and found this," she said, holding out a ragged hood covered with dried blood.

"Uh…" He had that deer-in-the-headlights look.

Removing her other hand from her back, she smiled and tossed a new hood to him. "You might need this if you're going out for a while."

GENE LA VINESS enjoyed playing football and fishing while growing up in Oklahoma. As an adult, he has worked in the machining industry and spent almost twenty-five years as a sports official on days off.

After raising his family, Gene found himself building custom pool cues, specializing in masse' cues for artistic pool players. He has sponsored some of the world's top trick shot artists.

He likes to play tag, fly kites, or just have lunch with the grandchildren.

Although he has written snippets of nonfiction in the past, a fictional muse recently invaded his life.

Everyday Heroes

DON MISKEL & PAMELA MURRAY

T THE AGE OF FIFTEEN, I knew I was in a bad place. And I don't mean the tiny South Side apartment I shared with my father. Mama had left us for good, chasing a rock in a glass pipe, though she still made cameo appearances in my nightmares, her face twisted into a scowl, cursing both me and my daddy.

Pop was one of the walking wounded, his eyes sunken and hollowed-out, a man who would have checked out if he hadn't had me to raise and guide. "Junior," he would say, dragging in after a double shift, "You stay outta them streets!" Then he would slump down on the couch in front of the TV and pass out in his work clothes.

I would hear his snores before I could get the grilled cheese and scrambled eggs out of the frying pan. Shaking my head in disgust, I'd put his plate in the fridge and pick up my book. After spending my summer mornings immersed in novels of fantasy and science fiction, it made me angry to come face to face with the reality of my crappy life and my loser father. He preached that with my smarts I could do anything—but I knew it wasn't true. Like I said; I was in a bad place.

"GO AHEAD AND PASS ME, YOU JERKS," she shouted, daring to take one hand off the wheel and shake her fist. "I didn't get old being stupid!" With the windows rolled up and the vents making more racket than cool air, no one would hear her, but it felt good to yell. Margaret Trumble—a 76-year-old widow from the middle of the mitten—had been driving mad for hours, except for two potty stops while still in Michigan. After hundreds of miles, she wasn't even halfway to her destination, but she was already beginning to regret her hasty departure. What was she thinking, driving off like that? No navi. No cell phone. Alone!

Truth be told—and Margaret wasn't afraid of the truth—she had a nasty habit of making impulsive decisions; especially when angry. *I'm too old to change now.* She took a ragged breath, staring at the license plate of the camper ahead, but thinking about that morning.

The call had come around ten, long after her daughter Beth had gone to work. It being summer, both the grandsons were home; Danny, the youngest, brought her the phone. As soon as she hung up, Margaret asked his brother Patrick, who was lounging around eavesdropping, to get her traveling bag down from the high shelf and lay it open on her bed. It didn't take her long to pack a week's worth of size XL white cotton underpants, pajamas, and a few outfits—including her black dress and pumps—and of course, the veiled black pillbox she always wore to funerals. Finished, she closed all the zippers and looked around for one of the boys to carry it out to the car for her. Funny, everyone had disappeared. No matter, she wasn't helpless.

The arthritis didn't help, but Margaret dragged the luggage out to the driveway, just as Beth's car pulled up. Some tattletale had called her to come home from work. Margaret scowled at her grandsons, noting that both teens had materialized on the front porch, each wearing headphones and trying to act nonchalant.

Margaret was frustrated but not thwarted. She jerked open the back door of her trusty sedan, and tried to wrestle the suitcase onto the seat. *Why was everything so damn difficult?*

"Mother, give me a chance to help you. Tell me what's going on," said Beth, jumping out of her car in her business suit and heels. *Here she comes, as usual, trying to control my life.*

"Don't just stand there, give me a hand," she said to the nearest grandson, who looked to his mother before taking the suitcase and lifting it into the trunk.

"How am I supposed to get it out of there by myself?" Margaret shouted at Patrick who lowered his head and hunched his shoulders like he was afraid she was going to hit him. "Put it in the back seat like I said!"

"Sorry, Gram," he mumbled, and she glared and huffed.

"I'll go with you on your trip, Grandma. Just wait 'til I can get my shifts covered for the next few days," volunteered Danny. *As if their trivial summer jobs were so important.*

"I can't wait. My baby brother is dying," said Margaret, hating to say it aloud, choking on the words. She saw the shrugs and puzzled looks. "Your great-uncle Billy." Turning to her meddlesome daughter, Margaret told Beth about the phone call, and thus the urgency.

"I'm sorry about Uncle Billy, Mom, but you can't drive all the way to Iowa by yourself," said Beth, in that overly patient voice Margaret so often heard from her daughter these days. *She treats me like a child.*

Beth folded her arms and pressed her thin lips into a line. Her sons stood on either side of her, mimicking her pose, like little sentinels.

Hours later, Margaret played the scene over and over while she drove. She could still see them standing in the driveway as she sped off, empty promises blowing across the lawn like trash in the wind.

We will see what I can and can't do. Margaret flicked on her blinker, and pulled out to pass the slow moving camper she'd been following for too many miles.

I KNEW THE KNOCK WOULD COME: two light raps on the door, so as to not wake my old man. Grimy was good like that. Dad was splayed out on the sofa, his work boots still on. With all that snoring, it sounded like Paul Bunyan was working overtime cutting down trees.

"You comin' out today?" asked Grimy as I stepped into the dim hallway that wreaked of piss and dried vomit. Alfonso Grimes hated his first name, so the handle was his preferred *nom de guerre* and nobody dared call him any different. He grinned a dark smile and added, "Or are you gonna just stay in the house reading those dumb-ass books like some little pussy?"

"Yeah," added Theo, a younger kid perpetually in tow, who also lived in my apartment building off 55ᵗʰ Street. Theo would go along with anything the other two of us agreed to do. As the *de facto* leader, Grimy was always looking for ways to live up to his nickname. Me? I rounded out the trio and just wanted a reprieve from the four walls and my father's snoring. "Books ain't dumb," I declared, "and I ain't no pussy!" I chuckled, elbowing Grimy in the ribs and giving Theo a complimentary sock in the arm. "It's hotter than hell out there. At least I got enough sense to stay inside where it's a little cooler."

The dog days of summer had set in, with the heat index soaring into triple digits by noon. It was so hot that people wanted to unzip their skins and walk around in their bare skeletons. But it was after five now and the lakefront breeze made its way from the east, granting us a stay of execution by heat stroke. Truth be told, I sequestered myself indoors during the hotter hours of the day, enjoying the coolness of the apartment, and devouring page after page of books borrowed from the library.

I remember that July, as if I stood on a narrow wall with my arms outstretched, teetering between a childhood wrought with disappointment and a future bleak of opportunity. I missed my mama and all my preachy pa did was sleep and go to work. What did he know? He couldn't even hold onto his wife.

No matter how bad I felt, I wouldn't dare step up to Pop—I at least had that much sense. Though I was tall enough to look him eye to eye, weighing about the same as he did, his stringy muscles were like steel cables, his hands calloused and rough from years of honest toil. As cock-strong as I wanted to be, he could've unscrewed my cap in a couple of moves. He'd earned a bachelor's in street-fighting, then mastered his technique in the military. The former tutelage prompted his warnings and unwelcome advice to "keep outta them streets".

"Yeah, man," Theo parroted Grimy, "Bring your butt on out... and don't be usin' none of them big words on us, either."

I smirked at my running buddies. "Yeah, I'm coming out," I said halfheartedly.

"Well, bring yer ass, negro," Grimy added, rubbing salt in the wound. Ever the hothead, he was the most troublesome of us three.

SHORT GRAY CURLS PLASTERED HER FOREHEAD and sweat rolled down her ample arms. Margaret clutched the steering wheel with both hands, her stiff and swollen knuckles aching as she hugged the right lane. Traffic sped by on her left. Every vehicle that appeared in her rearview mirror soon pulled out and zoomed past. She worried that a tiny flick of the wheel would steer her mid-sized sedan under the grinding wheels of the semi-trucks just inches away.

Margaret hated this part of the road and wished she could pull over. The next stop would have to be for gas, but she wanted to get past Chicago first. She had just negotiated the interstate mess in Gary, so it would be another half hour or so before she could take a rest. The changes in traffic patterns and glut of people in a perpetual rush had her mind spinning. All this was new since the last time she'd traveled this way.

Brooding about the morning's argument while she drove, Margaret thought of what her daughter had said that had really ticked her off.

"Mother, just wait 'til tomorrow. I can get someone to cover for me. We can take *my* car."

To this, Margaret had turned in fury. "You'd like that, wouldn't you! Then you'd be in complete control, Beth."

"No, Mom, it's a newer car, it has a navi… I just want you to be safe."

But Margaret suspected it was all a ploy to sideline her. Little by little, they took away your independence, until one day, you found yourself sitting in a nursing home, drooling on your slippers.

The caller had been Luella, Billy's second wife. Margaret didn't recognize her voice—she barely knew the woman Billy had married after Vera died in childbirth. Even now, decades later, Margaret missed her deceased sister-in-law. With her fair, freckled skin and red hair, and her lilting laugh, Vera's friendship had colored Margaret's world with joy. In all the years since, she had never found another such friend.

As she drove, Margaret's mind drifted back to those idyllic summer weeks spent on Billy and Vera's Iowa farm, Beth and her brothers playing in the fields and creeks and forests with their cousins, while their mothers preserved tomatoes, pickles, and pears. The women exchanged letters all year, looking forward to their summer weeks together, their heads bent together laughing while they snipped beans or sliced cucumbers, usually one or the other or both of them pregnant or nursing a baby. But then, in the short span between two summers, Vera had died, and Billy had married Luella. The following summer was the last time she ever went to Iowa, until now.

Margaret's attention jerked back to the present when she saw the sign for a toll-stop up ahead. *Odd. Do not recall toll roads on this route...*

The quarrel with her new sister-in-law was inevitable, Margaret supposed. Between the harvesting of beans and squash, they had argued over some stupid thing, prompting Billy to declare his loyalty to his new bride. Margaret was shocked and hurt. She had collected her family and stormed off to Michigan. In the decades since, an entire generation had grown up without knowing their cousins. Margaret missed her baby brother and, if it were just him, she told herself, she would have reached out. For the second time that day, Margaret tasted the bitterness of regret.

THE THREE OF US ARRIVED AT THE GAS STATION that bordered the Dan Ryan Expressway on 55th Street. That was our hangout when there was nothing else to do. We'd go inside the convenience store, grab a few ice-cold pops, and take up roost near the spot where the pay phone used to be. It smelled like busted bottles of malt liquor and dried urine, but we'd learned to ignore it. We each assumed our positions; me and Theo leaning against the guardrail, with Grimy standing out front. He was the catalyst: catcalling to pretty girls, talking smack to nosy passersby and instigating the occasional scrap, all of which we welcomed out of sheer boredom.

I spotted Claudette, the neighborhood tease, showing off her wares in tight shorts. She was thick in all the right places—mainly her ample butt and healthy thighs. Word on the block was that she'd begun letting some of the older guys cop feels for a few bucks. I'd thought she was kind of cute before that rumor surfaced, despite her penchant for talking mess.

I couldn't help but imagine my mother walking the same street just months before, wearing similar attire, in search of a drug to make her forget how hard life was. She, like Claudette, had once been beautiful. But that was before her pretty, smooth skin became pitted with blemishes. In a matter of a year, I watched her deteriorate from comely and upstanding into a monster that would turn a trick for a hit of rock. Made my stomach sick to think about it... made me angry to know that if the rumors were true, Claudette might be heading down a similar path.

Carlos Davis, Sr., my father, had his own take on it. He praised ladies for their curves and talent to nurture but warned me against the trouble they could bring. Without him outwardly badmouthing Mama, he was referring to the shame he felt at the streets claiming her. I saw him as one of those automatons I'd read about in my borrowed books: good for little more than unwanted advice and necessary provision.

TRAFFIC GREW HEAVIER YET, and industrial buildings sprung up on either side of the road. Something wasn't right. When the road widened into multiple lanes waiting for the tolling station, Margaret finally had a chance to reach over to the passenger seat, grab the road atlas, and confirm her worst fear: she was on the wrong highway. Her only option was to pay the toll and next chance she could, take the I-94 South. She'd lose a couple of hours, but Beth would never have to know.

She searched for change and finally had to break a twenty. The toll-taker asked if she minded ones. Margaret's reach through the window was awkward; she was afraid the dollars would blow away before she could get her grasp around them. She snared the bills, but several coins clattered to the ground. She momentarily placed her hand on the door latch and considered getting out of the car to search for the dimes and nickels that had gotten away. Sometimes she forgot that she had become an old lady, heavy and stiff. She stuffed the notes into her purse, which sat there open on the passenger seat and stomped on the gas pedal. *At least now I know*

I'm going in the wrong direction, she thought, feeling more hopeful than she had all day.

GRIMY STARTED OUT WITH THE CATCALL, which was half-insult. Everything he said had some sort of barb attached. Deep down, though we'd been boys since our days in grammar school, I was beginning to like him less and less. "Hey, sweet thang," he said, giving Claudette a lascivious once-over.

She slowed but did not stop. "What you want, fool?"

"I wanna ride," he said, grabbing his crotch and licking his lips.

"Yeah," Theo echoed, "we want a ride, woman! Time to do some community service work!"

She rolled her green eyes and sucked her teeth. "Your broke asses don't even have money," she responded, confirming the rumor, "and nobody rides for free!"

"You don't know what we got, girl. Tell you what, though," Grimy said, thumbing in a direction behind a nearby building, "why don't we dip back in the alley and I'll show you what I got!"

I laughed out loud—maybe too loud, considering I didn't find the exchange amusing in the slightest. I wanted to fit in with the crew, being more of a follower like Theo than I cared to admit. In Pop's impromptu sermons, he'd repeatedly tell me to be a leader. "If the trend is wrong, son," he'd say, "then don't follow the trend."

Claudette could verbally give as well as she got. She tossed out a lewd comment about the three of us combined not having enough to measure up to anything that would interest her. And that's when my laugh became genuine. She was like a frill lizard, putting on a display to make the predators find another target. Good on her.

"What you snickering at, Junior?" I paused as she stopped and put her hands on her hips, rolling her eyes at me. She even smacked her lips for emphasis. "I mean, I wouldn't crack up too much with that big peanut head of yours!"

It was Theo's turn to hoot and holler. "Oooooo," he called out, barely able to contain himself. "You gon' let her talk to you like that?!"

I paused and stared at her for a moment, a storm brewing behind my eyes. I'd only laughed to keep things light, so she could carry on with her dignity intact. The last thing I wanted to see was her being dragged down the alley so that Grimy could add sexual assault to his repertoire. I knew Theo would go along and I didn't know if I would be able to stop it. Now I was getting pissed.

"You should slap her ass," our *de facto* head stated flatly. He wasn't talking about a playful pat on her backside, but a backhand delivered across the face.

"Nah, man," I dismissed her with a casual wave of my hand, quietly putting my attitude in check. "I ain't thinkin' about that trick."

"If you don't," he said, "I will."

The look in Grimy's eyes was serious. He could be that way sometimes, his temper taking things from zero to sixty in seconds. As his chest puffed up and he stepped forward to mete out his version of justice (at least the kind of justice his father dished out to his mother whenever the gin-induced mood hit), Theo egged him on in the background.

The young woman, just a couple years older than we were, had stopped to hold her ground, which was crumbling beneath her feet. She said nothing, her smack-talking turned to silence, suddenly sensing the threat was real. She looked like a gazelle that'd sniffed out the lion's intent a minute too late.

I thought about my mother, who would goad my father, begging him to kick her butt for stealing the rent or light bill money to get high. And, though I could see the frustration as his face darkened, he never lifted a hand at Mama, despite her taunts. If he could do it...

"Nah, man," I repeated, waving my hand as if she were nothing, "let that heifer go." I stood in Grimy's way, pretending I didn't notice how he towered over me, his expression steely and unforgiving.

"We should take her out back and make her give us all free rides," he said.

"And catch something that'll have us blowing smoke signals?" I chuckled. "Man, we got better things to do 'sides going to the doctor!"

Theo cracked up at that one but Grimy did not. I gave Claudette a look that told her to get her butt out of here. She kept her mouth shut and crept off without running. A sudden burst of speed, the potential prey innately understood, would only cause predators to give chase.

Disaster diverted, I breathed a sigh of relief. Grimy stepped back toward the old pay phone station, cursing and fussing, but let the girl head to her destination.

ARGARET COULD FEEL HER PULSE beating in her head like a drum. This was all so frustrating! Caught in a storm of traffic across many lanes, she had missed her chance to exit from the Dan Ryan Expressway before it ducked underground, heading closer and closer to the big city of Chicago. Then she jumped as a noise inside the car began to sound: *Bong, bong, bong!* Something on the dash had turned neon orange; she couldn't focus through tear-smudged glasses, but knew it had to be the fuel gauge. The annoying alarm continued. She slowed down so she could think what to do. There were signs for gas, hospitals, parks, and schools. She was mostly worried about getting lost. She would just get off the highway, fill her tank, and get right back on the road. Margaret was not helpless, no matter what her family believed. The exit for 55th Street was coming up. She pushed her wire rim glasses back up on her sweaty nose, clicked the blinker, and took the plunge.

RIMY WAS ITCHING FOR A FIGHT after what happened—or, more accurately, what didn't happen—and Theo's constant hype was making things worse. I tried to distract him with stupid jokes, but the pall had already settled when a nondescript blue sedan, carrying an old white lady sputtered into the gas station. People of the Caucasian persuasion didn't venture into our part of town unless they came with badges and at least two guns each. When his eyes zeroed in on her, I knew the scene with Claudette had just been a warm-up.

"Oh, snap!" Theo exclaimed, pointing at the car's occupant.

The woman parked just a few yards from our perch, and was looking through her purse for something. She was either crazy or didn't know what neighborhood her time machine had placed her in. The car bore out-of-state plates but I couldn't believe she could be that ignorant. Hell, from where we stood, we could clearly see the dollar bills sticking up from her purse like leaves of lettuce, beckoning.

Grimy was fixated and set to drool at all that salad…

LUCKILY, MARGARET FOUND A GAS STATION right off the interstate, and coasted up to the pump on fumes. Beggars can't be choosers, but this place didn't look too safe. The convenience store had bars on the windows and door, and there was a lot of trash strewn around. It wasn't deserted; far from it. Customers came and went; she didn't see any white people. From where she sat at the pump, she noticed several teenagers standing around. More than anything, as she sat there with the gauge pegged at zero and the warning light glowing, Margaret wished she'd never left home.

She couldn't remember the last time she'd pumped her own gas. These days, her grandsons drove the car more than she did. It would sure be nice to have Patrick or Danny with her now, but she had had her chance. She had been in too big a damn hurry. Surprised, she acknowledged the truth. She was a hot head. Always had been.

Well, she wasn't helpless yet. She cut the ignition, extracted the keys, and lay them on the seat while she rifled through her handbag, singles from the tollbooth fluttering and flying out. Searching for her gas credit card, Margaret's arthritic fingers were clumsy stiff after clutching the wheel so long. She glanced out through the passenger window and noticed the nearby loitering teens were all three looking directly at her. She felt a chill in the humid evening and reached over with a shaky hand to click the door lock.

"You see what I see, right fellas?"

"Yeah," Theo muttered, "and ripe for the pickin'."

I was on the fence, scoping out the situation like a hawk on a wire. The scene before me reminded me of the two races in H.G. Well's Time Machine. Granny was an Eloi, we were the Morlocks. She was about to become dinner. Hell, what did she expect would happen when she wandered into this part of town? And, as much as I didn't want the lady getting robbed, I couldn't afford to lose face with my crew.

It was bad enough they saw me as some faggotty bookworm (Grimy's words, not mine), who thought he was too good to walk to the neighborhood school like everybody else. But none of my uppity classmates out at Kenwood Academy had to subsist on sandwiches made from blocks of government cheese. I couldn't deny my reality; I was an outcast and needed to belong to something local. Dang—the old lady had left me little choice.

"I got this," I said with confidence, though I didn't know my next move. I took a step toward the elderly woman's ride.

"Hey, Carlos," I heard from the direction of the convenience store. I spun toward the familiar voice and to the fact that all my friends called me Junior. It was Uncle Ray, who really wasn't my uncle at all. He and my dad had come up in the neighborhood together. Like Pop, Ray was still stuck here, working a dead end gig, barely hanging on.

"Hey, Unc," I said with a wave.

Ray talked and acted like he was still living out his heyday in some blaxploitation flick. "What's goin' on with you, youngblood," he asked, walking up and giving me five.

"Nothin', man. Just hanging out with my partners."

Ray, who had once been known as Cat Daddy in his storied days as a knucklehead, took a general look in the direction of my compatriots and turned back to me with a frown. "You know your father would whoop yo' ass to find you posted up on the corner with these clowns. What you doin' out here, Junior?"

Echoes of my daddy; I just couldn't get away. Ray, like my father, had long ago shed his street status for more legal, if less profitable, ways of earning a living. His epiphany had come with two slugs, some fragments of which were still lodged close to his spine. Maybe that's why he still rocked an afro and thought he was living in the '70s. Though his played-out style of dress and speech may have been stuck in a time warp, his good sense was never in question.

"I already see you sizin' up that old gray girl with all that dough fanned out in her car. Now, you can either go with the crowd," he informed me, looking over his shoulder with disdain toward my friends, "or you can go against it and choose to do right."

I grunted at both his advice and the hand he had clasped firmly to the back of my neck. This is what he did when he wanted to "pull my coattail". Though slightly embarrassed, I was glad I'd run into him just then.

Suddenly, I knew what I had to do and why I'd been relegated to the street corner that sticky summer evening. "Thanks, Uncle," I told the man whose relation to me meant more than blood kinship.

"Now, that's what I'm talkin' about, youngblood," he nodded, looking me straight in the eye. His mission accomplished, he gave me a "Later, baby", dapped me up with some antiquated handshake, clutched his brown paper bag, and strolled off. He still walked like a pimp and may have looked at life through a 40-ounce bottle, but his heart was made of pure gold.

The lady, who was propped up in the driver's seat with her swollen knuckles gripping the steering wheel, turned her head to look when I approached. She flinched when I tapped on her window and asked her to bring it down. "Evening, ma'am," I stated in the most unthreatening voice I could muster.

MARGARET SAT IN THE CAR, paralyzed with indecision. She could sense eyes on her from all directions. Especially obvious was a tall, lanky man with a huge sphere of hair on his head, looking like something from the 60s, which Margaret remembered well. She had been a young bride and then a mother when she used to see people wearing afros and beads on TV. He'd walked over to one of the youths, grabbed him by the neck and whispered something to him. *Probably giving the boy pointers on how to stick up an old lady stranded at an inner city gas station.* She watched the two in her rearview mirror.

The youth nodded and the older man walked off, clutching a bottle of beer, no doubt. She expected it, but still jumped when the youngster knocked on her car window.

Not wanting to show fear, she matched his gaze. He had a baby face, couldn't have been more than fourteen or fifteen, and he was smiling. She frowned back.

"Let down your window," the chosen emissary insisted, tapping. His two cohorts loomed in the periphery. Margaret went against her better judgment and lowered the window a couple of inches. She mentally surveyed the contents of her purse, considering what she would lose. She just wanted to get out of this unharmed.

"Hi," he said with a friendly smile.

"Hello, young man," she answered, careful not to look at him directly. She'd heard that cooperating increased your chances of getting out alive.

He leaned in close and lowered his voice. "My name is Carlos Davis, Jr. My friends simply call me Junior. That's what I want you to call me."

"But we're not…" she started, looking at him straight on.

"Shhhh," he warned. "I don't want my boys to hear us. What's your name?"

"Margaret," she said, wondering where this was all going. It was a carjacking, she realized. He'd order her out of the car, and she'd make a run for the convenience store. She might have a chance, if she didn't fall or get shot in the back.

"Hello, Miss Margaret. My friends have been looking for trouble," Junior said and, of course, though she'd vowed not to show fear, she gasped right out loud. "Relax. I'm not gonna let anything happen to you, okay?"

She nodded.

"What's that fool over there doin'," I heard Theo complain.

"I dunno," Grimy mumbled, eyeballing me go to the pump with Margaret's card. "Let's see what happens."

I was thinking the same thing, to be honest.

They watched from the sidelines as I set the nozzle, pocketed the credit card, and grabbed a squeegee from the cesspool. I worked my way around the sedan, wrestling with myself over how I would ever escape my destiny, and whether I should just stop fighting it. Finally, I got to the driver's side and leaned in close to speak in confidence to my would-be victim.

"Now listen, Miss Margaret, my friends are expecting me to rob you."

She flinched and her many wrinkles gathered into a look of disappointment.

"I should have known," she said, staring at me with those faded blue eyes gone cold. "You told me you'd pump my gas like you would for your own grandmother—and I *trusted* you, Mr. Carlos Davis Junior!"

I panicked just a little, hearing her state my name like that. "No, no, you've got it all wrong." I chuckled, half-nervously.

But Margaret was on a roll: "I expected more. For a moment, I saw potential in you, but you're going to waste it all by making us both statistics. Here," she said suddenly, her face red with anger, "you can have my entire purse if you want!"

"I'm not—I'm not a thief", I mumbled, my head bowed, and when she ran out of words, I told her my plan.

"You want me to do *what?*" she responded, her voice so loud and strident that I saw both Grimy and Theo's necks straighten and their ears flap.

WHEN THE YOUNGSTER ADMITTED THE ROBBERY PLAN, Margaret felt deflated. She kept thinking of Danny and Patrick, and wondering how it would feel to have a grandchild who hung with the wrong crowd and got into trouble. Beth had done well, raising the boys on her own. *But our small town is a totally different world from what these kids deal with.*

Across the street, a small group of teenagers gathered on the steps of a graffiti-covered building, its doors and windows boarded up. She observed, as a person dressed in a coat—*in this heat?*—pushed a grocery cart full of rags and bags past the gathered teens. At that moment, a sense of wonder at her own family's good fortune washed over her, as Margaret began to realize something that she'd never even thought about before.

She let her window down all the way, then grabbed all the bills sticking up from her purse and handed them over.

Junior leaned in the window, grinning sheepishly. He accepted the bills, stood up and thumbed through them proudly, so his buddies could see.

Damn thugs, Margaret thought, as they both smiled big in response.

But when he leaned back down to finish their little transaction, Margaret was ready with a little surprise for Junior.

ROM GRIMY AND THEO'S VANTAGE POINT, I seemed to pocket the bills. In actuality, I dug Margaret's credit card out and folded the cash around it, palming the bundle. Yeah, that should satisfy my so-called friends, I thought. Get them off my back while I figure out this destiny thing.

Cuz like I said, I'm not a thief.

When I leaned once more into the window, my summer buzz cut head ducking down, and my hand ready to give Miss Margaret her dough back as planned, she grabbed my forearm with both her puffy hands and yanked me towards her. It startled me so bad I bumped my head on the frame.

"Junior," she said, very close to my ear. "I'm just an old woman from the country, but I can see your struggle." I could've gotten away, sure, but I let her finish. I didn't want to be rude. "I have to tell you," she continued, "pretending won't work for long. Pretty soon, your fate will be decided. If not by you then by your associates." Her eyes slid sideways towards the guys. With that, she planted a big fat kiss on my fuzzy head and let go of my arm.

ARGARET COULDN'T BE SURE, but she thought she saw Junior wearing a blush as he stepped away from the car and began explaining the way to the interstate. After tucking the credit card safely in her purse, she insisted on giving him a five-dollar tip for pumping her gas and washing her windows.

"Have a safe trip, Miss Margaret," said the boy, stepping back. A glance out the passenger window showed the other teens on the move towards the sedan.

She cranked the engine, and made for the light. A last look in her rearview showed the gang of three collected where her car had just stood. A moment later, she was on the Dan Ryan Expressway, going in the right direction and wondering what had just happened.

"WHAT THE HELL WAS THAT?" Grimy asked, coming off his perch as the blue sedan pulled off. "Sure took you long enough. How much did you get, anyway?"

"Yeah, how much did we get?" Theo chimed in. I wanted to punch that kid dead in his nose to shut him up.

I handed over the single note with Lincoln's face, to which Grimy frowned. "What happened to all the paper you were counting after pumping her gas? What about the credit card?"

"Sorry guys. That's it."

"But you had the card in your hand—we saw it. You holding back on us Junior?" demanded Grimy.

"Nah, I gave the old lady her card back." I said, knowing this could not end well, "and she gave me a tip for pumping her gas."

"Wait. Lemme get this straight: you gave it back?!" Grimy could not believe his ears.

But it was Theo who stepped toward me first, realization of being duped stitching his face. "You faggotty mother—"

Before he could finish, before I could think, I landed my right fist in his punk-ass face.

Grimy froze, eyes wide, mouth agape like a dumbfounded cartoon character.

Theo was sliding backward in slow-mo, globules of blood flying from his top lip and snot locker. When his travels ceased, he held his hands over the gusher, howling like the flunky he was.

Alfonso Grimes took a step forward then paused. Though he had about 20 pounds and two inches on me, I wasn't scared of him. In fact, the crazed look in my eye dared him to say something. I even flashed a smoldering grin at the bully.

"Consider that my payment for exit from this little bitch-ass crew, Grimy. You're going down the wrong road fast, and I'm not going with you." I said.

My former best friend winced at my words, while bloody Theo sat trying to regain his bearings. If his nose wasn't broken it would be sore for a while, giving him something to remember me by.

I turned to go, which may not have been the smartest thing to do, but I was no longer afraid. To quell any urge to jump me from behind, I spun on my heel with a dark glance. "Run up on me or knock on my door again and you're gon' find your ass at the bottom of the staircase. Test me."

And with that, I was gone. If I hurried, I could get home to talk to my daddy before he left for work. I suddenly had a lot of questions, and I had a feeling he knew the answers.

DON MISKEL co-authored "Everyday Heroes" with Pamela Murray, breathing life into characters from opposite sides of the track. Of his protagonist he says, "I injected a lot of my DNA into Junior. Minus some molecular details, I was that bookish kid from Chicago's rough-and-tumble South Side."

Known more for provocative works of horror and comedy, "Everyday Heroes" is a far cry from his typical gigantic cockroaches, flesh-eating zombies, and tongue-in-cheek technology. "Miracles happen against mundane backdrops. We pointed the figurative camera in the right direction so the reader wouldn't miss it. Not all champions wear capes."

As a military and police veteran, some might consider Don cape-worthy. Though outwardly joking and gregarious, he downplays any notion of heroics. "Nah, my wife is my hero. She's used her superpowers to give life to our wonderful children. On second thought," he says with a naughty smile, "Because of the kids, we pay college tuitions, higher insurance premiums, and get gray hairs. Scratch that—my wife is the maker of villains!" And to that he snickers heartily... while nervously hoping his lady love never reads this write-up...

For more laughs, rants, and creative projects, please follow Don on Facebook (**www.facebook.com/DonMiskelOfficial/**) and his website (**www.donmiskel.com**).

THE YEAR 2000 was the last 'normal' year that Pamela Murray remembers; working as a critical care nurse, raising four kids, gardening and renovating their suburban home in Tennessee. The youngest child was in kindergarten when her husband was offered a job opportunity in Asia; it was a daunting decision to leave the comfort of the familiar for the unknown and the strange. That move led to thirteen years of interesting experiences overseas, and changed the perspective which inspires her fiction.

Recently, that youngest child graduated from high school, coinciding with the family's repatriation to America. During this transition, while Pamela decides whether or not to return to nursing, she writes short fiction, studies editing, and is working on a novel set in Japan.

As a writer, Pamela is fascinated by the power of perspective, and tries to get under the skin of her characters to let them speak their own truth. Her stories take the reader by the hand and introduce another culture or set of experiences. "Everyday Heroes" is her first collaboration on a realistic fiction piece. She feels blessed to have worked with the talented Don Miskel, whose authentic voice and powerful imagination made it a joy to write the story together.

Pamela Murray may be reached through her website: **www.transitionsquared.com**.

The Matchmaker

RYLAN PARTCH

YOU GET SO YOU CAN READ PEOPLE IN THIS PROFESSION—idiots, schemers, dangerous folk. It's all in the body language, and the eyes. Truth is, though, that you can't always depend on that. Some people are just too good at looking harmless, which is why I always take the least threatening people the most seriously. If they really are weak-hearted, you're overreacting—but if they're setting you up, you won't be caught off guard. And so today's fourth visitor immediately put me on the defensive.

He comes in and lays out his proposal like a chump—my girl came down, I haven't seen her since blah blah, almost crying. Looking like a damn pussy. "How did you get my name?"

"We have a mutual friend," he says.

"Who?" I ask, and he's silent, wiping his eyes.

"You got a picture?" I ask. He hands it to me and I look at it, but not twice.

Just your average stunner of a woman, swallowed by this hungry city. It's a big place, and one can easily fall into the clutches of unsavory characters while in its grids. I am supposedly a detective, but everyone knows what my real use is—I know many of these characters. Half the time we have a history; we might even be friends. So if somebody's missing, and you haven't gotten a ransom note, you might want to give the Shao Agency a call. A lot of the time the kidnappers don't know who to send the note to in the first place. In some ways I'm a vital part of the kidnapping industry—a matchmaker, if you will.

But most people don't know about my little connecting service, and many of the ones that do are less than savory themselves. Maybe the emotion is real, but this guy is trying to play me pretty hard. I pause, but I know what I'm going to do. "I'll take the case," I say. I'm pretty broke, setup or not.

"Thank you Mr. Bosan," he says.

"Mr. Shao," I say. "Bosan's the first name."

He smiles awkwardly, slightly more in control of his emotions. "Sorry," my client says, and puts well above my rate on the desk—they all overpay. "I just want her back," his cash says.

"I'll get right on it."

As the door shuts, I count what I got upfront and wonder. Once he's long gone I pull a folder out of my desk: another case from earlier today. I take out the picture and put it faceup on my desk, next to the one I was just given.

Now I'm not so good with faces, honestly. I couldn't tell you if a person in one photograph was the same as someone in another, usually. But it's the same girl.

I sigh and check the clock—it's close enough to noon for my lunch break. I lock the door, come back to the desk and open the bottom left drawer. I pull out the baggie of my most dependable companion, and empty the dark orange powder onto a book, feeling half the high already.

I couldn't tell you exactly how I ended up dealing with the absolute trash of society in one of the worst places in existence—honestly, I can't remember a lot of things. But I've been at this desk for a hundred years, doing this job and sniffing the same drug every damn day. And not just for lunch.

Two men separately walk into a detective agency, on the same day, tell the guy working there a convincing sob story and ask him to find their partner of centuries—and give him the exact same picture. I try to guess the punch line, but then my mind is wiped clean and I lean back, unable to think of anything.

Anything but peace.

Once I come back to this reality, more or less, I consider leaving again, right away—but I need to save my stuff. Given current economic trends, it may have to last a while.

Sometimes I wonder if the Edge is just a dream I'm having, just a vision—but the city is too persistent. Its layout never changes, and its essence stays the same dull shade of mundane. Slightly in control of my body and mind, I make my way to the open window and down at the scene of February street—pedestrians, people playing football on the rough pavement, if it can still be called that... the same, never-darkening sky. No, LEC has been my home for over three hundred years, and it's not going anywhere. I step away from the view.

Life sucked, and like many I thought death would end the suffering. But here I am instead, another punk in a city hugging the coast of a giant lake of fire, a city where Angels come on vacation and end up missing, and oh, let's call Shao Bosan and see if he can get her back. Send her back up to Heaven, where I'd much rather be.

Instead I'm here in Hell.

And I know right then the drug has worn off—here I am hating myself.

...oh well. I stand up and grab my coat, knowing that for me thinking is bad for my self-esteem. Time to solve this mystery.

I lock the door behind me, and almost make it to my car before a nonchalant glance down the block makes me notice a man in a sedan a few parking spaces back, openly watching me leave my office. I refrain from waving, and as I start the engine I think about the local gang I'm on bad terms with—but Gong's guys are too professional to be that obvious. Then I shrug; I don't really care who it is. I pull away from the curb and am on my way.

This part of Lake Edge City is relatively quiet right now, in terms of trouble—criminals are just waking up, and the party has ended for the tourists. Because of this traffic is okay, and it only takes me a minute to pass through two stoplights and park at my local convenience store, Grady's. It's pretty run down but they sell everything you could ever need, if you're willing to settle for cheap goods at high prices in exchange for 'convenience'. The guys here know me well, and as I browse the aisles, Ronaldo makes small talk.

"Where's the money, Bosan?" he asks.

"Check your girl's g-string," I say.

He laughs, not funny. "I'd better get it soon or I'm cutting you off." Yeah right.

I purchase some hardware and leave via the back entrance, where they sell the truly convenient stuff, but I haven't run out of my stash yet and am not desperate enough to sniff whatever they cut their drugs with these days.

As I sneak around the block, its many eyes lazily watch me, until I've made my way full circle and am creeping towards the rear end of the tail; I'm almost to the car in question with the just-purchased hammer and nails out when he sees me in the rear view mirror.

He jumps out of the car as I quickly I puncture both the back tires. I ignore him and his angry questions as I walk quickly back to my car and start her up, leaving the lot fast—he's pissed and pulls out his phone, but he knows better than to follow me on only rims. Later, jerk—Bosan wins this round.

My feeling of victory is short-lived, however, as I notice that round two has begun. I'm being followed again, this time by a black van I somehow hadn't initially noticed—who looks for two tails? A slip up and now I have to think about how I'm going to lose these clowns. Then they speed up, and I can see they want to dance.

I hit the gas, but I can't outrun them in these narrow streets—that's one thing I don't like about February Street and its surrounding maze. It's never a good place to get chased, and it's possible that one of the fifty witnesses that are always there to see every little shootout will turn. So I pull over in the nearest tow zone—I can't afford to damage my car right now; a crash would be worse than whatever they have planned for me, and this way I'll get my baby back with a small bribe. So I exit and put my hands up.

The van's driver is the crybaby that came into the office earlier; he unbuckles as muscle jumps out of the passenger seat, and the van comes to a stop. "Hey there," I say.

The large man doesn't say anything as he approaches me, doesn't ask any questions or give me directions. My hands stay up as he lands a thick blow to my face, then he pulls me off my knees and drags me towards the large black vehicle. Crybaby, now out of the car, handcuffs me as I'm held by the brute.

"Drive," he tells the muscle, and we all get in.

There's a chair in the expansive back of the van—surrounded by old torture equipment.

"Nice museum," I say. "Haven't seen some of these in a hundred years." Crybaby picks up a powerful electric prod and circles it around in the air. I know from experience that this one scars. "What do you want?"

"I know you know Bethany," he says. "But I seriously doubt you're going to lead us to her. So," he says, hovering the prod above my neck, "Plan B."

I dodge as he lunges, and stare him in the eyes. "Look," I say, "I know a lot of people."

He smiles; he seems to have made up his mind that I'm her new best friend, or a squeeze. "Well," he says…

"Cops," muscle says from the front, and the antiques collector turns.

"What?"

Muscle looks back. "Checkpoint. We're gonna need a bribe."

Misty eyes sighs, and puts the prod down. "They said you were an addict," he says.

"Yeah, so?" I say.

"Take this time to clear your head." He reaches for his wallet and turns towards the front seats. "When this is done we're gonna have some–"

He spasms as the prod touches his head right in back of his ear, which I know is an incredibly painful spot for contact. He's weak, and falls instantly—as he hits the floor his associate turns in the driver's seat, but neither one has a chance to stop me as I push the back doors open and bolt out, running down the street with the handcuffs dangling from one wrist and the teary man's wallet in my fingers. Good luck guys—I'm sure those cops have questions, and you'll be answering downtown.

I learned a few things during this hilarious attempt at intimidation—for one, I would assume that those goons are not from around here. It isn't like locals to use prehistoric electronic torture techniques; I would guess they bought their tools once they got here, and took whatever they could get.

Secondly, this man referred to her as Bethany, which shows a certain level of intimate knowledge. It's logical that he represents an interest in her coming from an angle of actually caring, which would make sense—someone had to genuinely be concerned about her disappearance. Maybe the tears were legitimate; it helps when there's truth in the lie.

I have an idea which angle he's coming from, but I have other questions. One of these is how exactly two separate groups magically found out I knew the missing girl, and both came into my office on the same day. Information like that doesn't come out of thin air, and I wonder if someone a little more serious wants me out of the picture.

I hate this neighborhood. The Barrio Rojo is an old part of Lake Edge—you can tell because the streets haven't been paved in a few hundred years. A hill blocks any view of the lake, and it's all cobblestone and dilapidation, a good combination for those barely making rent, or trying to hide a profitable operation. The cab charges me extra to drive here, and I'll have to walk a while to find a street where I can catch a return ride. But this visit had to be made.

His door opens and I watch his face carefully. He's a good actor, but not incredible, and I can tell it wasn't the vulture that set me up. "Bosan," he says.

"Mbunu," I reply. No, I provide this man with too much business for him to be selling me out. "You clean the place up?"

He turns and we look out over a dirty room with piles of discs reaching to the ceiling. There's barely a place to stand. He turns to me. "I'm busy," he says. "You have a problem?"

"I do," I say, and pull out a disc of my own. "I need you to track these faces."

"How many?" he asks.

"Three," I say. Crybaby, the other man that had earlier dropped Beth's photo off in my office, and Bethany Lin herself. "And if you make it a priority I'll make it worth your while."

"I've got some pretty high priorities," he says.

"Two grand."

He takes the disc. "Right."

My vision is never complete, but Mbunu is a valuable set of eyes in the Edge. He trades in dubbed security footage—enterprising souls at just about every establishment in LQ sell their camera feed for a much needed extra buck, and in Mbunu's cramped room here he sifts through them all. You never know what you'll find in last night's visual observations—or how much someone will pay to keep it a secret. "I have another question," I say.

"What's that?" he asks.

"Two people found out I knew the woman on there," I say, "on the same day."

He nods. "You want me to ask around at the next association luncheon?"

I smile.

"We don't have friends, in this industry," Mbunu says. "I can't help you there."

"Just if you hear anything."

I leave Mbunu's place willingly; it always smells in there. I can't go back to my office, right now—so I figure I'll go catch some sleep in a cheap hotel, a species of lodging all too rampant in the Barrio Rojo. But something eats at me suddenly.

A cheap hotel...

It took me a few minutes to remember where we had gone together—but it came to me. The Grand View Lodge, which is, despite its name, very, very trashy. There is a grand view though, and as we snake up the street leading to the place I get a panorama of the south shore of Lake Jezebel, flames burning endlessly and the coastal parts of the city responding with a faint glow. I don't remember seeing it on the way up with Beth, though; I hadn't been able to notice much with my tongue in her mouth and my hand in her pants. My lack of concentration was costly—with both of us high, the taxi driver had taken the long route getting there, and when I looked at the meter I got into a yelling match.

At least I remember that.

Once we arrived and got our room, there were a lot of drugs and significantly less clothing. Things get blurry, real blurry, and the next thing I can recall is us leaving. How someone would take that and assume we knew each other, I don't know.

But I'm positive this was the source of the footage. Everywhere else we'd visited had guarantees that no vultures would get their talons on your doings—that's why I frequent them—and even the Grand View held things back for me. It is, however, the weakest link in that chain.

But I know people at the Grand View, and they know me. If something happened, I would get a major apology. In fact, someone is coming out of the office to give me one as I pay the cabbie in the parking lot.

"You!" the man says; I forget his name, but then again I may never have known it.

"You too," I say, and step out of the car.

The man is apparently angry and before I know it I have been slammed against the taxi—then it takes off and I fall to the ground as I'm kicked. I grab a leg and twist, and John—there, I did remember—he hits the ground with a snap.

"What's your problem?" I ask as he writhes on the asphalt, groaning in pain. I step a threat towards him and he forms an answer.

"Cops were here looking for you," John says in wheezes.

"Looking for me?"

"About you and one of your girls. Ow…"

I step towards him. "When?"

"Left an hour ago." He tries to stand; it doesn't work.

"I wouldn't do that," I say. "Beth, right?"

He laughs. "You knew who she was, didn't you?"

"What?"

John shakes his head. "What, you get off screwing mob girls?"

"Hmm," I say. "Who'd you give the feed to?"

John shakes his head. "I didn't. It was Vlad."

"Vlad?" Then I remember him too. "Why? That's highly against your policy."

"He wanted some extra money, got fired, took footage, so on." My eyes express my curiosity. "He's taken care of. He won't cause more problems." I open my mouth. "Neither will you," John says. "You are no longer welcome."

"I am gonna miss the vista," I say. We pause, and he winces, still in pain. "Any way I can get a crack at old Vlad?"

"Undertaker took him," John says. "You know the deal."

I do. No killing, but an anonymous burial, no questions asked and no records kept. He won't die, but that means he won't be around again, either. Vlad is gone.

"Can't say it was a pleasure, John." I turn to walk away.

"It's Jack," he says to my back.

So now I have the cops on my trail as well—and who knows who they're working for. Lake Edge is getting a little too hungry for me, and it's time to play my card. I don't know which undertaker John used, not that it matters; mine's name is Galio, and I wave down yet another cab to pay him a visit.

The seemingly high man outside reaches into his bag, where he keeps his pistol—"I'm here to see your boss," I say.

"Who you mean?" the man asks in a sideways tone, then the door behind him opens. No head pops out, nothing is said, but it stays cracked.

Invited, I walk up the steps to the house past the guard, who continues to convincingly act strung out—maybe he is.

The room is dark, and you can hardly make out any details—probably the point. "I assume this is about your temporary," Galio says, walking towards his desk. Temporary meaning the body is buried somewhere retrievable—usually when you have a person buried alive, they never come back. "You want me to dig it up?

I nod, and he stares.

"When do you need it by?"

"As soon as possible," I say.

He slowly puts out his hand. "Seven grand."

I look to his face. "I don't have that on me."

"Then why are you here?"

Galio stares into my eyes, and I realize that, for the moment, I'm screwed.

I leave the undertaker's office and start to walk. This neighborhood is safe enough for that kind of thing—but just barely. I focus on putting one foot in front of the other; I don't know what to do exactly, which makes this a rare moment. I have half the city looking for me, so if I withdraw money anywhere it will pounce, and quickly—but I need that money to cool things down.

The phone rings. It's Mbunu.

"Yeah," I answer.

"Look, this is a hot one so I'll just tell you. The two men are mob guys from Heaven."

I nod. "Different families?"

"Right."

Hmm. "She's a member of the Lin gang, someone high up's partner. The other family is the Traps," Mbunu says. "That's all I got. Got any other work for me?"

"Nah," I say.

He hangs up, and I think for a minute before calling another number—not a friend, and not an acquaintance. I don't like to have enemies, and I figure a lot of money might settle a score or two.

"Gong," I say.

"What the hell do you want?" he says through his broken teeth.

I look around at a hostile city, and know that this is the right move. "I've got a proposition for you."

I thumb through the money—a solid amount for a day of dirty work. I sold the rights to the temporary burial to Gong, boss of the local gang that had been dying to get its hands around my neck. I told him to contact the families involved, and start a bidding war. Whoever wanted Bethany the most could reach deep into their pockets to dig her up. Whether it was her gang or another one, someone would walk away with the prize and Gong would walk away with a fortune.

All's well that ends well, as they say. There are definitely loose ends, but they're no longer mine to tie; I'm in the clear.

John was right—I do get off on dangerous girls. It's my Icarus complex; sleeping with women that could have me buried. It's only when they actually threaten me with doing that that I become a dangerous person myself.

Drugs make you forget things. Things like safe words, or what safe words are. And after that night, Bethany hated me. She told me I was as good as buried. So, logically, I had little choice but to bury her first.

As a person of some importance, I knew she'd be a useful asset one day, and if things had happened the way they were supposed to, I would have made a killing; instead I got a mere finder's fee. The matchmaker once again.

But right now I'm sitting here with a decent amount of money, enough to get my next fix from my favorite dealer and not the convenience store. So I'm happy. Well, soon to be happy, I guess you could say—I'm not smiling yet. I'm still a little pissed off as I chop my lines.

But the Edge is a bad city, a real shithole; I can't stand it here, that's the truth.

And I'm about to escape.

WHILE I AM primarily an author trying his hand at a multitude of fiction-based mediums, I also make music via audio collage and am a travel writer currently specializing in San Francisco Bay Area locations. When I am not creating, or somehow gathering resources for a project, I am usually extremely bored.

The story in this anthology, "The Matchmaker", is the first in a long and growing series of shorts based on the Shao Bosan character and his city of residence in Hell, a series entitled 'Lake of Fire.' So if you like this particular misadventure, there are many more, and you can find them in some form on the Lake of Fire facebook page. Just search for Lake of Fire and click on the coolest link that shows up.

Peace!